ME AND FIVE GUYS

A novel by

Trish Doolan

Me and Five Guys is published by Source Point Press, a division of Ox Eye Media, Inc.

www.SourcePointPress.com

Cover Design by Joshua Werner and Martha Webby.

Printed in the United States of America
First Printing Edition, 2022
ISBN: 9781954412538

SOURCE POINT PRESS

ME AND FIVE GUYS

Chapter 1: ME AND JFK

It was November 22, 1963, 12:30 p.m. Central Standard Time and all the good democratic Americans of Dallas gathered on the streets to see John F. Kennedy and his elegant wife, Jackie. The forecast predicted a cold and rainy day, but they were wrong. It turned out to be warm and sunny for the arrival of our 35th President and the First Lady. Jackie Kennedy wore a double-breasted, raspberry pink Chanel wool suit with a navy trim collar accompanied by a matching pink pillbox hat and white gloves. They looked dashing as they rode in their motorcade smiling and waving to throngs of loyal fans. JFK was the inspiration for America, the man who saved everyone from the Cuban Missile Crisis and invoked citizens to take pride in themselves and our nation. He represented hope for our country. Everyone was in awe of the President who would change the future for their families and put men on the moon. He was my father's hero, especially because he was Irish.

Me, I was in Queens, New York, 1:30 p.m. Eastern Standard Time, pushing myself through a very small passageway called the birth canal. The pressure was great, and my mother was howling in pain. All of a sudden, a special bulletin came over every television and radio station. JFK was shot.

The world stopped. My mother's labor stopped. Nurses and doctors were hysterical, crying and running around the hospital aimlessly. My mother was screaming bloody murder;

everyone had jumped ship. The televisions were on everywhere catching the scoop on the assassination, even in Astoria General Hospital where I was trying to be born.

My father, Ryan Finnegan, with good looks that gave James Dean a run for his money, was at his home away from home, McTierney's Ale House. His gorgeous pale blue eyes were glued to the news broadcast and his hand was glued to a glass of whiskey. My oldest brother Ryan, named after Dad, went to tell him Mom was in labor, but he didn't care. JFK was much more important to him. He needed to know if his hero was going to pull through.

The whole world awaited the unfortunate conclusion to this day. It was confirmed, JFK was pronounced dead at 2:00 p.m., New York time, and Mom had a baby girl at 2:01 p.m. As JFK was gasping for his last breath, I was inhaling my first. Born into this unfortunate time of uncertainty was how I entered into the world. I was told the only one happy to see me was Mom. And no one was happy to witness Lyndon B. Johnson sworn in to fill JFK's shoes; an impossible feat and everyone feared the worst.

For the rest of my life, my birthday was a day of mourning. In my father's heart, his daughter was not another year older, but Kennedy had been dead another year.

My mother was my hero. Isabella Finnegan was, of course, her married name. Five foot five, green eyes, red hair, which she styled exactly like Sophia Loren and had the face and figure to match. Mom was off the boat from Naples, Italy where she was known as Isabella Juliano. I was the only child my father allowed her to name. Mainly because I was a girl and he had already named the four sons they had before me. Mom told me she longed to have a baby girl and that my birth was the happiest day of her life, despite the horrific day that God sent me down. My name came easily to her, Francesca. It rolled off of her tongue so beautifully in her Italian accent. Francesca! It was like music when my mother called me. From her lips my name became a song that my ears longed to hear, but from her lips only did the song reach my ears. No one else could sing my name the way my mother did. There is nothing I wouldn't do for her because I felt her love so strongly. When Mom told Dad my name, he said, "Alright, I guess that will do. Frankie." To him I was just another one of the guys.

From a very young age, my mother taught me Italian, but it wasn't proper Italian, it was Neapolitan dialect, which is kind of like slang. Neapolitan dialect was frowned upon by true Italians, but in Naples it was the language of the street peasants. Mom could pretty much understand most Italians and converse, but when her and Nanny Juliano went at it (fast and furious with the hands and all) no one could understand them. It was fantastic, their very own secret code, and I wanted in. It was really fun in the food department. For example, MOZZERELLA would be pronounced MUTZ-A-DELL and RICOTTA was pronounced RA-GUT, SOPRESATTA SALAMI, was SOUP-A-SAD. For whatever the reason, things were added and changed in dialect. I didn't know why, and I didn't care. It was the way Mom talked and I loved it. None of my brothers wanted to learn. My father told them that it was for sissies. "These stupid Guineas come to our country and expect us to speak their language. You want to be in the U.S. of A. then learn our language and don't be pushing that crap on my sons."

My mother would shake her head and tell me in Italian, "Your father is a very ignorant man and tonight I'm gonna pee in his soup and he won't even notice!" We'd laugh.

"Hey, what the hell did you say to her?" Dad would get all defensive.

Mom would just smile. "You don't want to know my stupid language, remember? So, don't ask me what I said."

He wanted to make sure she wasn't talking about him and she always was. It was the only way she could release her frustration about Dad; out loud, in Italian, passionately and angrily without him understanding a single word. We were comrades, Mom and I, girls against the boys. We were constantly fighting for our rights. Bathroom privacy was an impossibility. I would be in the middle of important business on the bowl, and they would think nothing of coming in, grabbing the Colgate toothpaste and brushing their teeth, while scratching their balls and I'm trying to take a dump. They would even start having a conversation with me, rip off their 'Fruit of the Looms' and jump in the shower. I saw it all, and I do mean every body part a guy has all day long. Who could possibly take shit while all that was going on? Not me. My bowels got shy and shut down the factory. Too much traffic going on. When dinner hit the table, the cannibals were attacking anything with a smell. I was so little I couldn't seem to get a forkful. My mother started putting a plate aside for me before she put out the guys' food. No one spoke at the table. They just swallowed, drooled, and smiled.

Mom's food was something to behold. Pure deliciousness. A true culinary artist in the kitchen. Mom in her cotton peasant dress, every day a different color, prepared Italian food like nobody's business and let me tell you, there were no complaints about my mom being a guinea when it came to her cooking.

Even though we lived in the Boroughs, a real shithole neighborhood in Queens, under the El, Mom managed to have the most beautiful garden in the backyard. There was basil so green it was Irish; rosemary, oregano, sage, red and yellow peppers that glowed like a sunset. Her tomatoes were so red and juicy you could squeeze them over spaghetti. There was zucchini, portobello mushrooms, parsley, garlic, eggplant, and spinach. The woman brought Italy to Queens.

Breakfast was like a small Italian wedding. Salami, provolone omelets with fresh garden herbs, hand shaved

Parmesan cheese, and mom's homemade pork sausage. On the side we had French toast made with homemade Italian semolina bread that she baked every night. I lived for that bread. Probably my favorite thing on the planet. Mom would make one little loaf just for me. Then she made her signature dipping concoction in a ceramic bowl from Tuscany. She'd start with fresh chopped garlic, pour cold pressed virgin olive oil on top with some fresh cut basil, thyme, oregano, and rosemary from her garden. For the finale she would add just the right amount of hot crushed red pepper. Presto. Magnifico. I was in heaven. If I was on death row all I would want for my last meal would be that special concoction and Mom's homemade bread. I could die a happy girl. The neighbors would always ring our bell and make believe they just wanted to say 'hello,' but really, they were hoping Mom would give them a loaf. She did when Dad wasn't home. They always knew when he was there because mom, standing before them in her red and green apron, had a secret code, she would wink twice if he was home and if not, she would say, "Un minuto, ho una pagnotta calda per te." Their faces would light up like Christmas, because by now they understood that she just told them in one minute they would have a fresh hot loaf of homemade bread. Jackpot! But, when Dad was home, he would always yell that he wasn't made of money and let them go somewhere else for a handout. What he didn't understand is that this was Mom's pride and joy.

We all asked her why she didn't open a place of her own. She said it would drain the love out of her, especially if she had to do it for money. See, Mom believed her cooking was a gift. Something she could give people. Pouring a piece of herself into every meal, mom was a true magician in the kitchen. The kitchen was always my favorite room in the house because that's where I saw Mom thrive. It became my sanctuary. A place to escape all of the testosterone and connect with my feminine energy, which was my mother.

The black and white Zenith TV, framed in light brown wood with rabbit ears adorned the living room, but was off limits to me and Mom during peak hours. The boob tube was monopolized by the guys so they could watch sports, sports, and more sports. If it wasn't a game of some kind, it was a show talking about a game that would be coming on soon. Dad's mood would change dramatically depending on which team won and so would his alcohol consumption. Mom said it was because he made bets with some bookies and it would determine what would be on the menu for the upcoming weeks. If he won, we could eat Steak, maybe veal, but if he lost, we were looking at Oscar Meyer hot dogs, or peppers, eggs & onions, a popular dish in our house. I didn't care because Mom could make Spam taste like prime rib. Sundays were the worst for TV domination, especially during football season. Mom and I couldn't wait until all the games ended so we could snuggle up, finally, and watch our favorite show together; Ed Sullivan, 8 o'clock on CBS, every Sunday night, it was our religion. Thank God there were no sports on early in the morning because that was our time to spend with Jack La Lane and his fancy one-piece spandex jumpsuit. I figured I needed to buff up so I could become big and strong like the guys. It was no fun being the runt of the litter.

I learned at a very young age if I wanted to fit in with my brothers, I'd better learn to play sports. I wanted desperately to be part of them. I even let them rough me up to prove I could take it. One time they played hot potato and I was elected the potato. It was initiation time. I was five, Patrick was eight, Seamus was ten, Ian was twelve, and Ryan, thirteen. Ryan and Ian were Irish twins, eleven months apart. Ryan picked me up like I was a potato. He was so strong. Dad said he took after my Uncle Jim, his brother, who fought six men at once and sipped on whiskey in between. We weren't allowed to see Uncle Jim or talk to him. We had to take an oath. If we accidentally bumped into him, we had to pretend we didn't see him and run the other way as quickly as possible. We weren't allowed to ask why. All we knew was he was built like an Irish plow, demolished anything in his path, and had a terrible drinking habit. It seemed to run in Dad's side of the family, like diabetes.

There I was in Ryan's big strong hands, then he tossed me to Ian who tossed me to Seamus and then to Patrick who wasn't as big and strong as the others. He dropped me flat on my face. Out popped my two front teeth and blood was everywhere. As I lay on the concrete, I felt the pressure of my gums sticking to my lip. The taste was comforting for some reason. It hurt like hell, but all of a sudden, I felt tough, special. Secretly, I had wanted to get hurt, collect a scar or two to prove I was strong enough to fit in with the guys. I was just afraid of how it would happen. All my brothers had stitches, cool scars, bruises and war wounds to show off. This was my moment.

Not a sound was made. I couldn't speak. I think I was in shock. I could hear my brothers arguing. Ryan thought maybe they killed me because I wasn't moving. Ian said, "Dad is gonna kill us all and Patrick shouldn't have been playing 'cause he's too weak." Patrick got defensive and said that he was just as strong, but his eyes were closed. Seamus didn't say a word. He knelt down beside me, felt my pulse. "She's alive!" All my brothers cheered, "Thank God, whoa, that was close." Seamus placed his hand on the back of my neck. The touch of Seamus' hands on me was so comforting.

My brothers were all concerned about me. For the first time in my life I knew they loved me. I didn't feel like their stupid kid sister.

Seamus asked Ian to help him turn me around. They moved me ever so gently, like I was a wounded baby bird. As my eyes hit the light I squinted.

Seamus was relieved. "She's conscious. How you doin' kiddo?"

Ian said he couldn't believe I wasn't crying and that if that was Patrick he would've been. Ryan told Ian to shut his trap, or he'd shut it for him. Ryan was very protective about Patrick, who was so little.

Seamus softly said, "Can you hear me Frankie?" I smiled as big as day. I was so proud to be wounded. Seamus saw the gap in my mouth as his eyes widened.

Ian screamed, "She has no teeth!" then turned to Patrick; "You knocked her fucking teeth out."

Ryan smacked Ian in the head, "I'm gonna knock your fucking teeth out if you say another word." Ian zipped up quickly. When it came to fighting, no one would cross Ryan.

Patrick stood crying, "I'm sorry Frankie. I didn't mean it." I was so touched by his little face.

"Don't worry, Patrick. I'm okay."

"Let's get her to the hospital, her lip is split, and stitches are definitely necessary." Seamus insisted. I was queasy and wanted to cry, but no way in the world would I shed a single tear, not when I was being honored for my heroic qualities. Gladiators don’t cry.

When we got to the hospital the lady at the desk immediately called for a doctor then took our information from Ryan explaining that she had to call our parents. The doctor showed up, took one look at me and cleared a room.

"I'm Doctor Silver." His name sounded shiny and pretty, so I trusted him. He asked that the boys wait outside, but Seamus said,

"I have to stay and make sure you do it right. I'm gonna be a doctor someday."

Then Ryan said, "That's my baby sister and I ain't leaving."

Ian said, "I have to stay because wherever they go, I go.

Patrick pouted. "I'm the one who did this to her, so I have to be here." The doctor smiled at all the love they showed and told Patrick he must have some right hook. Ryan laughed and tousled Patrick's hair. Patrick didn't get it, but since Ryan laughed, he knew it was okay to laugh. We were all together, a family, and I was one of them, even if I was a girl.

Twelve stitches later, I was ready to go home. Mom and Dad ran in and saw my lip. Mom started swearing in Italian. Dad wanted to know how it happened. I couldn't speak too well because my lip was swelled up like a golf ball. Ian started to tell the story as Patrick hung his head low.

Ryan jumped in, "I had her on my shoulders, Dad, and she fell."

We all looked at him in amazement, knowing Dad was gonna give him a beating. Dad told Ryan he was a careless ape, just like his brother Jim, who we were never allowed to speak to, and shouldn't go near me because he didn't know how to be gentle with anything. Dad called Ryan a 'bull in a china shop.'

That night we all waited atop the stairs as Ryan took his beating with Dad's infamous belt, thick, dark brown leather; the third notch wider than the rest. You could smell the musty hide of the animal as it whipped around your skin like a leech. That old belt seemed to get a lot more use on us than it did on Dad's pants. This time Ryan was the victim. He never even said ouch, but he walked upstairs slower than usual. Patrick asked him why he lied to Dad.

He answered, "He can't hurt me, but he can kill you."

Dad was like two people. When he was drinking, he didn't even know what he was saying or doing. He could give Mom a beating so bad and the next day ask her where she got the black eye. He'd even go as far as to tell her that she looked like shit. He had no recollection of any of it.

When he wasn't drinking, he was kind, funny, a true philosopher. You just never knew which one he would be on any given day. It was like Russian roulette. Mom used to tell me that someday he was going to kill her. I believed her.

I always seemed to be at the wrong place at the wrong time. Particularly when it came to Mom and Dad. All the boys were in school, but I hadn't started yet. I didn't want to 'cause I knew it was going to take away my special time with Mom, so I wanted to enjoy every minute of it while I could. More often than not Dad came home drunk, and I would be dancing with Mom. She loved her Victrola and her dancing. She had boxes full of 45 LP records and bags full of the yellow plastic disc that went in the hole in the middle so they could spin round and round on the turntable. I loved popping those little yellow suckers in and getting the next record ready for me and Mom to dance to. I was her DJ of choice and knew all of her favorite songs. There we were dancing and singing to "What A Difference A Day Makes" by the great Dinah Washington. It was such a hopeful song about how twenty-four little hours could change anything. I wanted to believe that, but then Dad came in sloshed, saw us dancing, as he did so many times before, and ripped the needle across the record scratching the vinyl. He wanted to make sure Mom wouldn't play that one again, and then he threatened to break the goddamn Victrola. I never understood why my happiness with Mom made him so furious. He told her that she turned me away from him and that she loved me more than him. "You're being ridiculous Ryan." That was all he needed.

"Ridiculous, I'll show you ridiculous." He'd smack her in the face; she would hit him back and start swearing in Italian. Then it became punches, "You guinea bitch. You ever raise your hand to me again and I'll break it."

She was down, I would jump on him, but he would fling me off like an insect.

The rest of the night would be silent. No singing. No dancing. No music. Just the sounds of forks hitting the dinner plates as me and five guys sat around the kitchen table eating my mother's Italian food while she wept upstairs, longing for a better life.

Chapter 2: BIRTHDAY

It was 1970. The ugly, lying, long nosed 37th President of the US of A, Richard Nixon was in the White House and Dad was still pounding back the whiskey's at McTierney's Ale House. It had been seven years since JFK died, and my seventh birthday. The Vietnam War had really taken a toll on our country. A lot of guys in our neighborhood went off to war, but never returned. Some came home, but they were never the same. Every night when Mom tucked me in, we would pray to God, starting with the 'Our Father,' then the 'Hail Mary,' and we would always end by saying, 'God Bless the boys in Vietnam'. It was just something my mother added, and I learned it as if it was always part of the prayer. It became a habit and still to this day I say it. Everyone was talking about Nixon trying to bring all of our troop's home from Vietnam and praying he would be able to, but Dad said Nixon was full of shit and he didn't have the balls that JFK did 'cause if he did we wouldn't have lost so many of our boys and this damn war would've been over already. A war America shouldn't have gotten involved in to begin with. He now used the Vietnam War as a worthy excuse for drinking and claimed that no President would ever compare to his Irishman, John Fitzgerald Kennedy, a true statesman. The rest were all a bunch of liars. Despite this day of mourning and the state of our country my mother had planned a birthday party for me. My best friends were invited: Teresa McGuiness, Patty Bennett, Angela Caruso, Mimi Mordente and some other boys and girls from the neighborhood. The party was at 4:00 p.m. and my mother had prepared a feast. All the kids' parents were invited, too. A fitted A-line blue dress cinched mom's hourglass figure. For an extra touch she had her make-up and had her hair done at the beauty parlor. She looked like a movie star. I was so proud. She bought me a blue dress to match hers. It was heavenly. I looked just like her.

My brothers were there and some of their friends. Ryan and Ian got bored and left. It was nice outside so Mom brought the Victrola out into the yard and had picnic tables set up with decorations everywhere. We played, 'Red Light Green Light,' 'Twister,' 'Musical Chairs,' 'Pin- the-Tail-on-the- Donkey,' and 'Mother May I.' Everyone was having so much fun, the kids, the parents, even Seamus and Patrick. My mother put "Let's Twist Again," by Chubby Checker, on the Victrola. We were all doing the twist and laughing. Me and Patrick jumped up on one of the tables and twisted up there.

Mr. Mordente, Mimi's father, came over to Mom and asked her to dance. She gladly accepted and they began to tear up the dance floor. It appeared that Mom hadn't a care in the world, but that carefree feeling changed rapidly when Dad came stumbling through the door after his day of mourning JFK at the bar. Rage came over him as he saw my mother dancing with Mr. Mordente, the widower. All of a sudden, it was as if the whole party turned into a slow-motion movie. I saw Dad leap toward Mr. Mordente.

I cried, "Look out Mom!" She turned as Dad crashed a Coca-Cola bottle over Mr. Mordente's head. Blood gushed from the side on Mr. Mordente's head, but that didn't stop Dad; He moved in for the kill. Mom tried to pull Dad off, but he punched her in the chest with his fist full of fury and murderous intentions. She fell backwards and hit the floor. The sound of her head striking the concrete was similar to that of a wrench hitting a water pipe. Everyone stopped in horror and stared down at my mother lying on the floor unconscious. He knocked the wind out of her. The other fathers at the party ripped Dad off Mr. Mordente and held him until the police and ambulance got there. He kicked and cursed the whole time.

When the ambulance arrived, they tended to Mr. Mordente's wound, but mostly were concerned about Mom. There was blood running down the side of her mouth. They put her on a stretcher and carried her out. I looked at Dad with contempt and silently said, "I hate you." He heard me loud and clear. It showed in his eyes. This time he would remember because there were too many witnesses to let it go. Dad wanted to go to the hospital with Mom, but when the police got there, they handcuffed him.

He yelled to Patrick and Seamus, "Call my mother, tell her I need her to bail me out." Nanny Finnegan was always bailing Dad out of his messes. I never understood how she seemed to make excuses for all of her son's bad behavior. One time our Irish neighbor, Debbie Collins, went to her quietly and said that she was concerned about all the abuse she heard coming from our house. She wondered if Nanny Finnegan knew, and said she was thinking of calling child services. Nanny promptly pulled her in for a spot of tea and some Irish Soda bread, a recipe from the old country, to keep good old Debbie quiet. Why cause trouble by sticking your nose into other people's business? Nanny appealed to her and persuaded her to keep quiet, then warned Dad to watch his temper. She said if he couldn't do that at least keep it down so the neighbors couldn't hear. Family matters should be kept private she stressed.

Seamus was very concerned about Mom. He knew the blood coming out of her mouth was a bad sign. His fists were clenched so hard the whites of his knuckles glistened like light bulbs. Walking over to Dad, he whispered through clenched teeth, "Call her yourself, I'm going with my mother. You make me sick!"

"Patrick," he yelled, "Patrick, come here son." Seamus pulled Patrick by the hand. Dad was left alone with the two arresting officers who were actually friends of the family and Dad's drinking buddies - John O'Shea and Bill Dugan, only they weren't drinking, and they were in uniform. They told him to come quietly to avoid further damage. Dad saw them putting Mom in the ambulance as they pushed his head in the back of the cop car. He resisted and cried out, "Isabella, I'm sorry. I didn't mean to hit you." I couldn't believe Dad was sobbing like a baby.

John said, "Ryan, c'mon, stop making a scene. The whole neighborhood is watching you."

And they were all watching like they were at a sporting event. Some of them just shook their heads and walked away because it was the same old story. There he is, Ryan Finnegan drunk and belligerent as per usual. That was my dad and there was nothing I could do to change that.

"I don't care, John. What would you do? I come home to get some comfort from my wife on this awful day and some guinea bastard, who we all know is looking for a new wife, has got his hands on her in my home." Dad tried to defend himself to no avail.

"You're piss drunk, Ryan. Now get in the car and shut up." Officer John O'Shea warned him and opened the back seat of the police car. Of course, Dad fought them like a good drunken Irishman, but they finally got him in the backseat.

As the car pulled away from our empty house full of abandoned birthday decorations, his head was turned looking out the back window. My eyes were locked on his. In that moment I saw the lost little boy inside of my Dad, scared and fragile like my brother Patrick.

Seamus, Patrick, and I tried to hop in the back of the ambulance, but the medic said there wasn't room for all of us. Seamus said he had to be there because he had to make sure they did everything right and that he was going to be a doctor. I told him it was my birthday and that the only present I want God to give me is to be by my mother's side. Somehow, I believed if I was with her, she wasn't allowed to die.

Patrick said, "Can I please come? I'll squeeze in the corner. I don't take up much room."

The medic was in a hurry and didn't have time to waste arguing with us, so he crammed us in next to Mom.

As we rode to Astoria General Hospital, we all stared at Mom's tiny body, lifeless, sad, and lonely. Her beautiful blue dress now had puddles of blood that would forever stain the very fabric of her. I felt my short life slipping away. If anything happens to Mom, I don't think I can go on. I became acutely aware of everything around me. Seamus must have felt my fear. He grabbed my hand gently. Somehow, he always knew what to do and had impeccable timing. I noticed how handsome and distinguished he was. He had Mom's bone structure, but Dad's coloring, blonde hair, blue eyes and pearl white teeth. I knew someday he would be a great doctor. When I looked over to Patrick, I noticed his small delicate frame, his pretty face, curly golden locks that dripped into his sad gray eyes. He was lost, as he quietly wept. My fears were buried deep, my struggle was something I couldn't explain to anyone, not even to Mom because I felt like I had to take care of her. But Patrick's struggle was apparent to me. Maybe I saw myself in him. It must be so hard to be the youngest, smallest, weakest boy in the family. What goes on in his mind? I wanted to comfort him, save him. I wanted to comfort Mom, save Mom. I wondered who would comfort me, save me?

When we arrived, they took her right in and we were instructed to wait in the lobby. Seamus told us his diagnosis. Dad struck her so hard; he probably punctured her lung. She'd be all right, he assured us, but he could kill her someday.

Patrick and I listened to Seamus. Even though he was only twelve he spoke with intelligence and confidence beyond his years. While other kids were reading Captain Courageous, Willie Wonka and the Chocolate Factory, and Alice in Wonderland, he was reading 'Gray's Anatomy.'

Dr. Silver, the man who stitched me up when I was five, came walking by. I'll never forget his face. I cheered up for a moment. "Dr. Silver," I shouted, "It's me, Francesca. Remember?"

He smiled. I folded my top lip up for him, revealing my scar, which I was very proud of. He laughed and looked at my two brothers. "Where are the other two troops?" he asked me.

"We're not sure." I told him.

He inquired about why we were here. I told him Mom was hurt at my birthday party. "I'm so sorry to hear that. Is it your birthday today?"

Yes, I smiled with my two front teeth. "I'm seven. This was the birthday dress mom picked out to match hers."

"Oh boy, that's a beautiful dress. You're growing up to be a fine young lady. What's your Mommy's name?"

Seamus popped up, "Isabella Finnegan. Will you please check on her? I think she may have a punctured lung."

"That's pretty serious son, what makes you think that?"

Seamus explained. "She had blood come up after."

Dr. Silver realized there was more. "After what?"

Seamus hung his head as his mouth twisted to one side. I could feel the shame wash over him, and it splashed all over me and Patrick. Dr. Silver looked at Patrick and Patrick dropped his head quickly. He then looked at me. I couldn't hold it in.

"My father punched her in the chest. She fell on the ground."

Seamus was embarrassed. He scolded me, "Frankie, you shouldn't say that."

“But it’s the truth.” I protested.

“It’s private.” He whispered.

Dr. Silver felt our whole situation in a nano second. "I'll go check on your mom."

A little later Ryan and Ian came running into the hospital. Ian was sporting a black eye while his biceps were popping out of his Rolling Stones t-shirt. They were his favorite band and Mick Jagger was God as far as Ian was concerned. It was not unusual to see some evidence of a fight worn upon his face. When Patrick saw Ryan, he jumped up. Ryan immediately came over, lifted Patrick, "Hey champ." Now Patrick felt safe.

Ryan knew Seamus was the one to talk to. "What's the story, Dr. Seamus?" Ryan tried to make light of the situation.

"How's Mom?" Ian asked.

"What the hell happened to your eye?" asked Seamus.

"Nothin' Seamus. It's a flea bite, how's Mom?"

"We don't know yet, but she got whacked in the chest pretty hard.

"He punched her in the chest, that fucking animal. Excuse my filthy mouth, Frankie." Ryan was so pissed off. "He could kill her like that. Do you know how strong that Irish bastard is?"

If anyone knew, it was Ryan. Dad beat on him all the time, but he was not as frail as Mom. Ryan and Dad were built the same, like brick shithouses.

Hours went by. Patrick fell asleep on Ryan's lap. Seamus got some ice for Ian's shiner. He held it on his eye, while he laid on the couch, spread out so comfortably. Ian had such a freedom about him. He was a rebel and seemed to make peace with even the worst of situations. Worry didn't seem to plague him as it did the rest of us. If it did, he never showed it.

Dr. Silver came out to talk to us. Everyone jumped up and stood at attention. "Your mother is going to be okay. She needs to rest. There is some damage to her right lung."

Seamus interrupted. "Was it punctured?"

"Yes. We took some x-rays that confirmed the puncture." Dr. Silver looked at all of our faces. "Where is your father?"

"In jail," I blurted out. I couldn't help myself. Ian smacked me in the head. Ryan calmly replied, "We're not really sure where he is, why?"

"Well, I'm just curious why he isn't here. Does your mother have any family here?"

"We're her family," Ian replied.

"I mean her mother, father. Does she have any sisters or brothers?" "Yeah," Ryan jumped in, "Her mother lives around the corner and she has a sister in Jersey."

"Good, good," Dr. Silver smiled, "They need to know about her condition. She could use some love and support around her right now."

I thought to myself, I love and support her. I guess that's not enough. Then I thought, how's Nanny Juliano going to see her? Dad won't even let her in the house. They don't get along. She never wanted Mom to marry Dad. Nanny said, even though he was very good looking he was a no good drunken Irish bum. Nanny had a point, but Mom lost her heart to Dad. She couldn't resist his magnetism. She always said he could charm the habit off a nun. All the mothers in the neighborhood wanted to be my dad's wife. All the women would say, he's drop dead gorgeous. They used to say to me, "I could've been your mother if your father picked me." I sneered back at them defending my Mom,

"No you couldn't. You could never be my mom, my Mom's the best." Later I found out that Dad had screwed around with all these women who said they could've been my mother, but Mom was the one who got pregnant. That's why they got married. Nanny Finnegan didn't want her son marrying some guinea off the boat either. No one wanted it. Mom was very religious. Always at church doing her novenas and talking to Father Haggerty about Jesus and Mary. She would never dream of having an abortion. She would rather die.

Nanny Juliano lived around the corner one way in a one-bedroom rent control apartment infested with cockroaches and water bugs the size of my foot. Nanny and Grumpy Finnegan lived around the corner the other way in a beautiful three-story house. We were never allowed upstairs. I don't even know what it looked like up there. It was like some big secret that we were forbidden to see. Either it was a pigsty and Nanny was embarrassed or she was hiding a dead body. My father told us if we ever disrespected his mother, he would kick our little asses, so we just chalked it up to be a mystery. We called my grandfather Grumpy because he was always smiling. Known as the champion walker of Queens, he set out every morning, no matter the weather, and marched all the way to Sunny Side, which was good five-mile jaunt roundtrip. There was a bakery called Lowry's and it was his daily ritual where he would get his favorite bread, rye with caraway seeds. Yes, they had great bread, but I don't think that's why Grumpy went there religiously. It was that walk that he needed so desperately. He said, 'it's my time to talk to God and tell him my sins.' Then he would flash me a weak smile. He didn't seem to talk much, always letting Nanny Finnegan have her way. Behind his silence I suspected something, but I couldn't put my finger on it. His eyes told a different story than his constant smile.

Then there was Mom's sister, Carmella. I loved her but we hardly saw her because she lived so far away. Dad didn't like to drive. It didn't mix too well with drinking. Aunt Carmella loved to cook too. Desserts were her specialty. One in particular was my all time favorite. She called it icebox cake. It was made with bananas, cookies, ice cream and sponge cake. Whenever we went there, she would show it to me as soon as I walked in.

"Guess what I made for you, Francesca?"

I smiled as my belly danced with joy. I would run to the fridge, open the door and there it was in the middle shelf as if it were on a throne. Ice Box cake just for me. I always felt like I was special at Aunt Carmella's and Uncle Louie's. They treated me like a little girl. They bought me pinafore dresses and Barbie dolls. I would leave the dolls there so I could have them whenever I went and also because I didn't want my brothers to make fun of me for playing with dolls. Sometimes I was allowed to stay the whole weekend and Dad would pick me up on Sunday.

I would dread the car ride back, me and Dad all alone. He would start quizzing me on those long car rides, and I would freeze. It was as if I couldn't speak. He would tell me the answers and stress how important education is. 'If you're stupid in this life it's a lot harder.' Then he would talk to me about life and its struggles, it's lessons, the highs, and the lows. It was hard not to be intrigued by everything he was saying. As much as I hated to admit it, the Irish bastard was full of wisdom. I know he thinks I never listened to him 'cause I stared out the window the whole time, but I did. I listened to every word but pretended that I didn't 'cause I wanted to punish him. However, no matter how hard I fought it, his words were locked in my mind, imbedded in my memory from those long car rides home. He taught me so much.

All this flashed through my mind when Dr. Silver asked about Mom's family. Seamus assured him she would get plenty of love and care.

We tried to stay in the hospital, but they wouldn't let us. We visited with Mom until they kicked us out. Seamus read her chart, checked all her vital signs. He took a stethoscope from one of the stations to check Mom's lungs. They weren't too strong.

Mom was so happy to see all of us together. She told me how sorry she was that my party got ruined. I held her small face in my small hands. "Don't be sorry, you didn't do anything wrong, Mom."

Seamus told Mom, "Don’t talk too much, it uses up too much strength. You need to sleep."

Ryan kissed Mom. "I love you, Mom."

Patrick quickly added, "Me too, Mom."

Ian muttered "Yeah."

Mom asked Ian, "Have you been fighting with Sean Murphy again?" Ian just nodded yes. Ian and Sean were fighting partners. Every time they saw each other they would stop whatever they were doing and start punching the hell out of each other. They never even knew what they were fighting over. It had become a routine. It was one fight that lasted for about twelve years. "Stop being such a tough guy. Fists never solve your problems."

Seamus took her hand, "Mom, we'll be back in the morning. Get some sleep." I didn't want to go. I felt scared. I've never spent one single night in that house without Mom.

She whispered to Ryan as she grabbed his big hand, "Ryan, I want you to do one favor for me, will you promise?"

"Sure, Mom. Anything."

"Make sure you take Francesca's birthday cake out of the ice box. The candles are in the top drawer in the kitchen. You and your brothers sing to her. She needs you."

Ryan smiled, "You got it, Mom." All the boys turned and left.

I waited one more minute. I looked into Mom's eyes. She touched my curly red hair. Both me and Mom had red hair. Mom said I got it from her. Dad argued that it was from Nanny Finnegan, because she had red hair too. I think mine was from Mom. In Italian she said, "You are so beautiful, my little Francesca. Your heart is so wild like an antelope and this is good. You must be free. Do not let anyone put chains on you, then you are no longer yourself. I see greatness in you, my child. Don't be afraid to be yourself. So many boys around you can make you scared, but don't let them. They are more afraid of you than you are of them." Mom was getting sleepy and her words were almost coming out as if she was talking in her sleep. She continued, "Don't be a prisoner like your mother. So much fear keeps me in prison."

She was asleep. I was confused. I touched her red curly hair. It felt lovely like a silk scarf. I wanted to wrap myself in her hair like a bird in a nest. I didn't want to leave. Dr. Silver tapped me on the shoulder. I don't know what came over me, but I lifted my arms to him and asked him to hold me. He picked me up and comforted my broken heart for one small moment. He then handed me a little stuffed monkey with a red bow around it. "Happy Birthday, Francesca."

"Thank you, Dr. Silver."

He took me out to my brothers. We all left Mom and were going home. We didn't know what we would find there, and it didn't matter as long as we were all together. We felt strong for Mom. Patrick grabbed Ryan's hand. Ryan grabbed my hand. Seamus and Ian walked with their hands in their pockets. Whatever may come, we were ready.

The house was dark when we got there. Ian turned the lights on, and we started to clean up a little. I went to the backyard. As I took a deep breath, I wished I could turn back the clock. Earlier that day I was happy. It was my birthday, a celebration for me. People came and gave me presents. Laughter and dancing filled our house for a change. Why did Kennedy have to get killed on my birthday? I walked over to the spot where Mom fell. Kneeling down, I touched the bloodstain on the cement. It was somehow a way to touch Mom. All of a sudden, the lights went out. I got scared. When I looked up a candlelit cake was approaching me with my four brothers behind it. As they started singing, I laughed, then cried. I missed Mom. I even missed Dad. The Dad I wished he could be. He never even wished me a happy birthday. I let it go. I had Ryan, Ian, Seamus and

Patrick smiling at me. I was going to milk it for all it was worth. Before I made my wish, I looked up to God and noticed a shooting star. I made my wish. All I wanted was for Mom to get better. Then I blew out my candles. A chill passed through my heart. This was going to be a very hard year. I heard a voice whisper to me. I shook it out. Ryan lifted me up and all the boys sang. "For she's the jolly good marshmallow." I'll never forget that night and how much love I felt for my brothers. I also noticed how good-looking they all were. Ryan, with his sandy brown hair, green eyes and muscular body. Ian looked like the spit out of Dad's mouth, a real heartthrob. Seamus was so handsome, but never lead with that. It was more important for him to appear intelligent, and Patrick was just the prettiest boy I had ever seen. Everyone used to say Irish and Italians make the cutest babies. I don't know if that's true, but to me, my brothers were the cutest guys in the neighborhood.

About two in the morning Dad strolled in. Nanny Finnegan bailed him out yet again. I was wide-awake. He was grunting and groaning. My bedroom was right next to Mom and Dad's. As a matter of fact, I could see right in their room. There was no door separating us. I saw Dad fall to the bed and bawl. He leaned over to Mom's side of the bed and began talking to her pillow as if she was there. "Forgive me, Isabella. You're just too good for me and too gorgeous. I get so jealous. If only you knew how much I love you, then you would forgive me." I couldn't believe my ears. Does Mom know? I wondered if maybe Dad leaned over my bed and said he loved me when I wasn't there. If perhaps he whispered 'Happy Birthday' to my pillow hoping I would catch his words in my ear when I rest my head at night. Why can't this man express himself to us? What has got such a deep hold on him?

As soon as I heard him snoring, I went to his pants by the side of the bed, saw his brown leather belt fastened through the loops, reached in his pocket and borrowed a five-dollar bill. I went downstairs and cut a piece of cake. It was a Napoleon sheet cake, with chocolate and vanilla cream and almonds all around the sides. It was Mom's favorite. I thought of her words "Don't be afraid to be yourself." Well, myself was saying, 'Bring your mother some of your cake. She needs you to be there for her.' I grabbed my stuffed monkey that Dr. Silver gave me and headed out. I was scared, but nothing could stop me. I hopped on the Q19 bus in my flannel Bugs Bunny pajamas, red converse sneakers, and handed the bus driver the five. He was crusty but nice.

"Where you goin', kid?" Cracking his gum.

"Astoria General Hospital. My Mom is there, and she needs me."

"Keep your five, have a seat." I think he was just happy to have a little company. "What's your monkey's name?"

I looked at my monkey and realized I hadn't named him. It came to me, "Silvio", I said.

"Good name," he said. No one else got on the bus. "You really shouldn't be out at this time of night alone."

"I know that, but I have to bring Mom a piece of my birthday cake. If I knew you were gonna be so nice I would've brought you a piece too. We had so much."

He laughed and grabbed his fat belly. "Thanks. I'm on a diet anyway." He told me his name was Jerry and he rode the Q19 from midnight to eight a.m., Tuesdays through Saturdays and if I need a ride, I could ride for free. I liked Jerry. "How old are you kid?" He asked out of the side of his mouth.

I felt mature and proud. "Seven years old."

"Wow, you're practically a grown up," he laughed. "You know usually I wouldn't do this, but I want to make sure you get to your mommy safely. I'm gonna drop you right in front of the hospital." Wow. I felt special. Door to door service from Jerry. He waved good-bye to Silvio and me and took off in his big bus.

When we got inside, I pretended to fit in so I wouldn't look suspicious. That's why I left my pajamas on. It was very quiet. No one seemed to notice me at all. I crept into Mom's room, bare and sterile. She was sleeping peacefully. I sat in the ugly green chair beside her bed. I figured when she woke up, I would be there. I fell asleep. Early in the morning the sun glared through the hospital window. I woke up. Mom's eyes were still closed. Slowly she opened them. She smiled softly. I thought she was looking at me, but she was looking just past me at the doorway to her room, 317. I turned to see what grabbed her attention and there in the doorway stood Dad, wearing a gray pinstriped suit with a royal blue pressed shirt, sparkling from head to toe and looking like a stud. He must have just got a haircut and shave too. I was shocked. Carrying an exquisite bouquet of tulips, his eyes filled with mist as he smiled at Mom. Suddenly a surge of energy permeated through the dead air that occupied the room. Delighted to see him, she stretched her hand out to him. That was his cue to go to her.

In that moment he knew all was forgiven. He tried to speak but she silenced him. "Kiss me, Ryan." He handed the flowers to me and went to her like a puppy. For a moment I wondered if he brought the flowers for me. Maybe they were to make up for spoiling my birthday.

He reached over, smiled at me and grabbed the flowers.

"These are for you, Isabella." They were for Mom, not me.

"Go find a pitcher with water, Francesca," Mom excitedly asked. Great, I thought, I've been here all night with my Napoleon birthday cake and Rudolph Valentino strolls in and gets all the attention. I was angry. This is too easy. How can she forgive him so quickly? I wanted her to yell at him or punch him. Do something besides, 'Kiss me Ryan." Then I remembered last night as he spoke to her pillow. Maybe she heard him. Maybe she got the message in her dream. They were so connected that they communicated even when they were apart. I guess I was too young to understand their relationship, but if this was love, if this was what it meant to be married, I wanted no part of it.

All the charges were dropped against Dad. Mr. Mordente said if it ever happened again, he would have Dad locked up.

After they kissed and laughed for a while, I gave Mom a piece of my birthday cake. Turning to me she took a bite and smiled as if she just turned seven years old. Was it the cake or because of him? I'd like to think it was because of me, but I realized in that moment that Dad had a power over her that was beyond my reach. She became a little girl in his presence. Dad had a bite of my birthday cake too, even though I didn't want him to. He didn't deserve it and he never did wish me a 'Happy Birthday.'

Chapter 3: THE CUBAN MAN

Something shifted inside of Dad after my birthday. We didn't know if it would last, but we enjoyed it for the moment. Winter had come and the snow was falling. As the flakey white powder fell from the sky, I felt hopeful that things were changing.

Dad was light and funny and was laying off the booze since the incident. He even looked more handsome. It was the first time I ever saw the whites of his eyes, no red lines hiding how pretty his blue irises were. Cheekbones popped through where there usually was puffiness. Mind you he was not a fat man, just swollen in his face from the drink, as the Irish would say. Looking closely, I could see all the blue and red blood vessels forming a trail around Dad's nose, but that bulbous look was subsiding. I finally got why all the women in the neighborhood, including Mom, would fall for him. This guy was full of charisma and a boyish innocence that made you want to squeeze him. It was as if he was young again, before he had five mouths to feed. I wonder what he was like, and if it was our fault that he drank so much. Did we suck the fun out of him? I hoped maybe, now that he was off the sauce, he could see the good in all of us. Perhaps we could bring him happiness.

Even Nanny Juliano and Dad were putting up with each other. She was over for dinner and dancing every night, who knew Nanny had all that rhythm inside of her. I even caught Dad getting a kick out of Nanny a couple of times. Suddenly Mom's old Victrola was the prized possession of the house. As part of his amends Dad showed up with duplicate copies of all the 45 LP records that he scratched so that Mom could have her favorites back and enjoy them again. It really seemed that he wanted her to be happy, but more than that, he wanted to be the cause of her happiness. Mom and Dad could really cut the rug. He told us the story of how they met.

"It was 1949 and Harry S. Truman, our 33rd President, was in the White House, with Alben W. Barkley as his Vice President. While serving as Vice President to Franklin D. Roosevelt, Truman succeeded and became President after FDR died on April 12, 1945 from a hemorrhagic stroke." Dad always started his stories with who was running our country and commentary about them. Throwing details in about their background, war stories, families, you name it, Dad knew it all. All I really cared about was how he met Mom and why they fell in love.

"Tell us about Mom." I laughed impatiently.

Usually, he would tell me to shut my mouth, pay attention and learn something for a change, but he just smiled, gazed at Mom and took me back with his fascinating ability to paint pictures with his words. Damn, he was a great storyteller.

He was eighteen and she was sixteen. There was a neighborhood dance at St. Patrick's auditorium. Mom, Aunt Carmella and Nanny Juliano had just come off the boat from Naples the year before. They came with Nanny's sister, Josie (Josephina, pronounced Ho-sa-fina back in the old country) and all of her kids too.

Mom went to L.I.C (Long Island City) High School because they couldn't afford a Catholic School, but Nanny Juliano worked at St. Patrick's as the lunchroom lady in the cafeteria. One of the women she worked with gave her some extra tickets to the school dance. Mom and Aunt Carmella got all decked out in their finest skirts that landed just below the knee and graced their feet with closed toe high heel Mary Jane shoes. They were ready to strut their stuff on the dance floor. As fate would have it, Dad was there.

From the time Mom was a little girl in Italy, dancing was her dream. Nanny Juliano said she would dance around the house saying, 'I'm going to New York someday to become a Rockette in Radio City Music Hall.' She could watch a dance once and do it better than the person who showed it to her. Rhythm and style were her middle name.

All the girls at the dance gathered around the best-looking guy in town, Ryan Finnegan, otherwise known as my dad, in the hopes of possible having just one dance with him. Then they can die happy. He wasn't interested in any of them. His attentions were being pulled to the dance floor. Breathless, he found himself mesmerized by the red-haired girl ripping up the dance floor with her sister. These two stunning Italian girls that no one recognized from school, were jitterbugging to 'In the Mood,' by Glenn Miller as they dominated St. Patrick's School auditorium dance floor. Their skirts were spinning, their leather shoes clapping on the hardwood floor, and their hips were shaking with a thunderous freedom. Watching the two of them made the whole place want to dance. But watching Mom made Dad want to sing, fly, and cry. The feeling that came over him terrified him because he couldn't control what happened to his body. Breaking out into a sweat, he didn't understand why just the sight of this girl made him feel so weak. Remember, Dad was as cool as a cucumber and no girl could make Ryan Finnegan crumble, until now. He said Mom's energy filled the whole auditorium, the whole school, the whole city and at that moment, his entire world. Carmella was a good dancer and pretty, but Mom was a royal queen. Her red hair was shooting beams of light to every corner of the room. Even the band commented on Mom's dancing. She stopped the whole room. And it was that night, at that moment that Mom captured Dad's heart. He knew he must meet her, but believe it or not, Dad, the coolest guy in Queens, was too shy to ask her to dance. He was intimidated. He had two left feet. Mom noticed him because he was the most beautiful boy she had seen since she arrived in America, but they never spoke that night. They just stared at each other through a sea of people as twinkle lights beamed magical possibilities before their eyes. Dad mysteriously disappeared.

He found out who she was and where she lived. Leaving school early each day, he would perch himself in position under the El, as the trains rumbled above him, then check his watch and wait for her to descend from the Court House Square train station. She took the number 7 Flushing line to school every day. Watching her every move became his favorite pastime. Nothing else existed for him except the Italian red-headed flame that ignited his soul with her exquisite beauty and magnificent dance steps.

One day when it was cold and the ground was icy, he hid behind the corner of her apartment building, where she lived with Nanny Juliano, and waited for her. Timing it perfectly, he rounded the corner and came sliding into her, causing a major collision. Falling on top of him, her books went flying everywhere. He helped her up. "I'm sorry, excuse me, I didn't see you."

Mom laughed nervously and then saw who it was. "It's all right, don't worry."

He noticed she had an Italian accent, "Are you from Italy?"

"Yes I am." She smiled causing him to practically slip on the ice for real. Mom had a smile that melted everyone's heart, but completely stole Ryan Finnegan's that day.

"So, listen, uh, I was wondering if maybe, you know, you can teach me some of those fancy steps you were doing down at St. Patrick's."

She was smitten. "Sure, you want to learn to dance?"

"Yeah, why not." Dad was still playing the tough guy.

"Why not, sure. I'll teach you if you like." She played tough back.

Dad's heart was about to burst. Mom brought him home and pulled out her records, Tommy Dorsey, Bing Crosby, The Ink Spots, Ella Fitzgerald, Frank Sinatra, you name it, Mom had them all and she spun them on her favorite Victrola and began to teach her future husband how to dance. It was love at first sight. Dancing brought them together. Maybe it could keep them together.

Our house was filled with laughter and dancing that winter. We all learned the Cha-Cha, the Lindy, and the Jitterbug.

Mom and Dad were like Fred and Ginger. Patrick was the best dancer out of all the boys. This was the one area where he really shined. He would pick me up, straddle me from side to side, spin me, and flip me, whatever it was. He was so confident with every move. Mom said he was a natural.

* * *

Spring came, and Patrick and I decided to start our own business; a shoeshine business, since Dad was always talking about the state of our country's economy and how he had to take on extra jobs because we can never have too much money or work hard enough. 'You always have to have something stashed away for a rainy day 'cause you never know what's gonna happen in this crazy world.' Well, I, for one, wanted to have some money. I loved the feeling of having cash in my pocket. Whenever I swiped a few bucks from Dad for being such a drunken asshole it always made me feel powerful knowing I had money at my fingertips. But now that he wasn't drinking, I figured I'd better get my own stash going. Patrick and I found an old shoeshine box of Dad's in the basement. It was wooden with the shoe-shaped foot holder on top. There were round tins with black and brown polish, three cotton cloths, and a thick bristled brush with a wooden handle. We still needed to find another kit. We went to Grumpy's house around the corner. We told him of our business plan together. He thought it was great and gladly lent us his old box, which was even more ancient looking than Dad's, but surprisingly had more provisions in the shoe-shining department. We decided to split all the profits and put the money in a secret hiding place until we figured out what we wanted to do with it.

Business was great. Waiting at the bottom of the stairs at the Court House Square Train Station, we wore corduroy pants, button down man-tailored shirts and suspenders, accompanied by salt and pepper caps backwards with big smiles on our freckled faces. All of our clothing ordered from the Sears Roebuck catalogue. And I, of course, dressed just like my brothers because I was, after all wearing their hand me downs. Dad said they suited me just fine and he wasn't made of money.

"Shine Sir?" "Shine Ma'am?" We charged 50 cents a shine, but they always gave a dollar and said keep the change. Freckles go a long way when you're a kid. At rush hour we'd pull in twenty dollars a piece. The more we made, the more we wanted. We became very competitive with each other and had contests. It was great incentive and upped the ante. A lot of ladies would let Patrick shine their fancy pumps and patent leathers just because they thought he was so cute.

After a rush at the train station on St. Patty's Day, we were walking by Dom's Bar on the corner of 45th road, Court House Square, Queens, and happened to peek in. Decorated with green Shamrock's, Irish flags, and piss drunk Irishmen, celebration was in high gear, as it was packed to the gills. Then, we saw Uncle

Jim. Spotting us, he waved for us to come in. Patrick and I knew we were betraying the family rule put in order by Dad, but both of us were intrigued by the possibility of danger. I had never stepped foot inside a bar. Neither had Patrick. Walking in slowly with our shoeshine boxes, the great Jackie Wilson was singing one of the most famous Irish songs ever, 'Danny Boy.' Here's this amazing black man with the voice of an angel pouring his soul through the jukebox as it pumped a new lifeforce into my heart, it felt like he was singing just for me. For the first time I felt proud to be Irish, but not because of any Irish people I knew. It was because of Jackie Wilson. I always heard people talking about 'The Black Irish,' maybe this was what they meant. To me, Jackie Wilson was by favorite black Irishman. I wondered why Jackie was so passionate about this song in particular and why it made him summon such a melodious tenor from the bottom of his feet to reach the heavens above. My God his voice was hypnotic and the ambiance in the bar energized me like some sort of drug. I thought to myself, I have to get me a jukebox at home, music never sounded this good. The cigarette smoke wafted like storm clouds through the bar. You needed a knife just to cut through it. There was a musty smell that felt toxic to my seven-year-old body, but at the same time, it excited the hell out of me. Uncle Jim started yelling to the bar, "Look at these two, their fathers got them working already." He started laughing with all the other drunken fools. Uncle Jim hated my father, and this was his bar, his home, his gang. They all knew that he and Dad fought all of the time and were not on speaking terms.

I shouted above the music, "Dad didn't make us do this, he doesn't even know."

"Well, what are you doing with the money?" he asked.

Patrick yelled, "We're saving it for something special."

Uncle Jim smiled, "Okay, well just don't tell your old man or he'll keep it for himself." Jim yelled again to the whole bar, "Listen up you drunken idiots, your shoes are all needing a good shine so line up and give these kids some business." Wow. It was unbelievable. One by one all the drunks stepped up with their dirty shoes to support our business. They were throwing their money at us. We couldn't shine quick enough, shoe after shoe. I even shined one guys' bare feet, he was so drunk, but didn't want to be left out. He gave me five bucks. The drinks were flowing, the music blaring and our brushes polishing. Uncle Jim raised his glass of whiskey, "Give us another round of Napertandy."

All at once the entire bar broke into an ole Irish song, loud and proud.

'Oh I met with Napertandy, he took me by the hand,

he asked me how was Ireland, and how did she

stand? The most distressful country that you have ever seen. They're hanging men and women for the wearing of the green!'

Then they all roared with laughter and sang it again and again. Ordered more drinks and hugged like it was the last time they would ever see each other. I didn't know what the hell the song meant, but it obviously meant a lot to them, and I couldn't get that damn song out of my head for the rest of my life.

* * *

We learned that people were more generous when they'd been drinking. We made two hundred dollars in honor of St. Patty. Uncle Jim slipped us twenty bucks each. He made every single person in that bar get a shoeshine that day, even the bartender. It was epic. Truly a day to remember and without a doubt the best St. Patrick's Day to date.

Patrick and I figured maybe we could hit up other bars in the neighborhood and maybe even travel a little and explore other neighborhoods. Queensboro Plaza was loaded with bars. We were raking in the bucks and having fun at the same time. People respected what we did and didn't mind paying us. We would fool around with the customers and make up sad stories to assure a good tip. They were always asking us questions about our family and why were we shining shoes at such a young age. Sometimes I would say that my father ran away from home and left us with nothing. Patrick would tell some of the women that he was trying to save enough money to buy his mother a washing machine. Boy did that go over well, especially with the moms. It became an art, knowing just what to say and what not to say was the key to a good tip. On the average, we would make a few hundred a week.

Unfortunately, as the weather changed, Dad started to change back to his old self. He was back to drinking at the Ale House and resumed his abusive behavior.

Dad had strict rules in the house. Dinner was always at 4:30 p.m. sharp, no exceptions unless he had to work late. No talking at the dinner table unless it was him speaking. You had to hold your fork and knife properly. If not, you would feel the point of the fork digging into your hand, sometimes that meant a little blood. No sweets, no soda, no dessert and no crying.

One day Patrick and I were on our way home after shining shoes. It was about 4:00 p.m. The train let out a slew of businessmen, about forty of them. They all went into Dom's bar. Patrick called to one of them "Shine Sir?"

"Sure kid. Let's take it inside so I can get my fix too."

We followed him into Dom's. There was some sort of convention going on in there. All these well-dressed men in fancy suits, laughing and drinking. They weren't locals. You didn’t see guys dressed like this in these parts unless they were going to a funeral or a wedding. We didn't know why they were in our neighborhood. But we didn't care; we could smell the money. These guys had nice fancy shoes, imported from Italy or Paris or somewhere special. It was a pleasure shining such expensive shoes; they came out looking great. I felt a sense of pride in my shoe-shining talents. It was like we graduated in the shoe-shining department. Dom's Place was a lucky spot for us. He always let us in, as long as we kept a low profile in the back. After we shined almost everyone's shoes, we noticed it was dark outside. We got carried away and 4:30 dinner came and went, and we missed it. I felt the terror fill my heart, but Patrick was more afraid than I was. We plotted and practiced our story, what we would say. Dad knew we had been shining shoes in the neighborhood, but he didn't know we went into the pubs.

When we got close to the house, we took a deep breath and blessed ourselves. We hid our boxes in the usual place, down the steps that lead to the basement outside the house. We found a bunch of leaves and branches and camouflage the crap out of it.

As I turned the doorknob and pushed open the front door, my heart banged beneath my sweaty T-shirt. Patrick was close behind with his hand on my back. He didn't want to walk in first. Waiting behind the door was Dad with a Heineken in one hand and his belt in the other.

We froze when we saw him. "Where were you at 4:30 while your dinner was getting cold?" Think quickly, lie, and remember your story. I was blank. Fear erased any and everything in my head.

"Well, answer me Goddammit."

"We were playing in the park." I lied.

Patrick mustered up a "Yeah."

"You lying little fucks, come here. "

We walked over to him. He started sniffing us like a dog. I wondered if he was trying to smell if I was lying. "Have you been smoking?"

"No, Dad. I swear."

"You reek of cigarettes."

"Everyone at the park was smoking," I lied again, but the kind of smoke lingering in our clothes was only attainable by a regular drunk or someone who has to work in a pub. It becomes part of you.

"Bullshit!" He cracked the belt against the wall. Patrick and I jumped out of our skin. "You've been shining shoes at Dom's Pub, haven't you?" Before I could lie again, he warned me, "If you lie again, you're gonna get this belt across your face." That didn't sound like fun to me. Maybe I should tell the truth. "Well?" He shouted.

"Yes, we were at Dom's shining shoes because this guy called us in." Dad went nuts. "I never want to hear another word about Dom's bar. My brother goes there. Don't you know that?"

"No, Dad." I lied again.

"Did you ever see him there?"

"No, Dad." Patrick shook his head to confirm.

"If you ever see him, you're not to say hello or smile or look at him. Is that understood?" Dad was in so much pain, like a child, as he was saying this. I wasn't afraid anymore, I was curious.

"Why Daddy?" I asked him. He smashed his beer to the ground, took me by the neck and threw me up against the wall.

"Because I said so. That's why. Because I hate him! That's why. Because whatever I say goes, you little piece of shit. That's why. Do you understand me?"

My calm curiosity turned once again into panic. "Yes," I squeezed through the lump in my throat. "Yes, Daddy." He dropped me, turned to Patrick who was frozen with fear in his eyes.

"Pick up this glass and both of you go to bed. No dinner, no talking and no crying, and if I ever hear about you shining another fuckin' shoe, I'll kill you both."

Where was Mom? Where were Ryan, Ian, and Seamus? I didn't know why no one came out of the kitchen during this whole time to stop Dad or help us. Patrick and I got ready for bed in silence. I counted my money when I was alone. $123.00 dollars...I focused on that, the money. I had to. If I thought about anything else. I would cry and I wasn't allowed. I couldn't chance getting killed. So, I swallowed my tears, stuck my money in my small wooden dresser drawer under my Sears hand me down clothes and went to bed. I wanted to talk to Patrick and tell him not to worry and to be strong. Because with all this money we saved, maybe we could get out of this house soon. I wanted to hold him. I knew how deep his despair could get. I worried more about him than myself. Maybe that's what got me through. No matter how bad I felt, I always knew Patrick was feeling worse.

The next morning, I got up early and woke Patrick up. We had a couple of hours before we had to go to school. We took our shoeshine boxes and got the early commuters. We agreed this would be our last morning of shining shoes. We pulled in $50 and then sold one of the boxes to Joey McVee for $20. He was thrilled and had been trying to get in our business from the beginning. Now he could run the show by himself and make all the money that we would be missing out on. We took the other shoeshine box and we hid in a secret place that only the two of us knew about and pinky swore to keep to the grave. It was the end of our moneymaking enterprise. Patrick was sad and so was I, but I told him we would come up with something else. We got on the train and headed to St. Mary's, where we went to school. While we were on the train, Patrick counted how many pairs of shoes we missed out on. I told him that would only make it worse. I saw his little eyes fill up with tears, so I started to imitate Dad. "You lying little fucking kids, you ever see my brother? Uh, no, Dad. What does he look like, you?" Patrick started to crack a smile. "Uh, Dad, do you even have a brother? No, we never saw him, did we Patrick? Nope. You're not lying again are you? No, Dad, of course not, would we lie to you?" Patrick couldn't hold it anymore and he busted out laughing. I did a great impression of Dad. I became the clown for Patrick whenever he was down. I felt like it was my job. He put his arm around me and said, "You're the best, Frankie." I smiled and said, "I know," and we both laughed. Our train arrived at Vernon Jackson Boulevard station. We got off, walked to St. Mary's and went our separate ways to our respective classrooms.

Summer was in the air and I was excited. It was my favorite time of the year. I loved the sun staying out longer because it meant I could stay out longer. I felt more freedom in the summer. I was more optimistic.

I would go down to 12th Street Park where all of my brothers played and where all of the cool kids hung out. Seamus and Patrick loved baseball. Ryan and Ian preferred basketball. I loved them both equally. I was really good, and I don't mean for a girl. I was just really damn good at all sports. My brothers would pick me on their team before some of the guys, which made me feel special.

One day when we were playing basketball, all the guys took off their shirts because it was sweltering. I, too, was very hot so I ripped of my t-shirt without even thinking about it.

Ian got embarrassed. "What are you doing? You can't take off your shirt."

Right back at him, "But you can?"

"Yeah. I'm a guy."

"So, I'm a girl."

Ryan pulled me aside, "Frankie, it's not polite for a girl to take her shirt off outside."

"But why can you?"

"Cause I'm a boy."

"I don't get it."

"Well, you will someday. Just trust me Frankie, it's not cool, okay?" "Okay, Ryan." I put my shirt back on as all the boys stared at me. All of a sudden, I felt ashamed. I yelled out, "I quit!" and went home. Sean Murphy yelled out, "You're a little shit." Ian went at him and they had it out once again. I didn't stick around to see who won. I was too humiliated.

It was 3:00 p.m. and Dad was still at work. Mom was getting dinner ready. She was always cutting up something and preparing long before dinner. I had no one to play with. I got my Spaulding ball and went out to the front stoop. In Queens, when you're bored, you throw a Spaulding against the stoop. It helps you think things out. There I was, trying to pass the time and this strange looking man came over to me. He had very dark skin. A cold chill crawled through my entire body. I remembered last week a bunch of Irish guys were playing cards down at 12th Street Park and they let me in on a few hands of Blackjack. They were all laughing and saying that this fat Cuban man named Oscar had moved onto the Spanish block. The Irish and Italians had their section of the neighborhood and then the Puerto Ricans and Cubans had theirs. But the park, of course, was free turf and everyone would mix. The guys were saying how the fat Cuban man had no wife, but he had two daughters. They started making jokes that the fat bastard probably killed his wife in Cuba and was on the lamb in Queens. I realized this must be the fat Cuban man that the Irish guys were taking about. "Excuse me little girl. How are you today?" in his best American accent.

"Good," I answered without taking my eyes off my Spaulding.

He held out a piece of paper to me. "Do you know where this address is?"

I stopped throwing my ball and looked at the paper. I recognized the address because my friend Eddie Lopez lived there. "Yeah," I said. “It's around the corner, it's a brown and white apartment building.”

He smiled. "Oh, what time do you eat dinner?"

"4:30," I answered, "Why?"

"Well, I was just wondering if you could show me where it is."

"It's the apartment building around the corner," I said again.

He started to get impatient, "You show me, please."

"I can't."

"Yes," he insisted.

The trains started to rumble into Court House Square, one from each side. We were right under the El, and it was so loud when the trains pulled in and out. He took advantage of this moment and began pulling me under the El and around the corner.

"Let go of me," I pulled and yelled, but I was no match for him. My little feet dragged on the floor as the weight of his heavy body forced me. I fought him as he smiled at the people who passed by staring. I never understood how not one person stopped him-this fat Cuban man, dragging a milky white skinny girl with bright red hair. Clearly, I did not belong with him. As I screamed, "Let go!" the train drowned out my cries. I could see fear in peoples' eyes as they looked at me. Maybe they knew there was something wrong but couldn't find the courage to save me.

We finally got around the corner. It seemed like it took forever. As we stood in front of the brown and white apartment building that he asked me to show him, I felt relief. Okay, now I can go home and watch my mother stir her sauce, smell the garlic as it sizzled in the pan browning and filling the house with comfort. I wanted touch my mother's hair and feel safe and peaceful. I said, "Well this is it. Now I have to get home to eat dinner. My father gets very angry if I'm not home for dinner."

He shut me up quickly, "You don't eat until 4:30, you liar."

Thinking quickly, I blurted out, "We're eating early today."

As if he didn't even hear me, he dragged me into Eddie Lopez's apartment building. A look came over his face that scared me. Maybe the Irish guys were right. Maybe the fat Cuban man was a killer. My armpits began to leak with sweat as heat spread through my entire body and my heart fluttered beneath my t-shirt. I kept trying to yell, but he covered my mouth. The smell of his sweaty hand was dangerous to me. I have never been this close to a real man. I wonder if Mom feels this way when Dad grabs her. He threw me against the wall with his hand pressing hard into my mouth. My lips were piercing into my teeth. I felt my scar on the inside of my upper lip. I remembered the day that happened, the pain, my brothers. Where were they now? I wished they were here. I still didn't know what he wanted from me, but something told me it wasn't good. He stared into my eyes, which peered out above his fat sweaty brown hand. I didn't want to look directly at him, but he kept shaking me. He reached down to his crotch and began to touch himself quickly, like he was vibrating. I didn't know what to make of this. An evil smile filled his face as his mouth started to drip with saliva. He removed his hand from my mouth and pressed his wet fat mouth on mine. I froze as he slobbered all over my face. I thought I screamed, but no sound came out. Please, someone come home. There were four floors in the apartment building, and I prayed that just one person would come home soon and save me. He pulled away and grabbed my hand in his.

"You come upstairs with me," he demanded. I tried to knock on the first door we passed but he caught my hand before it hit the door and jerked it back, then he laughed. As he dragged me up the stairs, he kept shoving money in my pants. "Here. Here's some money, be a good girl, you like money, right? I'm gonna give you lots of money." I was so confused and terrified. I couldn't speak. "Now," he said, "You touch me like this." He started touching himself, smiling and moaning. "Now you do it."

I was trembling, as I stood there lifeless in the middle of the first and second floor. I prayed my friend Eddie Lopez would come home soon. I prayed my mother would notice I was missing. I prayed someone under the El would call somebody to help me even if they didn't have the courage to help me themselves, but nobody came. He was impatient. He twisted my arm back. "Do it now!" I closed my eyes and left my body as I slowly reached between his legs. "Open your eyes and look at me or I will break your arm off." He jerked my arm hard, and I opened my eyes. He groaned. I noticed how dark his skin was. This was not the first time I saw a guy's thing because I saw my brothers changing a few times. He then pulled my hand down and made me touch it. My stomach filled with nausea, strange excitement and fear. "Play with it," he demanded, "Don't stop." It got harder and I didn't understand, but the harder it got, the happier he got. Then he stopped.

He pulled me up another flight against my will. I refused to walk up, so he dragged my tiny body as my legs smashed against each step like a chisel hitting a stone. I knew my shins would be bruised tomorrow, but honestly was wondering if I would see tomorrow. My body was breaking in more ways than I knew. Everything hurt and I felt nothing all at once. His clumsy hands reached in his pockets and shoved more money down my pants, but this time his hand didn't come out. "Ha, you like that. It feels so good, right little girl? Now, I'm gonna play with you." I could smell his perspiration like a poison, as the walls of the apartment building started closing in one me. I have never been touched in this spot. Not even by myself. His fat, dark stubby fingers rubbed in between my legs. He rubbed me so hard it hurt. He stuck his fingers in his mouth, looked into my eyes and then licked them. He smiled and then spit onto the same fingers he was rubbing me with. He then went back down in between my legs and started rubbing me again. I was choking on my tears. My heart was hammering, and I felt myself slipping away. Without warning, he thrust his fingers into the place I pee out of. I squealed, "NO!"

He covered my mouth. "Ssshhh it will only hurt for a second, here's some more money." An ache came over me so deep I thought I would die right then and there. I heard more loose change falling to the floor as his pants dropped, money in my pants, against my skin, on the ground. There was money everywhere. I wanted my Daddy. I knew he could kill this man. Please Daddy. I'll be good. Come and save me. As he thrust his fingers in and out of me, he started playing with himself again. "Oh, isn't that good little girl, isn't it fun?" No words would pass my lips. My head started to spin. Was I still breathing? How could this be happening to me? I was just playing in front of my stoop. How did I wind up here? "Now you touch me while I touch you."

I obeyed. He stared into my face, so close I could smell his stale breath. "I know your father. You're gonna tell him. I can't let you." Fear grew deeper and deeper. "I must take you to the roof. You're gonna tell."

A power came over me to help me speak. "No, I won't. I swear."

"Just shut up. Do what I tell you. I'm gonna throw you off the roof."

My traumatized body was quivering in terror. His big fat body was quivering in delight. He handled me like a toy. His pants were down, and his thing was hanging between his legs as he leaned into the corner. "Come here. Give me your head." He took my head and pressed it on his penis. "Now kiss it, lick it."

While I did that, he held my head in one hand and rubbed himself right below my mouth. I could feel his sweaty flesh rubbing on my chin. It was disgusting. He was disgusting. His thing smelled dirty, and it was fat and thick and sweaty. I wanted to throw up as he moaned with pleasure. "Oh yes little girl. Lots of money for you."

I was thinking, 'Money for what? He's going to throw me off the roof, so Daddy won't find out. What do I care about his fucking money.' I wanted to kill him, and I knew I had to come up with a plan to save my life. He reached under my t-shirt and started playing with my nipples. I heard my brothers talk about girls and what nice titties they had, but I didn't have any. I also heard my brothers talk about being horny and laughing. Now I knew what horny meant. This fat fucking Cuban bastard was a horny pig who was raping me. I heard that word, rape, on the news. But no one ever talked about it. It must be a sin or something.

So here I was in this apartment building being raped and committing a sin. My life was over. When would it end? It must be close to 4:30. Will they come and look for me, or will Daddy be mad and think I'm out shining shoes?

White creamy liquid started pouring out of the tip of his thing and all over my plaid hand me down pants from Seamus. I got scared. Maybe I hurt him. He held my face in it. I almost threw up. It smelled so strong and unlike anything I've ever smelled. He let out a deep grunt, like a fucking animal. I hated the sight of him.

He gripped me tight and got even crazier; more, more, another flight. I tried to knock on another door as we passed by, but again he caught me and hit me, each flight, a new position, a different thing. We were getting closer to the roof. This was the last floor. I wondered what he'd have me do this time. It was dark and quiet on this last floor. More fear surged through me. He dropped his pants once again. His thing dangled. Oh no, I can't do this again. I couldn't cry. He pulled me to him and angrily pulled down my pants. He started to touch me and made me touch him. He started to pound my small body hard up against the wall. I felt the bones in my back crunch from the weight of his big fat body thrusting into my small frame. He grabbed his thing and started to push it into my vagina. I couldn't believe this was happening to me. No, no, no, no I begged him to stop. This just wasn't right. He covered my mouth. "It will only hurt for a second little girl."

I bit my tongue and pictured my mother's pretty face, Mommy and Daddy dancing, tasting Mom's spaghetti and meatballs. Tears streamed down my face and the pain intensified. I wanted to be home. I had to get away. I couldn't die here, with this pig being the last thing that touched me. I knew I was more than that and that God didn't put me down here to die this way. I knew I had to be strong like my brother, Ryan, my Uncle Jim. I prayed for his strength. "One more flight" dragging me again as I hit the floor. He pulled me up the stairs as my body took the blows from each step. Anger filled me. I was going to fight. If I were going to die on this summer day, I wouldn't do it without a fight.

"Come on little girl, I got to make sure you won't tell Daddy."

He started laughing. While he was pulling me, my hands dangled alongside of me. As if it were a gift from God, a piece of glass swept into my hand. It must have been an old broken bottle. I closed it into my fist. We got to the top of the landing. The doorway to the roof was before me. He stood there sweating and out of breath, but still horny. "One more time, little girl. You're gonna do me one more time. "He dropped his pants as he held my arm. His ugly dirty smelly thing dangled. I took all the hate and rage I felt and channeled it through my right hand. I rammed the glass into his thing and pulled it along till the end. I felt the blood squirt out, covering my hand. His eyes exploded with pain as he yelped like a dog. I began running away. I saw him drop down, holding his dirty bleeding crotch. As I got to the staircase, I fled for my life. I did not touch one single stair. Each flight was four sets of seven stairs in a square shape. I leapt down, smashed into the wall, then the next flight the same thing. I got down to the bottom in about thirty seconds. I burst through the front doors and the daylight startled me. I was dizzy, nauseous and bleeding. I saw a cop standing in front of the bus stop. I went over and just stood by him with my bloody hand in my pocket, wondering if he could smell the sin on me or see the disgusting creamy stuff that stained my clothes. I turned to the building and saw the Cuban man run out of the building. He was adjusting his pants and holding his private parts. When he saw me by the cop, he ran his hand through his hair, and went the other way.

The Q19 bus pulled up and the cop got on. I looked to see if Jerry was the bus driver, but he wasn't.

I ran home, snuck upstairs, threw up, rinsed my hand, rinsed my face and hid my clothes for now. Later I will go to the dumpster by the Court House and get rid of the evidence. That wasn't enough. But I couldn't take a bath in the middle of the day. They would know something was wrong. The cut in my palm was pretty deep. I poured peroxide on it and it stung like the devil, then I applied five Band-Aids. I went in my room and started sticking all the dirty money in my piggy bank. I don't know why, but I kept it all. Dad's words swirling in my head, 'gotta save it for a rainy day.'

Dinner was ready. Everyone sat down to eat. Mom had on WNEW, her favorite radio station, 'Happy Together' by the Turtles was playing, but nothing could make me happy at this moment. I didn’t think I would ever feel happy again. Dad was in a good mood and my brothers were all laughing about how much fun they had at the park and how if I would’ve just behaved like a lady I could’ve stayed and played with them. It was like silent echoes around me. I couldn't eat a bite. Dad looked at his watch. 4:30 sharp. I wasn't even late. I kept my right hand in my pocket throughout dinner and used my left hand to push around the food with my fork. I was so afraid someone would notice me and see what happened. I felt like it was so obvious, but no one recognized my pain. No one noticed how sick I was or that there was anything different about me at all. I'd been raped, beaten and almost killed, but I was still on time for dinner and that’s all that seemed to matter.

Chapter 4: SURVIVING

Our usual 4:30 dinners took on a whole new meaning for me. I learned to become a lefty and hid my right hand as I hid the truth. Every day I rinsed my wound out with peroxide. Every day I prayed to God to help it heal quickly. Not just my hand, but the wound that burrowed deep into my existence. Looking at the food on the dinner table every night made me sick. My appetite was gone, and I would just stare at my plate, which looked like a black hole.

"Francesca you are not eating," my mother complained. Ryan dug his fork into my plate and swiped three raviolis'.

"Don't worry Ma it won't go to waste." They all laughed.

"I even made your favorite. The least you could do is taste it."

"It's great, Ma." She didn't seem convinced. I felt like I couldn't look anyone in the eye, not even Mom. If I did, I risked them seeing the truth in me. I knew I was alive because my body was breathing and moving, but I felt dead, numb, lost and I had no clue how-to carry-on living. A piece of me, the biggest piece of me, died in Eddie Lopez's brown and white apartment building the day the Cuban man made me show him that address that was on his little piece of paper. I became separate from everyone and everything, especially my family.

* * *

Mom was worried because I was getting skinnier - which was not good, since I was already skinny enough - and I was looking pale all the time. Seamus told her I might have the stomach flu, so she took me to the doctor. I was so afraid that the doctor would be able to tell that I had been raped just by looking at me. I was afraid of everything and everyone. I looked at people differently. I didn't trust anyone. The doctor didn't find anything wrong with me but told Mom that maybe I was under stress at home. She didn't want to get into that whole mess, so she thanked him very much and bye-bye.

If only I had said I didn't know where that address was then maybe this would not have happened, but then I realized that fat Cuban bastard never intended to go to that address for anything except raping me. He probably watched me go over to Eddie's and knew that I would recognize the address. He probably watched me play with my ball on the stoop too and had the whole thing planned. The more I thought about it the more it drove me crazy. I couldn't get his fat little stubby hands out of my mind. They haunted me and I felt like I was suffocating every day. Whenever I thought of him and the things, he made me do I would have to run to the bathroom to throw up.

I was trying to hide the deep gash in my right palm everyday by keeping my hand in my pocket. I also found this to be a weird comfort for some reason. Watching peroxide fuzz up with white foam in my palm every day became a ritual. It didn't seem to be healing and neither did I. The Cuban man haunted me. It seemed as if his face was everywhere, I turned. I saw him so much in my mind that I couldn't even see myself anymore. I would look in the mirror and not recognize the person looking back at me. I wanted to break the glass and shatter my image because it was not me. I looked at my right hand and realized that for the rest of my life, a scar would be there to remind me of what happened to me that day in the brown and white apartment building around the corner from my house. I would never be able to look at my right hand again and not think of the Cuban man. I would always be carrying him around in my right hand. I swore never to set foot in that building again.

***

One day Ryan and Ian said they were going to play a game of handball, so I followed them.

Ian turned to me, "Frankie go home. You're always hanging around us lately. You're like a wart."

Ryan laughed. "Leave her alone. She likes being with us. Maybe we'll choose her to be on our team."

"Pain in the ass." Ian muttered under his breath.

But I didn't care because Ryan liked me around and I felt safe with him. I knew he would protect me, no matter what. They were walking fast, and I was trying to keep up, but I was confused, because they were walking into the Spanish section of the neighborhood.

"Hey, where are you guys goin'?"

Ian got even more annoyed. "We're gonna play the Spics."

Ryan chimed in, "Yeah, we have to go to their neighborhood and beat them on their own turf."

They started laughing with confidence. I didn't know what to do because if I ran home like a baby, they would know something was wrong. I started to sweat and shake, and I felt like my legs were coming out from underneath me. I could hardly believe it, but when Ian and Ryan walked up to the Spanish stoop to meet their opponents, Pepe and Jose, there he was, the Cuban man, walking out of the apartment building. He was holding the hands of his two little daughters, one on each side. They must have been his daughters. I recognized one of the girls from my class. She was the new kid. I freaked out and ran into the middle of the street without even thinking of looking. A car screeched to halt and came within inches of killing me, which might have been a relief and an easier path than the life I was trying to survive. Ian and Ryan ran after me.

Ian was furious. "What the hell are you doin' Frankie?"

"You could've been killed." Ryan yelled too.

"I know. I'm sorry." I waited in the middle of the street and watched as the fat Cuban man hurried up the block. His daughters looked at me and I saw it in their eyes, terror, and anguish, secret scars. 'Oh my God, I bet he makes them touch him too.' Those poor little girls... one was about my age, but the other looked younger.

Ian and Ryan lifted me up and turned to the Cuban man because he had stopped to look.

"She's fine don't worry." He dismissed the Cuban man. He turned away and pulled his girls with his fat chubby hands. I felt sick. Ryan threw me up on his shoulders. He was lucky I didn't puke right on his head. "Now you can't run away." He laughed.

* * *

I was terrified that I might bump into him again and I won't have my two strong brothers with me to protect me. What if I'm alone next time? Would he do it again? Would he kill me next time? I knew I was in deep trouble and that maybe I should tell someone, but I was too ashamed. Everyone would think it was my fault. I somehow even thought it was my fault. I was so confused.

I tried to cope in school but could barely stay awake because of the nightmares. I had not slept more than twenty minutes at a time since the whole Cuban incident. My teacher called my Mom down to school and told her that my participation in class and my grades had dropped significantly. She was worried and thought it was because of Dad. I assured her that I was just going through a rough patch and that things would change soon. I asked her to keep it between us. I would prove to her that I was okay. I could not risk Dad questioning my intelligence and venturing to figure out what might be going on. She agreed.

***

I kept falling asleep on top of my desk. My teacher would wake me up and all the kids would laugh at me, all except for one, Yolanda, the new Cuban girl, his daughter. We would just stare at each other, and our eyes would exchange sadness. One day at lunchtime, I went down to the cafeteria and grabbed my yellow plastic tray as I let the lunch ladies serve me franks and beans. I knew I wouldn't eat it, but it made me look like the other kids. As I tried to find a place to sit, I noticed the Cuban girl, Yolanda. She sat alone everyday. Nobody ever talked to her, but they would whisper and giggle whenever she walked by. There was an empty chair next to her.

"Can I sit here?"

She looked up at me and almost smiled, then nodded 'yes.' I sat down. All the other kids stared at me like I was crazy, but I didn't care. Yolanda's food was untouched like mine. She pushed her food around with her fork, but I never saw her take one bite. I wanted to tell her what had happened to me and ask her if she was so sad because her father forced her to do things she didn't want to do. I wondered if either of us would ever enjoy lunch again or even enjoy living. I wanted to hug her and take her away somewhere and talk to her about what we had in common. I was perplexed about what I felt toward her. We sat side by side in complete silence, but when she was leaving, she looked in my eyes and I smiled at her and I don't know why, but it made me feel happy.

Chapter 5: CHURCH MOMENTS

The August humidity sat on my skin like a wool sweater. The days seemed to go on forever and my nights were infinite. I couldn't fall asleep without having nightmares about the Cuban man. Mostly about his fat stubby hands, reaching for me, strangling me. I'd wake up in a pool of sweat and a bed wet with urine. I was filled with so much shame and guilt I thought I would die. Quietly as I could, I would remove the purple cotton sheets mom got from the thrift shop, so Mom and Dad wouldn't find out I peed the bed. I'd tip-toe downstairs to the basement where the Maytag washer and dryer were. This was the hard part. The basement was scary, even in the daytime. My brothers and their friends would talk about it being haunted.

Ian and Ryan set up a haunted mansion the summer before and charged kids a buck to get in. They had to come down through the entrance outside of the house. That's where the ride began. Ryan and Ian had the outside stairs decorated with spider webs, fake spiders, rubber snakes and a black cloth you had to push aside to enter the basement itself. Watching ‘Creature Features’ and studying the art of scaring the shit out of people was their favorite pastime. I remember every episode opened with one single decrepit hand pushing through a box, as the word ‘THRILLER’ spilled through the screen like a slimy lizard. They had Mom's Victrola on in the background with some creepy Transylvanian music. Every once in a while, a voice would come on saying, "I vant to suck your blood" and then a blood-curdling scream. It terrified the kids. Then, when they entered the basement, it was pitch black. You could barely see your hand in front of your face. There was a purple bulb in one outlet toward the back, and a black light bulb toward the front. This way Ian and Ryan could see them as they came in, but the kid’s eyes weren't adjusted from the sunlight so they would jump when Ryan and Ian would grab them. They always wore black and laughed sadistically. "Ha, ha, ha. I'm going to kill you and torture you." They would toss them into these empty refrigerator boxes they found in the neighborhood. Every time Ryan or Ian saw a new family getting a fridge or a stove delivered, they'd wait until they threw away the box and snatch it.

First, they would spray paint them black with some red drippings for a bloody effect. Then they would hang those rubber spiders and lizards and any other creepy critters they could find on the inside of the box. They punched holes all around so they could reach in the box, grab the kids and scare the hell out of them. Ryan and Ian would shake the box while the victim was inside trying to catch their balance, screaming, "Let me out. I'm scared. Let me out." For a big finish when they opened the box to let the victim out, they would throw a dummy at them. The dummy looked like a dead man. It had a noose around its neck with its tongue hanging out. The eyes were rolled up into its head. Ian designed it himself and was very proud of his creepy creation. He called the dummy, Mr. Stiffy. It worked very well. After the paying customer was finished wrestling with Mr. Stiffy, they had one more obstacle to overcome before they could get out into the real world again.

Ryan and Ian would move the box as they shook it all the way to the back. When they opened the flap to the box, it was strategically placed before a floor of small rubber balls. Pillows were thrown all around so that kids wouldn't hurt themselves when they fell. Skeletons hung from the ceilings and a giant net was cast over them.

Even the toughest kids left traumatized. The line to get in was ridiculous. My brothers had to make them wait across the street at Sanders Candy Store so that Dad wouldn't find out. Ryan would send me, Patrick or Seamus to collect the next kid. They let us watch sometimes, but we had to sit perfectly still. We weren't allowed to laugh.

I never understood why these kids would actually pay my brothers to scare the living daylights out of them, but they did. The whole neighborhood was talking about how crazy the Finnegan bunch were and how we had a haunted house in our basement. The boys racked up on the cash that summer. The real tough boys came back five or six times just to prove they weren't sissies. But Ian and Ryan would make sure they did a little extra spooking for frequent victims. Just to keep it interesting. They wanted everyone to get their money's worth.

Ian and Ryan told Mom they would help her with the laundry all summer. This way she didn't have to work so hard. Meanwhile, they just wanted to keep her out of the basement. She knew something was going on, but Mom was very lighthearted and loved when we had fun.

So, she let them do the laundry and let them be. They actually did a pretty good job. Ian folded clothes like the Chinese laundry. Anything he did had to be the best.

I was sad when the Haunted Mansion closed. Not because I missed the ghosts and goblins, because I secretly was afraid of it all. I was sad because Mom started doing the laundry again. It wasn't that I didn't like the way Mom folded my clothes, but it wasn't the same. They even smelled different. I don't know what Ian did to the laundry, but it really comforted me.

I wished he would wash my sheets with his special touch and make my bed safe and warm. Maybe he could chase away the nightmares of the Cuban man that caused me to be in the basement at three in the morning with smelly sheets and bloodshot eyes.

It always took a long time just to muster up the courage to go in the dark haunted basement alone.

The first test was opening the door. It was old and creaky. The house itself was a hundred years old. I don't think the basement door had ever been replaced. I pulled the door open and jumped back quickly, just in case a monster was waiting for me on the other side. When I was in the clear I would switch the light on quickly, still no sight of anything. I would look down the stairs and see the cockroaches scatter as the lights hit them. Then I counted the steps. There were thirteen. Bad luck. I took a deep breath and flew down all thirteen stairs in under five seconds. I told myself if I make it down all the steps in 5 seconds, I would be safe from the boogieman. I used to like making up little games with myself. As I reached the bottom, I checked around quickly. There was a stillness that was overwhelmingly peaceful. It was eerie. I could smell the dust and mildew that lived in the basement and hear the walls crackle as night settled into them. The light seemed brighter than ever. It was as if all my senses were more alive. Was it because it was three in the morning and maybe I was still dreaming a little, or was it because of what happened to me? I felt more aware of every little thing. I threw the sheets in the washer and pulled out the knob. Ian taught me how. I knew I had to wait at least twenty minutes before I could put them in the dryer. I would take a short nap in the red velvet chair that we had down there and wait until a buzz went off signaling that the clothes were finished being washed. It always woke me up with a jolt. Then I would stick the sheets in the dryer and go back upstairs because they took about an hour to dry. If I fell asleep in the red velvet chair for a whole hour, I would be giving the boogieman an open invitation to get me. I couldn't get back in my bed yet, so I'd go to Patrick's bed. I'd shove him over and tell him I had a bad dream again. He'd grunt and let me in. It was hard to fall back asleep knowing the sheets were in the dryer. My mind would race, and I'd count the seconds. Somehow, I always woke up before Mom and Dad. I would run to the basement to collect my sheets and then I would race back upstairs to remake my bed. I would act like nothing happened when Mom would come to get me up.

I'd say, "Good morning, Mom."

She'd ask, "How did you sleep?"

I would lie, "Oh great, Mom."

She'd smile and go prepare an amazing breakfast. If only she knew how hard I worked all night long to keep my secret safe within the torturous corridors of my being. If only she knew that my existence revolved around how I would get through all the lies today and if anyone would notice how much I was dying inside.

Mom was a big churchgoer, which meant we all had to be. Dad never came to church but made us go with Mom. Her rosary beads were always wrapped around her hand like a tattoo that had been branded into her skin. Even around the house she'd hold onto them as if they were going to save her or something. She'd mumble in Italian as she went from bead to bead on the rosary. Mom preferred to go to mass on Saturdays, at five o'clock. This way she could cook and clean on Sunday mornings. Sunday was always a big meal. She'd get up at the crack of dawn and stick Puccini on the Victrola. As Puccini filled the house with echoes of emotion, the garlic and herbs would pass through the air. I would wake with my mouth watering. I imagined what Mom was like as a little girl in Italy. I wanted to see the place where she grew up. She said it was beautiful, so different from Queens, New York. She seemed sad when she spoke of it, even though a reminiscent smile would pass her face.

Somehow Mom transported herself through cooking and music right back to Italy. She took me with her. Her green and red apron looked just like the Italian flag and she wore it proudly whenever she cooked. I could see the piazzas and vineyards. I could picture the shopkeepers and townspeople. I felt like I had been there just from the stories Mom told me. I know it meant a lot to her that I listened.

I used to catch Mom singing like she was in La Boheme. She would crush tomatoes in a big pot as she swayed back and forth. She wouldn't know that I was watching because she was so involved in the food and Puccini. I felt as if I was invading her privacy, but I couldn't help myself. I was witnessing this beautiful woman, my mother, expressing the depths of her pain to a saucepan. There she was singing, *Che-Gilida-Manina* which means, "your tiny hand is frozen" as she cried onto the tomatoes. One hand clutched her heart as the other squeezed tomatoes. There are so many things I didn't know about Mom. But I knew Sunday was her favorite day. She got to travel someplace in her mind, someplace that gave her peace. Still, she could not relax and enjoy her Sunday ritual if she missed mass on Saturday night.

During mass we would get bored. It seemed to just drone on and on. I would find myself asking God to forgive me for showing the Cuban man the brown and white apartment building. For whatever reason, being in church would bring up all of the sleeping monsters that were trapped inside of me. Who the hell needed all that? I needed to laugh a little and forget all that serious stuff. My brothers were a perfect escape. All we would have to do is look at each other and that was enough to send us into a fit of laughter. There was really nothing funny most of the time, but we would get the giggles constantly. Mom would separate us and stand in the middle. She got very upset when we caused a scene. Seamus had one of those laughs that were very contagious. It would build like a wave; first Seamus, then Ryan, Patrick, me, and finally Ian. All the older people would "shoosh" us and give us dirty looks, which cracked us up even more.

One day we were in a non-stop roar over absolutely nothing. Father Haggerty, an alcoholic who had no trouble backhanding a kid for being a wise ass, was saying the mass. As he lifts the chalice and says, "Take this, all of you, and eat it, this is my body," Seamus and I are holding ourselves laughing and Ryan can't even look our way, or he'll lose it. Patrick has his hand over his mouth and Ian is trying to control it. We called these outbursts of laughing fits, 'Church moments.' Father Haggerty stops in the middle of the offering, takes the microphone and points directly at us.

"Will the woman in back with those five annoying children please shut the hell up!"

We all ducked down in the pew, leaving Mom standing alone as a church full of people turned to stare at her.

She smiled uncomfortably and whispered to us, "You're all going to get it when we go home."

Mom's bark was bigger than her bite. She even laughed when we left, but she said we weren't allowed to go to church with her anymore if we were going to laugh the whole mass. We were all relieved. This was our ticket out. However, she said, we must go on Sundays on our own. She did not want to be embarrassed anymore. To make sure we went she made us come home and tell her what the gospel was about and what we learned from it.

At first, I would go with all of my brothers and try to pay attention. It was very hard. My mind would wander. I didn't understand the Catholic Church. I know that the priest and nuns were married to God. This concept alone was enough to confuse me about the Catholic religion. It did not make sense to me. How could you be married to someone you never see? And priests are men, but so is God. Is that a sin? And how does Jesus come down and fit his body and blood into the chalice every mass? I would drift off and with my eyes go from station to station of the cross. As I looked at Jesus I wondered if he had a girlfriend. If he did, she must have been very upset at the way the soldiers tortured him. I still didn't know why they did that to him. I only knew I had to pray to him on the crucifix, kneel when the priest said the "Hosanna in the Highest" prayer, and when the Gospel was said, you were supposed to take your thumb and make the sign of the cross on your forehead, your lips, and then your heart.

I noticed Patrick really starting to enjoy mass. The rest of us couldn't wait until it was over.

Every Sunday right outside St. Mary's church, there was a stickball game. It started at ten o'clock, the same time as mass. Ryan, Seamus and Ian wanted to play.

Patrick looked scared. "C'mon you guys, we gotta go to church."

Patrick went to mass. We played stickball. It was great. All the big guys were impressed with me. I could tell my brothers were proud.

When mass ended, we ran up to Patrick, "So tell us what the Gospel was about."

"Oh, it was very good today, you really should've been there."

Ian grabbed him, "Cut the crap and tell us what it was about."

He said, "It was according to Luke, and that's all I'm saying."

Seamus screamed at him, "I don't care who it was according to, what the hell was it about?

"You shouldn't say hell when you're referring to the Gospel." He was being such a pain in the ass.

Ryan made us all leave him alone. "Listen buddy, you don't have to tell us what it was about. Just don't tell Mom we skipped church. You got it?"

Patrick nodded, "Got it."

We had to figure out something. Mom would kill us if we missed mass. This was a big sin. Ian came up with a great plan. Since I was the youngest, I had to go up to a sweet little old lady and say, "Excuse me can you please explain to me what the Gospel was about? I didn't understand it." Well, it worked like a charm. So, our one sin of missing mass turned into two sins; lying to Mom was the second.

We did this every week until old lady Marge went up the block and told Mom she saw us outside playing ball while Patrick was in mass.

We all got punished for a whole week. We couldn't go out to play, but worse than that, we had to go to church every day for two weeks straight and we had to go with Mom.

Patrick would come even though he didn't have to. He decided that he wanted to be an altar boy and ring the bells at communion time. The church was happy to have him. He got his little outfit. It looked like a dress. My brothers teased him and called him a sissy. Ryan of course, shut Seamus and Ian up as soon as Patrick told on them. Patrick was Ryan's baby. Nobody could do or say anything to Patrick without answering to Ryan. There was a real comfort in that for Patrick. The truth was he needed Ryan.

Patrick became a hot shot altar boy. He was doing special services and getting good tips for it. Weddings were about ten to fifteen bucks and funerals were an easy twenty. All of a sudden Seamus wanted to get in on the action. It seemed that all the girls thought altar boys were cute. Before too long both of them were Father Haggerty's altar boys. I asked, but they didn't have any alter girls. Ryan, Ian and I would sit up front and tease whoever was doing the mass. They would rotate masses. Mom couldn't be happier. Her two sons were helping God.

They told us that Father Haggerty would drink two glasses of whiskey before each mass. There were two other priests, thank God, because by ten in the morning Father Haggerty was sauced. Father Joe was my favorite priest. There was also Father Tom.

Father Joe was funny. After church he would talk to me. He wanted to know how it felt to be the only girl in the family. I told him Mom was a girl. He laughed. We were friends. I wanted to tell him about my big sin, but I had to wait until I received the sacrament of Penance. Maybe next year I'd tell him that I felt like a prisoner trapped inside of my own skin and that no matter how many times I scrubbed myself, my sin left me feeling dirty.

* * *

One day after church we were walking home. It had been a little over three of weeks since I sinned with the Cuban man. Seamus and I were walking behind the others. He was telling me that next year he would be starting high school and that Patrick would be the only brother I'd have in school. He told me if I had any problems that Patrick would be there for me.

"I can handle myself." I boasted.

"I know you can, killer, but just remember your family is always there for you." He reached down and grabbed my wounded hand. I pulled away in pain. "What's wrong Frankie? Let me see.

Oh my God, I started to panic, "I cut myself."

He looked at it carefully as he always did any medical situation.

"When did this happen?"

"Oh, I don't remember, like a few weeks ago." I pretended that I didn't know the exact day, time and place.

"It must've been pretty deep. Frankie you should've gotten stitches. Why didn't you tell anyone?" He looked at me so lovingly.

I wanted to tell him. I wanted to wrap my arms around him and tell him that I couldn't handle myself. I do need my brothers. My heart was racing. My knees were quivering. Seamus being the doctor recognized me slipping away.

"Frankie what's wrong? Sit down."

We sat on a stoop. The others looked back. Seamus yelled to them to go ahead and we'd catch up. Seamus touched my wound.

"You're gonna have a scar kiddo. I know you like having your war wounds to prove how tough you are."

I smiled weakly. This was one war wound I was not proud of, one that I wanted to make disappear.

"So, are you gonna tell me how it happened?

If only I could, but I lied, "Okay, but you have to promise you won't tell anyone. Especially Mom and Dad."

"Okay I promise." Seamus agreed.

A story came to me quickly, "I was down at 12th Street Park playing 'King of the Hill' with Michael and John-John, the two toughest boys my age. Well, I got up to the top and was king, so naturally they wanted to take the throne away from me. They came up to get me. I lost my balance and fell on a broken bottle."

Seamus was confused, "Why didn't you tell anyone, especially me?"

"Getting in trouble? Getting stitches?" I tried to play it off.

He wasn't stupid, "C'mon Frankie."

I started crying, "I was afraid okay, I'm afraid, please don't tell on me Seamus, please."

"I won't tell, I promise. But you have to let me put some anti-bacterial cream on your hand when we get home. I don't want you to get an infection. It will be our secret."

I held him tight. For a moment all my pain went away because I felt Seamus taking care of me. I needed someone to hold me. The last time that anybody held me in their arms was the Cuban man and it wasn't in a way that gave me feel comfort. Seamus comforted me and I surrendered into his loving arms, hoping some of my pain would melt into him.

* * *

Fall arrived and I welcomed it. The cold felt refreshing. The leaves on the trees turned color. My brothers and I would crunch through the piles of leaves that fell to the ground. I loved the sound as they buckled under my buster brown shoes. I think Dad loved the fall more than any other time. He used to sit by the window with his beer and draw the trees as they changed. He was a gifted artist. Ian took after Dad. Every Halloween Ian made the most fabulous costume in the neighborhood. Halloween in Queens was more tricks than treats.

The older guys would fill their socks with flour, get cartons of eggs, and torture all the girls. This was their idea of fun. The streets were covered with eggshells and drippings. It was a battlefield. You had to run for shelter. When the eggs came flying from across the street they hurt like hell. Sometimes they'd come right up to you and smash it on your head, add some flour and you were ready to bake.

Well, I couldn't just be a victim. A few friends from school, Teresa, Patty, Angela, and I got six cartons of eggs and fought back. The guys killed us, but we got some good shots in. John-John, Michael and Sean were all very cute, so we threw eggs at them. Big mistake. They ran after us, cornered us in the alleyway and bombarded us. We were in the alley, smothered in eggs and flour, laughing hard at how stupid we looked, when Sean comes running back to smash one more egg on my head.

"Hey Frankie, here's one more because you're so cute."

All of my friends snickered, "Oohh he likes you."

"Get out of here. You're all crazy, he's eleven."

"So what, he likes you." They started singing.

'Sean and Frankie kissing in a tree, K-I-S-S-I-N-G, first comes love, then comes marriage, then comes Frankie with a baby carriage.'

"No way, not me." I said, "I'll never get married."

They all laughed, "Frankie has a crush on Sean."

I guess I kind of did. I know I was blushing.

Teresa teased me, "Look at your face. You're beet red."

I had so much egg and flour on me that I thought it would hide it, but it didn't. I didn't know what to do with myself. I reached into my carton for an egg and smashed it on Teresa then one on Angela. They chased me and we all had a good laugh.

The cops were around the neighborhood trying to keep things under control, but it was impossible. Guys were out windows throwing eggs. Even the cop cars were covered with eggs. Some of it was fun, but some of it was dangerous. It made me angry when kids would throw eggs at old people or mothers wheeling a baby carriage. The worst part of Halloween was the older guys, Peter, Thomas, Whitey and Francis. They went on the roofs and poured bleach over the sides of the buildings. Cars were skidding, people were falling, some kids got it in their eyes and had to be rushed to the hospital. It was not funny. The cops eventually got up there and chased them away. Peter and Thomas had to go to the 12th Street Precinct down at Vernon Jackson, near our school. They got in big trouble. Whitey and Francis got away. Nobody ever snitched on them. That was a no-no in my neighborhood. The consequences were great. You learned to keep your mouth shut and take your own beatings; kind of like home.

When I would finally get home, I would bolt upstairs so I could jump in the tub before anyone saw me. No such luck. My Mother ran up after me.

"Look at you, Francesca. You look like a little birdie that has just been hatched."

"I know, the boys trapped us and egged us really good. We tried to run. I wanted to get cleaned up before Dad sees me. I swear Mom, we didn't do anything. It's a zoo out there."

"Don't worry he's not home. I don't expect him for a while." She looked so sad, so I thought I should say something. The truth is I didn't care where he was or if he ever came home, but I pretended.

"Where is he?"

"At the bar." She looked down at the floor.

"Doing what?"

She laughed, but not in an amused way. "There's only one thing anyone goes to the bar for...to drink."

I thought of Dom's bar, all the old fools who couldn't even count their money. I pictured Dad at the bar drinking and acting like an asshole with his buddies. My Mother washed my hair in the tub. She could not believe how many shells were stuck in my head. I asked her why she didn't go out to the bar with Dad? She said she hated bars and the people in them. A bunch of wishbones and jawbones, but they got no backbone. I didn't know what she meant. She explained, "They get a little liquor in them and then they start talking a lot about nothing and everything. Promising you things that will never happen. That's the jawbone part. Then they start wishing they could do this or be that, but they had such misfortune happen to them. Still, they have big dreams that they're gonna make come true some day. That's their liquid courage talking. That is the wishbone part. But ya know what none of them have, Francesca, especially your father, is backbone. They're all wishbones and jawbones, but they got no backbone." Mom always had a way of telling me something, which made it sound beautiful. Maybe it was the accent. Maybe it was her gentle nature. Maybe it was because she was my mother. I could listen to her talk all night long. I was so happy that Sean came back and smashed an extra egg on my head because Mom had to take more time to get it out. I didn't want her to stop touching my head. She got out every single shell.

"Would you brush my hair mommy?" I loved the way she did it.

"Ah figlia bella, of course I will." It was dialect, meaning my beautiful daughter.

I stayed up with Mom until Dad came stumbling in. He would barely look at me, "Go to bed, NOW, Frankie, Bed! I kissed Mom and went upstairs, but I couldn't sleep until I knew Mom was safe in bed.

"Why do you have to keep her up with you?" He slurred through his drunkenness.

"She can't sleep sometimes. We talk. It's nice." She tried to avoid any confrontation.

Dad started screaming, "Nice, nice for who? For you? You sit here with her talking about me, don't you? Don't you?" His fist banged on the table. I could hear the silverware jump up and down. "Well answer me. Do you talk to her about me? About what a bad husband I am? Why, you ungrateful bitch."

My heart started racing. Why was he picking on her? What did she do? How can I save her? And why does he keep calling me, “her?” As if he can't say my name. Mom still didn't answer. Then, I heard a smack.

"Answer me now!" Another smack. I can't stand it. I run up to Ryan's bed. I hear Mom crying.

"Leave me alone. You're drunk." Mom tried to get through to him, but he wouldn’t stop.

"Ryan, wake up. Dad's at Mom again." Ryan, who sleeps like a bear in hibernation, pops up like he's been waiting for this moment. He reaches under his bed and grabs a bat. He shoves Ian who sleeps right next to him. "Let's go buddy. Mom needs us."

I was so excited I could hardly stand it. They were going to rescue Mom. Maybe they would kill Dad. Then we could be a family. The sound of chairs banging against the walls filled the house. Glass was being thrown. Mom was crying. It got louder with each descending step we took. I woke Seamus up just for back up. We all let Patrick sleep. As we got to the kitchen Dad took a full swing at Mom's face. She fell down to her knees as blood spouted out from her nose. Her small body went limp. Wailing in anguish, she moaned like a wounded animal.

"Bastardo, I hate you." She managed to spit out with contempt.

"Oh yeah, take that back, tell me you love me."

Ryan wound up and went at him. "Mother fucker, no more."

Dad turned around and whipped the bat right out of Ryan's hands. Ian jumped on Dad's back and Seamus tackled his legs. Dad fell to the ground punching and kicking, but no one gave up. I couldn't help myself; I started to pull his hair. I wanted to rip it all out, but then the strangest thing happened. I couldn't stand that my hands were touching his hair. It seemed weird. I wanted to be a part of Mom's redemption, but I didn't want any part of me to touch any part of him. I saw Mom holding her nose as she moaned. I had to hurt him. I took a frying pan and whacked him over the head. He screamed.

"All of you get the fuck off of me right now." None of us moved. Ryan and Ian had him pinned down. He couldn't move.

Ryan warned him, "If you ever hurt Mom again, we're gonna kill you. That's a promise. Do you hear me you drunken piece of shit?"

Dad looked scared like a child who just got caught doing something. Everything got quiet, except for Mom. She was covered in blood. Dad looked at her like he saw her for the first time. The he looked up at all of us.

"What's going on? Isabella, what happened?"

"You beat the shit out of her again. Don't pretend you don't know." Ryan was pissed.

We let him up. He collected himself slowly. Ryan was ready with the bat. He crawled over to Mom. Seamus ran to the freezer to make an ice pack. Mom was too weak to fight him, but she pulled away. Seamus came over and shoved Dad away.

"Get away from her, you animal." Dad had no response. Seamus ran to the medicine cabinet and cleaned her up. We waited to see what his diagnosis was.

"Well, it's definitely broken. We got to get you to the hospital. They have to set it. I'll take you."

Ian jumped up, "I'm coming."

"Well, I gotta go too." I insisted.

"Someone has to stay with Patrick."

We all looked at Dad crying with his head in his hands.

"What have I done, what have I done?"

Seamus had no sympathy, "You broke my mother's nose."

She had one of those beautiful Roman noses. It wasn't too big, but it had that great Italian bump in it.

Ryan asked Dad for his car keys even though he didn't have a license. Dad didn't fight him. All of us piled in Dad's Red Chevy Impala SS Matador and drove over to Astoria General Hospital. I was getting really familiar with this hospital. I knew that wasn't a good thing.

Having been through this before we knew we would be asked a million questions and wanted to get our story straight. We used the time it took to drive to the hospital to plot our strategy. Mom insisted we lie. She was too ashamed to tell them her husband beat her. She said they could arrest him. We didn't care, but she did. Why did she protect him so much when all he did was treat her like shit? It was so frustrating. She begged us to keep quiet. She said it was nothing and she wasn't even in pain anymore. As much as we hated to, we went along with her request.

Seamus checked her in. He told the doctor that Mom went to get a can of tomatoes out of the cabinet and it fell on her nose. The doctor looked at him. "At two o'clock in the morning?"

Ian laughed, "You know those Italians. They like to start cooking their sauce early in the morning."

The doctor didn't laugh. Mom had two shiners. I looked at her face but didn't recognize her. It scared me. Where did my mother's beautiful face go? Would she ever look the same? I had to touch her hands to make sure it was her. Those hands, strong yet delicate, knowing and giving, yes, they were Mom's hands, the safest most gentle hands my being has ever known. Just touching her hands restored me for a moment. Somehow, I felt this was my doing. If I didn't stay up talking to Mom, maybe he wouldn't have gotten so pissed. Maybe he really wanted to hit me. I ran into the hall. I wanted to cry, but I knew it wouldn't matter. I wanted to run away, but I couldn't leave Mom. I looked for Dr. Silver, but he wasn't there. I thought he lived in the hospital.

When we got home, Dad was sleeping on Mom's side of the bed, hugging her pillow. I'm sure he was probably whispering, 'I love you' into the pillow and apologizing, but I didn't care how sorry he was. His apologies were running thin and meant less and less each time. He was a fucking JAWBONE and my ears were tired of hearing the shit that came out of his mouth. He made me sick and he was killing my mother a little bit more each day.

Chapter 6: THANKSGIVING 1973

Every Thanksgiving, we went to Nanny and Grumpy Finnegan's house. Dad demanded that we all looked our best, dress up real nice, as if the clothes would hide the evidence of a family tortured by an abusive alcoholic. We were under strict orders to pretend to be happy on this very special day. It was on this day that Abraham Lincoln, our 16th President, who abolished slavery, the greatest President in history, declared a national holiday back in 1863. Lincoln chose the fourth Thursday of every year as a day that families would come together and give thanks for all their blessings. Both of Dad's favorite Presidents were murdered, assassinated, shot in the head on a Friday and both were particularly passionate about civil rights. Too weird for me! Then we had to listen to Dad complain about the Watergate scandal and how President Nixon is lucky someone hasn't shot him by now, but he's an asshole, so he'll live. Only the great ones get killed. He said, whenever a true leader steps up to the plate people get scared and when people get scared, they hurt other people. He threw in Martin Luther King, and what a great leader he was. Poor guy didn't stand a chance. Dad was passionate about civil rights and hated when someone would hurt or even kill an innocent person who is trying to do good for all, yet he did this to my mother. She kept trying to be a leader in the family, but Dad just kept trying to kill her. Now, we were in front of the Irish side of the family celebrating this American holiday of gratitude, it was time to act our parts as happy, grateful children. 'God forbid if his parents or brothers thought anything was wrong. That would be a sentence worse than death for your father.' 'From Mom's mouth. I remember asking her why Dad never tells us he loves us "The Irish have their pride and they'll never tell you how they feel, you're supposed to know, and God be with you if you don't." She said.

Mom was informed on what she could and couldn't talk about. She would just throw up her hands and say, "Don't worry, I won't speak."

Dad was paranoid that Mom would slip and say something that made him look foolish.

Uncle Jim would be at Nanny and Grumpy's house as well, with his three kids, my cousins, Joseph, Elizabeth and Brian. My other cousins would be there too. Billy and Bobby were Uncle Bobby's boys. Margaret and Virginia were Uncle Joe's girls. I loved it. The house was crawling with kids, twelve all together.

As soon as I walked in, I could smell the turkey wafting through the air. Stuffing, mashed potatoes, gravy, sweet potatoes baked with marshmallows and brown sugar. All the aromas swirled into one delicious temptation. I couldn't wait to get it all in my belly. I was always the first there. Nanny and Grumpy let me come over to help. It never really worked out that way though. As soon as Laurel and Hardy's March of the Wooden Soldiers (also known as Babes in Toyland) came on, I was glued to the television. They would get a kick out of me pretending I wanted to help cook when all I really wanted was to watch my show, alone, no brothers, no fighting, and no noise. It was the only place I remember feeling peaceful as a child.

I didn't care about anything at this moment, except, Laurel and Hardy and their six-foot tall wooden soldiers. It was the highlight of Thanksgiving. No one else could share my adventure, my secret journey to Toyland where all could be forgotten, even the Cuban man. I would forget where I was, who I was and the family I was born into. I didn't think about my brothers, my father or the Cuban man.

When the credits rolled and the doorbell rang, I was back. Nothing had changed except the clock. The relatives strolled in one by one. It was exciting. Mom and Dad always arrived last. I think Dad liked to make a big entrance.

The two tables were set. One was for the grown-ups and one was for the kids. We always had more fun at our table. We would joke and say it was the Last Supper and we were the Twelve Apostles. Every year Nanny and Grumpy would have a contest before dinner to see which two kids got the turkey legs. We all wanted them. It was like eating power. It made you feel like a caveman. All the boys would say the contest should just be for them because eating a big old drumstick while it's dripping down your face wasn't very ladylike. Who cares? I wanted the drumstick. Well, this year, me and Virginia won, and we enjoyed every last morsel. I don't know about Virginia, but I got a lot of satisfaction out of winning the drumstick. I knew all the boys wanted it. I smiled the whole meal. We also had a contest to see who could make the best farm, created by using mashed potatoes as your land. You'd take the fork and make different roads or hills, then decorate with corn, peas and other various vegetables. The gravy served nicely as a mudslide.

Ian was always the most creative. He would have the most elaborate farm. He was such an artist, even with his food. He would line up the broccoli to make it look like trees all around the farm. Then the carrots would outline the farm like borders, with a mixture of sweet potato and mashed potato. It gave it the color of soil. His roads would be carefully structured. Each pea and kernel of corn had a purpose. His farm was meticulous. Mine was one big mushy piece of glob, but it tasted great. Ian's was so exquisite you didn't even want to eat it. You wanted to frame it.

Mom knew we did this every year so she would come over to see this years' competition. She praised all of them, even our cousins. They all loved Mom. Especially Virginia. She used to say Mom looked like an Italian movie star. It's true. She did.

She stood over Ian's farm and gazed deeply into it. She smiled so softly. "That reminds me of back home, the farm in Italy."

***

When dinner was over all the ladies and little girls would help clean the tables. The women were in the kitchen, the men in the living room, watching football, drinking and swearing at the tube. The kids got to play games. If it was too cold, we would stay in and play 'Operation, Don't Spill The Beans or KerPlunk,' but if it was warm enough, and it was that day, we got to play in the backyard.

I realized that year that two of my brothers were already drifting away from me. Ryan and Ian weren't kids anymore, they were 17 and 18 and I was just a scrawny 10-year-old. They didn't play in the backyard. They watched football with the men. Brian did too. He was now 16. I felt a small ache in my heart. Even though they bullied me, and I could never win against them, they made the backyard games special. It was part of our Thanksgiving tradition together. I asked them to come out and play red light, green light. Both of them laughed at me as if to say, "How silly, that's only for kids."

They said, "Go ahead Frankie, have fun. We'll be inside."

Now the Twelve Apostles were down to nine. It wasn't the same I missed them, even Brian. Did this mean that next year Ryan, Ian and Brian would sit at the adult table? I discovered something that day. I hated change. It didn't seem to bother the others, only me. They were playing and laughing. So, I pretended, but I wasn't happy. I looked in the window. The women in the kitchen were washing and drying dishes as they laughed and gossiped. That looked like fun. I could hear the football game and the men cheering. That sounded like fun. I didn't want to miss anything in any room. I wanted to be three places at once. As I watched my mother laughing with Aunt Mary, a dodge ball cracked me in the head. This brought me back Patrick and Seamus yelled, "Frankie are you playing or what?"

I shook it off and yelled back, "Hell yeah, I'm playing!"

I played harder and better than I ever had. I was unstoppable. It was dodge ball at its finest and everybody wanted me on their team. My anger actually helped me play better. Sometimes I think my anger was the only thing that pulled me through. It was a very useful yet dangerous tool. I could feel

Dad's Irish bloodline flowing inside of me. His rage. His hate. I was cursed. No matter how hard I fought it, I could feel him stirring in my DNA. I was part of him, and he was a part of me. No matter how much I wanted to be different than the things I hated in my father, my mother, my brothers, when I looked in the mirror, I saw them in me. I saw my mother's fear and insecurity. I saw my father's hate and rage sitting in my eyes. I saw all of my brothers struggle to be strong so that they could win Dad's approval. I despised myself.

Unleashing my wrath, I took the dodgeball and went after my cousin Joseph. I don't know why. Maybe it was because he was Uncle Jim's kid. This might make my father happy, I thought. Maybe it was because he was a big crybaby. I mean, he was 11 years old... get over it already. His Mother coddled him all the time. It made me sick. Whatever it was, something came over me. Something evil. I ran full speed as I wound up. I thrust the ball right at his face. The moment I released it I felt regret. It was too late. The next sound I heard was a crack, then a shriek. Joseph was on the ground. All the cousins huddled around him as blood gushed from his nose.

I ran over shouting, "I'm sorry Joseph, are you alright?"

Seamus was checking him out. Patrick looked at me and shook his head. Elizabeth ran inside to get Uncle Jim. Billy and Bobby were trying not to laugh.

Margaret yelled at me, "You're such a little bully, Frankie."

Bobby defended me, "It's a game and Frankie's good. Joseph should have protected his face."

"Yeah," I chimed in.

Next thing I knew Uncle Jim and Dad were running out to the backyard. They were already arguing on the way out.

Uncle Jim took one look at Joseph and yelled, "Get up you sissy. Hit her back!" I couldn't believe my ears. He was encouraging him. What happened to that nice guy at the Dom's pub who got all those drunks to give me money for shoe-shines? Oh well, I guess we were on different turf.

"Yeah, go ahead. She'll kick his little ass." Dad and Uncle Jim started their own fight. Joseph slowly got to his feet. He wiped his nose. I did feel really bad. I put my hand out to make peace. He pushed it away and punched me right in the mouth. That was it, my invitation to pound my poor innocent cousin into the pavement. My adrenaline was flowing like Niagara Falls. Get your ringside seats.

Dad was yelling, "Punch him back."

No one discouraged this fight. They stood around like an audience who paid admission. I kind of got excited, because I was the center of attention. I didn't want to let anyone down who was rooting for me, especially Dad. Here I was in a fistfight with my cousin who was a boy and it all seemed normal. Is this how all families are? On Thanksgiving? A day of gratitude. I took the punch like a man. It hurt like hell. I shed some blood, but I was ready. I put up my dukes and went at Joseph like a bull at a matador. I connected with his face quite a few times, real professional punches. He fought like a girl. He was pulling my hair. He tried to smack his way out. I tackled him to the floor. I felt invincible. The more I hit him, the less control I had over my fist. It felt so good. Too good. Why did it feel so good to strike another? I couldn't stop. Obsessed. Uncle Jim couldn't take anymore. He grabbed my arms and lifted me off of him. Just as he did, Joseph punched me as hard as he could in the stomach. He knocked the wind out of me. Dad grabbed Uncle Jim and they started beating the crap out of each other. It was a free for all. Virginia and Margaret ran for help. Nanny and Grumpy and the whole Thanksgiving party came out to break up the rumble. It was messy as usual. Every family gathering ended in disaster. Uncle Jim came out with barely a scratch. I had a fat lip and a couple of scratches. Dad and Joseph both left with bloody noses.

Nanny and Grumpy were not happy with my behavior. They hated the fighting between the brothers. They wanted more than anything for everyone to get along. Nanny had this way of talking to me as if she was a Queen, superior, but always with a delicate smile. She warned me that it was time for me to become a young lady, and ladies don't fight, not even if they're hit first. Uh, wait a minute. What? Nanny encouraged me to solve my battles with words instead and leave the hitting to the boys. Well that explains a lot. I couldn't believe my ears. It was Mom and Dad in a nutshell, but not me, no way. I wanted to scream BULLSHIT! I'm breaking the mold. I'm never letting any man hit me! I don't give a crap what Nanny Finnegan says or thinks.

Wearing Laura Ashley from head to toe, Virginia came over to me when everyone left. Brown leather loafers peeked out beneath her chocolate tailored slacks. I almost asked if I could polish them. She said she admired how brave I was. Virginia was stunning, the kind of beauty that the Ivory girl embodied, the homecoming queen. We were complete opposites. I was a tough, little tomboy with ratty hair and a runny nose, but she wanted to be like me. I didn't understand this. I wished I could be like her. In any case, it made for a great friendship.

I told her I felt like Thanksgiving was ruined because of me. She felt completely opposite. In her opinion, Thanksgiving was exciting and fun because of me. She was bored until I livened up the party. She wished she had the guts to punch that little Momma's boy in the face years ago. He bugged the hell out of her.

Before I knew it, we were tearing every relative to shreds. We found out we had much in common, the things we loved and hated and how we felt about our family. Not only was Virginia my favorite cousin, but on that day, she became my best friend. The question was how would we arrange to see each other again? I wasn't allowed to talk to her if it wasn't a family gathering.

Virginia was twelve, a little bit older than me. I asked her if she knew why my father and Uncle Jim hated each other so much. She asked if I could keep a secret. This was my first chance to prove my loyalty to her. Of course, I said yes and held my pinky out for a 'pinky swear.' Wrapping her pinky in mine, deal. Taking a deep breath, she looked over each shoulder to make sure no one was around, then she leaned in. Her hair smelled like a cozy pair of pajamas that were fresh out of the laundry. I wanted to snuggle inside of it. Lowering her voice, she made it sound like this was official FBI business that I better take to the grave. She had such a way of commanding my attention. I hung on every word she said.

"Well, a long time ago when your father and Uncle Jim were younger, they both fell in love with the same girl. As a matter of fact, all the boys in the neighborhood wanted to be with this same girl. Even my dad says he had a crush on her at one point. Anyway, it was clear that her heart belonged to only one lucky boy, your dad. Then your father joined the army and went away for a year. While he was away Uncle Jim tried to steal the girl away. She was innocent and liked Uncle Jim, but not like that. Just as a friend. They became very close, and then Uncle Jim went too far. He made her do things against her will. He asked her to marry him. He told her Uncle Ryan was no good and made up lies about him. When Uncle Ryan came home, she seemed different. He was broken hearted. He didn't know what to do. My Father wanted to tell him but didn't want to betray Uncle Jim. Everyone was confused. Finally, she told Uncle Ryan. He lost it. He wanted to kill Uncle Jim and her. My Dad said he's never been the same."

I was fascinated by the story. I could see why Dad hated him. It made me hate him too. It all made sense now. I wanted to know more.

I looked at Virginia and asked her, "What ever happened to the girl?"

"Your Father married her. It's your mother, silly."

My heart sank. I felt like I just met one of Dad's demons. A demon that lives with me and my four brothers every day.

Virginia went on a little while longer, "Your mother was the talk of the neighborhood. My Dad says she was a real looker. She still is."

There was a question burning deep inside of me. I had to know. Even though I was afraid to find out the answer. "Virginia, what do you mean by he made her do thing against her will?"

Could it be like me and the Cuban man? Could Mom have passed that on to me, like Dad passed on his anger? Was Mom keeping her dark secret from all of us, even Dad? I awaited the answer with dread.

"You know," she said.

"No. I don't, please tell me."

"Well, my Dad said it was bad. He won't tell me exactly. Says I'm too young."

She didn't need to say anymore. I could tell what she meant. I wasn't too young to know. I felt my secret stewing inside, and I wanted to tell Virginia. After all, she'd just told me a secret. I wanted to tell her how I was like Mom and I know how she feels, but I couldn't. The words wouldn't come out of my mouth. My stomach was nervous. I must have turned white.

"Frankie, what's wrong? You look sick."

It was too big a risk. She'll have to prove her loyalty to me before I could tell her.

"I think I ate too much turkey."

She laughed, "Yeah, and that fight probably stirred you up."

I had to leave, get away, but where could I go? I didn't want to go back home. They would be there. I didn't want to go inside with Nanny and Grumpy because I felt their disappointment in me.

It was just Virginia and me in the backyard after a long and depressing Thanksgiving Day. It was getting dark. Virginia would soon have to leave. They had a long drive back to the Hamptons. I was sad because I knew I wouldn't see her for a while. I didn't even know where the Hamptons were, never mind how I would get there. She said maybe she could talk her mother and Father into letting me come for a weekend around Christmas time. I smiled with excitement, until I realized Dad would never let me.

"We'll see." I told her.

She got up and gave me a big hug and kiss. I was filled with excitement.

"You are my favorite person, Frankie."

Wow, no one has ever said that to me. I didn't know how to respond. I felt like crying, but that wouldn't be acceptable, especially because she thought I was so brave. How could I let her know that her departure was breaking my heart? How could I tell her she's the first person beside my mother that made me feel special? I didn't say anything I felt. I said what I thought she expected from me, something funny. "Good thing Brian wasn't out here. I would've beat the shit out of him too."

She laughed hard, "I love you, Frankie."

"I love you, too." And I did with every ounce of my broken and scarred heart.

"Well, I better go or my father's going to get mad." She ran off. I sat in the yard listening to the next-door neighbor's dogs barking. What were those dogs trying to say with all the noise they made? It must be terrible not to be able to talk, to say what you're feeling. How frustrated they must be. Just like me.

Everyone was gone. I always stayed late. Since we only lived around the corner, Dad didn't mind. It was getting cold and any trace of light had disappeared. I didn't care. The stars were dancing above me. I found the ones that winked at me the most and made my wishes on them. I had lots of wishes this night. I wished that I could see Virginia again soon. I wished Uncle Jim never did that to Mom. I wished that Dad could forgive Mom and they could love each other again. Maybe it was different between them before that happened. I wished I could have a sister, so I didn't have to be the only girl. I wished that the dogs and I could stop barking and really talk. At that very moment the dogs stopped barking. It gave me chills. This gave me hope.

Nanny came out with a cup of hot cocoa with marshmallows and a blanket. She sat next to me without saying a word. I knew she loved me, but I never expected her to say it ‘cause she’s Irish. She handed me the steamy mug and wrapped the blanket around me. Peace swept over me. We sat and gazed at the stars together. I figured she had a few wishes to make too, so I kept quiet for a while and sipped on my delicious cup of cocoa, with all sorts of secret spices that made for a magical treat.

When she finished placing her order to the violet sky, she turned to me and said, "You're a pistol."

I didn't understand what she meant by this.

"You're a son-of-a-gun, just like your father."

These are words I never wanted to hear. Defiantly, but with respect, I rebutted, "I am not."

"You are so. You're feisty, hot tempered, thick headed and witty. I know Joseph is a pain-in-the-ass, but you can't go beating every pain in the ass up. There are a lot of them out there. Girls shouldn't fight. It's not ladylike."

Again... with this ladylike thing. How can I be ladylike when I'm suffocated by boys? I have to fight for dinner for God sakes. I explained to Nanny that I was playing, and I didn't mean for anyone to get hurt.

"I know, I know." She said, "It's hard for you with all your brothers bullying you. You need someone to bully. Why don't you find some friends, girls, to play with? You're too much with the boys. You're starting to look like a boy."

As I looked down at my clothes, I realized I was wearing hand me downs from my brothers. "Dad doesn't have money to buy me new clothes."

"Do you see the way Virginia and Margaret dress? Like pretty young ladies, Elizabeth too."

Virginia, my God! Does she look at me and see a little boy too? I don't know if Nanny knew she was hurting my feelings, but I couldn't tell her. After all she was a grown up. The dogs started barking again.

I took a risk, "Nanny, Virginia wants me to come and visit her in The Hamptons. Do you think you can talk Daddy into letting me go?"

She smiled, "We'll see. That would be good for you. Maybe she can give you some of her old clothes. Then you can start to look like a little lady."

Great, more hand-me-downs; more old smelly ripped clothes that no longer fit their original owner. Give it to Frankie. She needs clothes. I looked up at the stars again and caught one winking at me. I wished someone would understand me.

Nanny looked at me, "Frankie, it's Thanksgiving. It's a time to count your blessings and show thanks. What are you thankful for today?"

Oh boy! Why did she have to ask me this... anything but this. She waited for an answer while I searched myself. Let me think of something that will satisfy her. "I'm thankful for the Pilgrims. I'm thankful for all the food you cooked. I'm thankful for you and Grumpy and some of my cousins, especially Virginia. I'm thankful for my hands and feet, eyes, ears, my nose."

She was still looking at me like I was missing something. I had to come up with one thing that would make her happy. I had it! It was a lie, but nonetheless I knew it would please her and I would be off the hook. "I'm grateful that I'm Irish." Bingo. She loved that one.

She laughed and told me, "You don't know how lucky you are to be Irish."

As if I'd just been handed fame, fortune and an easy life. "There's no better nationality in the world. You'll see one day how lucky you are."

I hope she's right. I hope someday something good will come out of my being Irish. Maybe I'll cash in on my luck. So far it felt more like a curse.

When I got home that night Dad was waiting for me. I never received such a greeting. "That's my girl." He said, "Frankie, you did good. I'm so proud of you." The boys all chimed in. They were cheering, like I was some kind of hero. Mom looked disgusted.

"Frankie, tomorrow I'm gonna start giving you boxing lessons, you boys too. We'll get some gloves and we'll have matches right here in the basement."

Mom walked away in silence. The boys all hugged me with excitement. I know boxing isn't ladylike, but Dad was suddenly interested in me. I needed to do it. If I were good maybe Dad would love me. Maybe he would even say it one day and break the Irish rule.

Chapter 7: RUN, CATCH AND KISS

Boxing was harder than I thought it would be. Dad built a ring with Ryan. It had rubber mats on the ground and a double set of ropes that squared us in. Each corner had wooden poles wrapped with towels. First Dad would demonstrate a few fancy foot moves with Ryan. He showed us how to throw a punch, how to take a punch, how to block and duck, the power of the follow-through, the Rope-A-Dope. He made us jump rope all the time and explained that boxing was more about mental strategy than physical strength. I never saw Dad more alive and eager to teach me. He seemed to really have a passion for boxing. "Boxing is the only true sport alive today. No luck, no errors, no relying on your teammates. All you have in that ring is yourself. It's the ultimate test of sportsmanship and only the strong survive."

"How do you know so much about boxing, Dad?" I asked.

Dad lit up with excitement. "I was fourteen years old when I had my first real fight. This guy, Pauly Murk, was picking on my brother." He didn't say which one, but I had a feeling it was Jim. "Now Pauly was a lot bigger than me, but I didn't give a shit. All I knew is nobody touches my family. I grabbed this guy and gave him a beating he'll never forget. Everyone in the neighborhood was there, including a trainer for the Golden Gloves, Shotsy. Shotsy was a crusty old bugger. He told me I had the hunger and coached me for the Golden Gloves. I won the city nationals three years in a row." He danced around and threw a few quick jabs and hooks as he told his story. "Anyway, back to business. It's time to work on you. My time has come and gone."

He showed me how to break the opponent's nose. You had to hit them precisely on the bridge. I guess he got the exact spot when he broke Mom's nose. Then he showed us how to knock the wind out of someone if they were a smoker. Now, as a ten-year-old, these facts confused me. Part of me was so interested in learning all this, but part of me thought it was crazy. Am I supposed to look around for ten-year-old's who smoke and knock them out?

We had two pairs of gloves. They had Everlast written across the wrist. Whoever was in a match would wear them. Dad and Ryan would have great matches. Dad said Ryan had the hunger. He had that animal quality it took to make him a professional boxer. They had a look in their eyes, like they were going to kill each other. Sometimes I believed they wanted to. Mom would come down with snacks and drinks, but she would never watch. She felt it was a ridiculous sport. Two men beating each other to death was not her idea of fun. She was angry that Dad had me doing it, too.

I never boxed Dad, Ryan or Ian. They would only work on my punches with me. They never punched back. Patrick and I were paired up against each other most of the time. I would always tell myself, 'Just let him win one, it'll make him feel good.' But when we were in that ring my competitive nature got the best of me and I would blast him with my right hook, and he was down.

Once in a while Seamus would box me, but he always won.

Dad encouraged us to get other kids in the neighborhood and we could charge admission for boxing matches. Everyone loved the idea. No other girls boxed, but Dad said it was because they knew I was too tough for them. I took this as a compliment.

Christmas was coming up and Virginia called me and said Uncle Joe agreed to let me come to the Hamptons. Now I had to get Dad to agree. I talked to Mom about it first and she thought it was a great idea. I think she wanted me to get away from the boxing for a while. Dad said no. He said he needed me around and that Christmas was going to be a busy time for boxing. I felt like a freak in the circus, a slave to my dad's wishes. I wanted to be treated like a girl and go do girlie things with Virginia, but that was not a possibility.

The boxing caught on quickly. Before we knew it, our basement was packed every night. Dad was racking up cash, not only on admission, but he was taking bets on the side. Sean was among the boys who came to box. He was there every night. The more we saw each other, the bigger my crush got. Still, I begged Dad to let me go to Virginia's.

He said, "No way. I scheduled a match for you to box Sean."

I couldn't believe it. "I can't box Sean, Dad."

"Why not."

"He'll kill me! He's older and bigger."

Dad smiled, "But you're tougher, Frankie. Trust me. I watch you and I watch him. You're smarter. You can beat him."

I had a week before Sean, and I were scheduled to fight. The bets were coming in. Dad and Ryan worked extra hard with me. They wanted me to be fully prepared for the big match. Ryan taught me a lot of fancy footwork. He put on inspirational songs like 'Feeling Stronger Every Day' by Chicago and 'Live and Let Die', by Paul McCartney and Wings. Then he made me dance around the ring to them as I punched the air, pretending that it was my opponent.

I went down to Sanders candy store to play pinball with Patrick. He told me he was quitting boxing. He felt like it was against God to hit people over and over, knowing that you're hurting them. He told me he was thinking of being a priest. He always seemed so sad and lonely. I apologized for beating him all the time in boxing. I didn't mean to hurt him. I just liked to win. He wasn't mad at me. He felt like he didn't fit in. I knew that feeling; I was boxing so I could fit in. I didn't know if I liked it or if I was doing it for Dad.

Patrick and I loved to play pinball. He was really good. He had the high score all the time. The big guys would come in and challenge him, but he would always beat them. It was nice to see Patrick have confidence in something. Sean came in and stood by me. I got a tingly feeling inside. When I looked at him, I felt like I might throw up. I didn't know what to say. He smiled at me. I could feel my face go red. "Hey, when you two finish here you wanna come over to the park? We're playing a big game of RCK. Everyone's gonna be there."

RCK stood for Run, Catch and Kiss. I was dying inside.

Patrick quickly answered, "No thanks."

Then Sean turned to me, "What about you, Red?"

At this point, I didn't know if he was talking about my hair or my face. I was red all over. Something came over me and I blurted out,

"Sure, I'll play."

It was like an alien popped out of me. Patrick looked at me in shock.

Sean smiled, "Great! Come over when you're done."

He glided off with his blue eyes, blue jeans and platinum blonde hair. I couldn't wait until Patrick's game was over so I could go run, catch and kiss Sean. Patrick lost his concentration and the ball whizzed by his flippers.

He smacked the glass, "So are you gonna just flat leave me to go play with Sean?" I couldn't believe how sensitive he got. He went on, "We haven't even had our egg creams yet."

Patrick and I would go to Sanders every day and drink at least three egg creams each. No one made them like Sammy. The glass was a tall sundae style, narrow at the bottom and wide on top. There were deep grooves that ran up and down the sides. When I touched the glass and saw the foam on top, my mouth would water with anticipation. My favorite flavor was chocolate. Patrick's was vanilla. First, Sammy would grab the special glasses out of the freezer. Steam would spill out as they hit the air. Then he would splash just the right amount of syrup in each glass, grab the long skinny spoon and stir in the milk slowly. He would finish it off with a powerful shot of seltzer and they would puff up like a cloud. I couldn't get my straw opened quickly enough. Patrick liked to gulp it, but it didn't taste the same. I had to sip it down through the straw without taking a breath. At the end, after I made sure I got every drop, I would let out a big satisfying sigh.

"Okay, let's get our egg creams, Patrick. Then I'll go."

I figured I could probably use some extra running energy. We ordered our egg creams, but Patrick had a puss a mile long on his face. Sammy even noticed.

"The usual." I smiled at Sammy.

"Why the long face, Patrick?" Sammy inquired.

"Ah nothing." Patrick lied.

"Girl trouble?" Sammy tried again.

"Nope, just want my egg cream and then I'll be happy."

Sammy got our egg creams. We downed them in our usual fashion, and I told Patrick I'd see him later. He didn't move. He didn't respond. As I started out, I heard Sammy tell him the next one's on the house. I wanted to stay and talk to Patrick, but I didn't want to miss out on the game.

When I got to the park everyone was just getting ready to play. I saw Sean sitting with Seamus and my heart sank. How am I going to play with my brother? As I got closer, I saw Teresa, Angela, and Patty. They were so excited to see me. Did Sean ask them too? I thought I was special. There were a lot of older boys. Boys I definitely didn't want to kiss. As soon as I got there, Sean took charge. He went over the rules. They were pretty easy. The boy chases the girl of his choice and tries to catch her. If he does, he wins a kiss. That didn't seem fair to me. I raised my hand. Sean called on me as if I was a student.

"Hey, how come the girls don't get to pick who they want to kiss and chase them?" All the girls shouted with support. Sean laughed along with all the other boys.

John John yelled, "'Cause boys are faster than girls and you would never catch us."

I came back quickly, "I'd never wanna catch you."

I immediately got back-up support and laughter from the girls.

Seamus couldn't help himself, "I think Frankie could catch a lot of you lard asses." There were some older girls there too. They liked me sticking up for our sex.

Sean agreed, "Okay, first the girls will chase the boys, but if they don't catch anyone we switch." He put his hand out to me, "Agreed?"

I shook on it, "Agreed."

Seamus winked at me. All the girls had to sit on the bench and count to ten while the boys ran in all directions. My eyes were set on Sean. I was determined to have my first real kiss. When ten seconds passed, I headed for Sean. So did two other girls. Both older, but I was faster. Angela and Teresa went for Seamus. Sean started teasing us. He went up on the slide and jumped off when I started climbing up. Then he went on the monkey bars. This was my favorite. He got to the top and jumped again. Then he went onto the baseball field. A straightaway. No swings, no slides, just him and me. I left the two other girls in the dust. He was mine. He was surprised I was still behind him. I could see him getting tired. No way would I give up until I win. As he got to the end of the field, he jumped on the fence, but couldn't climb quickly enough. I grabbed his foot and pulled him down. He was panting.

"I got you, I got you." I jumped up and down with joy.

He laughed as he rolled on the ground, "I let you."

"Yeah right." I laughed.

He looked at me quietly for a moment. It scared me.

"Frankie" he said, "I wanted you to catch me." His voice went through me. I was frozen in time. Oh my God, it hit me. Now I have to kiss him. I thought this was what I wanted, what I ran so hard for. Fear filled my sweaty, shaky and maybe stinky body. Even though it was cold out, I was boiling inside.

He took my hand, "So you caught me. Are you gonna kiss me?"

He was so cute I was melting. "Yes," I said weakly. "Where should I kiss you?'

"On the lips," he said.

I laughed, "I know that. I mean should we go somewhere, or should I kiss you on the ground?'

"I think you should kiss me right here where you caught me."

I sat on the ground next to him. Smoke was coming out of our mouths as the cool air filled our lungs. I felt like we were all alone in the park at that moment. I couldn't hear or see anything else. He was so gentle and sweet. He waited until I was ready. He said if I wanted to, I could close my eyes, but he was going to keep his open so he could see me. I took a breath, leaned into his face. I made sure my mouth was lined up with his and then I closed my eyes. I melted into his lips. They were so soft, like pillows. I wanted to stay this way forever. I didn't know how long the kiss was supposed to last. No one mentioned that in the rules. I felt like we were there for hours. I opened my eyes slowly, but I didn't pull away. His eyes were open looking right into mine. They were deep blue and soothing like the ocean. They were kind and warm as if they were smiling at me. I got shy and pulled away, not too far, but our lips weren't locked anymore.

"That was nice Frankie. You're a good kisser."

"Thanks." I said, but then I got a sick feeling. He seemed like he's done this before. How did he know I was a good kisser—as opposed to whom? How many girls had he kissed? Did he kiss those two older girls who were chasing him? Did he play RCK all the time? Who would he kiss next? Would we ever kiss again? My head was swimming. Oh no, what had I done? I am going to box him next week. How could I punch a boy I'd just kissed? My Father was going to kill me. What if Seamus told? I was sinking fast.

Sean was still quiet, "Do you want to kiss again."

"Yes, but I don't think we..."

Before I could finish, he was kissing me. I didn't fight him. It felt too good. My second kiss was with the same boy as my first. They were both unforgettable. I could feel the tip of his cold nose pressed against mine, like Eskimos. Reality crept in and I could hear voices again. As I pulled away from Sean the whole game was running toward us. The boys were now chasing the girls. John John was running right toward me. Sean and I were both still lost in our moment. As soon as Sean realized what was going on, he grabbed me and yelled, "I caught you." John-John grabbed me right after yelling, "I got her." They started to argue over me. John-John said Sean wasn't playing fair, hogging me all to himself. You're supposed to catch and kiss as many girls as you can. Sean said he only wanted to kiss me. I was so happy. I didn't know what to do with myself. Sean winked at me. John-John left defeated. When I saw Seamus, he had a girl on each side. Back and forth he went. They didn't seem to mind. When I got a closer look, it was Patty and Angela. Sean and I started laughing. Everyone was kissing everyone. Who made up this game anyway?

Well, the game ended, and it was time to go home. Sean asked if he could walk me home. I agreed even though I was afraid of my Father seeing me. He kissed me on the cheek and asked if I'd meet him tomorrow after dinner. I felt like putty in his hands. He could've asked me to fly to the moon and I would have done it.

When I got home, Dad was not in a good mood. He was drinking and yelling at Mom. I tried to sneak upstairs, but he caught me.

"Get in here." He demanded, "Where have you been?"

"At the park, playing," I answered.

Mom looked at me as if to say he's in one of his moods.

"You're supposed to be practicing. You got a big match coming up."

"Dad, I don't want to fight Sean."

"Well, you have no choice. The bets are in and you're fighting.

Patrick snickered. He knew I had a crush on him. I guess he felt like if Sean and I fought, I wouldn't flat leave him anymore.

I ran upstairs and Mom ran after me. I went and grabbed my monkey, Silvio. I always held him when I felt sad. Mom sat on my bed.

"Where have you been tonight, Francesca?"

"I told you. Playing at the park."

"Don't lie to me. You have a certain look tonight, that I have not seen before."

"Tell me Bella Figa," (my beautiful fig), "I need to know why you glow like this?"

She looked at me and I knew I was caught. I must tell her the truth.

"Mom... today I kissed a boy. More than once."

Mom was still. "Who was it?"

"Sean."

"Sean Murphy?" She asked with surprise.

"No," I assured her quickly. Sean Murphy was Ian's rival. The guy he was always fighting. "Sean Carol." I explained, "The blonde hair, blue eyes."

She smiled, "Yes I know who he is. How did you like it, Francesca?"

"Well at first I was scared and sick and then I felt like I was dreaming."

"Yes, that's a first kiss alright." She laughed, almost childishly, but then caught herself. She came back at me with more authority this time. "Francesca, you are too young to be kissing boys. There will be plenty of time for that and plenty of boys believe me."

"But Mom..." I argued.

"No buts. You are not to kiss this boy anymore."

My stomach dropped. It was like letting a kid have a big slathering lick of ice cream and then taking it away. She began brushing my hair. I think this was to make up for the disappointment. When she calmed down, I popped the question.

"Mom, how old were you when you first kissed a boy?'

Silence. The strokes of the brush on my hair became softer and slower. She took a moment.

"I don't remember," she replied.

I would not accept this as an answer. "Come on Ma. If you don't remember you must've been pretty young."

"Ashpet," she scolded.

"Why won't you tell me?"

"Because it is none of your little business."

I decided to take another approach, manipulator that I was. "I bet all the boys wanted to kiss you. You're so beautiful." She laughed. "Who was the first boy you kissed?" I couldn't believe it, but Mom was blushing.

"Pasquale D'Amato."

"How was it?" I was curious.

"You know, like you say, scared, sick, then dreamy." We both laughed. In spite of herself, Mom liked talking about this. "It was a very hot day and I was in front of the house hanging laundry. I still remember the dress I was wearing. It was pink with a cranberry trim and cranberry laces up the front. My hair was still wet, I had just washed it. I felt very pretty that day." She started whispering. I guess she was afraid Dad would hear her. He was very jealous. She continued, "He popped out from behind a long sheet and smiled. He said, in Italian of course, 'Isabella you look as fresh as the laundry.' Then he came up behind me and sniffed my neck. The feeling of him behind me gave me chills." I knew exactly what she meant because when Sean's little pinkie touched mine on the pinball machine one day, I got weak inside. "Then Pasquale said, you smell as fresh as the morning air off the sea."

"Oh my God," I said. "He was a poet."

"Yes." Mom was tickled. "He was quite romantic. Without me asking him, he began hanging laundry with me. We hardly spoke the whole time. We didn't need to. His eyes were full of conversation and I answered with mine. His face was in the bright sun facing mine. The way the light caught his eyes made them twinkle."

"What color were they?" I blurted out, caught up in the moment.

"So many colors I could not say for certain. They look like that thing you hold to your eye and turn."

"Kaleidoscope."

"Yes. One moment they were green, then gold, then amber."

I was thinking of Sean's beautiful eyes. "Were they ever blue?" I asked.

"No, never." She giggled at me.

"So, go ahead. Finish! What happened with Pasquale D'Amato? Did he tackle you in a big sheet and wrestle you to the ground?"

"No, Francesca. You are ten years old. Where do you get such an imagination from? When all the laundry was done, he took my hand and so softly asked me to come to the sea for a walk. I could not even make a sound. I just took his hand and walked. I felt like I was walking on a big white cloud. On the way, he told me he wanted to show me the most special thing in the world to him. I must say I was very scared. When we got close to the water, he sat me on a big rock. The day was cooling off and I knew I couldn't stay very long. I was not allowed out after the sunset.

I couldn't help myself. "So, you must've been really young, right?"

She gave me a look and continued as if she didn't hear me. "Pasquale looked at me with those kaleidoscope eyes and said, 'Isabella you are the most magnificent flower I have ever set my eyes upon. I have watched you for a long time.' I felt embarrassed, but I kind of liked it. It was flattering. See he was older than me, so I thought he would prefer to be with an older girl."

"How old was he?"

Again, she continued as if I said nothing. She filled up. "It was like nothing existed except Pasquale, that rock, the air, and God. Then he said, 'Look, Isabella the sun is dropping around the crown of your beautiful red hair.' He touched my hair. 'Now I will show you the most special thing.' He touched my face gently and turned it toward the sun. We watched as the water slowly swallowed the last bit of daylight into its body. The orange and yellow hues filled the sky. Purple streaks spilled in the horizon. It was the most beautiful sunset I have ever seen. Then he turned my face back to him. He looked at me a moment to make sure my eyes welcomed him, and they did. So, he kissed me."

She paused for a breath. I took one too. Wow! Wow! I was so happy.

"That was even better than me and Sean. We were cold and sweaty on a concrete baseball field with dog shit all around us. You were on a cliff in the Italian Alps, surrounded by the sea."

"Oh Francesca, you are hopeless."

"Mom, please let me kiss Sean again. He's such a good kisser."

"No. Kissing leads to other things. Things that you are not ready for."

"Did you do other things with Pasquale D'Amato?"

"You ask too many questions."

"You told me whenever I want to learn to ask questions."

"Yes, but I meant in school."

"Mom, what happened to Pasquale?"

"I saw him for about two years, but it was a secret because my father would not allow it. Then his family moved."

"Were you sad?"

"Yes, I was very sad, even more sad because I could not show my sadness. If I did, they would know our secret and I would get in trouble."

I saw a side of Mom that night that made me feel closer to her. We were a lot alike. We both had secrets.

Mom's story satisfied me. Cozy in my bed, I felt safe for the first time in a long while. She began to sing me an Italian lullaby. I felt like I was on the cliff with Mom and Pasquale. I could see the sunset. Then I could see Sean. Mom's song got softer and softer as my breathing got deeper and deeper. She must have thought I was sleeping. She kissed me and whispered, in Italian, as she always did, "God bless you and sleep with the angels." But then she continued, "My child, I know you will do what you want, just be careful." I was filled with delight. My heart started beating faster.

I bolted up and kissed her. "Thanks, Mom."

She laughed, "You little faker, go to sleep."

I hugged my pillow, hugged Silvio and prepared myself for happy dreams about Italy. Just as Mom was almost out of the room, I tried one more time. "Ma, how old were you?'

"Good night." She commanded, as she switched off the light.

* * *

The next morning, I woke to the smell of Pancetta sizzling in a pan. A hungry smile passed my face. I stretched my frail body out as long and big as I could. I could feel my little muscles growing inside, yearning to explore. I ran my hands along my body and liked the way I felt. I was soft and lean, my body taut, strong, and alive. I was slowly starting to pull the Cuban man out of my skin, thread by thread. Excitement filled me as I went down to breakfast. I thought it must be eight or nine o'clock, but much to my surprise it was 6:00 a.m. Mom had her music on as she prepared breakfast. I kissed her good morning, but she was cold, short. Not happy to see me.

"What are you doing up so early?"

“I couldn't sleep anymore. I woke up so excited.”

"Huh," she mocked me. "I know what you're excited about."

"What's wrong, Ma?"

"Nothing. Go back to bed."

"I'm not tired."

"Well, I am," she yelled. "I've been up all night waiting for your father, but he's still out somewhere."

The pots and pans clattered together as she threw them in the sink with the food still in them. She grabbed clean pans and began cooking some more. It was as if she didn't know why she was cooking, but it definitely wasn't to eat. I couldn't help it; the smell was making me hungry. I reached into the sink and helped myself to breakfast. When I turned around Seamus was standing in the doorway scratching his privates.

"Smells good, Ma. What it is?"

"Everything!" I yelled. I was just happy to have company. Not too far behind were Ian and Ryan, scratching their privates as they squinted, with sleep still in their eyes.

"What time is it?" Ryan questioned.

"Early." Mom snapped back.

Ian was confused. "Is it Christmas already?"

"No." Mom slammed another full pan of food into the sink. Ryan and Seamus made a beeline to the sink. I must admit, for some reason the food tasted better than ever, maybe because I was happy. Finally, Patrick strolled into the kitchen. Not like the other guys, he came in scratching his head and shivering.

"It's freezing down here."

"Stand by the stove," Mom told him.

It was a Saturday, so none of us had school. Mom didn't pay much attention to us. Ian knew she was disturbed.

"Hey, where's Dad?"

"Not here," Mom replied angrily.

"Well I can see that. Has he been out all night?" Ryan asked Mom compassionately.

"Yes, Ryan." Mom began to cry. "Will you go look for him?"

"Sure, Mom." Ryan motioned to Ian and Seamus. "Let's go."

They all got dressed and went out to look for him. I wanted to go just to be out with the guys early in the morning, but I really didn't care where he was or if he ever came home. Secretly I prayed he didn't.

I was too energized to go back to sleep. I told Patrick I was going to 12th Street Park and wanted him to come. He assured me it was way too early to see Sean. That wasn't why I wanted to go. I wanted to be in the first one there, before anyone else. I'd never been in the park that early in the morning. I thought it would feel amazing. He was still mad at me and played hard to get. I was determined to go, with or without him. I got myself dressed. He didn't want to be left alone, so he got dressed too. We walked toward the park as the sky peeked with a thread of sunrise. The streets were still and empty. The neighborhood looked different to me. I felt big.

When we arrived at the park it was empty except for the birds singing their morning melody. They seemed happy to me. I felt happy. I raced Patrick to the swings. There was no waiting to get on. We went up really high. I loved to touch the leaves on the trees with my feet pushing out from my swing. I felt the way the morning birds must feel - free, awake, and alive.

Patrick was happy he'd come. We went on the seesaw, the slides and the monkey bars. The sun was out, but it was cold. I hit Patrick and yelled, "You're it," as I ran away. He laughed and started chasing me. I ran by the sandbox and noticed a body face down. It looked like a dead man. I stopped. Patrick tagged me. He was so happy because usually he couldn't catch me. "Got you," he jeered with delight. I couldn't speak. We both looked in silence as we moved closer to the sandbox. An empty bottle of Jack Daniels was attached to the man's hand. The closer I got to the sandbox, the more familiar the figure looked. I couldn't believe it. It was Dad. Patrick and I looked at each other. The same thought passed both of our minds. Is he dead? I was afraid to touch him, but I knew Patrick was even more terrified. As I knelt down beside him, I waited for him to breathe. There was throw-up by the side of his head. His back rose a with little breath, so I knew he wasn't dead. I must say it was a relief to me.

"He's not dead," I whispered to Patrick. Patrick and I looked at each other and it was like one of those church moments. We busted out laughing. I was laughing so hard I couldn't breathe. Through his laughter, Patrick said, "Shh, you'll wake him," which made us laugh even harder. Well, I should hope so. I wanted to get him out of the sandbox before the whole neighborhood came to watch, like a freak show. I told Patrick to run to Sanders and get some coffee. I knew Dad needed coffee whenever he woke up after having a few too many. While Patrick was gone, I shook him gently. Although he looked and smelled like shit, there was something serene, unthreatening about him.

"Dad," I whispered. "C'mon, wake up."

"Isabella?" He mumbled.

"No, Frankie."

"Frankie, what are you doin' in my bed. Get out."

"Dad, I'm not in your bed."

"Am I in your bed?" he asked immediately.

"No. We're in the sandbox. You fell asleep here."

He took a while to become aware of his surroundings. He seemed so lost, like he wanted to cry. I felt sorry for him. "I sent Patrick for some coffee. He should be back any minute."

I'd been a coffee drinker since I was seven. Mom had that old-fashioned espresso pot, the silver one that looked like a double-decker chimney. You cooked the coffee on the stove. It came out perfect every time.

"Did anyone else see me like this? Your mother, where's your mother?"

"She's home cooking enough for the Sicilian army."

"Oh boy. She must be mad. That's what she does when she's real mad, Frankie, she cooks."

"At least it's safe. She's not killing anyone," I said.

He laughed. He started wiping the sand and dirt off his back. He looked at me and I saw him fill with shame. "You must think I'm a real bum, huh?"

I didn't answer him. I didn't feel like it was a question. I think he felt that way about himself. Patrick arrived with the coffee. He gulped his down. Patrick and I sipped ours. He was blue with cold from being out all night. The three of us sat in the sandbox as Dad finished his coffee. It felt like we were three little kids. No one spoke for a long while. We just looked at the sky, listened to the birds and watched the steam spiral up from our Styrofoam cups. Finally, Dad shifted uncomfortably and said, "Great coffee, huh?"

"Oh yeah," I agreed. "Nothing like a good cup of coffee in the morning." What I really wanted to say was, "You drunken bastard. You could be drinking a cup of turpentine right now and you wouldn't know the difference." Dad went on to tell Patrick and me all about coffee beans in Columbia, Italy, France and Spain and how big of a business coffee is. He said he was never really a big coffee drinker until he met Mom.

"You know how those guineas like their espresso."

Every cup felt like you injected pure adrenaline into your veins. It was the highlight of my day. I knew I was too young to be saying, 'I haven't had my coffee yet,' but I was already hooked. All of us loved Mom's espresso. We would fight over who got theirs first. The pot only made two cups at a time. Dad liked his with Sambuca and three coffee beans. He said the beans symbolized good luck. I don't know what the Sambuca symbolized, but I didn't see how the combination could bring anybody good luck. It seemed like a ticket to trouble; caffeine and booze. I mean, what could be worse than a wound-up drunk?

The day was getting on the way. A young handsome man entered the park with a little girl holding his hand. With the other hand he pushed a baby in the stroller. I had seen him here before. He always smiled at me. He was probably the same age as Dad, but he looked about ten years younger and a whole lot happier. He said, "Good morning," as he passed. Patrick and I said, "Hello." Dad just looked at him longingly and mumbled, "What's so good about it?"

The little girl threw her arms up to him. "Come on, Daddy, do the thing," she said as she giggled. "Okay," he smiled. He lifted her above his head and kissed her belly making a funny noise. She laughed so hard as he kept making this funny sound on her belly. Then she wrapped her arms around his neck and said, "You're the best, Daddy."

Dad turned to me and Patrick, "What do you say we go home and have some of Mom's espresso?"

"Sure, Dad." We were as uncomfortable as he was. I waved good-bye to the man and his daughter, wishing I could switch places with her for just one day. I wanted to laugh like that, play like that, but for now I would juice myself up with Mom's Italian espresso.

***

It was Christmas day and the smell of mouth-watering food permeated in the air as usual. Mom had Nat King Cole crooning "Chestnuts Roasting on An Open Fire," from her Victrola. She said his voice of velvet made her melt. I ran downstairs to see what presents were under our silver, fake, ugly tree. It looked like a space suit, with tinsel branches that fell apart a little bit more each year.

When I got downstairs, Mom and Dad were cooking together. They were laughing and singing the Christmas songs that were jingling through the radio. They seemed happy. Dad was excited to see me.

"Go see what Santa got you." My parents always said that even though I knew the truth. There were two boxes for everyone. I tore the paper from the bigger box first. I was excited. When I got all the paper off, I could read the letters on the cardboard box. It said 'Everlast;' a brand-new pair of boxing gloves. I didn't know how I felt. I was confused. What would I tell my friends when they asked me what I got for Christmas? I would be too embarrassed to tell the truth. I wanted to cry, but Dad stood behind me with a proud smile. "I figured you need your own pair. Aren't they great? They're the real McCoys."

"Yeah," I said. "They're ggrrreat," but I kind of felt like I was pushing myself to say it, like those Frosted Flakes commercials. I just blurted it out like Tony the Tiger as if to mock him, although he didn't catch on. "They're Great!" All of a sudden, I remembered I had to fight Sean today. Oh no, my heart sank. I wished I were at Virginia's house sharing secrets. She sounded so disappointed when I told her I couldn't come, but I couldn't tell her why. I was dreading the fight. Sean and I had been kissing every day and now we were going to be punching each other right in the kisser, perfect. Maybe it wasn't any different than Mom and Dad's relationship. There was one more box and I was afraid to open it. I thought it might be men's Everlast shorts. The boys all ran down scratching their balls. I wanted to see what they got. Seamus and Ian both got a pair of boxing gloves. Dad probably got a discount rate for buying in bulk. Ryan got gold silk boxing shorts and headgear. Patrick got a harmonica. Don't ask me why. Maybe when you bought three sets of Everlast boxing gloves you got a free harmonica. Everyone looked puzzled, even Dad. It was as if he didn't know what to get so he hoped for the best. All four boys also got a jump rope each, Everlast of course. So, I figured that must be my other present. I had no interest in opening it. I tossed it aside. Wow, what a great Christmas this was going to be. A house full of testosterone and Everlast equipment.... a perfect environment for a growing girl. Dinner was at two. This gave us plenty of time to digest and get prepared for the big Christmas match.

My stomach was nervous, so even though Mom's food was unbelievably delicious, I couldn't eat it because I had the runs. By six o'clock everyone started piling in the basement. Dad had beers for sale. It seemed like everyone was excited to be here on Christmas Day and could give two shits about being with their families. I didn't know why. I'd rather be playing with Virginia and watching Rudolph the Red Nose Reindeer, but no such luck. I had to buckle up and march to my battle like a man.

Sean walked in. My heart stopped. God, he was so cute. I turned red. I felt it. He winked at me. My knees wobbled. How was I gonna fight him when I could barely stand next to him without turning into a bowl of Jell-O? I guess Patrick had told all my other brothers that I had a big crush on him. They all stared him down when he walked in. Then they looked at me. I tried to be cool, but it was so hard. Especially when he pulled off his sweats. He had on blue and white trunks. His body was lean but muscular. His hair dangled near his shoulders. Just as I was lost in his blue sea eyes, Ian whispered to me "Sean's been seeing Joanne Castinello the whole time you two been kissing partners." My heart sank. Joanne was older than me. I'm sure she's more experienced. I didn't know what to do. How can he do this to me? He made me believe I was the only girl. He told me I was a good kisser. Why does he need to kiss anyone else? God, I was mad. I felt betrayed. I felt like a fool. Ryan and Ian rubbed my shoulders. It was almost time. We both stepped into the ring. From opposite corners we stared at each other. He smiled. I growled. He looked confused. I think it was just him trying to cover up his guilt. I felt Dad's temper boiling in my blood. I wasn't myself. The bell rang. It was fighting time. The crowd cheered. Dad chanted my name so proudly. “C’mon Frankie, you got this bum.”

Sean met me in the middle of the ring. "Hey, hot lips." This made me even more pissed off. I wanted to kill him. Round one. He was not really punching much. He was letting me jab at him. I was in my own world. I pictured him and Joanne kissing. I pictured him saying the same things to her that he said to me. I wondered if he liked the way she kissed better than me.

Round Two. I came out punching and so did he. He hit me so hard in the head I actually saw stars. I lost my balance for a moment, but then regained my footing. Everyone's voices cheering in the background sounded like faint whispers in the distance. I felt like I was in a Twilight Zone episode.

Round Three. He blew me a kiss and smiled. I hated him. How could he smile when my guts were twisted? All of a sudden Joanne walked in. She looked great. It looked like Mom and Dad Santa got her a lot of nice, new, feminine clothes. Clothes that guys liked to see on girls, not hand-me-down boy clothes or Everlast workout threads. I bet her parents didn't shop through the Sears Roebuck catalogue. Some guys whistled when she came in. She was a looker. She was beautiful. I was jealous. I'd never be like Joanne. From somewhere a bolt of lightning filled my body like a power that wasn't even my own. It raced through my blood and pumped the courage of a lion into my heart. My fists felt strong like a force field was around them. I wanted to be like Muhammad Ali. I danced around him like a butterfly and stung like a bee. I faked him out with some short jabs. He turned his head to look at Joanne and at that moment he was mine. Dead meat, dog food, yesterday's news. Wham, bam, kaboom, just like in the Batman episodes, I decked him. It was like this wild animal came inside me and possessed my body. I hit him with all the anger I had been holding inside me. He hit the floor like a dead weight. Everyone cheered as they rose from their seats. People always love to see someone get knocked out. And he was knocked out cold in Round Three. I was the winner. Dad went around collecting money. I looked at Sean's lifeless body. The anger left as quickly as it had come and then I wanted to kiss him. What was this? I had no control. I was just like Dad. I hated it. Sean left defeated. His eyes filled with pain as he stared at me, as if to say, "Why?" I couldn't go to him. I watched him leave, but Joanne stayed. I thought that was weird. Then she came over and kissed Ian. He laughed and said, "I had to lie so you could kick the shit out of him. It worked."

I wanted to knock Ian out. I didn't know if I was relieved or sad. I was happy Sean wasn't seeing Joanne, but sad because I hurt him. He must have thought I hated him. The truth was I loved him. All the feelings that were going on made me feel yucky. Dad was happy. My brothers were proud of me, the winner, but I felt like a loser.

Where was Mom? I needed her. I went upstairs to find her. There were two more fights scheduled for the night, but I had no interest. The moment I got to the top of the stairs I could hear Puccini serenading Mom. As I closed the door to the basement, I felt relief. I found Mom sitting by the window, gazing into the snow-filled sky. It was wonderful to see the snow. I felt refreshed after my big match with Sean. I wanted to go outside and stand naked in the in the white magic falling from the Christmas sky. I wanted it to swathe my body and wash me clean of everything that came before this moment. I wanted to be washed clean of the boxing match with Sean, the hatred I had for Dad and most of all I wanted to be washed clean from the scar that the Cuban man had branded into the core of my being. Could the snow have that much power?

Mom was wearing a pretty red dress with green flowers on it as she sipped her espresso and nibbled on Pignoli cookies, my favorite. Delight filled my small, sweaty body. Mom always made them on Christmas. She knew I loved them. I went to her and touched her cheek with the tip of my nose. Inhaling her aroma, I found myself home, in my mother's scent. She was my home and the only thing that made any sense to me. "Francesca," she pulled my head into her bosom. I wanted to cry but I felt like I shouldn't. I should be strong. I wanted to pour all my pain and disappointment right into Mom's breast. I knew she would take it from me, but the tears wouldn't flow. It was as if they were stuck. She held me for a moment and then pulled me away to look in my face. When Mom looked at me, I felt like I was a map and she knew how to read every lie.

"Did you like your present, Francesca?"

"Well, not really Mom. I don't want to box anymore. It makes me angry."

She smiled. "I hate that stupid sport. He is out of his mind. But I could not tell him anything. He insisted on you having your own gloves."

I told her about Sean. She didn't know whether to laugh or cry. I asked her if she ever beat up Pasquale. She didn't, but she had a feeling Sean would forgive me if I told him the truth. Just thinking about that made me feel better. I couldn't wait to see his blue eyes tomorrow and apologize. Mom was still wondering.

"How did you like your other present?"

“I didn't even open it because I knew it was a jump rope.” She couldn't believe it, "Francesca, this other present I picked out. You must open it."

My heart jumped with joy... a present from Mom? It must be something great, I thought. All of a sudden, I felt like one of those misfit toys trapped on the forgotten island when they looked up in the sky and see Rudolph leading Santa's sleigh to come and save them. Just when I had given up all hope like the misfits there was a possible chance, I was going to be saved on the Christmas night. I raced to the ugly silver tree and saw the present I tossed aside earlier that morning. I ripped off the paper and found a lovely handmade jewelry box. It was a cherry wood carved jewelry box straight from Italy. I went over each detail, savoring every edge of the box. It was magical. I opened it. Music began to play. The song brought a tear to my eye. Then I saw a gold necklace twinkling at me. Chills went up the back of my neck. I delicately grabbed it and lifted it up. An emerald dangled off the chain. My heart dangled from my chest. I could not believe this was for me. I was shaking. I did not know how to receive such a gift. Mom took it and placed it gently around my neck.

"I wanted you to have this. Great Grandma left this to me when I was about your age. It is very precious, like you, Francesca. Take good care of it always," she whispered. "You are my most precious gem in this world." Best Christmas ever.

Chapter 8: THE MOLACKS

Spring was in the air that filled the polluted streets of Queens. We all counted down the days until another school year was over. Sean and I were seeing each other all the time. We spent a lot of time at his house, which was a real pigsty. Empty vodka bottles and crammed ashtrays were scattered throughout and a stench I only recognized in Dom's bar. Old green shag carpeting lined the floors and shit colored wood paneling was slapped up on every wall. He didn't have a father and his mother was either out drinking or sleeping. Sean said she was a manic-depressive. Sometimes the only way to get through a day was to sleep. It seemed like a horrible existence, but it definitely gave us time alone; time to kiss and kiss and kiss, with lips and tongues. I had to keep my eyes opened when we kissed because every time I closed them I saw the Cuban man's face and felt his fat stubby hands on me. I couldn't let him ruin my kissing time with Sean, so I learned to kiss with my eyes open.

When his mother did emerge from the bedroom it was only for a short time, always scratching her ratted hair and barely revealing her rotted teeth when she saw me. Wearing her tattered terry cloth robe, she would mumble as she shuffled her fluffy slippers across the rotted linoleum in the kitchen. Making her way to the freezer, she desperately ripped it open and clawed for her big bottle of vodka. It was packed to capacity with vodka bottles, not even room for and ice cube. With trembling hands, she poured her healing elixir into a coffee cup and went back to her hibernation. Sean didn't like to talk about her. He didn't like to talk about his father either, who left when Sean was three 'cause he couldn't put up with his mom's drinking and depression. He did like to talk about his dreams and hopes. He wanted to be an astronaut. Walk on the moon. Float around weightless in a United States tuna fish can. He too was inspired by JFK's dream to put men on the moon. It scared me when he talked about it because what if he went up but never came down? What if his capsule exploded and he became dust? I didn't let him know how much I hated the thought of it because it was his dream. I didn't want to rain on his parade. At least he had a parade. The only thing I knew was that I wanted to get out of Queens. That was what we had in common, dreams of a better place. I don't know if the moon is a better place, but it was probably as far away from home as Sean could get.

Sometimes I wouldn't see him for days. Then he would come around. He said he was sick, but I knew it was something else. Sean always had bruises on his body, but he wouldn't talk about it. One time when we were kissing, I squeezed his back and he jumped. I pulled his shirt over and saw a very deep indentation obviously made by a set of teeth. I let it go. I saw the look of shame cover his face, a familiar look. I've worn it so many times. We were the same. Two misfits, trying to find some comfort in each other's arms, even if it was stolen moments in an abandoned car, a tree house, a dark alleyway, or in his living room while his mother was in her constant coma. It was precious. We had an understanding.

Patrick was getting ready for his graduation. He had been practicing making his tie all year long. Everything he did was executed scrupulously. His clothes were always washed and pressed. His shoes were shined like a sparkling dime. Never was a hair out of place. He carried one of those corny pocket brushes, the kind you put your finger in the hole and the round part was cupped in your hand. Now his new obsession was the tie. He had it down to a science. It was almost mathematical for him. He measured and pulled and wrapped and inched and inched until all the angles met properly. He stood in front of the mirror for hours at a time. In between he would brush his hair or notice a pimple, pop it, wash his hands and go back to his tie practice. My other brothers loved it because they had no patience or desire to have a perfect tie on. It was more of a nuisance for them. They could care less about looking neat and tidy. As a matter of fact, whenever an occasion called for a tie, they would be annoyed. As soon as it ended, they would loosen their collars and rip their ties off. Not Patrick, he would wait until bedtime, slowly remove his tie, careful not to wrinkle it. Then he would place it gently over a special hanger. Seamus made an okay tie, but Patrick was the master. All the occasions from then on were dressed with a Patrick Finnegan tie. Even Dad got in on it. We would be getting ready to go somewhere and Patrick became a human tadpole. Ryan, Ian, Seamus and Dad would throw their ties around Patrick's neck and he would smile and begin his mastery in the mirror. He had five ties around his neck. One by one, according to the size of each brother's neck, he'd measure. Ryan had the widest neck and Patrick used to tease him about it. Ian had a very skinny neck to match his very lean body. Seamus was average. It was beautiful to watch them having so much fun with this tie ritual, but I was jealous. I wanted everybody to depend on me to make them look good. I felt left out.

One day Patrick and I were walking to 12th Street Park. It was the middle of summer. He said, "It's so fucking hot out." I couldn't believe it. He'd slipped; we were forbidden to curse. Even though I had been cursing by myself for a while and Dad said "fuck and shit" every other word, we would get our heads bashed in if it came out of our mouths in front of anyone. He looked at me in horror.

"I mean, it's hot as hell."

I laughed. I was relieved because God knows I cursed every chance I got when I was alone. I said, "Hey, I won't tell. Shit, why should I?"

"Frankie, you said 'shit,'" he pointed out and then covered his mouth after saying 'shit' again. We both started laughing so hard we almost pissed our pants. I was excited. To curse out loud with someone made me feel strong and way cool.

I said, "Patrick, let's say as many curse words as we can today. And, of course, it'll just be between us."

"Okay, deal, but only for today. You go first."

I was glad to. I started with "Bitch."

He went, "Bastard."

Now me, "Mother fucker."

We both went, "Ooohh, that's a bad one." Then Patrick surprised me.

"Cocksucker."

Wow. I thought maybe there was a little devil underneath his goodness. "Okay, bullshit."

Then he said, "Cunt." Oh my God. He explained Ryan and Ian always say it. We continued with everyone we knew. "Piss, shit, fucking whore, cock sucking pig fuck, ass wipe, shit head, dick nose, father fucking prick, big fat assholes shitting and pissing on their fucking mothers." I mean you name it and we said it. We even came up with new ones. It was freeing. We shocked each other. I think we both let go of a lot of anger that day. We shed tumors from our system. Just spewing out all the toxins from our sewer mouths. If anyone heard us, we would be punished for life. We bonded again. The cursing bond. Patrick kept reminding me it was only for one day and then no more cursing forever. "Yeah, right," I thought to myself. Whatever. All I know is that after expressing myself with this curse language, I could never remove it. 'Fuck' was my new favorite word. It just had a way of really adding zest to a sentence.

Later that day, Patrick and I ran into one of the Puerto Rican kids, Jose. He lived around the corner and always picked on Patrick when he was alone. He wasn't stupid enough to start trouble if any of my brothers were around. I guess I didn't frighten him much because he started with Patrick right away.

"Hey, fag boy," he said.

Patrick whispered, "Keep walking."

"What? No way this little Puerto Rican fucking bastard is calling you a fucking fag. Let's kick his sorry cock sucking pig brown ass up the street." I tried to get in as many curse words as I could. Patrick was scared.

"Frankie, stop it. Please, let's go." Patrick got nervous.

Jose came up and stood in front of Patrick. "You can't pass, sissy pants."

Patrick stopped. His white skin turned flush and he trembled with fear. Jose pushed him. That was enough for me. I wasn't afraid of the little motherfucker. I pushed him hard. He was as shocked as Patrick.

"Listen you fucking asshole, you ever touch my fucking brother again, me and my brothers will kick your whole fucking family's asses back to shitty Puerto Rico, you little piss ant fuck."

Well, not only did I scare the shit out of Jose, who ran off crying, but Patrick ran home. I started running after him. "Hey, where are you going?"

"I'm telling Dad you cursed at someone."

I was confused. We had a deal, a cursing bond, what happened to that? But Patrick said it was just between us. When I cursed at Jose, I broke the rules. A third party was added. I thought I was doing something good, saving my poor helpless brother. But no, I was a sinner. He told my father and I got the shit smacked out of me. Dad said no lady speaks like that. He made me stand in the yard with a bar of Ivory soap in my mouth. Then he took the green hose and sprayed water in the side where spaces were between my teeth and the Ivory. I was sick as a dog. Patrick watched from the window as I threw up bubbles and suds. I didn't tell on Patrick and all the bold and innovative curse words that had rippled out of his mouth that day. I just took it like a man.

When Dad finished washing my mouth out, I looked up at Patrick. He turned away with regret. I kept burping up soap and my tongue felt like I would never get rid of the taste. My belly was sick, and I had a terrible headache, which started in my nose, burning all the way through my eyes and ears, up into my head.

I was punished for the rest of the night. When everyone was sleeping, I snuck out the window and went to Sean's house. He was watching 'All in the Family' and laughing until he saw me. I was a little nervous his mother would wake up, but I had to see him. I told him I wanted to run away with him. I was so sick of my father. He was angry about what happened. He told me I didn't deserve it and that I was special. He promised he would never hurt me. I believed him. He told me I must go home or else I risked more punishment. Before I left, he kissed me. I was afraid he would taste all the Ivory soap, but he never mentioned it. "Frankie, tomorrow I want to take you to a new place where we can be alone, and no one can find us." This sounded heavenly. I could hardly wait. I asked him if he could call me Francesca because that's what my mother called me, and it made me feel pretty. "Goodnight, Francesca."

I floated all the way home and through the front window, up to my bed without anyone noticing. I said my prayers and made believe Sean was holding me while I slept.

The next day arrived and I was up and out of the house without breakfast. I was too excited even for Mom's delicious breakfast and heart jolting espresso. My heart was racing enough. I ran to Sean's house. He was up and dressed. His hair was still wet and smelled like Head & Shoulders shampoo.

"Good morning, Francesca," he smiled; I got that funny tingle.

"Good morning," I returned his greeting. "So, where are we going?" I couldn't wait.

"You'll see." He went in to say good-bye to his mother. I waited and waited. I heard her yelling and throwing things. He came out looking a little disheveled but ran his hand across his blonde wavy hair and smiled, one of those smiles that always seemed to be covering a broken heart.

Off we went. I had no idea where, but I didn't care as long as we were together. I watched him walk as if I were in a dream. I was kind of floating, but he was on solid ground. His long, slender legs kicked out gripping the blue of his Levis. There were rips on both knees and a couple of bleach spots. Although he had on a plain white Fruit of the Loom t-shirt, he wore it cuter than any other I had ever seen. His skin was soft, and it turned copper as the sun worked on him. He was much tanner now than when we first kissed. His teeth looked whiter. His eyes were even more blue if that was possible. Could I be in love? My nose could smell his Right Guard deodorant. My tongue could taste the Colgate toothpaste. My hands could feel the Vaseline Intensive Care lotion that he wore on his hands. All my senses were awake with curiosity. I wanted to explore this feeling more. Is this what Mom meant when she said kissing leads to other things? His kisses left me satisfied at night and hungry for more each morning. I didn't tell a soul about Sean. Mom knew a little on her instincts. But no one else knew. I figured I would tell Virginia when I saw her again. We had been writing to each other, but this was something I needed to tell her in person.

Sean led the way as I followed closely behind. We arrived at an opening, which was camouflaged by trees and bushes. He climbed through first and waited on the other side. "Here, give me your hand." He reached out to me with a smile.

All I could think about was kissing him. I thought about Mom and Pasquale and their perfect sunset kiss. Maybe there was a blue coast beach covered with sandcastles on the other side of the opening. I grabbed Sean's hand and he pulled me through. A smile ran away from my face when all I saw was two manhole covers on a concrete floor. I tried to hold back my disappointment.

"Is this it? Is this the most special thing?" He looked at me confused.

"The most special thing?" he questioned me. "Who said anything about special? I said we could be alone here."

Once again, I was confusing my common life in Queens with my mother's perfect romance with Pasquale D'Amato on the beach in Italy. "I'm sorry, Sean."

"It's okay," he said quickly knowing very well this was no glorious palace. "You haven't seen it yet."

I was puzzled. We were surrounded by trees. There was nowhere to go, so what was I missing? Did one of these manhole covers lead to a secret kingdom? Would I open it and pass through another space and time like 'The Lion, the Witch and the Wardrobe?' Was Narnia on the other side? Maybe this was better than Mom's rock in Italy. Maybe I underestimated Queens and all of its fabulous charm and culture. I surrendered to the future of this new place with no expectations.

"You're right. I haven't seen it, so show me, Sean."

He lifted one of the lids on the concrete floor. It squeaked so loud it pinched my ears. He began to climb down. I lied down with my face looking in the hole as Sean descended into the darkness.

"Come on, Frankie. "He'd forgotten about calling me Francesca already, but it was fitting. Climbing down this dirty manhole, I felt like a boy once again. The ladder, which led down the hole, was not your basic wooden ladder; it was iron handle rails, which stuck out of the cement wall. There were about six inches in between each rail. As I lowered my body, I felt a strong wind blow up past me as the sound of a train rumbled by. 'Where the hell are we?' I thought to myself. 'Are we catching a train somewhere?' Maybe Sean was taking me away. Could you take a train to Italy? I didn't have any clothes. Neither did he. I only had a few dollars in my pocket that I'd stolen off Dad's dresser this morning.

Sean yelled up, "Hurry up, Francesca."

I smiled, he remembered. "I'm coming."

He reached up to help me down. His hands grabbed my waist before I reached the bottom. He lifted me down. His arms were wrapped around me from behind. I melted into his chest. He whispered into my ear, "Are you okay?"

"Yes," I whispered back.

"You ready to see it?"

I knew there was no castle down here. "Sure, I'm ready."

We climbed up another iron ladder. This one was much shorter. Sean went first and waited to help me up. When I got to the top, we were inside a huge train tunnel, on a platform. It was very narrow, probably two feet wide. The walls curved up to the top to form a round ceiling. I could see the opening where the trains came through. There were many tracks outside the tunnel. I had seen these tracks near my house. They were laid out behind the jail at Court House Square. I never knew where they led to and never cared. When I looked down onto the tracks, I could see small cubbyholes along the wall. There were about fifteen feet in between each hole. This wasn't Narnia, but it was exciting. Sean grabbed my hand and led me down the platform. "Are you scared?"

"No." I answered too quickly. We reached the big hole in the wall. There was a bar across the front. Sean ducked under the bar and I did the same. It was obvious Sean had been here before. He knew it very well. I hated to think about him kissing anyone before me.

"This is the six-man hole," he explained. "The ones on the tracks are two men holes."

I was getting educated in the size of holes and how many men can fit. I didn't know if this was a good thing or a bad thing, but it was definitely a thing. He proceeded to tell me the schedule of the trains and what kind came through. Amtrak's were the fastest trains. He explained that when the trains came by you could feel your whole-body tremble. He said it felt almost as if you were going to be sucked right out of the hole. I watched him as he taught me all about this place. The same excitement filled him when he spoke about being an astronaut. Maybe they were connected somehow. Dark holes with beams of lights trickling in. The silence filled the long tunnel. The clicking of the third rail echoed up and down this hollow place. I could hear the dust blow on the tracks. A train must be coming. Sean held me. "You ready?"

"Do I have a choice?" I thought. There was nowhere to go except in front of the train. Would the engineer see me? Would he be able to stop in time, or would I become a flattened pancake? "I'm ready," I assured him with an ear-to-ear, completely forced, smile. The light slowly glistened on the dirty concrete curved wall. The energy of the locomotive filled the tunnel. A horn howled. I covered my ears. Sean smiled like we were on top of a roller coaster and he was so excited to go down the hill. As the train got closer, the tunnel rocked. The wind swept up anything in its path. Our hair whizzed back as the train whipped by. Cha-Ching. Cha-Ching. Cha-Ching. Cha-Ching.

Quick, but rhythmic, like the pounding of drums to match the pounding of my heart. When the last car passed us, Sean howled, "Wow, isn't it great? Don't you love it?"

I must admit I felt a rush of adrenaline when it was all over. It was powerful, a near brush with death. Sean liked dangerous things. "Yeah, it's great," I said.

Then he kissed me long and hard, wet and wild. I could taste the dusty air on his lips. It was different than he'd kissed me before. There was something animalistic about it. I got warm in between my legs. I felt him press himself in my warm spot. Our clothes were on, so I felt safe. I wasn't worried about him going further. I had been touched before and I knew what the next step was. I wanted it to be different with Sean. He wasn't forcing me or hurting me like the Cuban man, but my senses were exposed just the same. It was exciting and scary, but I felt dirty for even having the thought. I felt like I must be sinning because anything that felt good must be a sin. When Sean pulled away, he looked in my eyes. "This is my secret hideout. I call it the Molacks."

The Molacks! Why he called it this, he couldn't explain. After a while the Molacks became our escape. The name somehow suited the place. We went every day. We brought nickels and pennies and placed them on the silver railings of the tracks. After the train passed, we would collect our Molack souvenirs. The residue of our summer afternoons left me dirty and smelly. I had to run to the shower as soon as I arrived home. As the water trickled down my white body, the streaks of brown Molack dust dripped down, making a circle of dirt around the drain. It wasn't that I wanted to get rid of the dirt or smell right away. I liked it. I found it comforting. I smelled like him, but if I didn't wash, I would get found out. I couldn't risk this. As I showered off the dust from too many Amtrak's, I felt myself. I thought about Sean showering. I pictured him cleaning himself. Just that thought kept me in the shower way too long. I started touching myself every day after my daily Molack shower. Did Sean touch himself? Did he want to touch me? Why hadn't he tried? He might have thought I was too young. He didn't know about the Cuban man. If he did, he'd know I was older than other girls my age. I was interested in sex. I was curious what it would be like if you actually liked the person who was touching you; if you knew his name, if he kissed you gently and made you feel pretty. What would it be like if I willingly let Sean put his hands on my hungry flesh that ached to feel love? I didn't have much to touch, certainly not as much as the girls his age. Maybe this was why he didn't make an attempt to reach for my breasts that weren't quite breasts yet.

That night at dinner everyone was quiet, which was very unusual in our house. I felt scared, as if they were all waiting for me to say something. Ian broke the silence. "So, how's Sean doin', Frankie?"

Oh boy, here it comes. They've been spying on us. My skin got hot. My armpits exploded with perspiration. Calmly I replied, "Fine, I guess."

Seamus jumped in "You guess? Don't you know?"

Then Patrick, "She should. She sees him every day."

Ian kept going. "Yeah, when are you getting married?" The three of them questioned me like I was a Russian spy.

Ryan let out a loud burp, "Hey Frankie, pass the salt please." I loved that. He could care less. It was a break in the interrogation for a moment. I elaborated, "Sure, Ryan, would you like the pepper too?"

"Why not," he muffled out through his veal cutlet Parmigianino. "Could you pass me some sauce?" I pretended everything was fine.

"Sure," I wished Ryan and I were the only ones at the table. We could eat all day and pass things back and forth to each other, but there was no escaping the other savages. Mom just looked at me as if to say, "I told you so," but she said nothing. Dad pushed my fork down. I guess dinner was over.

"What's going on with you and Sean?" He pounded his fist on the table.

"We're friends." That brought a roar out of the cheering Romans.

Patrick rubbed it in. "Oh yeah, right, friends. Come on. Who are you kidding?"

All of my brothers except Ryan were torturing me. "Kill her, slay her, off with her head. Let's burn her at the stake. Crucify her."

"Why are your brothers saying you're more than friends?" Dad wanted to know.

"I don't know." I knew that Sean was my boyfriend. I knew I loved him. I lied to protect both of us.

"That's not an acceptable answer." Dad got more pissed off.

"Well, it's the only one I have," I snapped back. He snapped back with a hand across my face, followed by a chair pulled from underneath my ass. I was on the floor. Veal Cutlet Parmigianino followed my descent. He threw it on me and stained my favorite blue jeans. I'd faded them perfectly with spots of bleach, torn each knee and tried to make them look like Sean's.

"Is that still the only answer you have?" Dad was standing above me. Mom tried to calm him, but he pushed her away. This brought Ryan to his feet. All the boys stood up above me. I felt like an ant, a worm, an insect that was insignificant and could be squashed away at any time. All eyes peered down on me. What would happen next? Ian, who started it all, put his hand on Dad's shoulder gently.

"Forget it, Dad. She won't see him anymore." Ian acted all cool.

What? Who was he to answer for me? I wanted to scream, "You fucking shit stirrer," but of course that would only get me in more trouble.

"I'll make sure of it," Ian assured him.

Dad took a deep gorilla breath as he grabbed some spaghetti out of the pot.

"You better not see him again or else I'll kill you." He threw the spaghetti on my head. All the boys tried to help me up. I couldn't accept their hands. Then Mom tried. Again, I refused. I felt ashamed as I stared at the ugly yellow linoleum floor. I groveled around in Mom's veal cutlet Parmigiana. I was afraid to get up. I didn't want him to hit my face again. Sean might not like me if I looked different. My face didn't hurt but I could feel the spot where Dad's hand had made impact. My ass was bruised for sure and my back felt like it had snapped, but I didn't cry. I could feel the spaghetti stuck to the curls of my hair, but I had no desire to wash them out. I was numb, caught in a stare. I never noticed the legs of the chairs in the kitchen before. I wondered who'd made them. Who'd chosen the color they would be painted and who'd invented the chair?

I could deal with all of this, but I couldn't deal with being without Sean. I must defy my father and be clever enough to outwit my brothers. It was clear, a girl was not allowed to make choices or have feelings. They knew what was best for me and my opinion didn't matter. My destiny seemed to be ruled by the guys in my life. Why were they so overprotective with me? How come they could date and kiss as many girls as they wanted and get praised, but I couldn't even think of a boy without getting the third degree? They were all princes and I felt like a mere servant.

That night Ian and Patrick were down in the basement. I felt okay to go down since they would be keeping me company. I hated Ian for starting trouble at dinner, but I had to make friends to get what I wanted. When I got downstairs it was dimly lit. Ian was painting as Patrick posed for him. Ian was always painting something. It was usually a thing, like a plant, the table, a cup and saucer, but I never saw him paint a person. Neither of them moved. It was as if I were a ghost. They were both so seriously involved in the art. Patrick looked like he was going to a Sunday dinner in Paris. I don't know where he got the ridiculous outfit that he was wearing. Ian probably stole it from a second-hand store or brought Patrick to the Salvation Army and made up some sob story. "Excuse me, this is my brother and our parents abandoned us. Could you spare some decent clothes because he loves to go to the Lord's House and pray?" Ian was the best bullshit artist in town, as well as the best oil painter. He may have even been better than Dad, but I'll never know because Dad won't show his work to anyone. Because Ian was so handsome, he could get anything he wanted from just about anyone. Patrick stood proudly against a wall that was dressed in some lace curtains that Mom had brought from Italy. Ian had placed flowers on a small table and a chair for Patrick to rest one hand on. In his other hand he held a book. I walked around the canvas to peek at Ian's painting. I was astounded. I couldn't believe it. Ian had captured Patrick's essence, his innocence and his spirit. He'd caught the fear that always sat in Patrick's eyes. Ian had a magical gift. I was jealous and proud at the same time, frozen with admiration. Ian stopped, and gazed into the canvas. "Enough for tonight, Patrick."

Patrick shook out his body. God only knows how long he had been standing there like a mannequin in Bloomingdales. It didn't bother him. He liked posing.

Ian grabbed my hand. "Hey, sorry about before, Frankie, I didn't think he'd hit you."

This was my chance to make him feel guilty. "Well, he did, and I'm bruised everywhere. See?" I limped across the floor, milking it just a bit. I showed him my bruises and he winced.

"Frankie, forgive me. It's just that I know what guys like Sean want and I don't want you doing anything you don't want to."

"Like what?" I asked.

"Never mind. Guys only want girls for one thing and you're not just some girl. You're my sister."

What the hell was he rambling about? Spit it out. "Sex? Are you talking about sex?"

His jaw fell to the floor. He wondered how I knew. "Patrick, go upstairs."

"No" I said. "He should know too."

Patrick turned red. "I'm never having sex."

Ian laughed. "Oh yes you will, buddy, and you'll love it."

"Ah ha, he'll love it, so it's great, right?"

"Wrong." Ian changed his tone. "Boys can love it. Girls who do it are sluts, whores."

This concept disturbed me deeply. Didn't a woman have to be there in order for the man to have sex? ‘If she enjoys it, she's a whore?’ It seemed to all be for the guy's benefit. Was I a whore because of the Cuban man? Could guys really care so little about hurting a girl’s feelings, that they used them for pleasure and then dropped them at the nearest dump? Okay, this wasn't working. I’d better go to Plan B.

"Okay, I'll tell you guys the best secret in the whole world if you let me see Sean." They looked at each other.

"If it's not good, no deal." Ian assured me.

"No, it's good. But both of you have to promise or I can't show you."

Patrick was interested. "Show us or tell us?"

"Both." I smiled. "But only if you promise." They both promised but Ian said he was going to have a talk with Sean. I begged him not to, but he wouldn't promise otherwise. I agreed. I figured kissing and hugging and making nice on each other was better than nothing at all. Making nice was what we called gently running your fingers up and down someone's skin. If you had a little length on your nails, it was even more enjoyable. I especially liked when Sean made nice on my face and head. I could look into his sad blue eyes forever.

I told Sean what happened at home. He was very upset. He started punching the wall in his bedroom. I was surprised at how violent he got, but I felt like he must love me, or he wouldn't have such a reaction. "If he ever touches you again, I'll kill him."

This was a phrase I heard quite often. "I don't care about them. I only care about us."

"Me too, Francesca."

I felt safe. Now I could tell him. "I told my brothers about the Molacks. I promised we'd take them down there."

"What are you, crazy?" He exploded. "Now you've ruined it."

I felt like I'd taken away his first shiny bike.

"I had to," I defended. "It's the only way to get them to keep our secret from my father."

He looked at me and realized the importance of our relationship. "Okay then. Let's take them." He smiled.

"One more thing," I told him, "Ian wants to talk to you."

"Fuck," he replied. "He's such a bully."

"Believe me, I know. But it's the only way."

Ian and Sean had their man-to-man talk and then it was off to the Molacks. Ian insisted we bring Seamus and Ryan. He said they would find out anyway. If we all knew, we could cover for each other when any questions came up.

***

The Molacks was a big hit. They took to it like rats to cheddar cheese. Slowly, but surely, Sean became best buddies with all my brothers. This was good and bad. Good because now they all liked him and accepted him. Bad because sometimes they all went off together and left me behind.

The Molacks was our meeting ground. If you were looking for one of us, you just had to check the Molacks. The two-man hole was my favorite. It was more exciting and dangerous than the six-man hole. When you sat in the two-man hole, the train was within six inches of you. If you stuck your hand out, it would be immediately amputated. Sometimes I would look up as the train sped by. Occasionally, I would see people in the train. Imagine if they knew we were down there peeking up into the trains they rode.

The six-man hole was definitely better for kissing. If the train came, you didn't have to run into your hole. You just stood up with plenty of room. Up there the train was about six feet away from you. My brothers discovered quickly that this was the ideal place for making out.

"I love it when they get scared. They'll do anything I want as long as I protect them from the big, bad train," Ian laughed.

I had liked being the only girl, but I actually didn't mind a little girl company. It was refreshing. None of them lasted too long. They either got scared of possibly getting killed by a train, or my brothers moved on to their next conquest.

In a way, the Molacks was like a drug: dangerous and addicting, an escape and a risk to your life every time you went down there.

One Sunday, my brothers and I went down to the Molacks. Sean couldn't make it because he had to take his mother to the doctor. She was always sick with something. He wouldn't tell me what was wrong this time. Ryan had his current girlfriend, Kelly, with him. Ian was entertaining two new girls from Greenpoint, Lucy and Terry, a blond and a brunette. Seamus had Elizabeth. They'd been together for almost a year. Patrick always brought his friend, Michael. The trains came through slower on Sundays. I put some nickels on the track so I could make them flat. Though I could have used the money, something compelled me to crush as many as I could. An Amtrak came through and whizzed by our cubbyholes. I was by myself. Ryan and Kelly were in the next hole down. Ian was over two cubbyholes and Patrick was up in the six-man hole with Michael. After the last car was through, I jumped out to collect my flattened coins. The tunnel was darker than usual; a few bulbs had gone out along the platform. I don't know how often they come down and check on them, but we've never run into any workmen so far. I couldn't find my coins, so I kept walking down the track. Out of nowhere, the tunnel filled with whipping wind. This was unusual for a Sunday. Trains never came back-to-back. I wasn't ready, the headlights from the train beamed through the tunnel. I was stunned, blinded and confused. It was coming at me so fast. My hands searched for my hole, but I felt only cold dusty walls. I had strayed too far from the hole. The clicks from the third rail were contracting fast. I was running as I held my hand out, hoping I would fall into the nearest cubbyhole. I looked up and saw Patrick and Michael screaming down at me. I could only see their mouths move, I couldn't hear anything, except the sound of the conductor's horn. I wanted to move as much as he wanted me to. If only I could find my cubbyhole. That was it. I surrendered. How could this be? I was going to die in a dark train tunnel with rats, dirt and my four brothers. A million thoughts flashed through my head, "Oh my God, Dad's gonna kill me. Oh wait, I guess he can't, I'll be dead already. He'll kill all my brothers. I felt sorry for them knowing the beating they're going to get. Maybe one or two of them will join me soon in heaven or hell, if Dad kills them. Mom, I'll miss you. I hope my emerald necklace doesn't get crushed like my nickels."

I held the necklace tight hoping at least that would be intact when they collected the remains of my body. The light got brighter, the horn got louder, my heart was beating out of my chest. I said good-bye to Sean, to Virginia, Nanny and Grumpy Finnegan, Nanny Juliano. I was sorry I didn't spend more time with them. I said good-bye to Angela and Teresa. The sweat poured down my paralyzed body. I thought of my brothers. How much I loved them even though they could be real shits sometimes, especially Ian. I forgave them all. Ian was the hardest to forgive because he'd always hurt me the most, but I knew my time was running out, so I better forgive him soon. The train was close. I was going to die and there was nothing I could do. The wind blew my hair all around my face and I prepared myself for death. At least I could finally be set free from all the torment the Cuban man caused me. All I could see was light and all I could hear even above the mighty horn was Patrick. "FRANKIE... NO... GOD, NO!"

Out of nowhere a hand grabbed me. I thought it must be God. It was Ian, he pulled me into his cubbyhole. I didn't even have time to sit. I stood crouched down as he held me. The train went by as my body shook vigorously. It was so close that my clothes were moving. When it passed, I noticed the blonde and the brunette; four of us in one hole. No one spoke. After the noise of the train vanished, I heard Patrick sobbing.

"Frankie's dead, Frankie's dead. I saw her get hit, I saw." He was flipping out. Michael tried to calm him down. We climbed up to the six-man hole. Ryan grabbed him.

"Frankie's right here, buddy. Look, look." He looked straight at me but couldn't believe it was me. From his point of view, he'd seen me get hit. He hugged me. Ian hugged me.

"Thanks, Ian. You saved my life."

"Hey, it was nothin'. No more crushin' those stupid nickels."

My brothers all kissed and hugged me and let me know how much they loved me and how sad they would've been if I had died. We left there that day changed, with one more secret we stashed into the Finnegan's lock box.

Chapter 9: THE PIE MAN

Summer always brought everybody in the neighborhood out of their houses. It was too hot and humid to stay inside, and chances were, if you lived in our neighborhood, you couldn't afford an air conditioner. We had a couple of fans, but unless you were standing right in front of one, they weren't doing much. I used to love to sing into the fan and listen to the way it made my lyrics vibrate. Mom said if I didn't get away from the fan, my lips would get cut off. I think the heat made everyone crazy. The younger boys would race their 'Big Wheels' up and down the street. Girls would jump 'Double Dutch' and sing songs that rhymed. Some of them jumped so fast it made me dizzy just watching. I preferred pitching pennies. The rebels would drink cold beer on the corner and smoke cigarettes all day, wolf whistling at all the girls that walked by, even if they were ugly. Drunk as skunks, they would screw anything with a pulse. The older guys would get their big wrenches out and turn on the Johnny Pumps, that's a Queens slang for fire hydrants. All the kids would run in and refresh themselves. Then Mr. Softy would come around pushing the soft serve from the truck with that annoying song shrilling through his crackling speaker. It would repeat over and over. I guess it was worth the payoff. Vanilla or chocolate, or if you wanted, half and half swirled together. My flavor of choice was chocolate. We played handball, softball, stickball and wolf tag. I could run all day, even in the heat, without getting tired. My brothers were fast too; Ian was the fastest. I had no appetite in the heat, but Mom made me eat. She said I couldn't live on Mr. Softy and I had to keep up my strength. Watching me walk up the street, "Francesca, you have no behind. Your pants are going to fall around your ankles." She would holler after me. I was skinny. I ate a lot, but I was always going.

The neighborhood was chock full of characters selling their wares. We had the 'Meat Guy.' I never knew his real name. He would pull up to our street and shout out on a megaphone, "Meat, come and get your fresh meat." They came out in groves, men wearing their wife beaters and trousers, women in halter-tops and hot pants, running to the meat truck. Now I don't know where the hell he got the meat from, but it was the best anyone in Queens ever had and it was only in the summer. Dad would take my brothers and a couple of coolers and stock up the freezer. All summer long the smell of the 'Meat Guy's' stash was grilling on

BBQ's throughout our neighborhood. Then we had the Dr. Brown's Soda Guy delivering the glass bottles in the wooden crates in front of our door. Black Cherry, Vanilla Cream, Root Beer, Cel-Ray and Orange. Oh boy, how I loved seeing those at our door. The milkman left cool glass bottles too, but that wasn't as exciting. Mom had us drinking skim milk to boot. It did taste a whole lot better out of a glass bottle, as opposed to the carton, but I still wasn't a fan. The summer seemed to bring out lots of strange guys selling stuff from the back of their trucks, some of it was good and some not so much, but the one that is most memorable to me and was the highlight of each summer day was 'The Pie Man.'

A little old bald Italian man with eyes that brimmed with kindness, his name was Giuseppe. I knew he wasn't related to me, but I wished he were. He and Mom would speak Italian. They were both Neapolitan. She spent more time than Dad would like, talking to Giuseppe. They would talk about Italy. How the Americans don't know how to make real Italian food in this country. They talked about crime, the pollution, and how they missed Italy, but this was home now. Giuseppe had four daughters who were a lot older than me. I told him maybe I could meet them someday. He said, "Maybe, someday. We'll see." His truck was dark blue and very wide. He would pull up to the curb and open the back. Then he would stand there and ring his bell. It wasn't a loud bell like the one in the schoolyard at St. Mary's.

That bell was so loud and heavy. I dreaded it. Giuseppe's bell had a little tingly inviting sound, like music.

Dad said, "What the hell is that guinea sellin' pies on the street for? If I want a pie I'll go to the bakery, stupid Wop."

This fabulous man would bake these pies at home with love. Just like Mom. As I stepped up on the back of the truck, Giuseppe took my hand to help me. "Whattya got today, Giuseppe?"

"I gotta you favorite flavor." He'd smile.

I didn't even know what my favorite flavor was. They were all so good. As soon as I stepped inside the truck, the smell of the pies punctured my nostrils. My mouth would water as I saw the fruits peeking out of their crust; cherry, blueberry, lemon, banana cream, coconut custard, strawberry, boysenberry, apple. How could I choose? Other customers would come, and I would watch their excitement as they paid their buck fifty. Giuseppe had a small stool in the back of the truck. I would sit on it and wait until everyone was gone. He would tell me stories about his family in Italy with the same longing that Mom had. Sometimes I imagined what my life would be like if he were my dad.

"Give-a this to your mama, it's a gift." Blueberry pie, always. Mom was tickled. It made her feel special. She put it on the bottom shelf of the fridge as if she were hiding it, saving it for a perfect moment. Dad didn't like her having sweets in the house. He didn't want to pay for five sets of cavity-filled teeth. I think he was jealous of her friendship with Giuseppe. After dinner I helped Mom clean up. I was hoping she would offer to share the pie with me. She never mentioned a word. I think she wanted to wait until everyone went to bed. She'd probably make herself some espresso, put on Johnny Carson and swim into that gorgeous blueberry pie that Giuseppe made early that morning. She was going to hoard that whole pie for herself. It made me crazy. I was dying for a piece. After all, he gave it to me - yes it was for her, but I was the liaison, the messenger.

Mom said, "Francesca, I am now going to take my bath." She took a long hot bath every night without fail. No matter how hot it was outside.

"I will put you to bed first."

"No, Ma. Let me watch Johnny Carson tonight, please."

She agreed. When she went upstairs, I couldn't resist. I couldn't chance that maybe, just maybe, she'd offer me a measly piece of pie. I went to the fridge. No one was around. Dad was out drinking in some bar. Ryan and Ian were out. Patrick was asleep and Seamus and Elizabeth were making out in the basement while they listened to the Beach Boys. I found the pie on the bottom, way in the back, behind the lettuce, mayonnaise, tomatoes, and broccoli. I was just going to taste it. I cut a little piece and stuck it in my mouth. Oh my God, I was dying. How could food of any kind be this good? I took a little more. It melted on my tongue; blueberry torpedoes bursting in my mouth with each bite. I graduated to using my hands; the fork took too long and seemed inappropriate for such a succulent dish. I lost myself. It was scrumptious. That Giuseppe put a lot of love into this pie. Wait till Mom tastes this, but all of a sudden it was gone. The whole pie vanished as if it were beyond my control. I quickly stuck the empty tin into the box and put it back into the fridge with everything in front of it. Before she got out of the tub, I jumped into bed and pretended I was sleeping. I prayed she wouldn't find out. A few minutes after she went downstairs, I heard her footsteps coming back upstairs. She whispered to me in a calm voice.

"Francesca, I thought you wanted to see Johnny Carson."

"Nah, Ma, I'm so tired. You watch it, let me know how it was tomorrow."

She clicked on the light and looked at me. For a moment she looked stunned.

"Francesca, did you see my blueberry pie in the fridge?"

"No, Ma. Why would I see it?" I acted dumb.

"Did you have some?" She gave me a sideways glance.

She was giving me an opportunity to confess, beg for mercy, but I lied through my teeth. "No, I didn't have any. I was so full, from dinner."

She walked up to me, "Then what is that all over your face?"

Uh oh. My stomach dropped. "What?" I said weakly.

"Go look at the mirror."

I went to the mirror. When I looked at myself, I barely recognized the blueberry face monster looking back at me. My face was smothered with blueberry pie. My teeth were blue. Mom stood behind me.

"You still gonna tell me you didn't see my pie?"

"No, I saw it. I saw it all. I'm sorry, I got so hungry."

"Francesca, you're like an animal. You did not have to be a gavone." A gavone was Italian slang for a big pig. "If you asked me for a piece, I would've given you one. Now you gonna be sick like a dog."

"No, I won't."

Well, a few minutes later it hit me, and I hit the bowl. Blueberry everywhere. It was blueberry hell. My stomach was churning. My throat was burning. Needless to say, I couldn't eat blueberry pie for a very long time after that.

Giuseppe was one of the many characters that flavored our neighborhood. It was mixed. You had your Irish, your Italians, then your mixed Irish/Italians like us, your Puerto Ricans and your Greeks. Manny, the butcher, was Jewish. He was the only one in town, so he was always busy. He used to get pissed off that the 'Meat Guy' came around in the summer 'cause it took business away from him. But Manny, the butcher, was a staple in the neighborhood and he was legal. Me and my brothers took turns going to the store every morning. When it was your day to go to the store, you were allowed to go in Daddy's pants and get money for the groceries. Then Mom would rattle off what she needed.

First go to Manny's and get the meat for dinner. Then right next door was the Spanish store. They had vegetables, household products and stuff you couldn't get at Manny the Butchers, and last but certainly most important to Dad was Sanders. This is where I bought Dad his cigarettes and newspaper.

There was one Italian guy in Manny's, Vinnie. He loved me. We used to talk about the Mets and the Yankees. I was a Met fan, but he loved the Yankees. If the Mets had won the night before and it was my turn to go to the store, I would go to Sanders, get the paper first so I could tease Vinnie. "Look, the

Mets won, and Yankees lost!" He got a kick out of me. Vinnie said I was a good luck charm for him. He was always gambling.

"Hey Frankie, who do you think will win tonight?"

I'd always go with my gut even if it wasn't my favorite team. I would always be right. One time I walked in and he looked so excited to see me.

"Frankie, c'mere." He pulled out a folded paper. "Look, these are the horses that are racing. I'm gonna place a big bet on whatever you say."

I took the paper and read all the names of the horses to see which one sounded the best. "Scarlet Fever," I blurted out.

He looked at me like I was crazy.

"She's a long shot, Frankie."

Long shot, short shot. Who knew the difference? He asked me to pick, I picked.

"Do you know what Scarlet Fever means?"

"No. I don't care. She's gonna win."

Come Tuesday, it was my turn to go to the store. A whole week had gone by since I picked the horse with the wrong name for Vinnie. I got the paper first cause the Mets won a double header against the Pirates. I wanted to rub it in Vinnie's face. When he saw me, he lit up like a Christmas tree.

"Frankie, Frankie, Frankie baby. Where have you been?" He pulled me to the side, reached in his pocket and handed me a hundred-dollar bill.

"Wow." I didn't know what to say. "What's this for?"

"She won. Scarlet Fever fuckin' won, excuse my language. Could you believe it?"

"Yeah, I could believe it." 'You big asshole,' that part I said to myself. Manny saw me, "Hey, Vinnie struck gold with you, kid." Everyone laughed.

"What do you need today? Chicken, veal, pork? Whatever you want, it's on me."

"Okay, how 'bout a leg of lamb, 12 filet mignons, 7 chicken cutlets, 2 lbs. of chuck chop, eggs, milk, cheese, butter and a loaf of bread." As I rattled off my order, Vinnie wrote it all down. I was just kidding, ya know, just testing him, but he wasn't kidding. I could barely carry all of the groceries home. He didn't charge me a penny. I went home proud.

"Ma, I got a surprise for you." Mom was shocked.

"Francesca, how did you get all these things?"

"Vinnie down at Manny's gave it to me, on the house, ya know."

"No, I don't know. What house?" Mom didn't understand slang too well.

"That means it's free."

"Nothing is free. I don't like this."

Here I was feeling like I did something good and Mom thought it was bad. Next thing I knew Dad came in. He saw all the meat. "What the hell is this, Isabella, we can't afford this."

"It's free, I got it." I smiled proudly thinking Dad would be happy.

"Oh yeah? The only thing you can get for free is a kick in the ass. What did you do, steal it?"

"No, Vinnie gave it to me ‘cause I picked a horse for him and it came in first. Scarlet Fever, she was a long shot, but I liked the name."

Dad lost it. "That fuckin' guinea bastard taking advantage of my daughter."

I was baffled by Dad's reaction. I got a hundred bucks and lots of free food. I didn't tell him about the money yet, I was afraid he'd take it from me. Dad grabbed me by the arm and marched me down to Manny the Butchers. I was sick. I felt like I was going to shit my Sears Roebuck plaid pants out of fear. What the hell was Dad gonna do? I knew Dad had a gun in the house because Patrick and I had found it one day. He hid it in the ceiling down in the basement. I was praying he didn't have it on him as we approached the Butcher shop. I didn't say a word as Dad dragged me. My legs felt lifeless. I said a quick prayer, "Please God, don't let Daddy kill Vinny from Manny the Butcher's place." Dad busted in, "Vinnie, get over here." I saw one of the Jewish guys go to pick up the phone. Dad screamed, "You get off that phone or I'll blow your Jewish head off." Oh man, he brought the gun. The phone went down quickly. Vinnie was white. "Ryan, what's the problem?"

"The problem, Vinnie, is you. Guineas like you see a young smart girl and you use her to get rich." Dad was losing it big time.

"Ryan, it was not like that. Frankie's lucky. I just asked her to pick a horse. You know, for luck."

"And you give her a leg of lamb as a token of appreciation? Cough up some dough you guinea bastard."

I was appalled, embarrassed beyond belief. I wanted to crawl inside the 'Boar's head ham' and hide for the rest of my existence. Vinnie probably thought I went home and complained to Dad. He probably thought I wanted Dad to come here and stick up for me.

"What about the hundred dollars I gave her?"

Dad stopped, looked at me. "He gave you a hundred dollars?" I shook my head yes. He smacked me clear across the mouth, blood shot out of my lip. "She didn't tell me that, but that's not the point. How much did you win?"

"None of your God-damned business."

Dad pulled out his gun. I shut my eyes tight. "Please God, help Vinnie."

Vinnie blurted out "A hundred G's."

My father laughed. "You won a hundred G's and you're givin' her a C-note and some meat? You betta cough-up some more cash buddy." Dad was trying to collect from this poor guy who'd been slinging meat for 20 years. He finally gets a break and Dad wants to rob him. They were all scared of Dad.

"I'll tell you what, you give her another $500 and I'll let you live."

Vinnie pulled out a wad of hundred-dollar bills from his pocket. His hands were trembling as he counted five and handed them over to Dad. Dad grabbed them, "Here, Frankie, put that in your piggy bank." Wow, I'd never seen that much money in my life, never mind holding it. I felt like one of the Rockefellers. Six hundred dollars! Not bad for picking a horse. As soon as we got far enough away from the store, Dad turned around to make sure no one was looking. "Give me that money."

"What?"

"Give me that fuckin' money. Whatya think you're gonna do with it?"

"Save it."

"Bullshit." He reached in my pocket and ripped away my Rockefeller feeling. Just like that, snap, I felt worthless again, like a piece of shit.

"And when we get home, I want that other hundred he gave you."

"But it's mine," I cried.

"Nothing's yours, you understand that? Everything you got is mine, your shoes, your clothes, your smelly underwear - it all belongs to me. You're nothing without me and don't you forget it."

I was punished for the night and Dad said I couldn't go out, but once he went out to the bar Mom told me to come and join her and Patrick on the front stoop. She even let us have some frozen 'Charleston Chews' bars that she had been hiding in the freezer for a special occasion.

Hedges surrounded our stoop; they were high, and they hid our house. I liked this. Mom kept them that way for privacy. It felt safe when we sat out at night. We could hear the noises that were around, but we didn't have to be exposed to them. Mom didn't like to see too many people. She said it overwhelmed her. "They always ask too many questions of me." Mostly about Dad.

Patrick, Mom and I were playing charades, enjoying Mom's homemade lemonade. The four snoop sisters, Betty, Barbara, Connie and Lonny DiGiovanni, were strolling by our stoop.

"Did your husband have another fight?" Betty smiled.

"I heard he hit you." Barbara added.

Connie threw in her two cents. "You really should leave him, there's a program for battered women, ya know."

"I heard he got fired again for being drunk on the job." Lonny finished.

"Well, you heard wrong. You should know better than anyone how much people gossip in the neighborhood."

"Oh, but some gossip is true." Betty let out a phony laugh.

They said things like this whenever they passed our stoop. It hurt me. Even though they were right, Mom should get help, I still felt like kicking them every time they opened their big mouths. Mom would always cover. She protected Dad like one of her children.

"Ryan is working a good job, thank you.” Dad was working construction as a steamfitter, local 22, and running numbers on the side. “My husband is very kind; you just do not know him." She unconsciously put her hand over her black and blue covered arm. I watched their eyes follow her lying hand. I felt sick. I was mad because I was helpless. I couldn't change my family. I was in the middle of it - a joke that the whole neighborhood talked about.

Mom would try to convince us when they left, "Those women have nothing better to do than to try to spread lies. They have no life, so they want to ruin mine." She looked so angry, but it was more toward herself. I could feel her shame running through her hand as she grabbed mine and put her arm around Patrick. We were her support. She tried to convince herself that these women who stopped at our stoop spoke lies. If she believed what they said and admitted the truth to herself, to them, to us, how could she stay with Dad?

"We were having such a good time, why did those horrible ladies have to bother my family?" Mom shook her fist in the air.

She took the dodge ball that was sitting by the stoop, went in front of the bushes and kicked it up the block. She cocked her leg back and followed through with a thunderous connection making the ball fly. She was hoping it would hit one of the women in the ass. I knew that feeling. She packed years of resentment in that kick. The ball took the brunt of her rage. Whether or not it hit them we'll never know. Mom ran back in after she fired it and laughed hysterically. It was such a release of laughter and tears. She was like a little child. She collapsed on the stoop and put her head in Patrick's lap. Her shoulders shrugged up and down. She popped up laughing, but tears streamed down her face. We went along with it.

"Let's play charades," She grabbed her lemonade and swallowed the remaining fluid in her glass. She brushed back her hair, straightened her dress and started to act out Cinderella for us. We went on as usual. I tried to enjoy the last few hours of our summer night together.

Chapter 10: BAYVILLE

For an escape, Mom took us to the beach at Coney Island. It was her guilty pleasure. She would pack salami & provolone sandwiches in aluminum foil, make biscotti's, buy Ruffles potato chips, cream soda, and a big jar of dill pickles. The boys brought a Frisbee and we baked in the summer sun as the Coppertone melted into our skin. After we were all worn out from the heat, Mom would take us over to the Cyclone, Coney Island's famous rollercoaster. She was crazy about it. Everyone was tall enough to go on the Cyclone, except for me. In a way, I was relieved. Mom got in line like a little girl. As the crash of the Cyclone ripped down the track, everyone in line roared with excitement. The passengers screeched with fear and exhilaration. Patrick was terrified, but always went on once, just to prove to my brothers he was a man. Mom giggled like a little girl, as the cars pulled up to board. Freedom flowed through her body. Her arms were waving loose and limp, like overcooked spaghetti. Mom and Ian would run for the first car. Patrick would go with Ryan because he knew that no matter what happened, even if the rollercoaster turned upside down, Ryan would find a way to save him. Seamus told me he couldn't wait until next year when I was tall enough. This way it would be even, and I could sit with him. As they pulled out and made their way up to the top of the Cyclone's biggest drop, my heart raced just watching them. Mom's arms lifted way up in the air as the car plunged a jillion-feet down. When the ride was over, Patrick came out to keep me company. Mom still had a lot left in her. After five times Seamus had enough. Ryan came off next and Mom and Ian would keep going. It was like a contest. Ian would get off after ten times. It wasn't that he was tired. It was just that he knew if he didn't get off, Mom would stay on forever. She needed to go one time longer than him. I don't know if it was sheer competitiveness or just that she needed that one time alone. Just for her. We would all stand together looking up at our mom, the Cyclone queen. None of us spoke as Mom welcomed each hill. Her face was serene. Her hair was blowing wild and free. Her smile met the summer wind, refreshed. The little girl that was locked inside of her finally got a chance to come out and play. It was the happiest we'd ever seen her. She came off looking ten years younger.

"Wasn't that fun?" The boys all laughed and agreed. "Next year, Francesca, you will come. We'll sit in the first car and you will love it." Uh, I wasn't sure about that, but smiled and went along. I had a whole year to muster up the courage.

It was a big treat for us to get out of the neighborhood. Besides Coney Island, the most excitement we had was going to Lenny's Clam Bar on the way to Rockaway beach. We did that every Fourth of July. It was the one holiday Dad got excited about. Even though we sat in traffic for hours, we were all together, squished in the back of Dad's Champagne colored Chevy Impala, and we were thrilled.

Nanny and Grumpy Finnegan had a summerhouse in Bayville. Bayville, to us, was like going to Paris, except we didn't have to get on a plane. Dad wanted to impress his parent's, so he rented a new car for the weekend; a big blue Cadillac. The car rides were always a bitch because I had to be passed from lap to lap. When one brother's knee would get tired, I'd be passed to another. My ass never felt the seats of the Cadillac, just the boney legs of my brothers. When we arrived, Nanny and Grumpy were at the door with open arms. The house was pretty, but sterile. It had a feeling of temporariness in it, like people coming and going, but no one really committed to put any love into it. Grumpy was going for his usual walk so Seamus and I went with him. Of course, he found a bakery to walk to. Grumpy believed that walking a few miles a day would keep him young and strong. I liked being with him, so I would walk wherever he wanted. Grumpy was a proud Irishman and I could see the beauty of

Ireland in his eyes. His stories were sad, but very captivating. His whole family had died in Ireland and he was the only one left, so he decided to make a new life and came to America. It was common for the Irish to have very large families. It was also common for a lot of them to die. Some families had more kids than they wanted. They did this for a couple of reasons. At least if some of the children died, they would still have the remaining healthy ones. The other reason was that they didn't believe in birth control and they used to fuck like crazy when they were drunk. This is what Grumpy told me. I don't know if it was true, but he used to make me laugh. All of his stories were off-handed and sarcastic. I never knew when he was telling the truth or just trying to make me laugh. It didn't matter. It was fun.

When we got back with the bread it was time for dinner. Tomorrow, they would take us to the beach. My freckles had doubled, and my skin was practically blistered from the sun, but I didn't care. I was having fun. Mom would cover me from head to toe with sun lotion and try to get me to sit under the umbrella, but I liked to be out in the ocean. Patrick was great at building sandcastles. Ian would help him with the style of the castle. He always added his artistic touch. Ryan and Seamus would race out to the buoy. It was pretty far out, but I knew I could make it. Ryan couldn't believe I swam out that far. Seamus wasn't surprised. Ryan and Seamus were doing tricks off the side of the buoy. Ryan would do a jump and then Seamus would have to imitate it. He would always go a step further, ya know, add a little something like an extra curl or a twist, something to make Ryan top him. Seamus had no fear in the ocean. He was like a fish. I was just happy to cheer them on and watch. I met a little blonde-haired girl on the buoy. Her brother joined in with Ryan and Seamus. Before we knew it, they were all doing tricks together. The blonde-haired girl and I just watched our brothers proudly. Her brother was good, but mine were better. We were all laughing and having fun. The blonde-haired girl's brother got really confident.

"Hey, I bet you guys can't do this." Ryan and Seamus smiled as they waited for him to show off.

Seamus shouted as the boy dove in, "Don't drown!" We all laughed, even his blonde- haired sister. It was all in good fun. He did a spectacular dive. We all clapped as we waited for him to come up. Seamus was preparing himself to top him. Of course, we had to wait, so the boy could witness Seamus topping his dive. After a while we started getting nervous. Ryan checked one side. Seamus checked the other.

The blonde-haired sister looked like she was about to cry. "Where's Frankie?"

"Hey, that's my name too." I tried to cheer her up. She didn't even hear me.

"Where's Frankie? Frankie? Frankie!" She started to cry. She grabbed Ryan. "Please help Frankie, please." There was no sign of Frankie. We all started to panic. "Help, help us, help!" Ryan and Seamus were waving to the lifeguard. We all lied down on the buoy, one person on each corner, searching the water for any sign of Frankie. It had been a while and I didn't know how he could hold his breath that long.

Ryan screamed to Seamus, "Look down here." Seamus leaned over. Under the buoy there were large barrels. I don't know what they were filled with if anything at all, but they were yellow. I guess they helped the buoy float. The blonde-haired sister was hysterical.

"Where's Frankie? Frankie, please don't be drowned." She started punching Seamus. "It's your fault. You wanted him to drown. Why'd you have to come here today?" Seamus felt so bad. He tried to hold the girl.

"Here, come here. Maybe Frankie swam into the shore. Maybe he's playing a trick on us." We all prayed to God that was true. Ryan and Seamus jumped in and searched the surrounding area. Unfortunately, there was no sign of Frankie. Ryan looked at me and shook his head. I heard him whisper to Seamus while the blonde-haired sister cried.

"If he tried to go under the buoy those barrels probably sucked him right in. There's no way to get out from under them."

The lifeguard reached the buoy, "What's goin' on out here?"

"This boy dived in, but never came up. We can't find him anywhere." Ryan reported with despair.

The lifeguard made a quick and thorough search. "Do you know if he went under the buoy?"

"That's what we think." Seamus shouted to him in the water.

The blonde-haired sister screamed, "No! God please, no, Frankie."

The lifeguard looked at her, "Who is she?"

"His sister." I said. The lifeguard's eyes filled with compassion.

He jumped up to talk to us. "Okay let's all get back to the shore. I'll get a search party out here." I was scared to get back in the water. I knew the blonde-haired girl was too. She was hysterical. Ryan said he would go back and get a small boat, so we didn't have to swim. Seamus and Ryan went back while we waited with the lifeguard. He tried to comfort the blonde-haired girl. She was in total shock. I knew in my heart Frankie was dead. I think we all did, but there was one little bit of hope that maybe he was such a practical joker and he actually swam to shore without us seeing.

We all went back to Nanny and Grumpy's that night. It was quiet at dinner. Ryan, Seamus and I were numb.

Dad was pounding back his green bottles of Heineken beer. "So how was the beach today?"

Ryan quietly, "We saw some kid drown."

"What the hell are you talking about?" Dad spit through his beer suds.

"We were doing tricks off the buoy and we saw this kid, Frankie, go under, but never come back up."

Dad laughed, "You're so full of shit."

Nanny grabbed his arm, "They said they saw it happen."

Dad didn't believe us, "Did you actually see the dead body?"

"No, because they had to find it," Seamus explained.

"Yeah, well I'll believe it when I see it." He popped open another green bottle of beer.

Grumpy watched Dad distastefully, "Aren't you going to eat something?"

"Later Dad, when they find the boy that drowned." He laughed, but no one laughed with him.

The next day, the Bayville headlines read, "16-Year-Old Boy, Frankie Bellifiore, drowned yesterday while his sister watched helplessly." Dad read the front page, "Hey look, you were right. They found the dead Italian kid. Poor bastard. He shouldn't be out there if he couldn't swim."

"He was a great swimmer," I defended him.

"He couldn't have been that great, he's dead. Too bad no one was smart enough to save him." Dad was talking directly to Seamus and Ryan without really talking to them. He had a wonderful way of cutting us down in front of his parents. And they would just turn a blind eye to his drinking, cursing and lack of respect for Mom and us. It was like they owed him something. Nanny said that Frankie's family came here every summer. She would have to go by Mr. and Mrs. Bellifiore's and pay her condolences. This was our first summer and probably our last summer here. Seamus felt guilty, like it was his fault that Frankie drowned. He thought maybe if he weren't there Frankie wouldn't have tried to do all those tricks to impress us. Poor Frankie was just dying to make new friends. Isn't that what we all want? I missed Sean. We had written letters to each other, but it wasn't enough. I needed to see his comforting eyes.

I couldn't go to the wake. The thought of seeing his body in a box gave me the creeps. When everyone came home from the wake, they looked changed. Heaviness surrounded them. Their bodies seemed to weigh two hundred pounds more than their normal weight. Their posture was as if an anchor had been hung from their necks. They walked in slow motion. I felt as if a part of them had died that night.

It was time to go back to Queens. Our week in Bayville was over. Nanny and Grumpy said this was the last year they would rent the house. Maybe Frankie dying was too much for them too. I don't know, but we all said goodbye to Bayville with relief and sadness.

As we got closer to our house in Queens, I was happy. I was actually excited to see our house, go to the park and play, see Sean, kiss Sean. All I wanted to do was kiss his puffy lips and sink into those pretty blue eyes that calmed my being.

Dad parked the Blue Cadillac and we unloaded our bags. I threw all of my stuff in my room and ran to Sean's house. When I arrived at his front stoop, it was sealed off with yellow Police tape. I ducked under and pounded on the door. My heart was now racing with panic. What the hell had happened? A violent rush of sweat began flushing through every pore of my body. I got a sick feeling in my guts. Please God; don't let anything have happened to Sean. I ran to Angela's house, maybe she knew something. When she answered the door and saw my face she started to cry.

"What, Angela? What's going on?"

"Didn't you hear?" She managed to sniffle out.

"Hear what? Please tell me."

"Sean... Sean's..."

I was going out of my mind. I grabbed her, "Spit it the fuck out." I didn't care if I cursed.

"Sean's mother killed him." She sobbed even harder.

I could not digest this information. My body shut down. The sweat now became puddles of water. I couldn't hear any noise, just my heart pounding like a drum on judgement day. I didn't believe her. "No," I said. "You're lying."

She could see my struggle, "I'm sorry Frankie. She freaked out on him with an ice pick. He's dead.",

My whole world stopped. My knees buckled underneath me. I fell to the floor and passed out.

When I woke up, I was in the hospital. My parents were there. Seamus was holding my hand. Patrick was crying in the chair. Ryan and Ian were just staring at the walls.

Seamus shouted, "She's coming to. Hey she's waking up."

A doctor came in. It was Dr. Silver. I cried as soon as I saw his kind eyes holding me. "Hey sport."

"Hi," I greeted him weakly.

"Don't talk right now." He urged me.

He told my parents I was suffering from posttraumatic stress syndrome. Ian came over, dropped his head on my stomach and started weeping. I never saw Ian cry. I stroked his hair, "Is it true?"

"Yes." His delicate blue eyes overflowed with anguish.

Dr. Silver suggested I stay in the hospital for a couple of days so he could keep a close watch on me.

Dad got crazy, "I'll keep a close watch on her. You doctors just want to rape me for some extra money. She's coming home with us. Come on, Frankie. Get out of that ugly gown and let's go home. I'm starvin'."

Mom looked at him in amazement, "If the doctor says she needs to be here, she needs to be here."

"Are you questioning me?" Dad threatened her.

Dr. Silver jumped in, "Excuse me. If this is about the money, I assure you it's not a problem. I will make sure it's taken care of." Why? Why would he do this for me? Why was he always so nice to me? His kindness made me sad and uncomfortable, but I knew it came from a pure place. Dad settled down and seemed relieved that he wouldn't have to pay a cent. Seamus talked to Dr. Silver about my condition and his feelings on the matter. Dr. Silver was very impressed. I asked Mom if she could bring Silvio when she came back. "Of course, Francesca." I was scared to stay in the hospital alone. Dr. Silver stayed with me for hours. We talked about Frankie drowning in Bayville. I told him that I loved Sean, but it didn't matter anymore. He was easy to talk to. He helped me feel better and he got me special food and sweet treats. I could never have this stuff at home. I wanted to tell him about the Cuban man, but I was afraid he wouldn't like me anymore. He might think I was a whore. Telling him could end our friendship. He'd find out I wasn't as innocent as he thought I was. The Cuban man should remain a secret.

My brothers and Mom came to visit. All the guys looked handsome in their suit and ties that were obviously crafted by Patrick, The Tie Master. They informed me that Sean's wake was tomorrow and asked if I wanted to go. I didn't think so, but I agreed to sleep on it. I couldn't think about Sean. It made me want to die. I still didn't believe it had really happened. I told Dr. Silver about my fears and how I didn't want to see Sean dead, in a box. I wanted to remember him the way he was. He felt I shouldn't push myself to go if I didn't feel strong enough.

Somehow, I felt like if I didn't go, he would always be alive for me. The reality never had to sink in for me, as long as I didn't have to actually see his lifeless body. These goodbyes people say to the dead, I didn't understand. This was not the person they knew. I refused to believe Sean was dead. My fear of death grew stronger and stronger. I was consumed by it. Dr. Silver assured me this was normal. The hole in my heart got wider and deeper. I told Dr. Silver I didn't want to go back home, how much I hated it there. He said I could stay in the hospital until the funeral was over. That way, I didn't have to be around while everyone else was getting ready to bury Sean and all of his dreams of walking on the moon.

Everyone came to the hospital to visit after the funeral. They all looked handsome, but so dreadful. All dressed up, with bloodshot, puffy eyes.

Mom had on a black dress. "Oh Francesca, the ceremony was beautiful." She touched my hand gently.

"I wouldn't use that word to describe it, Mom." Ian got pissed off.

"It was lovely. The flowers, all the people." Mom kept it up.

"You should've seen it. The whole neighborhood showed up." Ryan was happy about the turnout for Sean.

"Yeah, even Manny, Vinnie, Lou, everyone from the Butcher shop." Patrick added.

I started to feel guilty for not going. I even got a little jealous. Seamus came and sat by me. "It was good you weren't there Frankie. It was hard."

Ian looked like he was going to lose it, "Hey Ryan, you wanna go get a beer?"

"Sure. Not where Dad is. Let's go down to Astoria."

"Yeah, Seamus you wanna come?" Ian was in a rush to get out of there.

"No. I'm gonna pass." Seamus looked at me and knew I needed him.

"Patrick?" Ian didn’t want him to feel left out.

Mom jumped up, "Leave him alone. Must you try to corrupt him, too? If you want to go get stupid, do it by yourselves."

Ryan felt bad, "Ma, we just need a little release."

"Yeah, ya know with the whole funeral thing," Ian chimed in.

"Right, a release. I have your father who needs a little release every night. I am sorry poor Sean died."

"He didn't just die he was murdered by his mother! It's different." Ian reminded her.

"Yes, he was murdered by a crazy woman, but that does not mean you go get drunk and stupid and maybe murder yourself. That is what the drink does to you. It murders your soul. It drowns your heart." Mom started to cry. Seamus and Patrick held her.

Ryan and Ian looked at each other, "Let's go." They left.

"Can I spend the night with you in the hospital?" Patrick asked.

"That would be great. I'll ask Dr. Silver."

"Me, too." Seamus didn't want to be left out, besides the fact that he loved being around hospitals.

Mom laughed, "Maybe I'll stay, too."

Dr. Silver said it was okay, as long as we kept it a secret. After all, I had a big room all to myself with two beds. Patrick brought back Monopoly. Seamus snuck in a couple of pizza pies and ice-cold Coca-Cola. We didn't mention Sean again that night.

"We're here Frankie, and nothing's gonna happen to you." Seamus looked in my eyes and assured me.

"Yeah, you'll never get rid of us." Patrick laughed and jumped up on the right side of the bed. Seamus squeezed in on the other side.

Mom smiled. "Oh boy, they love their little sister."

My heart ached, but I was safe in my brothers' arms, but never again would I be in Sean’s.

Chapter 11: THE THIRD DEATH

Everything felt different to me. Food wasn't as comforting. Smells weren't as sweet. I was almost 12 and my life, as short as it was, felt like it was slipping away. I didn't understand what life was about, and why there was so much suffering? I decided by the look of things, I probably wasn't going to live too long. Mom kept talking about death always coming in threes. I was sure it was me who God had his eye on. I knew that I couldn't die without telling someone about the Cuban man. I felt like the rape had just happened all over again. I realized I was lucky to escape the death that the Cuban man had intended for me. Now, I felt like God was coming to get me for real. If I died with this secret, my life would be worthless. No one would ever know the damage that bastard brought to me. How many secrets did Sean die with? ...One too many. His silence was what ultimately killed him. I couldn't sleep because I was afraid of dying. I couldn't eat because I was afraid of telling the truth. Every time I opened my mouth, I was afraid the truth would spill out. I was working double time just to keep up with my secrets and lies. Who could I tell? How could I tell? I didn't know which was worse, actually dying, or the death I would feel after I exposed my secret. That, to me, felt worse than death. I locked myself in the bathroom and ran the water. The vomit was stuck in my throat. My body did not want to hold the sickness of ‘rape’ inside anymore. I was regurgitating all the pain and all the fear. It was causing me to feel terribly ill. I couldn't risk anyone hearing me. I looked at myself in the mirror. My eyes turned away from my own stare. I couldn't look at me. That sick feeling came over me as the sweat covered my skin like an oil slick in the rain. I could no longer hold my sickness in. I ran to the toilet and buried my head in the bowl. Everything that was in me came out. Trembling with fear, a knock on the door startled me.

"I'm on the toilet." I could barely speak,

"Frankie, are you alright?" It was Seamus. Should I tell him? Is he the one person I can trust with my secret before God zaps me from the earth? I rinsed my face and opened the door.

"Come in quick." I pulled him in.

"Frankie you're as white as a ghost. Are you sick?"

I nodded, "Yes."

He felt my head and neck and saw my body trembling. "Frankie, you're all clammy. Did you throw up?"

I nodded, "Yes," again.

He sat me on the toilet seat and looked straight in my eyes. It was so hard for me to keep direct eye contact with his soft green gaze. As a matter of fact, it was hard for me to keep eye contact with anyone. "Frankie, talk to me. What's wrong?" I looked away with fear and shame. I could feel the words wanting to come out, but how they would get out I hadn't a clue. They were clumped together, stuck, like a stone stuck in my belly. "Frankie, you know you can tell me anything."

I looked at him, "You promise?"

"Yes."

"Promise you won't tell?"

"I promise." He held his hand on his heart to convince me.

I made up my mind; he was the one I would tell before I died. "Okay." It was slow and hard, but he held me and rubbed my arm.

"Come on Frankie, tell me."

I don't know how it came out because it was like a dream. I could hear the words of my story floating in the air between us, but I didn't feel like I was saying them. I watched his face go white. His eyes filled with rage and confusion. He let me finish because he wanted to hear everything. My breath became shallow and I could feel myself come back into my body.

"Frankie, how come you never told this to anyone before?"

"I couldn't. I didn't know how. He said he would kill me. I was scared, Seamus. I still am."

He held me tight and kissed my forehead. "Don't you worry about anything. You don't have to be scared anymore. We gotta tell Dad." He ran out of the bathroom. I chased him.

"Wait! What do you mean? You promised you wouldn't tell anyone." I screamed after him.

"We have to Frankie. The man's a criminal. We gotta call the police."

Now I was freaking out, "No. The police, no, please Seamus, don't tell, please." I ran back into the bathroom and threw up some more. I had nothing left in me, but I thought with any luck my heart would come out and I could just die right then and there. No such luck. The moment I dreaded for so long was here. I was still alive, and my nightmare was a reality. Everyone knew. My shame encapsulated me. I felt myself shrinking into a small, black ball. My body abandoned me. I was naked before my family. I was sitting with all of them, but feeling separate, alone.

The interrogation started. Dad asked me a million questions. Ian was cursing. Ryan's fists were clenched. Patrick looked more petrified than I did, and Seamus was talking about taking me to a doctor for a test. He wanted to make sure there was no damage.

Dad said, "No way in the world is anybody gonna know about this!" Another Finnegan secret for the lock box.

"What happened to Frankie is nobody's business but ours. You all understand? No one needs to know this shit." My Mother kept cooking, with the music really loud as she cried in her food. I heard her praying to God.

Ian agreed with Dad, "I think we should kill him."

"Well, that's what we're gonna do," Dad said.

I couldn't believe my ears. It was scary, but it gave me a thrill to think that they were gonna kill the Cuban man. I would love to watch him die.

"Frankie, you're gonna point him out, make sure we got the right guy, and then I'm gonna blow his mother fucking Cuban head off." Mom's prayers got louder. Patrick started crying.

Seamus argued, "You can't do that. We have to report this. It's a crime. We can get him locked up."

"Oh yeah right. Do you want Frankie to go to court and testify?" Ryan asked.

Seamus looked at me, "Do you think you could, Frankie?"

"I don't know," I honestly answered.

"No," Ian yelled. "She's not going to court."

"Yeah, this is not gonna be a big show for the neighborhood. We'll finish him off and no one will ever know." Dad was frantic.

"Are all of you crazy, out of your minds?" Mom screamed at the top of her lungs. "You cannot just go and shoot someone. You will go to the jail for the rest of your lives.

"Oh yeah, then what do you think we should do?" Dad got in her face.

"I don't know. Maybe we should talk about it."

"Talk my ass. Talking is not gonna kill this son-of-a-bitch. What do you want me to do, talk him to death? He raped your daughter for Christ sakes!"

Mom turned the radio louder and covered her ears. Dad and my brothers continued to get riled up. Starting like a snowflake, snowfall then snowball, avalanche and we were buried. An unstoppable force began to build and there was no turning back.

"Yeah, the cocksucker deserves to die," Ryan agreed.

"Fuck 'em. That bastard. I want to pull that fuckin' trigger." Ian was ready.

"The last face I want him to see is mine. That'll teach 'em to be a fucking scumbag of the earth. How could he do this to my daughter? My fucking little girl. No, no, nobody gets to touch my little girl. How did this happen? What the fuck." Dad was drooling like an animal and tears were burning his eyes.

I'd never heard so many curse words in such a short amount of time, except for the day Patrick and I decided to say our first curse words. They were all pumped up. The adrenaline was flowing. Someone was going to die. Maybe this was the third death that Mom kept talking about. Maybe God would spare me and take the Cuban man.

Dad loaded his gun. He went to the fridge and pulled out a six-pack of Heineken. He took the bottle opener and popped the lids off all six of them. He grabbed one and chugged it back. Ian and Ryan did the same. Seamus still tried to convince them to report it. Dad finished his first beer. "If you mention one more word about calling the police, I'm gonna shoot your ass off. Then you can report that. You understand me?" Seamus backed off.

Dad grabbed another beer. Ian and Ryan caught up. The three of them drank their beer like it was a contest. Mom and Patrick cried. I was in shock. "You ready, Frankie?" Dad grabbed my arm.

"Let's go!" Ian smiled.

"Cuban fucker is gonna wish he never left Cuba!" Ryan yelled with excitement. I felt like they were getting ready for a sporting event, but the loser of this game would die. Dad took his arm and in one fell swoop, knocked all six empty beer bottles into the wall. The glass shattered everywhere. His arm was gushing with blood, but he didn't pay any mind to it. He roared like a wild lion. "Let's do this!"

"Please don't do this, Ryan." Mom grabbed him.

He pulled her face into his and for a moment everything stopped. "That bastard raped our little girl." Tears rolled out of Dad's eyes. Mom was frozen. He wiped his face quickly as if the tears were dust. Then he pulled me out. "Don't forget, Frankie, you point him out. That's all you gotta do." That's all I had to do. One motion of my little finger would seal this man's fate. Whether he was dead or alive, he would be a ghost in my life forever.

* * *

We went to the Spanish part of the neighborhood and sat in Dad's red Chevy Impala standing out like an eye soar, in front of the Cuban man's apartment building. The plan was, I would point, Ian and Ryan would grab him and take him into the hallway and Dad would blow his brains out. They went over it a bunch of times. The radio was on and the neighborhood was going on as usual. Nobody knew or cared what me and my crazy family were about to do. My Dad left the radio on for me and the DJ was in a great mood. He was talking about love and happiness. He sent out a love dedication on the radio.

"This one goes out to Johnny from Susie." Our Day Will Come, by Ruby and the Romantics, came flowing through the speakers, so hopeful and romantic.

"Our day will come, and we'll have everything

We'll share the joy falling in love can bring

No one can tell us that we're too young to know,

Oh, I love you so

and you love me."

I thought of Sean, of love. Our day would never come, but the Cuban man's day had come and here I was waiting, sweating, wishing I could be Susie on the radio sending a song to Johnny.

We waited for three hours. No one left the building. Ryan's friend, Pepe, came out of the apartment building.

Ryan called him over, "Hey, you see the Cuban man who lives in there?'

"You mean Oscar?" Pepe asked curiously.

"Yeah, whatever, I don't know his name."

"I saw him about an hour ago. He had a suitcase. Said he had to go to Cuba on business."

"Son-of-a-bitch!" Dad punched the dashboard.

"Is there a back exit?" Ian inquired.

"No, but the roof goes all the way to the corner. Why are you guys looking for him?"

"Because I want to kill him."

Pepe laughed, "Yeah, that's what he said. He saw you out the window."

We drove back home. No one spoke.

When we walked in, Mom had dinner waiting. She cleaned Dad's arm up. He stared into space.

"What happened, Ryan?"

"The fucker went to Cuba. He knew I would kill him. He'll be back. Someday, somewhere, I'll see him. He can't hide forever."

We ate in silence. It was the most uncomfortable meal I can ever remember. The silence was killing me. I couldn't eat. No one looked at me. I felt like a leper. Looking at me would mean they'd have to look at the truth. No one was ready for that. I was screaming inside, "Somebody help me. Look at me. I'm not a freak." I'd revealed my truth, it took all I had, and no one could handle it. There was something about keeping it a secret that was safe, because at least if nobody helped me, I couldn't blame them since they didn't know. But for them to still not be able to help, after I'd told them, hurt me so deeply I could barely breathe. Sure, they were willing to kill him, but now that they couldn't, it was put in a neat little box and sealed with an unbreakable bow.

Mom ate more than I'd ever seen before. Her face came out of her plate only for a refill.

When I went to school the next day, I noticed that Yolanda's, seat was empty. The teacher never mentioned why, and none of the kids ever asked where she was. It was as if she'd never existed at all. In a way I was relieved, because whenever I looked at her, I would see her fat father's face slobbering on me. But I couldn't help feeling sad for her and wondered what would become of her.

For the next few weeks Mom was cooking and cleaning constantly. She didn't have time to brush my hair or tell me a story at night. I never saw her sleep. Four a.m. the food was cooking, the Victrola was blaring with old Italian songs by Enrico Caruso that made me want to cry and Dad was still not home. Every night was the same thing. I didn't know what to do with myself. No one was there for me to talk to. I was trying to figure it all out for myself. I wished Sean were alive. I went down to the Molacks. It was weird to be there alone. I walked to the six-man hole. I wanted to take a nap. When I crawled inside, I was shocked to find Patrick, "Hey, Frankie."

"Patrick, what the hell are you doin' here?"

"Hey, Frank." Another voice whispered in the dark. It was his best friend, Michael.

"Is there anybody else here?"

"No, just us."

"What are you doin'?"

"Just hangin' out." Patrick said softly. "What are you doin'?"

"I needed to get away."

"Yeah." Patrick put his arm around me on one side and Michael on the other. I felt like Michael knew what had happened. Patrick told him everything. I didn't care. This was the first time I'd been physically touched since everything came out. It felt good. A few trains went by. We watched. We talked about the rats and the lives they must have. We all picked our fantasy places where we'd go if we could take a train to anywhere. Mine was Italy. Michael's was Paris. After Patrick heard about Michael's, he said he wanted to go with Michael to Paris. They took care of me that day, the way I wished Mom and Dad would have, but couldn't.

I went home and Mom was still cooking. I stood in front of her like a piece of furniture. She walked around me.

"Francesca, you are in the way. I'm cooking. Can't you see?"

"Yes, I can see. You've been cooking for weeks. Can't you see me?" I yelled. For two weeks straight I wore the same clothes without ever washing them. She didn't even notice.

"Please don't do this. I am busy." She turned away.

I was filthy from the Molacks and I didn't try to clean up. I wanted Mom and Dad to see my dirtiness. "Go wash up. You are so dirty."

"No."

"Don't talk back, Francesca."

"No." I said, "I won't wash up." I pulled on her blue knit dress, "Look at me. See how dirty I am. I won't wash up. You can't make me." I pulled her dress over and over. I rubbed my dirty hands all over her clean dress, her clean body. "Stop it!" She yelled.

"No." I jumped in front of her.

"Stop it!" She would not look at me.

"No!"

"God, please stop it!" She smacked me hard in my dirty face. It felt so good, alive. It was attention. "Why do you make me hit you?" She cried. "I've never struck you before. I didn't mean to." She knelt beside me and wept all over my dusty t-shirt. "Francesca, my baby, I'm so sorry." I held her. She couldn't comfort me about the Cuban man, so I had to make her hurt me so I could comfort her instead. It was a trick to make myself feel consoled. She was holding me, crying for me, to me, with me.

She said, "I can't help you, Francesca, I don't know how."

"I know, Ma. It's okay." I held her. “Just hold me, mommy, and I’ll be okay.” She rocked me back and forth as her tears spilled on my hair.

The Pie man rang the bell. “Let's go get a pie, Francesca. Blueberry.”

"No, anything but blueberry." I tried to make her laugh. If she couldn’t comfort me, I would comfort her, and in return, somehow it satisfied the need for her touch.

* * *

Dad came stumbling in at four o'clock in the morning. The only reason I knew was because Mom started yelling at him, "It's four o'clock in the morning, Ryan. I am tired and sick of you coming home this way." Dad just grunted. I watched from my bed but pretended to be sleeping. Mom picked up his shirt that he'd thrown on the floor. She pulled it to her face and smelled it. Her face became contorted with rage. "Are you wearing a new perfume, Ryan?" He grunted again. Mom inspected the shirt. "When did you start to wear lipstick, you pig." She threw the shirt at him. He hardly responded. Mom was not going to let this go. "Ryan, get up right now. Get out of my house, you cheat." She began punching him. "I knew you were up to no good, you son-of-a-bitch. I won't have this. Anything else, but not this." I guess the beatings and the drinking, screaming, coming home all hours of the night was okay, but cheating was Mom's breaking point. "How long have you been unfaithful? Who is she? Get up you fool. You're leaving. I don't want to be near you. I don't want you near my children. You disgust me." Dad started to come around. I was so excited, but scared. Mom was a woman in power. If she kicked Dad out, we could be happy. It could be a new kingdom, without the mean old drunken king. I wanted to run in and help Mom beat him up, jump on his head, grab a pillow and suffocate him. This was the moment I had been waiting for. Mom was finally sticking up for herself. She was relentless. The punches kept flying. "Get out or I'll call the police." Mom went for the phone next to the bed. Dad quickly grabbed her arm and bent it behind her back.

"Listen you bitch! If you don't shut the fuck up, I'm gonna break your arm."

"Go ahead." Mom did not flinch or show any signs of fear. She spit in his face, "You pig. I hate you!" Dad smacked her hard in the face. She smacked him back. "How long have you been betraying me?"

"For years." He shoved it in her face.

"Your hands will never touch my skin again." She went to strike him again. He forced her down on the bed and began ripping her clothes off.

"You think you can satisfy me. Show me. Make me happy." He kept trying to kiss her. She fought him, but he kept forcing himself on her. I couldn't stand it anymore. I ran in the room and grabbed the lamp. As I lifted it over my head, I prayed for the courage to follow through and save Mom. I whacked Dad in the head. He fell on the floor. Mom grabbed me. Ryan and Ian ran downstairs.

Ryan had the baseball bat in his hand. "What's goin' on?"

"Dad tried to kill Mom so I saved her." Ryan lifted me up and Ian went to Mom. Mom looked at us in shock. She looked at Dad on the floor. Blood dripped out of his head. Seamus ran in.

"Is he dead?" Mom asked with no emotion.

Seamus checked him out, "No, he's just drunk and unconscious."

Something clicked inside of Mom. She had a faraway look in her eyes. I didn't know how to reach her.

"Where's Patrick? I have to say goodbye." She looked like a zombie.

"Goodbye! Where are you going?" I tried to snap her out of it.

"Aunt Carmella's."

"Can I come?" I didn’t want to be there when Dad came to.

"No, not this time, Francesca. I must go alone."

"Ma, how are you gonna get there?" Ian couldn't believe what she was saying. She reached in Dad's pants and took his keys.

"You don't even have a license, Ma." Ryan pointed out.

"You could get arrested." Seamus tried to stop her.

"I don't care. I need to be alone. If he doesn't leave, I must. I cannot sleep in this house tonight. Do you understand?"

We all did, but we couldn't believe she was actually going to leave.

"Ma, I'll drive you there." Ryan insisted.

"No, no, no, no." She started to cry, "Can't you see I must go before he wakes up. It's over. It's ended! No more! This will never happen again. I am finished here." She was screaming, panting, pulling her hair. She ran to Patrick's room and kissed him. He didn't wake up. She kissed us all. "I'll call you when I get there. Francesca, take care of your brothers and you boys take care of your sister."

I couldn't breathe. "No Mom, you can't leave me here." I begged her. She hugged me tight and looked into my face, "Please don't leave me, Mom."

"I will never leave you, Francesca, it is not possible." She kissed me. I could smell her hair. A smell I wanted to hold for the rest of my life. "I must hurry." She kissed the statue of Mary by the door on the way out. She made the sign of the cross and left. Dad started moving, but Seamus pushed him down. "Just relax. You got a bad bump."

Dad looked at him confused, "Isabella?" He started yelling, "Where is she?"

"She went to Aunt Carmella's." Ryan was seething.

"Why?" He tried to get up.

"Because you're a fucking asshole," Ian informed him.

He rubbed his head, "Shit! How did this happen?" No one said a word. If he knew I did it he might kill me, but he never knew what hit him. He was in one of his blackouts.

We called Aunt Carmella's to let her know Mom was on the way and could she please call us the second she arrived. She assured us she would.

It was seven o'clock in the morning and still no word. We all sat around the kitchen table listening to Mom's station, WNEW, drinking pot after pot of espresso. I was sick in my guts, like someone had taken a serrated knife and carved out the lining of my stomach. Dad held an ice pack on his head but refused to go get stitches. I was happy I cut him and even happier that he would have a scar from me. I had so many from him.

It was nine a.m. when the phone rang. We all jumped and then froze. Everyone wanted to answer the phone, and no one wanted to answer the phone. Dad's eyes were brimming with fear and anxiety. It was as if all of our tongues were cut out. All the dialogue we spoke that morning, of September twenty-eighth, nineteen seventy-four, was with our eyes. The conversation was very clear, very deep and completely silent. The phone rang even louder! We all stared at Dad. He stood up and walked to the phone, as if he were walking to the electric chair, slow and dreadful. I watched his hand touch the pink telephone that was attached to the kitchen wall, just left of the stove. I'd never noticed how pink and ugly that phone was before. His hand was trembling, "Hello." He slurred out, "This is." He answered the voice on the other end. His face filled with horror as he listened. He started shaking his head and crying, "No, no, no." He repeated it over and over. He let out a guttural moan as he slid down the kitchen wall. The phone was gripped into his heart. The voice on the other end was still talking, "Mr. Finnegan, Mr. Finnegan, are you there, hello?" Ryan picked up the phone and took the information.

Mom had been killed in a car crash on the way to New Jersey. This was it. The third death she'd kept talking about was her own. It was almost as if she'd known in Bayville when Frankie drowned. Was that why she'd seemed so scared that night? I think she could feel her own death coming. The kitchen that once held Mom's cooking aromas, was now filled with a family hungry to taste Mom's love once more. We were all disconnected from each other, but strangely, connected more deeply than ever. Dad was banging his head against the wall like a ram, Ryan holding Dad as they screamed. Ian tried to punch Dad, "You killed her, you fuckin' worthless piece of shit." Seamus was holding Ian back. Patrick was holding his ears as he rocked back and forth singing as loud as he could.

'Row row row your boat gently

down the stream, merrily merrily

merrily, life is but a dream.'

Over and over. Faster and faster. Louder and louder. I was devastated beyond belief. I watched my crazy family falling apart before me. I couldn't go on without Mom. I felt as if I were going to die too. Ian finally got a hold of Dad and they started fist fighting. Ryan and Seamus just let them go. My body started shaking. Then came the sweats. My legs went out from under me and I hit the ground. This became my new way of dealing with overwhelming situations, faint and pray that I never wake up to face the truth.

When I did wake up, Nanny and Grumpy were at my side. But I didn't want to see them. I blamed them for having my father and then raising him to be such a violent animal. What did they do to him, to Uncle Jim? What secrets were in their lock box?

Nanny Juliano was sobbing and holding Patrick. She begged my father to let her have us kids, so we didn't have to be poisoned any longer with his wrath. He wouldn't have any of it and told her he was going to change.

"A leopard doesn't change their spots, and you will always be a leopard. It's a shame my daughter couldn't see you for who you truly are." All this from the sweet old Italian women who just lost her daughter. Nanny Juliano went to the police station hysterical after she heard the news about Mom and told them that Dad killed her and should be arrested immediately. Unfortunately, she didn't have a case because Mom was alone at the time of her death. No other cars were even involved. The police officer told her it was just her daughter and a tree. Nanny cried out, "He was the God damn tree. Please arrest him and save those kids." As much as some of those policemen down at the precinct knew she was right, their hands were tied. However, they did promise her they would keep an eye on him and check in on us kids every once in a while. It wasn't enough, but she thanked them anyway. She told me in private that she had a good mind to kill him with her own two hands. Dad wasn't about to defend himself. How could he? He didn't have a leg to stand on.

The house was turned upside down. Dad and Ian sat next to each other. Dad's face was cut in a few places. Ian's lip was busted open.

Seamus was crying, gripping my hand, "Frankie?"

I was hoping I was dreaming, "Seamus, please tell me Mom's okay, please Seamus. I had a bad dream." Seamus couldn't talk. I had my answer. "Nanny, I'm afraid."

She held me, "I know. Everything's gonna be okay."

"No, it's not. We're all gonna die. I hate life. It's not fair. I want Mom. I want Mom."

Dad came over to try to hold me, "I want Mom, too, Frankie."

"I hate you. I hate you." I started punching him uncontrollably. I didn't care if he hit me. I wanted him to. I wished he would kill me too. He didn't. He let me hit him. He cried more. "You killed her! You just couldn't stop! You couldn't stop! You killed my mother and she knew you would, she told me. I don't know why she loved you. I don't know how anyone can love you. You're a monster and I hate you!

He took it like a man, not one rebuttal, but then the tears began to fall. "I loved your Mother. I really loved your Mother." He tried to hold me, but I pushed him away with all of my might. I didn't want to hear it. It didn't matter any more, no words or apologies would bring back my mother.

"Why don't you die? I want you to die." I ran upstairs and Ryan followed me. Ryan seemed to be the only one who had any sanity in him. He held us all together. He sat on my bed, where Mom had sat so many times before. "It was an accident, Frankie."

"She wanted to die, Ryan. She hated it here."

"Mom loved you. She loved all of us, even Dad."

"You can say whatever you want. I know Mom wanted to die and she did it on purpose." He didn't argue with me, he couldn't. He knew I was right. Mom gave up. Her spirit had died long before this day. She was walking around in a body made up of flesh, bones and blood, but lacking a spirit. She was defeated, beaten down, broken. I got good and angry with her. What about me? The boys? Weren't we enough to lift your spirit and make you want to live?

* * *

Funeral arrangements were made. The wake was in two days. Nanny Juliano stayed over. She cooked like Mom and tried to bring us all comfort. Dad seemed grateful that she was there and for the first time, he was very nice to her. Aunt Carmella and Uncle Louie came over and made sure we all were taken care of. Friends and relatives were coming by and calling constantly, and the officers from the 12th precinct did check in on us and had a talk with Dad. The phone rang at all hours of the night. Dad hadn't been to bed since it happened. He slept on the couch or the chair or anywhere but their bed. I stared at that empty bed, picturing Mom's delicate face sleeping peacefully.

My brothers were trying to take care of Patrick, and me and at the same time take care of themselves. Ian was drinking a lot, but Dad didn't touch a drop.

I was faced with the dilemma again. The wake. How could I go? How could I stand to see Mom in that box? If I didn't go, it wouldn't be real. I'd never see her dead. But this was different. I didn't know if I would be able to. I got on the bus and went to the hospital. I needed to see Dr. Silver. He could help me. When I saw him, he got so excited to see me until he saw my face. I jumped into his arms and wouldn't let go. Tears poured out as I drenched his white doctor's coat. "Please don't let me go." I begged. "I really need you right now." I began crying like I've never cried before. He took me into an empty room and rocked me like a newborn. Oh, how I wished he was my daddy. I decided in this moment, I pretended, that he was, and if felt so good. I told him about Mom. The news shocked him. He stopped rocking me and gently sat down on the green couch with me in his lap. Looking in my eyes, he touched my face gently. "I am so very sorry Francesca, more than words could ever say." I felt safe. His words were so sincere. "What can I do for you? I'll do anything to help you." His eyes brimmed with sorrow. I said if he came to the wake, it would help me a lot because I didn't want to go. He agreed to come, and said it was very important that I go. He said I needed to see Mom again, to touch her and say goodbye.

"She would want that," he said.

"I know, but if you're there, I'll feel stronger. This way if I faint there will be a doctor in the house."

It was my first wake, my mother's. My body did not belong to me. It belonged to the air. I remember her telling me once, "Francesca, God does not give you more than you can handle." Well, this was way more than I could handle. How do I tell Mom, she was wrong? I can't tell here anything anymore, never. As I entered the funeral parlor, I took in the scent of this place of waking. Eerie, lonely, vacant air filled the room. Flowers surrounded the coffin. I stood in the back for the longest time. I couldn't bring myself to get close. From far away I imagined it was someone else. The whole thing still seemed fake to me. Dad sat up front. He brought her Victrola and played Puccini all night. All the women were in black dresses, the men in black suits. The Italian women wore black kerchiefs on their heads. My brothers did the best they could to keep it together, but it was impossible. Patrick did everyone's ties, of course. He said they had to be extra special tonight. They had to look their best for their mother 'cause she always did her best for them.

I hated that everyone wore black. As if we weren't all depressed enough. I refused. Instead, I wore white from head to toe. I made Ian help me bleach all my whites the night before the wake. I also made Patrick make a tie for me. I wore white slacks, a white button-down shirt and a bright red tie. My outfit was not appropriate, but no matter what Dad or Nanny or Grumpy or anyone said I didn't care. Mom's death was not appropriate either, but it had happened, and no one could change it, and no one could make me change. The people showed up to pay their respects. I was watching their faces as they talked to me, but I couldn't hear a word anyone said. I was in a plastic bubble and no one could puncture this wall I surrounded myself with. The owner of the funeral home was a good friend of Mom's, another Italian, Peter Vannelli. He saw these things all the time, so he'd gotten kind of immune to it, but Mom's wake was different. I was exploring the funeral home, while everyone else viewed my dead Mother's body, and I found Mr. Vannelli upstairs in a private office. He sat in a big brown leather chair surrounded by dark wooden walls, and family pictures, drinking a bottle of red wine while he cried softly. He invited me in. "Sit down, sweet Francesca." How lovely to hear the voice of an Italian, say my name. The only other one who said my name that way was Mom and the Pie man. I sat down.

"I like your suit." He smiled as a tear dripped onto his lip.

"Thank you, I do too."

"She was too beautiful, your Mamma. Sometimes they don't last in this place." The tears he shed were the most delicate I had ever seen. He didn't pant or sniffle. He didn't scream or whine. He didn't feel ashamed. He didn't wipe his face. At one point a tear, which he shed for Mom, fell right into his wine. He sipped it and swallowed his pain for Mom in that teardrop. "Would you like some wine?"

"I don't know if I'm allowed."

"It's okay, your Mamma won't mind. Just a bit. It's a special bottle from Italy." How could I resist? "I've been saving this bottle for years, but now I must drink it. I wanted to drink it with your Mamma, but she never came, too busy." I could sense Mr. Vannelli's feelings for Mom. I think he was secretly in love with her. He grabbed a wine glass from the shelf behind him. It was big, like a bowl. As he poured, I closed my eyes. It sounded like bath water running. Mom flashed before me, singing in Italian as she made my bath. "Come and let me clean those ears of yours Francesca. How does such a pretty girl manage to get so dirty all the time?" I could hear her laughing as if she were in the room with me. I opened my eyes, but there was no sign of Mom, just Mr. Vannelli raising his glass. He handed me my first glass of wine and I raised it to meet his.

"A toast," the tears streaming down his cheeks and curving underneath his chin. "To the prettiest swan in all of the lakes, the green-eyed girl from my homeland, to a woman who gave so much for so little, Isabella."

I toasted with him in agreement. I pictured Mom in my big glass as I gulped the Italian wine. He called it, Brunello di Montalcino. To me it tasted like blood, but after a few sips I liked it more. I started to feel warm and fuzzy all over. It hit me like truth serum, and I couldn't help myself.

"Dad killed Mom, ya know."

Surprised at my honesty, he held my eyes in his. I could see he believed me and that hurt him even more, but this was not the time or the place. Mr. Vannelli took my hand, "You must go see your Mamma."

We went downstairs. I felt a little better after the wine. I stood in the back for a few more minutes. Dr. Silver came in and picked me up, "Francesca, I'm here." I couldn't hold it in anymore. I started to cry. He held me. When I opened my eyes, Virginia was standing there with Uncle Joe. Uncle Jim and Uncle Bobby were there too. Uncle Jim went to Dad and hugged him. They cried in each other's arms. Virginia went up to the coffin and knelt down to say a prayer. She got there before me. I felt like a coward. I told Dr. Silver I hadn't seen her yet.

"Would you like me to take you?

"No, I must do this alone. She's waiting for me." I was shaking, but as soon as I heard the next Puccini song, Che -Gelida -Manina (Your Tiny Hand is Frozen), I knew it was my cue. I walked up to the coffin. Each step sent my heart into a quiver. Little by little I could see her. Her strong nose stood proudly on her face. I could see where it was broken. I followed the lining of her face around her sculpted cheeks. Her lips were full and closed. Her glorious green eyes were sealed shut forever. Her hands were wrapped, tattooed with the rosary beads, the same as when she was alive. Her dress was olive green, her favorite color. I knelt in front of her, grabbed her tiny frozen hand while Puccini played. It was so cold. It was the first time I had ever touched death. The last time I would ever touch my mother.

There were scars on her head from the accident. I thought about the police saying that there were no other cars involved, just Mom smashing into a tree. Did she think about me before she did it? I wished she had taken me with her. I touched her hair. It was still so silky and luxurious. I wanted to crawl inside Mom's hair, be buried with her, protect her from the worms that would come to feed on her flesh, save her from the process which rapes her human form. I was helpless. I didn't know what I was doing, but I crawled on top of Mom and laid on her in the coffin. I buried my head in her chest and wept. Ryan and Seamus came and lifted me off of her. I asked Mr. Vannelli if I could sleep at the funeral home. I couldn't leave Mom alone. He agreed. Patrick said he had to stay too because Mom wouldn't want me to be alone. Seamus said he had to stay to make sure no one got sick. Ian and Ryan explained that they had to watch us and protect the Funeral home in case any crazies tried to break in and steal Mom's body. Mr. Vannelli let us all stay. Dad went home with Nanny and Grumpy, they said he was having a nervous breakdown. Good, I thought, he deserves it and a whole lot more. I had no sympathy for him. My brothers couldn't stand to see him cry, but they weren't ready to forgive him. Patrick kept pulling all the God crap on us, saying how we needed to forgive and turn the other cheek. I said bullshit, I'm tired and I have no cheeks left to turn. I vowed that I would never forgive him. Uncle Jim offered to stay over and take care of Dad, which was a shock to all of us. Why was he getting pity from his enemy for causing such a tragedy?

The night went on forever. We all told stories about Mom and tried to keep from crying. I fell asleep next to the coffin and had a dream. Mom was running in a green field covered with all sorts of colorful flowers. She had on the same dress she was wearing in the coffin. She was waving to me, "Francesca, Francesca, I am so happy. It is magical here." She looked so young. "I love you." She started laughing. Then an Italian man was running behind her. He caught her and lifted her up. Then he kissed her, "This is Pasquale, Francesca, remember?" It was the little boy from Italy, Pasquale D'Amato; her first kiss, her first love. He waved to me, "Don't worry, I will take very good care of your Mamma." They both spoke to me in Italian. The field turned into an ocean and they were sitting on a rock. The orange sunset fell behind them. I woke up peaceful. Something told me Mom was safe.

Mr. Vannelli brought all of us coffees from Duncan Donuts and Entennman's pound cake for breakfast. I wished Mom could taste it. She loved pound cake. He opened the doors. Dad was waiting. One by one, the place filled up. It was the last viewing before the funeral. Nanny Juliano prayed in Italian while she cursed Dad out and held Aunt Carmella's hand. I understood every word. They cried together as they kissed Mom goodbye. The Pie man came. He brought a pie for each of us, and a blueberry for Mom. Manny the butcher and the whole butcher shop came. Sammy from Sanders was there. Dr. Silver and all our relatives. Everyone from church, all our friends from school. All Dad's drunken friends from the bar showed up to pay their respects.

The priest came to say a last prayer. Before they closed the coffin, I shouted, "Wait." I pulled out my favorite picture of Mom and me. We were rolling dough together. We were covered in flour, laughing and playing. I looked at the picture once more. I kissed Mom's smiling face in the picture and placed it on her heart. Then I put my monkey, Silvio, by her head to protect her. They closed the lid; the sound pounded in my ears as they sealed Mom in.

The procession was long. We rode in a limousine. All the cars from the neighborhood followed us to Calvary cemetery, the same place Sean was buried.

Everyone surrounded the coffin as the priest gave his speech. A hole had already been dug, just waiting to swallow my mother up. There were flowers everywhere, all from Dad. What a waste, I thought. I never saw him give Mom so much as a daisy when she was alive, except for that one time in the hospital on my seventh birthday because he almost killed her. This time he couldn't bring her back, no matter how many flowers he bought and no matter how sorry he was. It didn't matter. You cannot undo what was done. The smell of the carnations was making me sick. They smelled like death. After the speech, one by one, everyone threw a single rose on the coffin. I did not want to throw a rose. Instead, I made Ian take me to get a sunflower, a girasole. It seemed more hopeful with its happy yellow face. It was big and proud; it said so much. I put my sunflower, my girasole, on last. I didn't want any roses to cover the brilliant yellow petals. Goodbye my sunflower, my sunshine, my morning smile, my moonlit goodnights, goodbye fair woman who gave me life, goodbye red-haired angel who taught me to live and dream and cry, goodbye sweet woman who smelled like Italy. You gave me a language, a freedom, a wisdom that no one will ever be able to take from me. You gave me courage and saved me from storms. Goodbye to the mother of my brothers, the only woman I had. I will miss your eyes, so kind and sad. I will miss your hair; the ropes I climbed through to escape my pain. I will miss your laugh; it tickled my belly with delight. I will miss your scent, the calm it brought me. I will miss your cooking; it always comforted me and nurtured my soul. I will miss the mother who will never see me grow into a woman. I hope I am as beautiful as you. Goodbye, Mommy. I am dying inside to let you go. You said I have angels all around me. I hope you are one of them because I feel so alone, so lost without you. I don't know if I can make it in this world without you. You were the one person who understood me and now you're gone. Please help me, Mom. Help me to get through the pain of losing you.

Chapter 12: ANTOINETTE

A slow and dreadful year had passed since Mom's death. I was about to be a teenager and Mom was going to miss it. Therefore, it really didn't matter to me. It seemed like ten years and then again, it seemed like yesterday. There were days I felt as though I couldn't possibly go on. I would stare out the window and talk to the sky. I knew Mom was somewhere in those clouds. One day I had such a strong thought about her, and a bluebird flew right up to me. I know it sounds crazy, but I still think Mom was inside of that bluebird. It looked at me so clearly. It was so striking and alive. I talked to it and it kept me company for a short time and then it flew away. Just like Mom. From that day on bluebirds always seemed to follow me.

Dad tried to keep us all together, but we were all quietly falling apart. He started cooking and playing Mom's Victrola. He became obsessed with Puccini's life and wanted to learn Italian. He hung pictures of Mom everywhere and started to go to church. It was as if he were trying to be as much like Mom as possible, just so he could be close to her. He talked about her to all of his friends as if she were still alive. He spoke as if they had some kind of fairy tale romance. He was trying to be the man she wanted him to be when she was alive. Why did he have to wait so long? It was too little, too late.

We didn't talk a lot. It was like we all went our separate ways. Mom was the key that made all of us a family and without her it just didn't work. Ian practically lived in the basement. He became obsessed with painting. Instead of having Patrick pose for him, he had moved on to real nude women. The women he chose all had similar looks. They all looked like Mom, but even if they didn't, when the painting was done, he'd change their look to appear more like Mom. We weren't allowed down there while he was painting. He was like a mad scientist. Sometimes I would go down after I saw the girl, the model for that day, leave. Ian would be napping with paint speckled on him, an empty bottle of wine, and classical music softly playing in the background. The basement looked like a Parisian studio.

Ryan was boxing competitively. He was up at five in the morning, running and jumping rope. He was the toughest guy in the neighborhood. Dad was proud of him, but that's not why he was doing it. As a matter of fact, when Ryan hit that heavy bag, he imagined it was Dad. He looked like an angry animal claiming revenge. I wouldn't want to be his opponent. He became the heavy weight champion in Queens and was considering boxing professionally.

Seamus was in the library for hours. He knew every disease, every cure and who found it. He was a walking medical journal. He often visited Dr. Silver and they would talk about medicine. Dr. Silver liked having him around. He said he never saw someone so committed to the field of medicine. He told Seamus it was men like him who found cures for fatal diseases.

Patrick and Michael started taking dance classes together. They took tap, ballet and jazz. Patrick said you needed all of them to build discipline, correct form and endurance. Mom would be happy, Patrick said, because she loved dancing more than anyone. Dad and my other brothers weren't too thrilled about Patrick's newfound love of dance, but he didn't care. We all seemed to find some coping mechanism to escape the grief.

I passed the time by writing letters that I would never mail; letters to Mom, letters to the Cuban man and letters to Sean. I wrote poems and songs. They made me feel good. I said things to the paper in front of me that I could never say out loud.

My innermost secrets were shared with white lined paper. I began to discover how I felt. Knowing that no one would ever read these letters gave me a freedom to speak my truth and open the Finnegan lock box. It was better than confession. The sins these pages held could make the devil smile. Sometimes I was so proud of myself, I wanted to read them to Mom.

Dad stopped drinking, stopped yelling and actually behaved like a real human being. But I didn't know how to be with him. I wanted to smack him into reality, "You phony fuck. It's too late. You blew it." The nicer he was, the more I resented him. He said he was worried that I was spending too much time alone. He arranged for me to go see Virginia. I was bursting with happiness on the inside, but on the outside, I acted cool and aloof, "Sure, that'll be good." He drove me out to spend the weekend. Virginia was happy to see me. She was like the sister I always dreamed of having. We went for walks in the woods, stayed up late talking about boys, and she taught me how to put make-up on. I felt funny all made up, like I wasn't myself. I couldn't talk about Mom or Sean. She understood but told me if I wanted to, I could.

One Saturday night we went to a dance at her high school in East Hampton. There were lots of cute boys and the place was rocking. We were flirting and dancing and having a ball. The DJ cut the music and huge light show exploded on stage as a band began to wail, they were called Satan's Revenge. The lead singer began a rendition of 'Rebel Rebel' by David Bowie, with wild abandon and we ran over to watch. My heart stopped. I was in a trance, captivated. The dark-haired boy pounding on the blue

'Tama' drum set, made me get that funny feeling inside. "Oh my God, who's that?" I said dreamily to Virginia.

"Who?" She looked around.

"That drummer." I tried to play it cool and whispered in her ear.

"That's Ronnie Walker." She clearly disapproved.

My heart starting pumping love juice into my veins. Virginia must've seen the goofy look on my face. He looked right at me, winked, and went into a drum solo. He shook his head to the beat, scrunched his face, bit his lip and had a cute little style all his own.

Virginia tried to snap me out of it, "Uh, Frankie, hello! The guy is the biggest flirt in the world." I shut her out. I didn't want to hear it. After his set he came over to say hello.

"Hey, Virginia, who's the cutie with you?"

Before she could open her mouth, I put out my hand, "I'm Francesca, Virginia's cousin."

He kissed my hand just like Rhett Butler in 'Gone With The Wind.'

"Francesca. What a beautiful name." He was so charming.

"Thank you."

"Maybe we can all do something after the dance?"

Virginia tried to say no, but I jumped in, "Sure, we'd love to."

"Great, I'll see you after." He walked away with his faded blue jeans, white converse sneakers and a T-shirt cut around his shoulders. His arms had nice taught muscles that popped when he played the drums. Virginia said he was seventeen. I didn't care. I was a tall thirteen-year-old, taller than Virginia, so I could lie about my age. As I watched him walk, I imagined us walking together somewhere. I wanted to run my hands through his curly long brown hair.

"Frankie, Ronnie is bad news."

"He seemed nice to me."

"He's got a girlfriend and she's a lot older than you."

My feelings were hurt. I just wanted to have fun. I knew she was just looking out for me, but I didn't want to hear it.

The band started playing again. I watched as Ronnie pounded the drums. All of a sudden, I started to sweat. My head got light. I thought I was having a fainting spell, but this was something else. I had incredible pain in my stomach. "Virginia, I gotta find a bathroom now!" She saw my face and realized I was sick. I didn't want to leave Ronnie and his blue 'Tama' drums, but if I didn't, I was going to make a mess all over myself. All the bathrooms were locked. They were afraid kids were going to drink alcohol and hang out in them. We had no choice; we had to run home. It was about a mile. I don't know how I even ran because I felt like I was going to shit my pants. Maybe the movement was what stopped me. As soon as we arrived at Virginia's house, I thought I was close to death. As Virginia banged on the door and searched for her keys, I exploded all over myself, like Linda Blair in the Exorcist. I was so embarrassed. Here I was trying to act all cool and sophisticated with my older cousin and I shit in my pants. Virginia's face morphed, as if she were saying, 'Are you fucking kidding me or what? I can't believe you shit in your pants. Do you do this all the time?' But she didn't say anything. Now the smell started to waft up to the both of our noses. I wanted to cry, but this would just make me look like a bigger baby. I tried to break the ice. I stated the obvious,

"Virginia, I shit my pants."

"Frankie, I have eyes and a nose, I know." She cringed.

By this time there was evidence all around. "Do you think I can use the bathroom?"

"It's a little late, don't ya think?"

"Well, I'm still feeling a little sick."

Finally, she found her key. "Hold on."

She opened the door. She ran and got newspaper and made a trail all the way from the front door, up the stairs, down the hallway, to the bathroom. I felt like a puppy that needed to be housed trained. I ran to the bathroom and took off my pants. I asked Virginia if she could bring me a trash bag and if I could borrow some underwear and pants. "Okay, but we're not going anywhere else tonight. You have to stay close by the toilet." I agreed. I threw out my jeans and my underwear, too ashamed to wash them. Then I started throwing up. I was shaking like a leaf. Virginia and my uncle thought we should call Dad. I begged them not to. I'd never felt so sick in my life. Virginia was great. She told me not to worry. She promised she would never tell anyone, especially Ronnie.

"I guess I wasn't meant to meet him after all."

"Guess not." She seemed relieved.

I finally fell asleep. Early that morning I awoke with severe pains in my stomach. The sweats started to come back. I ran to the bathroom. When I wiped I couldn't believe it. Blood! Oh my God, I'm bleeding to death. No wonder I'm sick. "Aahhhh, Virginia." I started crying, "Hurry up, come quick!"

She ran in carrying a box of Kotex.

"I'm dying. Look, I'm bleeding internally." I couldn't believe she wasn't taking this seriously. I looked at this big thing she gave me to put on. "What is this, a diaper?" I thought she was teasing me.

"It's a pad. You got your period."

"My what?"

"Your period. I had a feeling."

What did that mean? Was I a part of a sentence? "Period?"

"Yeah, ya know, the monthly, your friend, ya know."

"No, I don't know. What the hell are you talking about?" How could this be a friend? That's what she called it. Something that comes once a month, makes me feel like I'm dying, sweating, shaking, shitting my pants and making me vomit is no friend of mine.

"Didn't your mom ever tell you about your period?"

"No, she never did." So, Virginia gave me two little pills called Midol for the cramps and told me about the birds and the bees and my period. "Oh joy, you're finally a woman," she said. I got really mad when I found out boys didn't get a period, only girls. Virginia said it was because we have the babies. "So, let me get this straight, we have to go through this nightmare every month, the period thing. We get pregnant, go through the pain of that and then we get to have the pleasure of being in severe pain while we give birth?"

"Yep, that's about right." She confirmed.

"Why do the women have to go through all the pain? What do the men have to do?"

"Well, I'm still trying to figure that out. I know they work, make money, and a lot of them cheat on their wives."

I told her about Dad and the night Mom died. She said she wasn't surprised. Her Dad cheated too. She said it was something in a man's blood, that men are made differently than women. She said it's easier if we just accept it instead of fighting it. That's what her mom had told her.

"No way, not me. I won't be like them." I got righteous.

Virginia told me she had a boyfriend right now, Tommy, and he'd already cheated on her. I didn't understand why she was still with him. She said he was cute and a good kisser. "Who gives a shit," I blurted out.

"Frankie?"

"I don't care. You're too good for that. So am I, so is Mom... was Mom."

"You're right Frankie. It's just hard. You'll see when you get older."

What a weekend! It was too much for me to digest. When I got home, everyone was waiting. We were going to have a Sunday dinner, just like the old days with Mom. I wasn't looking forward to seeing Dad or his cooking, but I was excited to see my brothers. I decided not to tell them about my period. After all, it was a girl thing. They couldn't possibly understand.

When I walked in the door Dad was waiting. Virginia and Uncle Joe walked me in. They couldn't stay for dinner. Dad smiled, "Frankie, I got a surprise, close your eyes." The only surprise that would even be acceptable was Mom. But I knew that was never gonna happen. I just stared at him defiantly. "I'm not in the mood for a surprise." He turned to the boys for help.

"C'mon, Frankie, just close your eyes." Seamus yelled and my other brothers chimed in.

"Okay, for you I'll do it, but not for you." I stared at Dad, intentionally piercing him and then I shut my eyes. Something jumped on me and started licking my face.

I opened my eyes. It was an adorable little puppy. "Oh my God. Is this ours?"

"It's yours. I got it for you," Dad said proudly.

"Wow!" Suddenly I didn't want it, even though I secretly did. "You never got me a gift before. Why now?

I didn't want him to think that this new puppy was going to fix everything. I was still mad as hell at him. The puppy was a girl. She had Mom's coloring, reddish, blonde and some white. My brothers said to lighten up and that Dad was trying. I should give him a break. But all I could say was, 'why?' And they didn't have an answer. They were trying to forgive him, and if that wasn't possible, they were learning how to bare living with him.

"I'll keep the dog, since she's already here and all." I said unenthusiastically but delighted inside.

"Good, good, that's great!" Dad smiled. "She's a collie mutt, I thought you'd like her." And with that he walked away deflated. I didn't even look at him.

"You have to name her," Seamus laughed. I thought really hard but couldn't come up with anything. It had to be perfect. I said I'd sleep on it. Dinner was terrible, as usual. All the boys said I looked different, glowing. It must've been all that womanhood going on in me.

Ian was going down to the basement to do some work.

"Can I come down for a minute?" I asked Ian.

"Sure, I'll be right there. I have to clean some brushes."

I walked down slowly. I wanted him to paint me, but I didn't know how to ask. I figured maybe if he saw me around enough, he'd see something in me that he'd find interesting enough to paint. When I reached the bottom of the stairs, I was startled by what was before me. It took my breath away. Mom was standing at the stove cooking. She was wearing her green flowy dresses, stirring her famous Italian sauce. It was her kitchen. The way she kept it. It was Mom. Every little red curl on her head was just the way she wore it...her brown leather shoes, her delicate hands and tiny wrists. The legs were just perfect. It was so real. I could hear Puccini crying through the painting. My heart ached for a moment. I thought it was Mom for real. "Francesca, go wash your hands for dinner," I imagined her saying.

Ian came down, "Hey Frankie, how do you like it?"

"It's amazing, unbelievable. Where did you find a picture like this?"

"What do you mean?"

"I mean to paint it from. Where's the photo?" I asked.

"There's no photo. It's from my memory."

I never realized he took so much notice. I thought I was the only one who paid so much attention to every little detail. Ian missed Mom as much as I did. I finally saw how much.

Maybe all the others did, too. I guess I was so consumed by my pain that I didn't see anyone else's. I looked around the basement. There were at least thirty-five paintings. I was proud, impressed, and intimidated by his incredible talent. He told me he was going to have a show someday. He was going to exhibit all his art and try to make some money. "Please don't sell this one." I stood before Mom at the stove.

"I love it. When I have enough money, I'll buy it from you, no matter what it costs."

"I don't know if I'll ever sell that one, Frankie. That one is my favorite." He looked at it longingly.

"Has anyone else seen this?"

"Yeah, they all did. They all wanted it." He laughed.

"Ian, do you think I look like Mom?"

He didn't even look at me, "Yes, you look just like Mom."

I figured that maybe if I hung around a bit, he'd ask to paint me. I found myself stretching on the couch, trying to be sexy like one of his models. "Well," he said, "your minute is up. I'm expecting someone."

"Can I stay and watch, please!"

"No."

"I promise I'll be quiet."

"No."

"Please Ian, I don't care if they're naked."

He loved painting nude women. They were all over the basement keeping him company. Ian and his many women. All the girls loved Ian and wanted to marry him. He couldn't do that. He said to be with one woman for the rest of his life scared him. He liked variety.

"Frankie, c'mon you can't stay." He grabbed my arm.

"Is it a repeat or a first timer?" I played with him.

He laughed at me, "It's a new girl."

"Do I know her?" I was curious.

"No, I met her at the museum last week. She's from Italy."

That was it. He should've never told me. I was compelled to stay. I didn't even know Ian went to the museum. That was all the way in Manhattan.

"Hey, can you take me to the museum one day?"

"Yeah, if you leave right now."

There was a knock on the basement door. This was the entrance all of his models came through. Good thing, because if they'd had to come in through the upstairs my other brothers might've attacked them. They were all drop dead gorgeous!

"Go, Frankie. Now!" He opened the door. There she was, the Italian goddess he would paint.

"Ciao, bella." She smiled at me.

I started speaking in Italian to her. She was very impressed. Her name was Antoinette Romano. She was from Roma and was an art student herself. She was doing an exchange student program. She talked about the Sistine Chapel in Rome, the Statue of David in Florence and all the great Italian art. Ian watched us speaking. He barely understood a word. I know he was wishing he'd learned Italian when Mom was alive. Ian became impatient.

"Okay girls, can we talk later? Frankie, can you leave us alone?"

Antoinette laughed, "Francesca, we'll talk more later on."

"Great. I'll make espresso when you're finished."

"Go, Frankie. Go now, go!" They both laughed.

I went upstairs. I couldn't wait to see the finished piece. I wondered what Ian would do with her. Did they just paint, or did they do other things? My mind was going crazy. I was so intrigued.

I fell asleep on the couch, with my new puppy on my head. All night I tried to think of a name for her. I was sad that it was a girl because I knew she'd have to go through the pain of getting a period, having puppies and being a woman. I kept on picturing Antoinette walking through the basement door, "Ciao, bella."

I decided to name her Bella. Bella and I put on a pot of espresso. I ran downstairs to see if Antoinette was still there. She was sleeping like an angel next to Ian. A large canvas sat in the middle of the room. It was not finished. This made me happy. Antoinette would have to come back. It was exquisite. She was lying on a white sheet with flowers all around her. Her body was long and lean, glistening like a bronze goddess. She reminded me of Mom.

The next morning, I made breakfast for everyone. I fried toast in the pan and broke eggs in the hole I carved in the middle, just like Mom used to do. Parmesan and basil on top. Italian sausage and Roma tomato sautéed with garlic, rosemary and cold pressed virgin olive oil. I was showing off. Everyone went nuts.

"Bellissimo, Francesca, this tastes like home," Antoinette said in Italian.

Dad was happy, but I think he felt bad because no one had commented on his cooking for over a year now. He's lucky any of us even gave him the time of day after what he did to Mom. Patrick wanted seconds, which never happened. Ryan couldn't get enough. His workouts were intense at the gym. Seamus needed more for studying power. I felt needed, loved. I knew I had it in me. I mean, I'd watched Mom every day. The way she pinched an herb here and an herb there. The funny thing was, it made me so happy to cook. I could see why Mom loved it so much. Maybe Ian felt like that when he painted. I was creating delicious food. I was an artist in the kitchen. I could hear Mom telling me to add more basil, more oil, not too much salt. It was actually easy for me. I told Antoinette to come for dinner. I was going to make something special.

I saw Dad's face drop, "I was going to make a meatloaf."

All the boys chimed in, "Oh Dad, it's okay, you've been cooking every night."

"Yeah, Dad, take a break."

"You deserve a night off."

"Let Frankie do it. You need a rest."

He knew they were giving him the brush off, but he also knew he had about as much talent in the kitchen as a termite.

Dad gave me money to go shopping for dinner. He said he'd take me, but I didn't want his company. I still hated him. Antoinette helped me clean up after breakfast. When we were alone, we spoke in Italian and listened to Mom's radio station,

WNEW FM. This was the happiest I had been in a long time. She told me stories about her family. I made her laugh. I felt like I'd known her forever. While we were washing dishes, a bluebird flew up, as if to say good morning.

We went to the stores to get our goods for the feast I was going to prepare. It was hard to find a lot of the fresh herbs and produce. I guess I'd taken Mom's garden for granted. Antoinette took me on the train. She said not to worry. She was old enough to be responsible for me. Ian was waiting at home for her. He wanted to finish the painting, but she could see this was important to me. That's what I loved. She was sensitive to my feelings.

She took me to Little Italy in Manhattan. Oh my God, I was in heaven. My head was spinning with delight. One store after another... Fresh basil, tomatoes, Italian parsley, salami, provolone, prosciutto, freshly baked Italian bread, still warm. I could smell Mom in every store. This was a whole new world. I spent all my money. Antoinette spent some of hers. We stocked up. All of the storeowners spoke Italian. We didn't speak English the whole afternoon. I pretended I was in Italy. Antoinette said she had to take me to her favorite dessert shop, Ferrara's. We had cappuccinos, which I'd never had before, only espresso. She said I could pick whatever I wanted. I had to get some pignoli cookies, a cannoli, and we split a napoleon and some biscottis, and then finished with a lobster claw. Wow! I never wanted to leave, but we had to make dinner. I made sure on the way home I took notice of the stop and which trains we took. I was definitely coming back to Little Italy again.

When we got home, Ian was pissed off. He said I was ruining his creative process. I had to admit I was being selfish with Antoinette, but I needed some girl bonding. Ian didn't understand that. She kissed him softly and stroked his hair, "Oh, now don't be so upset. I am here now." Ian blushed and melted all at once. She was forgiven. They went downstairs and I unloaded the groceries. As I looked at all the beautiful herbs, I became melancholy. I went into Mom's garden. I hadn't been out there since before she died. I was amazed to see how much life was still there. It definitely needed some attention, but there was so much vitality still in the soil. She left so much of herself behind. She was still living inside me, inside Ian, inside all of us, especially Dad. She was so alive in him that he actually changed. Did she sacrifice herself to save us kids?

* * *

Dinner was amazing. I started out with eggplant rolatini. First you fry your eggplant lightly in olive oil, and then you roll goat cheese, pine nuts and a thin slice of prosciutto inside. Next, a caprese salad, which is di mozzarella bufala, tomato and basil, with a gorgeous Dijon mustard dressing on top, then homemade ravioli, sweet and hot sausages, braseole and meatballs. For dessert, I made Tiramisu and Zabaglione over fresh berries. Dad put Puccini on the Victrola. It felt like we had all been transported to a cafe in Venice, Italy. There was very little conversation, just a lot of mmm's, ahh's, and grunts of approval. It made me happy. I felt proud, appreciated. Antoinette was beside herself. "Francesca, I must bring you back to Italy. They will go crazy for you there."

Everyone helped clean up so that we could get the Tiramisu and espresso going. Antoinette was joking that she'd gotten too fat from my cooking to pose for Ian tonight. Dad was fascinated by her. They spoke for hours. He must've felt what we all felt. Dad told her about Mom, his passion and regret. Antoinette tried to comfort him, "I can see you loved her very much. That is rare."

"I did, but I don't think she ever knew." Dad looked for sympathy.

"I'm sure she did." Antoinette had empathy.

"I'm not." Dad sipped his espresso.

Antoinette pulled out a bottle of port she'd bought. It was a present for the family. She poured a little glass for everyone. Dad had not drank since Mom died. He refused at first. I tasted it. It was so sweet, like cough syrup, nothing like the Brunello di Montalcino that Mr. Vannelli gave me. Ian didn't want

Antoinette to be insulted, so he insisted everyone drink as a sign of respect and for good luck. As Dad picked up the glass, my stomach dropped. I could see the longing in his eyes. It was like inertia; he'd just been reunited with an old lover. I felt like somebody had just punched my chest. I wanted to scream, "No Dad, please don't drink it!" But no words came out.

Ian smiled, "Wow, this is good." He refilled everyone's glass.

Seamus and Patrick felt the same way as me, "No thanks I have to study." Seamus put his hand up for Ian to stop.

"Yeah, I have to get up early for my dance class." Patrick also refused.

"So, you're a dancer, Patrick?" Antoinette asked curiously.

"Yes." She and Ian drank some more.

"Let's taste the Tiramisu." I changed the subject. I don't know why, but I didn't want Patrick to be on the spot, as he sat with his tight grey one-piece leotard and sparkling black Capezio's on his feet. It seemed to be the only thing he wore anymore. He had one-piece leotards in every color of the rainbow and a tights collection that could dress all the dancers on Broadway. Capezio, in Manhattan, was his favorite store.

"This is good shit." Dad downed another glass.

"Hey, Dad, slow down." Ryan patted him on the shoulder.

I was getting angry. Seamus pulled out the Tiramisu. Everyone had some except Dad. All of a sudden, food was uninteresting to him. Antoinette loved it. She fed some to Ian.

"Frankie, you really did a great job." Ryan smiled at me.

"I think Antoinette did a great job." Dad downed another glass.

"Too much port can make you sick, Mr. Finnegan. It is very sweet." She was amazed at how he was drinking it.

"Oh, don't tell me how to drink. All of the Guinea's have their fancy shmancy ways of sipping wine. It's bullshit. It all goes down the same way." Dad was turning from Dr. Jekyll to Mr. Hyde right before our eyes.

Patrick stood up, "Thanks for cooking, Frankie. If you'll excuse me, Antoinette it was so nice to have met you."

Dad busted out laughing, "What the fuck kind of talk is that? What have you been going to fucking charm school?" He laughed even harder and then tried to get close to Antoinette. "Patrick takes dance classes, ya know, he's charming." Dad was in stitches by this time. Ian chuckled a little, but no one else found it funny.

"He is charming, very charming. You are a perfect gentleman, Patrick." Antoinette got up.

"Thank you, good night."

"Good night." Antoinette kissed him on both cheeks. He blushed, and then sashayed away like Fred Astaire.

"What a dear boy. He is very special."

Dad laughed in her face, "Oh, please." By now Dad had graduated to drinking straight from the bottle. "He's a sissy." Dad started imitating Patrick, "If you'll excuse me, I'm a little asshole trying to be a ballet dancer. Do you like my tutu?" Dad was cracking up.

Ryan was embarrassed, "Dad, enough! C'mon."

"Enough, my ass." He was getting wound up.

Now Ian was even getting embarrassed, "Dad, have some coffee."

"Are you kiddin', and ruin how good I'm feeling. I haven't felt this good in a long time. I'm gonna enjoy it."

"Mr. Finnegan, you are drunk." Antoinette said softly.

"Oohh, what the fuck are you, the drunk police."

I felt myself getting smaller and smaller.

"I have to go study. Good night, everyone." Seamus excused himself. He kissed me and praised the dinner.

"Go ahead, Seamus. He's gonna be a great doctor ya know," Dad boasted.

"So, you are proud of him, huh?" Antoinette was trying to calm him down, but I also sensed she was giving him a dig about how ashamed he felt about Patrick.

"I gotta go too. I'm meeting some guys at the gym." Ryan left very upset.

Antoinette started cleaning the table. "Come, Francesca, we'll clean up."

Dad grabbed her arm almost in a violent way, "Don't you dare clean up. You're a guest. Frankie, clean up this mess."

Ian stepped in between them, "C'mon, Antoinette we have some work to do." They left the kitchen. She turned back and held my eyes for a moment. She sensed my fear. I recognized hers.

"Go, all of you! Go! A bunch of party poopers. I don't need any of you." Dad was shouting to the air. He sipped some port and turned back to me. I tried to talk to him from my heart, but I couldn't speak. I was hoping maybe he could understand what I could not say. It was just the two of us alone and I knew anything could happen. "Don't you look at me like that, you understand? I know what you think of me. You want me to die, don't you?" I couldn't answer. I thought I did, until he said that and then I got scared. What if both of my parents died? I would be an orphan. Maybe it would be better, but I sure as hell didn't want to find out. "I don't want to see your face it makes me sick." I thought he was going to start crying. His eyes were filled with water. I hated him. I loved him. I hated myself for caring about him, but I couldn't help it. I could see and feel how much pain he was in.

"Fuck this place. I gotta go," he mumbled.

"Daddy, please don't go. I'll make you something. You need to sleep." Someone had to take care of him.

"No, Frankie, I need, I need..." He couldn't speak. I waited to hear what he needed. I was praying it was me. I wanted him to say, 'Frankie, I need you. I love you.' Words I never heard from him. I went to him. It took all I had inside of me to go and hug him. I wrapped myself around him. My head was snuggled in his chest. I could hear his heart beating. It was fast and steady.

"I love you, Daddy." I didn't even know if it was true, but I figured if I said it first, he'd have to say it back. Isn't that the way it goes?

"I need... a drink." He pulled away from me and walked out the door. I was left with only myself to hold.

I ran downstairs to tell Ian that Dad went out. He was getting ready to paint and didn't care. "He's a big boy. He'll be fine."

Antoinette took my hand, "Francesca, you cannot help him. You cannot reason with a person like that."

"But he's lonely. He can hurt himself," I cried. I don't know what came over me. I felt like my mother.

"Don't worry yourself. You are too young to be so sad." Antoinette's words hit me hard. I'd never known when I wasn't sad.

"I gotta go." I ran out the basement door and followed Dad. He didn't know I was behind him. His walk was fast, but crooked. He was talking to himself, "What am I supposed to do? I got nothing. You left me and I got nothing." This is what I heard him say. He cried a little. When he reached McTierney's Ale House, I watched him as he took a deep breath, wiped his eyes and swept his hair back. He pushed the doors open and entered into the clouds of smoke. I ran to the window and peeked in. Even though it was a little bit more upscale than Dom's Pub the drunks pretty much all looked the same. Dad was smiling, walking proud. Everyone cheered and laughed as he walked in.

"Hey, look who fell off the wagon." "Look who's back." "We missed ya Ryan, don't stay away so long next time." "We knew you'd show up sooner or later." All the other drunks were happy to see him. It made them feel better. Misery loves company, Mom used to say. I didn't know what she meant, but now I saw it right before my eyes. They're all doing the same thing, hiding away from the real world. Escaping from their children, their wives, their husbands, pretending that this is fun, but I could see the unhappiness in all of their eyes. I could feel the loneliness in that bar. Dad was like some war hero who'd just arrived home. What a greeting he got, such approval for coming back to where he belonged. As I watched him laugh and hug all these strangers, I felt betrayed. They seemed more important to him than me, the boys, Mom. I was about to leave when I noticed a woman go up to Dad and give him a long kiss on the mouth. My heart sank. She sat down beside him. The bartender put two big drinks in front of them and then he gave them two little ones. They threw back the little drinks fast, made a face like they'd just swallowed rat poison, then they picked up the big drinks, clinked their glasses and drank some more. The woman was all over Dad. Her dress was short. Her breasts were popping out. She had on a pound of make-up and her hair was teased up to the roof. I was getting a crazy rush of violent fire piercing through my veins. Was this the woman who Dad was cheating with, the night Mom found out? I had to do something. I had to get Dad out of there. I walked in with determination. I felt like John Wayne in 'True

Grit.' There was a big-ness in my small body. I wasn't afraid. I had a job to do. Everyone was silent for a moment as I swaggered across the bar. I reached Dad and his dime store troll. "Dad I want you to come home with me." At first, he looked at me in disbelief. So did she. Then he burst out laughing. This gave all the other guy's permission, so they laughed along. "I'm not kidding. Let's go." For whatever reason, I felt like it was my responsibility to save Dad. He wasn't much, but he was all I had.

Some guy yelled out, "Hey Ryan, she means business."

Another shouted, "Looks like your old lady's putting you back on the wagon."

"Ryan's got a new wife." They all chimed in with what they thought were funny comments. I wanted to puke on all of them.

"Why don't you shut up, you drunken losers," I said to the whole bar.

Oohh's and aahh's came back at me.

"Give that girl a drink," an older woman shouted.

"Why? So you don't have to hear the truth about your pathetic selves?" I don't know what came over me. I had no fear.

"Frankie, go home now," Dad said in embarrassment.

"No, not until you come with me." I stood my ground.

"I said go home, you little pain in the ass."

"No." Defying him again.

"She's got a tongue on her," the tramp said to Dad.

"Frankie, if I have to say it once more, I'm gonna smack you."

"Smack her. She could use a good smack," another drunk blurted from the back.

"I don't care. I'm not going until you're with me." I stood defiantly. Dad lost it and he smacked me hard in the face. I didn't flinch. It stung a little, but it was nothing I hadn't felt before. At this point my desire was stronger than my fear. My desire was to get my father home and save my family. He smacked me again. I stood without emotion. I had become immune to physical pain. It was the emotional pain that ripped my heart out.

The bartender laughed, "Boy she could take it, huh, just like your wife." All the guys started laughing. This went through Dad like a straight edged razor. His eyes filled with venom and he was over the bar in two seconds.

"You ever mention my wife again and I'll kill you." Dad was punching the hell out of him. He grabbed Dad and threw him on the floor. The glasses were flying. Men were jumping in and trying to stop it. I grabbed a drink off the bar and threw it in the Tramp's face. She went at me and I was ready. Someone grabbed her from behind and escorted her out of the bar. I didn't care who won the fight. I knew Dad would be thrown out and hopefully forbidden to go into that bar ever again. The fight went on and on. Other fights started. I ran to the phone and called the cops, "Yeah, I'd like to report a murder at McTierney's Ale house in Queens. You better hurry up before more folks are killed. It's a free for all over here." I hung up the phone. Damn that felt good. Six cop cars were there within five minutes. The men in blue broke up the huge brawl and closed the bar. Dad was taken down to the station. He spent the night in jail. My mission was accomplished. I could go home and sleep peacefully knowing Dad was behind bars. I knew in the morning he would be mad at me, but I didn't care.

When I came home the house was dark and for the most part quiet. I heard a slow moaning sound coming from the basement. At first, I was afraid that Antoinette was hurt or crying. I snuck down without making a peep. As I got closer, I heard Ian moaning too. They didn't see me watching them. I was hiding behind the pillar near the stairs. The only bit of light in the pitch-black basement was flickering from two candles by the couch, which was now opened into a bed. I had seen Mom and Dad doing this before; it had never looked this beautiful, though. A soft piece of classical music whispered through the stereo.

Ian's masterpieces were all around. They kissed so passionately. I could feel myself blushing. It was like watching the most romantic movie of my life, except I felt like I was in it. I knew I shouldn't be watching, but I couldn't help myself. I was hypnotized. I thought of Sean and how nice it would be to do that with him. I made my mind stop because that would never happen. As I watched Ian, I realized what a gentle person he was. When they finished the moaning, Ian held her face.

"I don't want you to go. Stay with me."

"And live in the basement?" she laughed lovingly.

"No, we'll go somewhere else." My heart hurt as I listened to them.

"Your father does not like me." She was sure.

"You're wrong. He likes you too much. I think you remind him of my mother."

Antoinette stroked Ian's head as he nuzzled in her breast. "Do I remind you of your mother?"

"In some ways, yes. In some ways, no."

"How do I?" She wanted to get inside of his mind.

"You're both so beautiful, Italian, sexy, funny." She giggled with delight. "But you are much stronger than she was."

"How do you know that?"

"I just do. I can feel it. That's why she's gone."

"Maybe you do not know how strong she was. Maybe she never showed you. She must have been a very strong woman to have five children." Ian stopped and sat up. He looked like he wanted to cry. She sat in front of him. Their naked bodies twinkled in the candlelight. I had never seen two people talk so honestly. They kissed some more.

"I love you, Antoinette. I've never felt like this." He became so vulnerable. I had to fight back tears.

She took a deep breath, "I know." What was that? 'I know.' Say it back you jerk, I wanted to scream. She kissed him. She couldn't say it back yet, but I knew she loved him. I could tell.

"I did not expect to meet anyone Ian. I just wanted to see America, have fun and go back home."

"Well, tough. You did meet someone. Me. So, what are you gonna do?" As they talked through the night, I became sleepier and sleepier. I couldn't get back up the stairs without being heard because the loud moaning was finished. I fell asleep sitting up behind the pillar.

My drool woke me up the next morning. I looked over to the bed. Ian was sleeping like a baby. Antoinette was getting dressed. I pretended that I just walked down the stairs. Antoinette saw me and put her finger to her lips. She didn't want me to wake Ian. We walked upstairs together.

"Where are you going? I was just gonna make breakfast."

"Oh Francesca, you are such a dear, but I must go, bella."

"Why?" I couldn’t bear her hurting Ian.

"I must return to Italy." She seemed confused.

"Can I come?"

She laughed at me, "I wish you could, but I don't think your family would like that."

"They wouldn't care."

"Francesca, maybe someday you can come and see me there."

"Don't leave. You make Ian so happy. He needs you."

She looked so sad, "Francesca, your brother is very special, but I have a home. I cannot stay, as much as I would like to."

"Do you love him?" I had to know.

She was taken aback by my bluntness, "Yes I do, but it cannot be." She walked toward the door.

"I'll walk you out." We walked together to the train station. She held my hand. The sun was barely up. She wrote down her address for me on a piece of paper.

"We will see each other again someday." I took the piece of paper. I couldn't speak because the tears that I was holding in would spill out. She kissed me. "Ciao, bella." She left as quickly as she came.

I went home and put her address in my special jewelry box that Mom gave me. Dad was still locked up at the 18th precinct where he belonged. The house was quiet. I could hear the birds waking up the neighbors. I put on the necklace Mom gave me and I went downstairs and sat beside the bed just waiting for Ian to get up. When I sat down, I saw something I couldn't see last night, because I was behind the pillar. It was the finished painting of Antoinette. It took my breath away. I felt like she was still there watching over Ian. God, she was exquisite. Ian woke up and saw me. I told him. "She's gone."

Ian covered his face. "Frankie, go upstairs."

"Do you want me to make you breakfast?"

"No."

"Dad is in jail."

"What?"

I figured I'd change the subject. I could see his heart was broken. I left him alone.

I woke everyone up so we could have a nice breakfast before we picked Dad up from jail. I told my brothers what happened. They were laughing so hard they practically pissed their pants. Ryan was proud of me. He told me that he wouldn't let Dad hurt me when he came home. We had fun at breakfast. Ian tried to act like he was okay, but we all knew he wasn't. Patrick came up with a great idea. He thought it would be hysterical if we all got dressed up to go get Dad. As if we were going to a wedding or a funeral. We all agreed. He did all the ties for my brothers and I put on a pretty dress that Mom bought for me. Seamus took it a step further and stopped to get a bouquet of flowers and I pulled out the 'get out of jail free' card from our Monopoly set. Instead of making it so dramatic we made a joke of it.

Everyone in the police station looked at us like we were nuts. We made a pact that no matter what Dad said, we were gonna keep a big smile on and act happy.

We stood in front of the double doors waiting for him. When he came through those doors, we acted like those really happy, *Leave It To Beaver* families. We welcomed him like he was getting off a plane after a long trip, the loving family receiving him at the airport. He didn't know what to say. We looked great.

"Hi Daddy." Big kisses and hugs. He looked around as if he were dreaming.

"What the hell are you all doing?" He was mortified.

"We figured we'd go to church," Patrick smiled.

"Not before a good cup of coffee," Seamus added.

"You must be hungry, Dad." Ryan hugged him. He was in shock. All of his anger dissolved. Then I handed him the 'get out of jail free' card and he started laughing at how ridiculous we were and then tears streaked his cheeks.

"Why is everyone so happy?"

"You're out of jail, aren't you?" Ian put his arm around Dad.

"We're just happy to see you, Dad," Patrick laughed.

Dad grabbed my hand and squeezed it. I let him hold it for a moment, but I was uncomfortable, so I pulled away.

I know he was hurt. "Ya know something, I'm happy to see all of you too."

We walked down the street to get a coffee shop. It didn't matter if we were all pretending. It felt real. Pretending to be happy felt better than being sad. Every once in a while, some true happiness spilled through.

Chapter 13: BLACKOUT

It was the summer of 1977 and Jimmy Carter our 39th President, The Peanut Man was leading our Nation and 'Saturday Night Fever,' was leading at the box office. All the guys wanted to be John Travolta and all the girls wanted to marry him. If they couldn't do that, at the very least they dreamed of dancing with him. You couldn't even walk down the street without hearing The Bee Gee's blasting through storefront windows or from Eight Track stereos pounding in everyone's cars. 'You Should Be Dancing,' was the theme of the year and Discotheques were all the rage. I was thirteen approaching fourteen and changing every day. I felt awkward, like I didn't know how to live inside of my growing, maturing body. I shot up past Patrick and just two inches shy of Seamus. Ian and Ryan said I was turning out to be a perfect basketball player. Seamus was getting ready to go to NYU. He'd be the first in our family on either side to go to college. Ryan wasn't interested in anything but sports, mostly boxing. He was working as a bouncer at a disco in Manhattan called 'Studio 54'. He said it was like Disneyland and people would wait outside for hours just to step foot on that magical dance floor. He loved seeing all the crazies that would show up. Part of his job was sending home all of the minors and making sure no fights broke out, but more importantly, selecting whom, out of the crowd, looked good enough to grace the legendary Studio 54. There were certain types of people they wanted in the club, celebrities types, hot chicks and wealthy guys, while others could be turned away just because of how they looked or dressed. Girls used to dress to impress the bouncers, since their fate for the evening would depend on if they got in the most famous disco in the world. Ryan said guys and girls would rent limousines and make the driver pull up to the door, just so they could appear to be very important, hoping this would sway the bouncers. Ian knew he wanted to paint so school didn't appeal to him, not even art school. He felt that he had natural talent and if he studied, it would ruin his raw instincts. Patrick wasn't sure if he would go to college. He wanted to be a Broadway star. He wanted to sing and dance in big Broadway musicals. I wanted to go to a school far away, so I could live there. I wondered what my life would be like if I didn't have to have all these guys around all the time. In school, all the girls would giggle outside the boy's locker room. They'd talk about how they'd like to sneak in, be a fly on the wall. I'd say, "Not me, I live in a boys locker room. I've seen it all, heard it all, and have had enough."

Because I was the only girl, I had the most chores. I did the cooking, the cleaning, the sewing and ironing. I know my brothers said they would help with Bella, but now that she was older and dirtier, she was my dog. The only one who helped at all was Patrick, mostly with the laundry, because his clothes had to be a certain way. God forbid I added an extra drop of bleach.

It was hard living with five guys. Aside from all the housework and taking care of them, I felt inferior. They were constantly reminding me of just how insignificant the woman is out in the real world. Men were the heroes. Women are here to have babies and raise them. I had to come up with a way to survive in this environment.

One day I heard Ian and Ryan talking in the basement. Ian was showing him a tattoo that he'd designed. It was in honor of Mom. He wanted all the boys to get one. I ran down to see.

"I wanna get one." Just the thought of it excited me.

"Girls don't get tattoos. They're only for guys."

"Let me see it." I figured at least I could look. He had painted a picture of Mom in a heart with angel wings on either side of the heart. There were roses dripping down the heart with thorns coming out. It looked like a bleeding heart, but the blood was symbolized with red roses.

Ryan loved it, "Do you think the guy could draw this?"

"I found this amazing artist downtown in the Village. Right near Little Italy." Ian smiled proudly.

I was jealous. They got Patrick and Seamus and went to Little Italy, so I followed them. I stayed far enough behind so they couldn't see me. I just caught the train in the nick of time. I had to hide downstairs until it pulled in. I was in the next car so they couldn't see me. They were all excited, talking and laughing. Patrick looked a little scared, but he wanted to do it for Mom. When they changed trains, I successfully got on without being noticed. I had twenty dollars from Dad, which was supposed to buy dinner for tonight. All I could think of was cannolis, napoleons, pignoli cookies and a big frothy cappuccino. I missed Antoinette. Finally, we reached the big city. I stayed pretty far behind them, but it was easier not to be seen because there were a lot more people walking on the streets. In Queens you pretty much know everyone you see walking in the neighborhood, but here, a person could easily get lost.

Ian pulled out an address from his pocket. They stopped and walked down some stairs. The sign outside said Ivan's Tattoos. This was the place. I peeked in. There was a big fat bearded man, smoking a cigar and drilling a needle into someone's arm. The guy getting the tattoo had both arms covered in tattoos. I could hardly see any skin. When he finished with him, he got up and shook Ian's hand. Ian introduced all my brothers. He pulled out the tattoo that he'd designed. The fat bearded man seemed impressed. He offered all of the guys some liquor. It was a yellowish color. Ian drank some and so did Ryan. Seamus and Patrick refused. Ian went first. I watched for a little bit, but it was taking so long, I took a walk. I made sure I noted the street. I decided to go indulge in some Italian pastries at Ferrara's. I ordered all the same things that Antoinette and I had eaten together. It wasn't the same. I realized that all food tastes better when you're happy. I kept checking back on my brothers. I couldn't believe how long these things took. I looked in and Seamus was clenching his teeth in pain. The fat bearded man offered him the yellowish liquor again. This time he swigged some back. Patrick looked as white as a ghost while he awaited his turn. Ryan and Ian had a big gauze pad covering the place where the tattoo was. I figured I'd go shopping for dinner while I waited. I spoke in Italian to the shopkeepers and got them to give me a deal. I managed to get plenty of food for dinner with the little money I had left. I found that men like to give girls free food. Now the only problem was I had so many bags I didn't know how I would carry them all home. Mario, one of the owners of the Italian Deli, said I could borrow one of those shopping carts, the ones the little old ladies pulled behind them. I promised him I would return it next week. He trusted I would. He called me his little Paisan. I liked that.

I rolled my cart back to Ivan's tattoo parlor. Patrick was crying in the chair as the fat bearded man tried to hold his arm steady. Ian gave him the yellowish liquor. He drank it and made a face like he was sucking on sour lemons. My brothers all cheered him on. They were trying to make a man out of him.

Finally, they were finished. I hid until they walked a little and then I followed them home. I walked up to our house five minutes after them, pretending I'd just finished shopping. If anyone looked in my cart, they would know I could never have found this stuff in the neighborhood. But nobody was interested in my cart. They were excited to show Dad their tattoos. Ian thought he'd love them.

"Hey," I shouted. "Where'd you guys go?"

"Nowhere." Ian practically ignored me.

Seamus came over to me, "We went downtown for tattoos."

"Can you take me?" I didn't want to be left out.

"Forget about it, Frankie. I told you, tattoos are for guys."

"Just tell me where you went."

Ian was losing his patience; "You will never know where we went, so get that through your thick red head."

I laughed to myself. I already know, you big asshole. They took off the gauze and started looking at them. The one on

Ryan's arm was bigger than the one on Patrick's arm. Their arms were different sizes, so they actually looked unique on each one. My brothers were all glowing, with Mom on their right arms. We all waited at the kitchen table for Dad to come home from work. Ian proudly told him they had a surprise. They all revealed Mom painted on their arm. At first Dad was shocked to see her face. His eyes went from arm to arm. He looked at me almost expecting to see one on my arm. I was disappointed that I couldn't show him mine. He went closer to Ian's arm. There was blood in certain places. Ian said it would scab first, but in a few days it would be perfect.

Dad got quiet. His eyes filled with tears, "It's... it's... just a tattoo."

Ian pulled out the design to show Dad. He stared at it and then placed it on the table.

"I'm gonna go shower." Dad couldn't handle it.

"Are you alright, Dad?" Ryan went after him.

"Yeah, I'm just tired." He hung his head and walked away.

The boys went inside. I started to get dinner ready. I picked up Ian's design. "He really doesn't need it anymore," I thought. So, I kept it. Later he asked me if I'd seen it. I lied. I needed it. If I couldn't have it on my arm, I'd keep it in a special place, my jewelry box.

That weekend Dad let me stay at Virginia's. He was trying to be nice to me, which made me feel uncomfortable. I tried to be nice too, but it was very hard because I hated him. However, I knew if I wanted to spend time with Virginia, I had to at least pretend that I liked him.

Virginia was in rare form. It was time to party. She got me a phony I.D. and said we were going out dancing. Luckily, they didn't have pictures on driver's licenses yet. Because I was so tall it wouldn't be too hard to fool everybody. She did my make-up and dressed me up. I felt self-conscious, but I figured I'd do it so we could have fun. It was a breeze. The bouncers looked at the phony license, at me, at the license, at my eyes to check the color, my height – five foot eight inches, and then said, "Cool, go ahead."

What a scam. Here I was, fourteen, passing for eighteen. The lights were low, a silver ball spun from the ceiling and Donna Summers 'Love to Love You Baby' pumped through mega speakers that stood on either side of the dance floor. It energized me. Everyone was dancing, drinking and having a good time. Perfume and cologne interacted and overpowered the oxygen in the air. The guys were worse than the girls. The girls were dressed like hookers, including me, our hair teased as high as we could get it, then out came the Aqua Net. Heavy black liner and blue and purple shadows to decorate our eyes. The guys wore polyester shirts (three buttons open so they could adorn their chest with a gold chain) polyester pants and pointy leather shoes. Virginia ordered drinks right away. Alabama Slammers. She said they were sweet like soda and they were. My body started to feel light. I felt alive. We got on the dance floor as the energy pulsated from every corner of the room. You couldn't talk without screaming at each other. I hadn't danced since Mom was gone. She'd always get me to dance with her. There was a freedom I felt tonight that was exciting to me. I could close my eyes, stand under that spilling silver ball, and dance in my own world. The music carried me away. Now I knew why Patrick loved it so much. Unfortunately, my moment got interrupted by a big nerd. "Uh, excuse me, would you like to dance?"

I said, "No, thank you, not with you."

Virginia started laughing her ass off, " I can't believe you blew him off like that."

"What do you want me to do, lie?"

She was impressed. "I spend so much time dancing and talking to guys that I don't want to have anything to do with."

I didn't understand. "Just tell the truth." The next guy that asked her to dance was this muscle-bound, egotistical asshole. She blurted out, "I wouldn't dance with you if you paid me, you big muscle head jerk." His jaw dropped. She pulled me away. We cracked up, "That felt so good, Frankie."

We danced the night away. She knew so many people. I was introduced as her little cousin. Before I knew it, I was nicknamed Cuz for the rest of the night. The bartender kept giving us free drinks. I think he and Virginia had a thing going on. She was getting drunk. My head was spinning, and I felt like I took stupid pills. Then out of nowhere, Ronnie Walker, the drummer, was standing before me. He was still gorgeous. That tingly feeling came over me again. I was mad that I was feeling so silly from the Alabama Slammers, almost to the point of barfing right on his polyester pants. Now I wished I hadn't drank anything. How could I possibly have an intelligent and meaningful conversation?

"Hi." He smiled, as his voice vibrated through my vagina.

"Hi." I smiled back.

"Well, if it isn't Ronnie Walker. Why don't you keep walking, Walker?" Virginia practically attacked him.

"Oh come on, Gin, you're drunk. Be nice to me."

She stormed away. I wondered what had happened between the two of them.

"I'm sorry, I forgot your name." He looked at me.

"Francesca," I reminded him.

"Of course, Francesca, how can I forget such a lovely name? I will never forget it again. I promise!" I like the way he talked. He was so charming. "What happened that night? I looked for you everywhere."

All of a sudden, I flashed back to that horrible night when I got my first period. I couldn't possibly tell him the truth, "Oh Virginia got sick, so we had to leave."

"Drag." He was so cool.

"Yeah, big drag." I tried to talk like him.

"Well, you're here now."

"Yeah," I said, but I wasn't. The lights were flashing. Everyone was screaming. The music was so loud I felt like I might burst a blood vessel in my head.

"Do you wanna get out of here?" He grabbed my hand. Of course, I did.

"But what about Virginia? I came with her."

"Don't worry, I know where she lives. I'll make sure you get home." He was so cute I couldn't resist. I told him I felt a little queasy, so he took me to a diner to get some food. I loved to watch him talk. I forgot about everything, Sean, Mom, Antoinette. It was just Ronnie Walker and me. I felt like a puppy dog. We went out to his blue Monte Carlo and the rain started pouring down. He opened the door for me. That was a first. As the rain danced on the car, we listened to Led Zeppelin. When a good drum part came on, he would pound the dashboard and steering wheel as if it were a drum set. I thought he was the coolest of cool and here he was with me.

"How old are you, Francesca?" The windows were all fogged up. Should I lie? Virginia might tell him the truth.

"I'll be fifteen soon." He looked surprised, but disappointed. "How old are you, Ronnie?"

"I'll be twenty soon." He was proud.

"Oh." I was way out of my league.

"But you seem older." He really made me feel important and smart. “Most girls my age aren’t half as mature as you. You’re really special, Francesca.”

"Thank you.” I wanted to impress him. “Yeah, I feel older." I hoped he still liked me even though I was fourteen.

"Your cousin doesn't like me." He was feeling me out.

"Why not?" Hoping to get him to tell me.

"Well, it's a long story, but whatever happens between me and you, don't tell her, okay?"

"Okay." I said quickly without even thinking. I needed to be accepted by him.

"Okay." He whispered softly into my ear as he leaned into me, I could smell the 'Old Spice' on his neck. His long hair swept by my nose. I could feel his freshly shaven skin on my cheek. "I really like you, Francesca." He kissed my ear. My body got weak. He moved down to my neck. Oh my God, I'm in heaven. His eyes locked with mine, "You can't tell anyone. We could get into trouble." It was like anything he said was okay with me. We crawled into the back seat. I was just as scared as I was aroused. I wanted him to touch me, but I didn't want him to. It was nice just talking. It felt safe. Once we got in the back seat he went from a gentle boy to a rough man. I couldn't speak. I started to have flashbacks of the Cuban man. All of a sudden, I was seven years old and I felt his fat stubby hands groping at me. I became nauseous as Ronnie's hands rubbed on my small breast. I wanted to scream. I couldn't make a sound. It was like one of those dreams where you're being attacked, but you can't yell for help. I started to leave my body.

"Oh Francesca, you're so young."

I could feel him growing through his pants. He put my hand on him so I could feel his hardness.

"Do you like that?" He said as he panted. I was frozen. He didn't care. He didn't pay attention to my feelings. He just needed to take care of himself.

"Oh, I'm gonna make you feel so good." If only he knew how awful I was feeling. I wanted to run but couldn’t move a muscle. Please God, let me just get through this and go home. His pants were down and so were mine. He put himself inside of me, while I lay there. He reached the end, grunted and released his sweaty body on me. He didn't kiss me or hold me. He didn't touch my hair or my face.

"Oh baby, oh, that was so good. I better get you home." I felt dirty and alone, fooled by this smooth talker.

He dropped me off at Virginia's. He didn't mention seeing me again or ask for a phone number. He just said, "Good night, kiddo." No kiss, no nothing. As he pulled away, I threw up all over the curb. Then I rang the bell. Virginia came to the door, "Where the hell have you been?"

"I got sick."

I took a shower and tried to scrub Ronnie Walker off my body. My skin was crawling with disgust and shame. I couldn't look at myself in the mirror. I crawled in bed with Virginia. She wanted to know if he’d tried to make the moves on me. I lied again. I had to. I couldn't bear telling the truth. She made me swear to God I didn't fool around with him. After I did, she said, "Thank God, he's such a loser."

"Why?" I wanted to know what made her so angry with him.

"I'm gonna tell you something, but if you ever tell anyone, even a Priest, I will kick the shit out of you, and I mean it."

"Wow, okay, I swear, I promise."

"Okay. Ronnie Walker and I used to go out. I really liked him, and he said he loved me. So anyway, we did it, ya know, more than a few times." She started to cry, but then swallowed it and grit her teeth, "Well anyway, so, I got, uh, pregnant."

I was dying inside. No wonder she was so rude to him. "What? When?"

"A couple of years ago. He didn't even give a shit. He said he knew a clinic where his ex-girlfriend went. Maybe I should call her and get the number." This made me furious, "What a fucking asshole. Didn't you want to kill him?"

"Yeah, of course, but that wouldn't solve anything. I had to take care of it all by myself. He didn't even give me a cent to help out."

Now I felt even worse. God forbid I got pregnant from this jerk. I really didn't even know much about the whole pregnant thing. Just the stuff I heard in school.

“How did you know you were pregnant?”

“I missed my period.”

“Huh.” I didn’t understand.

“My period. The reason we get our periods is so that we can get pregnant.”

I felt like such an asshole. I didn’t know shit on shinola about any of this. I guess I was too young before Mom died, and in a house full of guys who was gonna sit down and talk to me about this topic?

Virginia was crying, "Promise you won't tell Frankie."

"I promise." I felt so bad for her and for myself. We were both used and dropped off at the curb.

She wanted me to know how much she cared about me. That's why she got mad at me for leaving with him. She knew how he was. Now I did too. I prayed to God not to make me pregnant. I couldn't sleep all night. I felt bad for Virginia. I knew what it was like to keep a secret. I could've told her some of my secrets, but I was afraid if I started talking about them, I'd fall apart and have to go back to the hospital.

When I got back home, I felt scared. If Dad ever knew what I did, he'd shoot me, and he'd go find Ronnie Walker and shoot him too. I went upstairs and unpacked my small bag, dropped to my knees and prayed to get my period. I took out the pants I wore the night I was with Ronnie Walker. I wanted to burn them. I emptied the pockets. There was a five-dollar bill, some change and the phony I.D. I forgot to give it back to Virginia. The name on it was Samantha Bennett, five foot eight inches, green eyes. I loved to pretend I was someone else. I didn't feel like I was doing a good job at being me. This was one of those days when I really missed Mom. I just wished she could brush my hair right now and pull Ronnie Walker right out of my roots. I went to my jewelry box and pulled out the necklace. I could see her sitting by the window on Christmas the night she gave it to me. I saw Ian's tattoo design staring at me through the open jewelry box. The phony I.D. practically winked at me simultaneously. I needed Mom. What could be better than branding her on my skin for eternity? This way, whenever I needed her, I could just touch my skin and feel her. I knew what I had to do, and I didn't care about the consequences.

The next morning, I woke up and got some money from Dad for groceries and took some of my own that I had saved. I got my cart and went downtown Manhattan to Little Italy. It was July 13th, 1977 and the most sweltering day I can remember from my childhood. I was sticking to my shirt by the time I reached the subway, but I didn't care I was on a mission. I hit Manhattan as the sun beat down on me like an insect under a magnified glass. Mario was happy to see me. We spoke in Italian. I told him about Mom. He would've loved her. He filled my cart and wouldn't let me pay for a thing. He said it gave him great pleasure to give me things. He told me to hold on to the cart. He liked my company and figured as long as I had the cart I'd keep coming to visit. He made me feel special. When I told him I had five guys to cook for every night he said the least he could do is help with vegetables. I told him about Mom's beautiful garden in our backyard in Queens. He had a garden, too. He encouraged me to tend to Mom's garden and bring it back to life. "It'll keep you young and strong," he said.

His theory was when you put your hands into the earth and create life - the garden - you connect yourself so deeply to nature that it enhances your DNA. I was afraid I didn't have a green thumb like Mom. She could make a basil plant grow out of cement. "Passion," Mario said. "Passion makes anything grow." Mario made me a deal. If I brought him a little home cooked meal every-once-in-a-while he'd trade me some home-grown herbs and vegetables. It was a deal.

I pulled my cart and headed toward Ivan's tattoo parlor. My hands were sweating. I was nervous, but so positive that I wanted to do it. When I arrived, the fat bearded man, who turned out to be Ivan, was working on some bald-headed bruiser with six earrings in one ear and tattoos all over his body. He was getting one on his bald head, while I waited.

Ivan smiled, "I'll be right with you, miss."

Miss? I'd never been called that. Oh well. Hopefully he thought I was older. The bald- headed man smiled. He had about three teeth in his head. I forced a smile back.

"Wanna smoke a doobie before you get drilled?" He laughed and then took a monstrous toke on a joint. I've never seen anyone inhale that deeply in my life.

"Uh, no thanks." I smiled politely.

They both laughed. When they finished, I froze. I was next. I showed Ivan Ian's design. He recognized it and told me how impressed he was with all the guys paying tribute to their mother that way. I explained I couldn't make it that day, but we all had to have the same tattoo. He asked for I.D. I showed him my phony go to license. He looked at me funny. I smiled hoping to distract him. "Hey, how come their last name is Finnegan and yours is Bennett?"

"Different fathers," I blurted out quickly, realizing I wish we did have different fathers. I wish anyone else was my father. Even Ivan. He bought it and told me he had the same thing, a half-brother and a half sister from a second marriage. I didn't want to talk because it made me more anxious. He assured me it was going to be painful. I insisted on feeling it before I drank any yellowish liquor, which I found out was called tequila from Mexico. Smiling with a gold-capped tooth in front, he pointed out the wiggly worm at the bottom of the bottle.

“Suit yourself, but she’s here if you need her.” He wiped my arm with alcohol and began the process. It hurt like hell. I clenched my teeth.

"You sure you don't want any tequila?"

"No." I wanted to feel the pain. I needed to feel it. I had been numbing myself so much. I needed to feel every second of glorious pain that it took to brand Mom into my pores for eternity. It reminded me of her. I was going through it for her. She wouldn't want me to drink the yellow tequila through this. It wouldn't mean as much. If I felt it, I'd never forget. I got off on the pain; it made me feel high.

Ivan was impressed. "You're one tough bitch. I've seen guys cry when I do them."

I looked at my right hand and saw my scar. It reminded me that I was a survivor. I didn’t just let the Cuban man throw me off the roof. I fought back. I was strong, very strong and I had scars to prove it. I clenched my right fist tightly and was ready. "It's all in the mind," I heard myself say, but I don't even know where it came from. Sitting in that chair, everything that ever happened to me came back. All of my loss and pain came pouring out of my arm. This was it, a new start. I decided that this tattoo was going to change my life and give me a clean slate. Ivan said I was the first girl he ever saw with a MOM tattoo on her arm. Usually, the girls did it in more subtle places. I liked that he said that; it appealed to my deep need to feel special. He said because I was so unique the tattoo was on the house, no charge. I couldn't believe it. It seemed like people were always giving me things for free. I gave him a big hug. He wanted me to come see him if I ever got any more tattoos. I told him from now on he was my main tattoo man. He laughed. It was dark out and I had been gone much longer than I planned, but I didn't care.

I ran to the train station with my cart. Without any warning, BOOM, the lights went out, everywhere. Every streetlight, store light, stoplight, everything. People started screaming. At first, I wasn't sure what was going on. I thought there was a big robbery going on. Everyone started running and pushing each other. Cars in the streets started flashing their lights, honking their horns. Traffic came to a halt. Guys were jumping over cars and breaking storefront windows. It all happened so fast that I didn't know what was happening. I was petrified. My arm was hurting, and I was feeling light-headed from the heat. I felt like an ant in a stampede. New York City was going crazy. There were gangs of guys breaking into stores and running out with TV's, stereos, clothes, couches, anything and everything they could steal. Some of the stores were closed. The ones that were open pulled out guns or knives to keep the thieves away. It was a free-for-all. I ran to Mario's with my cart. On the way, people were yelling, "Blackout!" "There's a blackout!" New York was in a total blackout. Holy shit! My family was gonna kill me. When I got to Mario's he was closed, but he was standing in front of the store, protecting it. He had a little battery-operated transistor radio on, trying to find out what happened. When he saw me, his face lit up, "Francesca, come here quickly." I ran to him. "What are you doing here?"

"I never made it home," I told him.

He looked at the big bandage on my arm, "Are you okay? Did they hurt you? I'll kill them."

"No Mario, I got a tattoo of Mom."

"Francesca, you had skin like a porcelain, why you gotta do that?" He scrunched his fist and his face at me.

"It was for Mom, Mario."

He saw my face and realized how important it was to me. He made me stay there because it was too dangerous to try to get home. There were car accidents everywhere. The police were catching as many of the looters as possible, but there were way too many. The whole city shut down. I wondered what was going on in Queens. I heard it was everywhere, not just Manhattan. All the boroughs were blacked out. The guys in my neighborhood must've gone nuts. I felt safe to be with Mario, but I knew my brothers and Dad were worried about me. I didn't care, I was excited. This was a major event in the history of New York, and I was in the middle of all the action with my brand-new tattoo. Mario was friends with all the neighborhood stores, so he introduced me as his little Paisan. We put together a bunch of food. All the stores chipped in; cheese and crackers, roasted peppers, eggplant caponota, Caesar salad, bruscetta. It was like an Italian candlelit, flashlight feast. We pulled out some beach chairs and crates and camped out on the sidewalk. It was way too hot to stay in the apartment without a fan. Mario lived right above his store. A lot of the storeowners did. All the old Italians were singing songs and laughing. They opened wine and played cards for money. We all pulled together and turned a crisis into an amazing and unforgettable event. I peeled off the bandage to show Mario what Mom looked like.

"Bella figa." He said, which meant a beautiful fig, but to the Italians it was like a huge compliment. When you think of a fig, symbolically, it is so feminine and perfect.

The power was out until the next day. I was bummed out when it came back on. I had to go back home. Even though I hadn't slept, I wasn't tired. We had some fresh-fruit, I got my cart and headed home. On the way home, everyone was talking about the blackout and all the crime that had occurred. I was alive: I'd survived the blackout of 1977.

When I got home, Dad was furious 'cause he was worried sick. My brothers had been all over Queens in the dark searching for me. I told them I was stuck in Manhattan. He forbade me to go there anymore. When he saw my arm, he ripped off the bandage. "For God sakes Frankie, what the fuck did you do that for?"

"They did it," I defended.

"They're guys. You're a girl. Everyone's gonna make fun of you."

"I don't care. I like it." Dad had no power over me, and he knew I didn't respect him anymore. He could hem and haw all he wanted, but he was dead to me.

"You ruined your body,"

"You ruined your body and Mom's body and my life so leave me alone and in case you haven't noticed it is my body and I'll do whatever the hell I want to it." Holy mackerel! I didn't even know where that voice came from, but it flew out of me. Maybe that's what the strength of a tattoo does to people. Dad was astonished but didn't say a word. He knew that no matter what he said or did he could never hurt me again. The ultimate had happened, and no threats, words or angry hands could penetrate my body, mind or soul. I was an impenetrable wall and immune to him.

Ian was amazed that it was the same as theirs. "Who did that for you?"

"Some guy," I acted stupid.

"Who? I'm gonna kill him."

"No one you know. I took your design and went to Brooklyn."

I shut them all up and it felt good. What felt even better is when I went upstairs to the bathroom, I got my period. Hallelujah! It was the first time I was happy to see the blood. Now I figured out why all the girls called it 'their friend.'

Dad cooked dinner that night. It was awful. No one ate. I sat with my tank top on, showing off my tattoo. I could feel Dad and Ian burning up, but there was nothing they could do. Can't undo a tattoo. I felt supreme. Patrick laughed. He was so happy I did it. Ryan and Seamus thought it was cool too. They knew how much it meant to me.

Ryan was telling us about all the robberies in the neighborhood last night. Fisher, which was the biggest electronic warehouse in Queens, got ripped off. It was full of TV's, stereos, phones, everything. The Rheingold and Schlitz beer factories got ripped off too. All the neighborhood establishments including the delis, Manny's butcher shop and Sanders Candy Store – All the people went crazy and robbed them all blind and not one of them got busted. The guys in the neighborhood were selling goods hot on the streets. It turned out to be a big score for them. Dad kept shaking his head and looking at my arm.

"I can't believe you did that to yourself, Frankie."

"Why? We all did it. Why shouldn't she?" Patrick's soft voice crept out. No one could believe he said it, so pure, so innocent. It just stopped everyone, even Dad. He didn't stop there, "She loved Mom just as much as us. I think it looks great."

Ryan saw Dad and Ian get red. He jumped in, "Me too, Frankie. That was really brave." He put his arm around me like I was one of the guys.

Seamus laughed, "Yeah, didn't it hurt like hell?"

"Well, yeah, but I didn't care. It felt good."

We all laughed, except for Dad and Ian. "You stole that from me."

"No, I didn't. It was on the table and I saved it." To be honest I didn't understand why Ian was so angry. I figured he'd be flattered that I put his tattoo design on my skin. Dad, I could understand, I was only fourteen.

Patrick put down his fork, "Hey, Frankie, are you gonna cook tomorrow night?" Seamus and Ryan laughed so hard they practically spit out their food. Ian couldn't help it. He cracked a smile. Everyone's plate was full.

"I don't know," I said. "Do you guys want a girl with a tattoo to prepare food for you? Aren't you afraid of catching the tattoo cooties?"

The guys all laughed. Dad was insulted. "What is wrong with my food?"

Ian looked at him, "Dad let's face it, you can't cook for shit."

We all joined in, "Yeah Dad, it sucks."

"If there was no food left in the world and I had to eat this or die, it would be a hard choice." Patrick was frank.

We all got a kick out of how outspoken Patrick was. It was like he was finding his voice. Maybe all that dancing was helping him express himself. Dad didn't argue. He knew it was true.

"Alright. I'll cook tomorrow, but only if Ian tells me how good my tattoo looks.

"C'mon, Ian, tell her." Ryan punched his arm.

Seamus and Patrick cheered, "Frankie your tattoo looks cool. It's the best."

Ian looked at my arm; "You really are one crazy girl, Frankie Finnegan."

"So?"

"I still don't think you should've done it, but it does look great. I mean whoever designed it is very talented."

Ryan went over to Dad, "When are you getting yours?"

"Yeah, Dad," Patrick laughed.

"Come on, Dad, then we'll all have one," Seamus egged him on.

"Oh no, forget it. I'm not marking up my body with that shit."

I looked at my arm. It was perfect. I looked around at my brothers. We were all the same. We belonged with each other.

I hated the way Dad referred to the tattoo of 'Mom' as shit. I got pissed off and turned to him, "But it's Mom."

He looked at it, then he touched it, "No it's not, it's a tattoo.

Chapter 14: LEAVING QUEENS

Ronald Reagan won the Republican Presidential Nomination in 1980 and picked George Bush to be his running mate. Dad said we were all in trouble. Not only was he a Republican but an actor to boot. It looked like The Peanut Man, Jimmy Carter, would probably be sent back to his peanut farm. We all tried to cope as best we could without our mother. I was seventeen now and I was used to my life in Queens. I went into the village, a lot to see Mario and all my friends in Little Italy. Bobby Fiorintino, a neighborhood guy, and I had been going steady for eight months. That was a record for me, and I was ready to move on. It was very hard for me to stay with a guy past a few weeks. I usually let them have what they wanted and then got bored. I couldn't seem to allow myself to become emotionally attached to anyone. I knew how to have sex and pretend that I enjoyed it, but the truth was, it was the most empty and lonely feeling in the whole world. I knew it made the boys happy. They were always running back for more, like little puppies, but I didn't feel anything for any of them. I let them touch me and do things because I thought that's what I was supposed to do. I went out with practically everyone in the neighborhood. The guys thought I was the coolest girl, especially because of my tattoo. In school I wasn't allowed to show it. The nuns called my father and said, "She has to wear long sleeves all year round, otherwise she will be expelled. She's a bad influence on the other girls." All the girls wanted to be like me, but they didn't have the balls because they didn't have the pain that I did. People do not just become a certain way overnight; it's the experiences in one's life that creates the personality. I couldn't teach all these girls to be cool, tough and seemingly fearless. I had been in the school of 'rough and tumble' for seventeen years now. I wouldn't wish it on any of them.

Dad decided he couldn't live in our house anymore. There were too many memories, too many things that made him miss Mom. In the beginning, I think it comforted him. The reminders made him feel close to her, but he finally realized he was in love with her ghost.

One morning, I went down to the kitchen and he said, "This is her house." He was in a trance. "It's her house. It never belonged to me. Every little corner has her touch, not mine. When I look at you kids, all the goodness I see is from her not me." I almost said, 'no, Dad that's not true', but I would've only said it to make him feel better because it was true. "We're moving," he said. "Out to Long Island, by my brother." We were going to leave good old Queens behind. Seamus didn't care because he was living at the dorms at NYU. Patrick didn't want to leave. He had just been offered a part in a Broadway show called, Chorus Line. I was so proud of him and couldn't wait until opening night. Ryan was with the same girl for three years, Sharon Shea; they were getting married and he didn't want to move. Ian didn't care as long as there was place for him to paint.

It would take a while for Dad to find a house, but he wanted us to prepare ourselves. He told us to say our goodbyes and complete any unfinished business. I really didn't know how I felt about the whole thing. In a way I was relieved to break up with Bobby. He loved me, but I couldn't say I loved him. I was afraid if I did love him or anyone, they would be taken away by some tragic event. When it came to relationships I felt like Ian. Love 'em and leave 'em and never let anyone in 'cause then you won't get hurt.

One of the things I wanted to do was write a letter to Antoinette. I had to tell her we were moving so she would know where to reach us. We had been writing each other ever since she left. Her letters were always filled with love and a longing to see me, and especially Ian, again. When I received her letters, I would read them to Ian. He listened, but they made him crazy. She wrote to him in the beginning, but he was so angry he didn't respond. I told her he loved her too much and that it was hard for him. She wrote about some guys she dated. Nothing was ever meaningful. She said it was just to pass the time. I watched Ian do the same. I told her there were so many paintings of her, she must come and see. She assured me she would return someday. I told Ian that and he said, "Yeah, and so will Jesus."

Dad had been saving all his money to buy a house. It was astounding how much he saved by not drinking. It seemed like this time he was really through with it. We could only hope. Ryan had boxed everywhere by now. He was forbidden to fight outside the ring, because his hands were considered lethal weapons. He was so physically strong, like I mean he could kill anybody with his bare hands but had one of the most kind and gentle hearts of anyone I knew. I was happy he and Sharon were together. She loved him so much. She didn't care where we moved, she said nothing could break them apart.

Patrick was at dance rehearsals every night in Manhattan. His dreams were coming true, Broadway, wow. Michael didn't make the cut, but he was happy for Patrick. He met him every night after rehearsal so they could come home together. Michael didn't like Patrick coming home late at night by himself. Patrick had to be ready to start his run on Broadway in three months. Patrick said if Dad found a house before then, he would just stay at Michael's until his run was over in Chorus Line.

One night at about one o'clock in the morning Patrick and Michael got off the train the number 7 Flushing line, which went from Times Square all the way to Shea Stadium. They exited at our usual stop, Court House Square. At the bottom of the stairs was a gang of tough guys just looking for trouble, which was pretty per usual in my neighborhood. They all wore leather motorcycle jackets, smoked cigarettes and thought looking dirty was cool. Patrick was carrying his turquoise dance bag, wearing his orange tights and tan bodysuit, as Michael walked beside him. They were talking and laughing about the show. They saw the troublemakers waiting as they walked down the stairs. They tried to act calm. But Patrick was very nervous. He hated confrontation. Michael was stronger when it came to that kind of thing. He knew Patrick was damaged from everything that went on in our house. He would protect Patrick no matter what. They ignored them and walked right by. One of the guys, creator face Jerome, flicked his lit cigarette at Patrick, "Hey fag boy, whatta ya got in your pocketbook?" All the tough guys laughed. Patrick and Michael kept walking.

Another guy, Augie, stepped in front of them, "He asked you a question, faggot!"

Michael pushed by him, "Look we don't want any trouble."

The other three guys surrounded them.

"Trouble? A couple of queers like you think you can give us any trouble?" Jerome came over into Michael's face.

"I didn't say that." Michael tried to remain calm.

"What did you say, huh? Tell me which one of you takes it up the ass?" They all laughed. Patrick froze with fear. Jerome wouldn't let up, "Hey dancer boy, I think I want my cock sucked. How 'bout you boys?"

They all cheered on Jerome. He started shoving Patrick into a corner as he reached for his zipper. Michael punched Jerome hard in the face. Blood shot out of his nose. All the tough guys started beating on Michael and Patrick.

Out of nowhere a pair of huge hands ripped each guy off of them. Punches were flying and heads were being kicked in. Like in a Bruce Lee film, the hero was standing in the middle of all these assholes, it was Ryan. Ready to kill every fucking one of those bastards who came near his baby brother. They didn't know what the fuck hit them, but they were scared shitless and praying for mercy. Sharon stood aside. He went nuts. He fought the way I always imagined Uncle Jim fought. I'd heard so many stories, but they sounded exaggerated. Now I knew where Ryan got his strength. It was definitely the Irish genes. Patrick said it was like Batman and Robin...only he didn't need Robin. He took out all five guys with his lethal weapon, bare hands. They were all bloody on the concrete. They tried to jump him from behind.

They went at him with knives, cracked bottles and chucks, but he swatted them off like flies. Ryan warned them that if they ever even looked at Patrick or Michael again, he would bury them without a funeral.

Patrick never told us he was gay. He didn't have to. We all knew for a long time. Once, when I was in the city visiting with Mario, I stopped by the theater where Patrick was working. I wanted to surprise him. I told the guy at the door that I had a meeting with one of the dancers. He wanted to know which one. When I said, Patrick Finnegan, he let out a high-pitched squeal, "Oh that Patrick, he's a cutie."

"He's my brother." I was proud.

"Oh well, why didn't you say so? Come on in and watch him do his magic. He's got such a tight butt. Don't worry, I know he's taken. That Michael is sure lucky. He's not half bad himself, aahh!"

He said all that with no pause in between, as he placed one hand on his chest, the other waved back and forth like a flag and oohh's and ahh's in all the right places. He let me sit in the back row. Patrick had no idea I was there. The music was pumping, and the dancers were tapping, jumping, stomping and moving like rubber bands. The blood in my veins was flowing with exuberance as I watched Patrick own that stage, with his toes and hands pointed perfectly. His body was lean, but solid.

He lifted this girl like she was a feather, straight over his head. The director would shout, "Okay from the top, a one and a two and a three." They would line up, take a breath and be in perfect sync with each other. It was fascinating. I was so proud of my big brother. He had more confidence than anyone I had ever seen, even more than Ian. That stage, those lights, the music, the steps, the costumes, the energy, all of it transformed him. It literally breathed life into his being. When I watched him perform, I knew dancing was what he was born to do. That same aching feeling of intimidation began creeping in on me, similar to how I felt when I discovered what a wonderful artist Ian was, painting was his calling. All of my brothers seemed to find their calling. I was still trying to figure out what I was supposed to be doing with my life. When the music stopped, the director yelled, "Let's take an hour for lunch." I saw this guy walk up to Patrick and touch him in a very sexual way, then he took a towel and wiped the sweat off Patrick's face.

I went backstage to see Patrick. He was so happy to see me. I was introduced to everyone including the towel guy, Simon. We all had lunch together. I kept talking about Michael, and Patrick got quiet, which made me think there was trouble in paradise and this towel guy, Simon had his eye on my brother.

I left them to go back home. On the way I thought about my brothers. How they were all so different. How they all knew exactly what they wanted. They were all doing what they loved.

But I was doing nothing. I didn't know what I wanted. Even Dad was clearer than ever. He wanted to move into a house and open a restaurant. He met two guys who were going to go in as partners.

Dad owning a restaurant seemed hilarious, since he was the worst cook in the history of mankind. Of course, they would hire a chef. It would be a lot of work and long hours, but he said it would be good for him. He had too much time on his hands. For Dad, too much time meant time to think and time to drink. He didn't want to do either. Both were deadly.

Mario was heart-broken that I was moving, but I promised I would visit. I told him Dad found a house in a place called Seaford, Long Island. It was really nice and not too far from the city. "There's a train called the Long Island Railroad, very easy, you bring the cart that I gave you on the train, come here to me and I fill your cart up extra since you can't come that often, okay?"

"Okay." I said with a big smile.

The week before I moved, we talked every day for hours and on the last night he pulled out a vintage bottle of Brunello di Montalcino. He remembered my story about Mr. Vannelli and knew how special that wine was to me. As a matter of fact, he remembered everything I ever said or did since the day we met. I feel like he understood me more than anyone in my life. He made me a feast to die for. Everything was home grown. I swear if I closed my eyes it tasted like Mom's. It had all the right ingredients, but the one that I tasted the most was love. Mario finally got used to my tattoo. He admitted it was beautiful. He laughed and said, "I think I would've been in love with your Mamma." I assured him he would have. When it came time to leave, he pulled out a box, "Francesca, a going away present for you." I opened the box. It was full of all different packets of herbs and vegetable seeds for me to plant. "I hear Long Island has big back yards. You grow a garden like your Mamma. It will bring you happiness." I hugged him so tight. How thoughtful he was. As I held him, I realized how tiny and frail he was. "My Paisan, you come back. I'll fill your cart."

I started to cry, "You don't have to fill my cart, Mario. I will come just to see you."

"You go now." He couldn't bear to see me shed a tear. In all the years I've been coming to see him, I've never paid for a single thing. He was too good to be true. I took my garden and my cart and headed for the train. When I looked through the cart it was packed. There was basil, oregano, Italian parsley, rosemary, Roma tomatoes, carrots, spinach, arugula, fennel, garlic, squash, everything. I could hear him saying as I left, "Remember to talk to the plants every day. They have big ears and love to listen, especially to music." He believed singing made them grow even faster.

As we packed up our house in Queens, I felt the years of pain and joy surging through my pores. Good and bad, it all filtered through. Dad put on the Victrola as we cleaned out every inch of the house. We had so much junk, so we decided to donate it all to the Salvation Army. Dad said Mom would have wanted it that way. He asked me to help him pack his room. "I'm terrified to do it alone Frankie." Reaching out, he grabbed my hand. I hadn't gone into their room in years. It was definitely haunted by Mom. I could still smell her scent. Her closet had not been touched. Her clothes were hanging as if she would be coming in at any moment to choose something to wear. The shoes were lined up neatly, all shaped to fit her feet. As I touched her clothes I fell apart. I folded each piece with a tenderness that only Mom knew. I didn't want to give her clothes away, but I knew Dad was right, she would want some poor family to have them. There were certain things I kept, like her dress in Ian's painting of "Mom at the Stove." A sweater she wore all the time. It was a green wool cozy one. Way in the back of the closet I found a hatbox. I was puzzled. Mom never wore hats. It was full of pictures, letters, and mementos. There were photos of her in Italy when she was young. Aunt Carmella, Nanny Juliano and I guessed, Grandpa Juliano. I saw the house where she lived. It looked exactly how I always pictured it. Digging deeper, I found a bunch of pictures of Mom with some guy. I bet it was Pasquale D'Amato". There were poems; he dated every single one in the right-hand corner, 1945 and they were addressed to Mom when she lived in Naples. There were pictures of all my brothers and me when we were little. Pictures of my dad, he was so handsome. There was one picture that affected me more than any I had ever seen. Mom must've taken it because she wasn't in it. It was on our front stoop. I was in front with my hands in my pockets, my brothers were in a row behind me, and my father stood behind them. Three separate rows, one family, no mother. Not one of us was smiling. I couldn't tell if it was before or after the Cuban man, but I know I felt separate.

I decided I would save everything in the hatbox, just the way it was. Obviously, all these things were treasures to Mom. Now they would become mine. I also knew that someday I would go to Naples and visit the house where my mother was born. Now I had the address. After reading all the letters from Pasquale, I felt his profound love for Mom. There were some letters I didn't understand. He explained that he knew he must say goodbye for now, but he knew they would surely meet again, perhaps in heaven. I guess Mom felt safe to keep all her mementos in this hatbox. Dad would never think to look there, but then again, he couldn't understand Italian.

Chorus line was all the rage on Broadway and Patrick was a major success. Every time he came on the stage, my heart sank for him. I think I was more nervous than he was. The audience clapped and cheered. He was part of something big and Ryan, Ian and Seamus were very proud. Dad wanted to be, but I could sense his resistance to Patrick's whole lifestyle; He didn't think his choices were appropriate. Dad would never say the word gay. He would always say, “I don't think it's right for Patrick to be a dancer; your Mother wouldn't approve.” And when Patrick told Nanny and Grumpy Finnegan, he was gay they said they wished he hadn’t told them. Nanny said they were old and could’ve lived the rest of their lives without knowing that bit of information. Patrick didn’t care. It made him feel better to tell the truth. He was tired of all the secrets and lies and wasn’t ashamed of who he was. When the play ended, there was a standing ovation. Patrick came out and took his bow. The crowd cheered. We all howled like a bunch of groupies from Queens. I hooted and hollered and then I cried with joy.

“Good for you, Patrick, good for you.” I whispered into the Broadway Theater.

There was a big party at Joe Allen’s afterwards. Our whole family was invited. Dad went home. When we saw Patrick there, he was so happy. "Where's Dad?" He wondered.

"You were great, man." Ryan hugged him.

"Hey twinkle toes. Fred Astaire, look out," Seamus laughed. Patrick smiled.

Simon walked over, "Is this the Fam?"

"The Fam?" Ian said with disgust.

Patrick jumped in, "Everyone this is Simon. Simon, my family."

"I heard all about you. All of you," he said in his best flaming way. We didn't stay too long. Ian was uncomfortable. Michael was there, but he seemed to be less and less important to Patrick. This was upsetting. I didn't care for Simon. I went over to Michael, who was sitting alone with his drink. "Hey handsome."

"Hey, Frankie." He wasn't his usual self.

"What are you doin' all by your lonesome?" I kept it light.

"Seems Patrick's found some new friends. I'm not sure where I fit in."

"I know what you mean. It'll pass. He knows you're the best."

"From your mouth to his ears."

"I'm gonna go, my brothers are restless."

"I'm gonna go with you, he won't even notice."

We all went to say goodbye to Patrick. He was laughing and celebrating. He kissed all of us goodbye, even Michael. He said if he didn't want to stay, he'd see him later. Michael was crushed.

Our house was completely packed in boxes and we were ready to move. Nanny and Grumpy Finnegan came, so did Nanny Juliano and Aunt Carmella. Friends from the neighborhood all came to see us off. It was a big deal. The Finnegan Clan was waving goodbye to Queens. The number 7 train rumbled above as kids played stickball under the El. As I looked at them, I couldn't help but fear for their safety in this cruel and unpredictable world. I asked God and Mom to protect all of these young innocent kids, protect them from perpetrators like the Cuban man and help them have a happy childhood. Then I realized I had one last thing to do before I said goodbye to Queens. It was time to face my demon, but I wouldn't do it alone. I went around the corner to the brown and white apartment building where the Cuban man raped me. I put Mom in my pocket and rubbed my thumb along the palm of my right hand. The scar was still there, but I was no longer willing to let the incident keep me in chains. I wanted to leave it all behind. I asked Mom to climb each flight with me and to help me be strong. I relived the whole thing with each step. Remembering the day, what I was wearing and how I was feeling. I watched it all flash in front of my eyes. I saw the spot where God left the piece of glass that saved me. I smiled and thanked him. I kept hearing Mom, 'It's okay now Francesca. Time to let go, move on and be free. He has no power over you anymore.' My legs pumped up the stairs to the very top. I promised myself I would even go to the roof, scariest of all. Thankfully I never got to see it before this moment. I spread my arms wide to the sky. Yes, I did it! The train roared by. I could see passengers through the windows of the cars because I was so high up. Everything looked different from up here. I lived in Queens my whole life and I always thought it was so big and I was so small, but today I realized how small it was and how big I was. This was a feeling I wanted to hold on to. When I turned to go back down, I noticed Dad standing there watching me. I was completely taken aback. He said he followed me because he was worried about me. After waiting outside the building for a while, he decided to come and make sure I was okay and then he started to cry.

"Francesca, I'm so sorry." He never called me that in my whole life. I let him finish. "I should've been there for you. I didn't know what to do. I thought your mother would know what to do and she thought I would, but the truth is we didn't know what to do so we did nothing. We left you alone and that was wrong. You were only a little girl..."

I couldn't believe what I was hearing. Dad could barely breathe as the tears poured out. "I hated what happened. I denied it to myself thinking if I pretended it didn't happen it would go away, but it never did and the one that suffered most was you."

"Dad..." I couldn't finish my sentence because I could barely breath. It was almost too much to see him falling apart this way.

"Please let me finish. I have to get this all out 'cause it's been eating me up forever and I don't want to drink again.'

"Okay Dad, I'm listening."

"I know you still hate me, and I don't blame you. You have every reason to. I did a lot of bad things and I am not proud of myself." He sat on the roof and held his head in his hands. "God, I miss your mother so much, she was my life, my love, my everything."

"Then why did you hit her all the time?"

"I didn't want to Frankie. It was like a disease, a cancer, eating me up, I had no control. Just like my dad."

"Grumpy?" I didn't understand. He was as quiet as a church mouse.

"Yeah, Grumpy. Nobody knows what I'm about to tell you, not even your brothers, but I think it's time."

I sat down next to Dad and he told me the story of his childhood as the trains rumbled by in both directions.

Turning into a little boy, Dad admitted that Grumpy was a terrible blackout alcoholic, just like him and Uncle Jim. Apparently, it ran in the family and he told me to watch out because it was in our blood. He looked at me long and hard in complete silence and then grabbed both of my hands in his for the next part. Dad had a little sister, Margaret, the cutest little thing he ever saw. She was a red head just like me and Mom. I felt Dad's hands trembling with sweat as he opened up the Finnegan lock box. "Pop had just been laid off from the telephone company and times were tough. He barely had two nickels to rub together and many mouths to feed. Instead of coming home he went to the pub and spent whatever he had on whiskey. My mother was feeding little Margaret in her high-chair, and I was making choo-choo train sounds, little Maggie loved that." He stopped to catch his breath. "Pop stumbled in drunk out of his mind. Nanny told him to go sleep it off, but he was in a mood and was going on and on about this country and our economy and how was he supposed to take care of a family. Well just at that moment my brother Jim ran in saying how he needed new shoes 'cause his had holes in the toes and all the kids in school were making fun of him. That was enough to put Pop over the edge. He went after Jim, but Jim started running around the table and around Margaret's high-chair. Jesus, it all happened so fast."

"What happened, Dad?"

"Jim pissed off my father and he was so drunk that he couldn't see straight. He picked up a paperweight and threw it at Jim, but hit Margaret instead, right in her little head. She was gone in an instant." Dad lost it. "I could still see her face, Mom's face, and my poor brother Jim's face. No one could move. Time stopped. Little Margaret would never see another day and we would never be the same, ever, even to this very day. My brother, Jim, blamed himself forever. I blamed myself for not jumping in front of it."

I couldn't believe Dad held that in for all of these years. He never even told Mom. The family shame was unbearable, and it was swept under the rug. They weren't even allowed to have a proper funeral because they didn't want anyone knowing the truth. Nothing happened to Grumpy, because it was an accident, and that is how they reported it to the police. Little Margaret accidentally banged her head and it killed her. And they all swore to carry that one to the grave, but now I knew. There was no point in letting Grumpy and Nanny know and what good would come of it anyway? Grumpy's sentence was a living hell and no chance for redemption. His long walks had nothing to do with getting fresh bread or keeping strong. They were strictly to keep him from losing his mind. No wonder he never spoke. I'm surprised he didn't kill himself. I know I would have. How can anyone live with themselves after murdering their own child? Accident or not, he killed her. And the reason no one was allowed on the second floor was because Margaret's room was still intact, and there were shrines with her pictures all around. Their silence was their prison, but somehow, they thought the lie would be easier than the truth.

"The Irish and their pride." Dad shook his head. "It kills you one way or the other."

Finally, Dad made sense to me. I could see him, the real him. I could start to try and love him. His truth began to thaw the ice on my heart. It was a start. I decided to keep Dad's secret. Not because he asked me to, but because it wasn't mine to share. I knew the suffering he went through to reveal his shame and I wanted to respect the sacredness of his trust in me.

***

Queens would go on just fine without us. Nothing ever changes and somehow everything does. I walked through our empty house once more. Bella ran through the rooms like she was a puppy again. She had never been in the rooms when they were empty, and neither had I. It was strange. Lonely air hung all around me, as did the fragrance of my mother, stabbing grief into my heart. The walls had echoes of memories passing through - screams of agony, peals of laughter. Each room brought a different memory. Each scent stimulated an emotion. How could one house bear to hold so much? If a stranger walked in, I felt as if they would know the whole Finnegan story; the secrets, the lies, the sorrow and regret. The never accomplished dreams and the broken promises were all held here. The energy was fierce. The house couldn't lie. I thanked that old house and prayed for it. It had been through so much and it was still standing, still proud, still willing to go on. Maybe it had its own dream. A dream that the next family who came inside would bring it happiness and it would do the same for them.

I yelled through the house as I ran with Bella. I climbed the stairs imagining Mom was with me. Maybe she'd always be here. The next family would feel her. "Goodbye Mom. We have to move. I love you, Mommy. Daddy loves you too. We all do." Bella barked loud, she agreed.

I went through the kitchen. Mom’s stove was still there. Dad said we were getting a new one. I don't know why, that one worked just fine. At least we had a painting of it. I let the kitchen fill up my senses, every one of them. My skin tingled. I looked once more at Mom's garden. I promised her I would start a new one in our new house. I grabbed Bella and walked down the long hallway to the front door. Dad was honking the horn, "C'mon, Frankie, we gotta go." I opened the front door and walked through. As I slammed it shut, I heard the familiar sound that only that front door had. Every door has a different sound when it closes. Some are peaceful, inviting, loud, or scary. And each door holds a distinct feeling. I knew I was closing this one for the last time and the sound penetrated my whole body.

Chapter 15: BELLA LUNA

Long Island was a whole different world than Queens. It was tranquil and clean with green lawns manicured to perfection and trees everywhere. Everyone seemed to have gardeners who came and cut their grass. The houses were fancy, and the cars were more expensive than the ones we had in Queens. The neighbors came over and introduced themselves. Smiling, they said if we needed anything to give them a holler and seemed genuinely happy to have us in the neighborhood. It made me a little uncomfortable at first. I was used to frowning, bitter, angry faces; faces that seemed to struggle through each day. Our new house was big and delicious with big windows all around so the sun could fill it up easily. Life looked a little brighter in this house. I never realized how dark our house was in Queens. The sun could never seem to shine through, but here the golden hues of sunlight spilled through the glass panes like a fountain overflowing with luminous possibilities. Ian had a great room. He loved the natural light, which affected his paintings; they really had a lighter energy. He was getting close to having a show. Maybe Antoinette would fly in for his big night.

I had my own room with a door that closed, which was fitting for a seventeen-year-old girl who now had noticeable breast. It was the first time in my life that I could actually have privacy. I didn't know what to do with myself.

There was a big pool in the back yard and lots of space for my garden. We had two kitchens. One upstairs and one downstairs. I still don't know how Dad could afford it. I knew it couldn't have been just from his construction job. Perhaps he got lucky with the bookies and a lot of his football teams won, but I never asked.

There was plenty of room for all of us, but Ian and I seemed to be the only ones around. Patrick stayed in the city most of the time, Seamus lived at the NYU dorms and came home on weekends, and Ryan and Sharon were planning their wedding.

Swimming became my new obsession. I would do a hundred laps a day. In the beginning it was the only thing that helped me sleep. Long Island was too quiet. I could actually hear crickets. It was dead silent at night. I was used to having the sound of the screeching train above our house and fighting, screaming drunks on their way home from the bars. Silence was foreign to me. That's why I started to swim. I would bury myself deep under the water. I'd scale along the bottom and push my way to the other side. I felt like a mermaid. The only sound I could hear was the beating of my heart. I was safe, free from the world. I'd hold my breath as long as I could. I never wanted to come up. It became my friend and a safe haven to work things out. Just me and the water flowing and ebbing through the constant changes my life presented.

Dad found a restaurant on the Upper East Side. He said it was a prime location and that if I wanted to work for him when I was through with school, I could. I was flattered that he asked me, but I was still struggling with letting Dad into my heart. I wanted to, desperately. And now that I knew his demons and struggles, I felt more compassion for him. More than I ever dreamed possible, but it was still hard. How do I let this man, my father, into my heart? I feared it wouldn't be possible. There was too much damage. Just because I now knew Dad's story, his deep wound, it didn't make mine go away. I prayed to Mom to help me forgive him and love him, but every time I looked at his face, I just couldn't help feeling that I wished he had died instead of Mom. He told me on the roof, the only reason he went on was because of us kids. Mom would kill him if he didn't do right by us. He swore he was doing the best he could and begged me to help him be a better father.

Dad's restaurant was Italian, and he asked me to help him with the menu. I agreed and thought it was worth a shot. Every night I would make a different dish for him to see if he wanted it on the menu. Dad loved everything I made.

Sundays were still a family day. We all ate together at four-thirty sharp. Everyone voted on the dishes I made, to decide what should go on the menu. It was fun. Dad really appreciated my enthusiasm. He said it made him realize how right his decision was about opening a restaurant. He really started to depend on me.

"You look more and more like your mother every time I look at you." Dad smiled at me after dinner. “And you cook like her too.”

"Thanks, Dad." It was the nicest compliment he had ever given me.

"I'll never be able to find a cook as good as you."

I didn't know what to say. He was trying so hard. It wasn't ‘I love you’, but it meant the same thing.

Dad consulted me on every decision about the restaurant. He would be opening in a few months and he wanted to be ready for anything.

"What should we name it, Frankie?"

"Bella Luna” just flew out of my mouth. Bella jumped on me as if I called her. "Yeah, Bella Luna, let's shoot for the moon."

The next few months I went to school, gardened, swam and prepared the menu for Dad. Virginia came over a lot because she lived closer. She loved to go skinny-dipping with me. She also loved to be the official taster for all the new dishes I prepared.

Ryan and Sharon decided to make the wedding sooner. I thought it was strange, but Ian told me she was pregnant, and she didn't want to walk in the house of God with a big belly sticking out of her white dress. I promised to keep it a secret. I was excited to learn I was going to be an aunt.

They got married at St. Mary's in Queens. All their friends from the old neighborhood came. The church looked so small to me, smaller than I had remembered it. Everyone looked different and I was changing. My brother's friends, who were always too cool for school, were now paying attention to me.

"Hey, Frankie, you really look great."

"Yeah, you're really growin' up nice."

"You got a boyfriend out there where you're livin'?"

"Yeah, I do," I lied. "I'm in love." I shut them all up. I tried hard not to be cynical. These guys never gave me the time of day when I lived here and now because I'd gotten bigger boobs and a nice ass, they suddenly saw that I was alive and breathing. What was even funnier was that they thought I might consider going out with them.

Ryan and Sharon found an apartment in Queens, but they promised they would still come to Sunday dinners. As much as it drove me crazy not to have any privacy in Queens because my brothers were always around me, now that they weren't, I missed them.

One day I took the Long Island Railroad back to see Mario. It had been a while since I'd visited him. I brought my cart. He smiled when he saw me wheeling it up the street. "Francesca, come look at these tomatoes."

It was as if I'd seen him yesterday. He hugged me as he handed me a vine of red Roma tomatoes.

"You must come and see the garden I planted with your seeds," I said enthusiastically.

"I can picture it in my head." He cupped my face with his hand, "Bella figa, you're growing up so fast."

"Dad got a restaurant. I named it Bella Luna." This excited him. We spoke in Italian, which I missed so much.

"I'm going to write the menu in Italian."

He said, "Americans are lazy, you better have the translation next to it."

"Once school finishes, I'm gonna cook there."

"Just cover your tattoo. The other cooks might think you are funny."

What he meant to say is they might think I'm a dyke, but he was being nice. A lot of people did think that, but I didn't care. I loved my tattoo, and never once have I regretted getting it.

On the grand opening of Bella Luna, the place looked great. Dad got a piano and hired two opera singers. There was a line outside the door because of the sizzling garlic and olive oil wafting from the kitchen. This was a trick I came up with to entice all the pedestrians on the streets. Every day at about 4:45 we opened all the doors, got the pans hot with olive oil and ready for action. We would throw the garlic in the pans and then put the fan on low. It would push the smell out and onto the busy streets of Manhattan. Businessmen and women leaving work would forget their day and smile with delight. And even if they weren't hungry, the aroma was sure to arouse their bellies. It was all about temptation. Perhaps they were thinking of another restaurant, but once they followed the scent and then tasted the food, we would have them hooked. The head cook, Luciano, said he'd heard all about my cooking and hoped he could do as well. He was superb. I realized that although this was not my dream, I had finally found something that made me happy; a family restaurant. Dad really did his homework. He ordered magazines from Tuscany and Venice, and had Ian paint the walls in an authentic style.

Dad's partners were thrilled. They were not very talkative guys. Mafiosa types. Dad said he needed them for the money and connections, but he was the brains behind it all. They looked around constantly as if they were waiting for something to happen. Their friends showed up one by one, all in Cadillacs. They kissed each other on the cheek as they entered Bella Luna. It was like one big family. Even Mario showed up. I was thrilled to see him.

As the singers belted out Puccini and Vivaldi, the food went around. The wine was flowing. We had everything from portabello mushrooms sautéed with garlic, tomato and radicchio, to linguini pescatore, pesto lasagna, and pasta al forno. From the grill we served rack of lamb, veal chop fit for a king and tournedos of beef in a cabernet peppercorn reduction sauce. Side table we served a Tomahawk steak for two, this was my absolute favorite, literally melted in your mouth like butter. It was a big-ticket item. From the brick oven we served pizzas and flatbreads. For dessert we had cannolis, napoleons, rum cake, berries with Zabaglione, pignoli cookies and ice box cake, my aunt let us use her famous recipe. The customers were beside themselves. "We will be back." "We'll tell our friends." "This is the best restaurant in the city." Everyone was delighted. But Dad's partners barely cracked a smile.

"I heard you're the one who came up with the menu." A dark mysterious man grabbed me as if I were going to be shot.

"Yes, I did."

"It's so good I wanna punch myself." He flashed a quick smile revealing crooked teeth and then went right back to being a stone-faced thug.

"Thank you, I guess." I thought it was a strange thing to say. Dad said it was the highest compliment I could get. Go figure.

"I'm Vito." One of his eyes looked at me, the other one was staring at the ceiling.

"I'm Francesca." Talking to the one eye that was looking at me.

"I can't believe a girl with a face of Ireland can warm a Guinea's heart like this."

"My mother was a hundred percent Italian." I made it very clear.

"Yes, I heard. God bless her." He made the sign of the cross and kissed his closed fist. Vito was strange, but I liked him. "Ya dunn good, kid." He walked away.

Chapter 16: YOUNG PATRICK

Ryan and Sharon had a baby girl, Isabella, in honor of Mom. Born on October 17, 1982. It was the first child born to start the next generation of Finnegan's. I was excited that a girl came through the gene pool, but I was sure she had a tough time fighting off the male DNA trying to dominate her existence. Perhaps she would be the one to get the Finnegan's on the right track. Dad was a proud grandfather and all of my brothers were uncles. Life was moving on. The following week I walked into Ian's studio and discovered a new painting entitled, "Birth." It was little Isabella in the nursery, a woman's hand outstretched to touch her, but she couldn't. What symbolism. It was clear that Ian thought about Mom almost as much as I did. There was a piece of her in all of his paintings. Ian called a man who gave him his card at Bella Luna; Zack Shumaker, was his name. He came to the house to view Ian's work. He was astounded and offered to set up a show for Ian. He said he would put up all the money and it would be in a gallery downtown, in the Village. Zack said it was the happening spot for new artists.

The show was going to open on my 19th birthday, which felt like a good sign. I knew Ian was excited, even though he never let on.

I was working at Bella Luna full-time as head chef. Dad said I was the youngest and best chef in New York City. I would take fresh herbs and vegetables from my garden every day and use them at the restaurant. I just pinched a little of my love in every single dish. I know that's what made the difference in my cooking; it was Mom's secret. A couple of weeks before his art show, Ian called me up to his room, which was also his art studio. "Frankie, I want to show you something." He had a white sheet covering a large canvas. "I wanted you to be the first one to see my last piece for the show." He pulled the sheet off, "Now I'm ready!" He said full of pride.

I stood before it frozen. My eyes began to stream with tears as the vision washed over my heart. I couldn't speak. It was Mom in her garden, kneeling down in the soil. Each herb and vegetable looked so real, it was as if you could pick it and eat it.

"How do you like it?" He waited for my answer.

"I love it." I cried.

He'd captured Mom once again - her beauty, her essence. He'd even captured the feeling of being in the garden. It was as if you were in the painting, feeling the serenity that the garden brings you. The sun was dancing on Mom's golden red locks.

"She looks so beautiful, Ian."

Ian looked confused for a second. He turned me toward him and looked into my face. "She's you, Frankie."

My heart split wide open. A rush of joy surged through every blood vessel in my being.

I was speechless. I had been throwing myself at him for years, wanting him to paint me like one of his models, but he knew that wasn't me. He saw me in the garden and documented a piece of myself that I never got to see because I was in it.

"Frankie, will you do me a big favor?"

"Anything." I wiped the tears off my face.

"Will you cater the show? Nobody cooks like you."

"I would love to."

"I'll get Zack to pay you."

"It's my present to you."

"Thanks, Frankie."

“Thank you, Ian." He hugged me tight as we stood before his latest masterpiece.

"What did you name it?" I knew Ian always named his paintings.

He answered simply, "Francesca."

The night of the show arrived, which also meant it was my birthday. I was nineteen. I was so excited for Ian, and I made all of his favorites.

I got to the showroom hours before anyone else. I had to set up. Ian's paintings hung on the walls. It was quiet. I could feel each piece speaking to me. They all had a story to tell.

Little by little the showroom started filling up. I saw familiar faces and new faces. Many of the people looked wealthy. I say that because they were very well dressed and wore very expensive shoes. Shoes say a lot about a person’s financial status. Zack was making the rounds and schmoozing. Ian called Patrick earlier that night so he could make a fancy tie for him. He bought a silk suit, blue with an orange silk tie and a white silk shirt. He looked like a painting himself.

Ian invited Michael because he was around through all the years. He never said it, but I think he liked Patrick and Michael together, too. Michael was so happy to be there. He looked dashing, but I could tell he missed Patrick. He admitted to me that he was having a hard time just getting through the day. They had been together since they were nine. I told him I couldn't imagine Patrick was really in love with Simon, but I thought he'd gotten swept away with the whole Broadway scene. I hoped he would come to his senses. Michael said he wouldn't be staying long. It was too hard for him to see Patrick with Simon. To all of our surprise Patrick showed up alone. He didn't look well.

Michael knew him better than anyone. "Something is wrong," He whispered to me.

"Maybe he and Prince Charming broke up." I was hoping.

"If Simon hurt him, I'll kill him." Michael got angry.

"Michael, don't you realize he's your competition?"

"I don't care. I can't stand to see Patrick hurt."

I hugged him, "You amaze me. How can you be so good?"

“I love him, Frankie," he admitted without shame.

"I know you do."

Michael went over to Patrick. I watched them. They were so connected. The moment Michael touched Patrick's arm,

Patrick broke down and pulled Michael into him. There was so much going on all around that no one really noticed.

I walked around and mingled, but I felt more like I was eavesdropping. I wanted to hear what everyone had to say about the brilliant artist whose work was being viewed, Ian Finnegan, my big brother. The vote was unanimous. He was the new hot artist. Everyone was going crazy, including Zack. Ian had a future as major player in the world of art. Now he would get paid for his work, his passion. He beamed all night as people came over to talk to him. He was humble, even shy. A few times I caught him blushing. The women were going gaga over him. I mean, the paintings were gorgeous, but when they saw the man behind the paintings they were smitten. He was flattered but didn't seem interested. So many times during the evening I caught his eyes turning up to Antoinette hovering over him, as she sat up on the wall, poised and inviting. Her eyes were on him all night, too.

The saddest part about the evening was that soon all these paintings would be sold. “Mom At The Stove” was up on the wall, but there was a little sign underneath, "Not for sale." I was relieved. I noticed a "SOLD” sign posted underneath a painting of Patrick when he was very young.

I grabbed Ian's arm, "Who bought, ‘Young Patrick’?"

He smiled at me, "Michael."

Dad came late. He had business to take care of at Bella Luna. He'd just been to the barber, and even rented a tux. He was the best-dressed guy there and the proudest. I heard him say to people, "That's my son." Dad put his arm around me. "Some night, huh?" He grinned.

"Yeah, some night. It's nineteen years since Kennedy was killed."

"Yeah, I know, but more importantly, it's your birthday."

All the lights went out. I was confused for a second. I thought we were having another blackout. Then I saw a huge cake being wheeled toward me. The candles were flickering in the darkness. All my brothers stood around me. Dad was by my side. Everyone started singing Happy Birthday. As they sang, my mind raced with thoughts. “It's Ian's night, not mine. I don't want to take away from him.” Dad remembered my birthday. Better yet he acknowledged it and JFK was second fiddle to me on this November 22nd. I found out the reason he was late was because he had to pick up the special cake he ordered from Zito's bakery in Little Italy. I looked in his eyes and could see how desperately he longed to be forgiven. I knew he loved me, even if he didn't know how to say it, and I was slowly starting to learn to love him. I flashed on the night my brothers sang to me in the yard when Mom was in the hospital. I caught myself drifting, so I focused on the candles, telling myself to get back in the moment, to surrender to what was in front of my face, which in this case happened to be a huge cake in the shape of a chef's cap which read, "Happy Birthday To The Best Chef In New York."

"Make a wish," my brothers all yelled. I took my time and thought of one. It wasn't a wish for myself really, but I figured since it was Ian's night, too, I'd make a wish for him, that if Antoinette was his true love, she would come back to him. I looked across my cake and caught Ian's eyes twinkling in the candlelight. Then I thought, "I hope it's not selfish, but I have more wishes." I wished for Patrick and Michael to get back together because I knew it was right. I wished for Seamus to change the world through his passion for medicine. I wished for Ryan, Sharon and Isabella to be healthy and happy. I finally caught Dad's eyes smiling at me and I wished that I could find it in my heart to forgive him. I inhaled with all my might and I blew them all out in one powerful gush.

The press snapped photos of Ian all night long. They asked some of the guests their opinions. They'd print the reviews tomorrow. As the crowd grew thin, we made a plan to go out for a nightcap. Zack was treating.

Although I was having fun, I didn't feel like I fit in. Zack wouldn't let go of Ian's arm and I trailed behind. For some reason I couldn't get Patrick's face out of my mind. There was something wrong. I could feel it. I had to call Michael's house to check in on him. I excused myself, but Zack and Ian were too busy to even notice.

As I dialed Michael's number, I got a sick feeling in my stomach.

Michael answered, "Hello?"

"Michael, it's Frankie."

"Hey Frank, I'm so glad you called." He began to cry.

"Is everything okay, Michael?"

"No Frankie, can you come over right away?"

"I'm on my way." I didn't want to hear what was wrong over the phone, so I didn't ask. I found Ian and Zack and told them I was leaving.

"Are you alright Frankie?" Ian noticed the color had left my face.

"Yeah, it's been a long day."

He kissed me, "Happy birthday," and I left.

It was a clear evening, cool and crisp with a crescent moon sitting in the sky. I could feel Thanksgiving just around the corner. I ran toward the subway. “That will take too long,” I thought. A taxi to Queens would probably cost me, but I didn't care. I hailed a cab. My heart was racing. As I got closer to Michael's, I thought of Patrick's face tonight. How lost he looked. It occurred to me that I had always thought of him as my little brother, even though he was older. I would say, "My little brother needs me, my little brother is in trouble. I have to save him." I was hoping it was just that he and Simon had had a fight and he was heartbroken, or maybe he'd been fired from the show.

It was 11:45 p.m. as the taxi pulled up to Michael's apartment. Fifteen minutes left of my birthday.

I knocked on the door, 3C. It was a humble apartment, but the inside looked like an art deco pad. Michael had great taste. "Tiny Dancer," by Elton John, was playing on the stereo. The lights were dim, and candles were lit. It was very romantic. For a moment I felt hopeful. Then I saw Patrick lying on the couch shivering under a blanket. I went to him. Covered in sweat, he looked at me helplessly.

"Hi, Frankie."

"Hello, my baby." I smiled at him. Michael stood on the other side of the couch with his hand over his mouth. Tears fell from his eyes.

Patrick grabbed my hand, "I'm sick, Frankie."

"I know baby, tell me what's wrong." I took the towel that was by the couch. Michael must've put it there earlier. I wiped his face and neck and stroked his hair. He wanted to tell me, but he couldn't talk.

Michael sat on the floor and put his head on Patrick, "C'mon Patrick. Do you want me to tell her?"

"No." He started sobbing. I held him. I knew it was bad, really bad.

Patrick took a breath, held my hands and swallowed hard, "Frankie, I... I..." He cried again. Then through his tears, "I have AIDS." I was in shock. We had been hearing a lot about this new disease called AIDS, but I didn't know much about it except that there was no cure and it was found mostly in gay men. They were calling it the gay disease.

"My God, Patrick. When did you find out?"

"Today." He continued crying.

I glanced at the digital clock as it turned from 11:59 to 12:00 a.m. Another birthday has come to a tragic end. What started out to be the best birthday ever transformed into the worse ending imaginable. What could I say to Patrick? I had no words, only pain and fear. Then beyond that, dread.

“Where's Simon now?"

"We don't know."

"What do you mean you don't know?"

Patrick got angry, "He split, left town without a trace."

He'd called Patrick a few of weeks ago and said he was sick, and that Patrick should get a test. No one had heard a thing about him since then. I actually felt sad for Simon because he was dying alone, but I was also angry that he did this to my little brother. Patrick was 22 years old, probably wouldn't see 23. I was sick to my stomach. I ran to the bathroom and threw up. I dropped to my knees and grabbed a towel to cover my mouth as I screamed to God in heaven, "WHY, WHY, WHY PATRICK!! Mom, please help us. I don't know if I can handle this." No towel could completely muffle my scream, but I couldn't hold it in. I felt like I would implode. Michael waited outside the bathroom door, "Are you alright Frankie?" I opened the door and we collapsed into each other's arms and cried. Our Patrick was sick and there was no cure.

Chapter 17: A NEW PATRICK

The night was endless. Patrick fell asleep, but Michael and I stayed up all night.

I knew I had to go home and break the news. I left Queens at 6:00 a.m. Dad would be at Bella Luna by 10:00 a.m. That gave me plenty of time to walk to Manhattan. It was cold, but I needed it. The morning couldn't have been prettier. The sky was blue with delicate clouds dancing about. It made me feel awake. Even after death, you can be sure that the sun will rise the very next day.

As I walked across the 59th Street Bridge, I heard the water inviting me to entertain it. I looked down into the cold fluid. I could jump, I thought. Even if I did, it might not kill me. It was not my time. I had a lot more to do in this world. This I knew deep in my bones. Mom had always told me I had a very special purpose and I finally felt it. She never worried about me. She knew I would be okay. I could almost hear her speaking to me with her sweet Italian accent. “Francesca, you are strong, not like me. You are a survivor." Why did I survive all I'd been through? How come I wasn't dead? I felt more alive than ever. With each car that passed, I became acutely aware of how alive I was. Everything seemed bigger, clearer, yet there was intense pain surrounding my heart. It was the pain of losing Patrick.

Dad showed up, all smiles. He was carrying a newspaper. "Did you see the paper, Frankie?" He proudly opened to a picture of Ian. "They loved him."

Indulging his excitement for a moment, "That's great Dad. He deserves it."

"I'm so proud of him. Ya know, I was a great painter too. He gets it from me."

"Why didn't you do anything with your talent, Dad?"

"Ah, it wasn't my calling." He laughed. "Mm, what did you make? It smells great!"

"Corned beef hash and eggs."

"My favorite." He started eating. "You make it better than my mom, but don't tell her I said so."

"Dad, we need to talk."

"Let's talk," he said through his chewing.

"Patrick is sick."

"I know, he looked like shit last night."

"Yeah, well, he's really sick, Dad."

He stopped eating, "How sick?"

"Well, you know that gay disease that's been all over the news?"

"Yeah, that AIDS thing."

"Yeah, well, Patrick..." A lump filled my throat and I couldn't bring myself to say the word, to name the disease that had no cure, which assured my brother an imminent death.

"Patrick has AIDS?" Dad grabbed my arm. "No." I watched him sink. "We gotta help him. Seamus can help him. We gotta do something. We'll call Seamus." He was very nervous and talking fast. "This can't be." I was surprised at Dad's reaction. You never knew how he'd react to things. I knew he didn't approve of Patrick's lifestyle, but I could see that it didn't matter. He started to cry.

"I know I fucked up with him. I just wanted him to be stronger." Brimming with regret.

"Frankie, call your brothers and tell them to come over here right now. We need to talk about this as a family." Every day he shocked me more and more. This was not the same man I'd grown up with. It's amazing how alcohol can change a person completely. It was a shame Mom didn't get to see the man who stood before me now. He was compassionate, loving, willing and ready to be our father. Maybe he was like this when Mom first met him and that's why she fell in love with him.

Before I made the call to my brothers Dad took my hand, "Sweetheart, I know I haven't been a good father. I know I was a terrible husband to your mother, but I have changed. I am so ashamed of all the things I've done and the way I behaved. I don't expect you to forgive me. All I know is that's not who I am anymore and every day I'm trying to be the father you never had. You deserve that, Frankie." I didn't know what to say or do. I just looked into his deep blue eyes that I used to think were cold and icy. Now they were soothing and sincere. They were inviting and loving. He smiled softly and so did I. "I'm trying to forgive you Dad, I really am." That was the best I could do for now. I turned to the phone and called my brothers.

They came quickly. We all sat together around a table, like a business meeting. We were a family taking care of business, very important business, the business of Patrick. Dad was the leader of the meeting. He spoke passionately and powerfully about his son. My brothers were devastated but determined to pull together as a family to support Patrick in any way possible. We joined forces to take this on with strength and committed to bring joy into Patrick's life right now. Seamus had lots of ideas for prolonging his life. We all had to stay positive. It was the only hope. As I looked around the table, I felt a profound love for all these guys in my life. Patrick was the only one missing, but his presence most powerful in the room. Today I was proud to be a Finnegan. I was proud of my father, my brothers, myself. Even if we lost Patrick, we committed to bring him peace. We were going to savor every moment. Dad wanted us to make a list of Patrick's favorite things—foods, movies, books, music, quotes, plays, everything. Michael helped us. We surrounded him with all the things he loved the most.

Seamus and I went to see Dr. Silver. He was definitely getting older, but his eyes were the same, welcoming. His heart was broken about Patrick. We wanted any advice he could give. He went to visit Patrick. It meant so much to both of them.

Seamus spent day and night doing research on medication. He got all the latest and best stuff available on the market. Because it was such a new disease, there was a lot of risk involved. Patrick was willing to try anything. Seamus said the most important thing was to love him and that people actually healed from love and laughter. Happiness builds your immune system like vitamin C. He told us stories about people curing themselves of incurable cancers. "It's all about a positive attitude," he said.

Patrick seemed to be getting a little better. We made a special photo album of him and put together cassettes with all his favorite songs. Thursday's became movie night and we watched all of his favorites. I stayed over at Michael's a lot and cooked his most loved dishes. He had a hard time eating, but he was happy just to see it in front of him. Michael got healing meditations on tape and we all did them together. I was healing things in my body too, things I thought were gone, but they weren't. They were lying dormant, waiting for me to pay attention to them, so I did. I meditated on healing my body from the Cuban man and getting rid of the body memories that haunted my dreams. I worked on releasing the pain my body had absorbed from Dad's angry hands and words. I prayed for the courage to open up my heart and allow someone to truly love me.

Patrick's doctor told Seamus that Patrick's t-cell count was up, and he seemed better, but not to get hopeful. Seamus told him to fuck off and found a doctor with a more positive outlook. We weren't in denial about Patrick's condition, we just didn't need a negative force sucking any more life or hope out of our Patrick.

One day I went over while Michael was out shopping. I sneaked in quietly in case Patrick was sleeping. Lingering through the hospital room, I heard Dad's voice softly telling Patrick a story. When I looked in the bedroom Dad was sitting on the bed reading a book to him. As I listened, I realized it was a children's book, James and the Giant Peach. Patrick said it was his favorite and he always wished Dad would've read it to him.

Dad never read to us when we were kids. I closed my eyes and made believe I was seven years old, in my bed in Queens. Dad read with such love and enthusiasm. He changed his voice when the characters changed. He put excitement in all the right places and read to Patrick like he was a little boy with his whole life ahead of him.

Patrick was never alone except when he asked to be. Sometimes he asked for an hour alone to write in his new big journal that he requested we pick up for him. Every day he wrote in it. He said he hated being sick, but in a strange way he was happy. He'd never felt so loved and appreciated. Dad was always strong in front of Patrick, but when he left him, he broke down.

"He's my youngest son. He was always so frail. I used to hate that about him. I just wanted him to be strong like the rest of you."

Patrick fought for almost two more years, but we could see that he was waning. Little Isabella was walking and talking. Ian was the toast of the town and in demand as an artist. Seamus was sleeping at Mount Sinai Hospital, on Fifth Avenue in Manhattan, a lot while he was doing his residency. Then he would come to be with Patrick. I was trying to decide what I wanted in my life. The restaurant, although it was doing well, was draining me.

***

The summer of 1985 was hot and difficult for Patrick, who was now twenty-four years old. His health took a turn for the worse, as he battled with pneumonia. We rushed him to New York Hospital. He was in and out of consciousness. We were all there by his side. Dr. Silver came to see him. Ian sat in a corner painting Patrick in his hospital bed. The nurse came in and said it was after-hours and we would all have to leave.

Michael explained, "He's my lover and I can't leave."

Then Seamus said, "I'm a doctor, I have to make sure he has everything he needs."

Ryan explained, "I'm his oldest brother and I have to take care of him."

Ian winked, "I have to stay, he's my baby brother."

She turned to me, "I'm his only sister. He needs me."

Dr. Silver smiled. He'd heard this routine before. The nurse didn't know what to say. She turned to Dad. "He's my son, my youngest son. I can't leave him ever again."

She didn't know whether to laugh or cry, but she knew we were serious. She left. A weak grin sprouted on Patrick's face as his eyes slightly opened. We all gathered around him. No strength of Ryan's could save him. No medical expertise that Seamus possessed, no artistic talent that Ian had, no regret that

Dad had, and no love that Michael or I had could do a thing at this moment. It was all up to God.

The energy that filled the room that night was magical. We were not of this earth but elevated to a higher level. It was getting close and Patrick knew it. He wanted to talk to each of us alone. When it was my turn, I held his hand.

"Hey, Frankie." He was so weak.

"Hey, handsome." Even with all the tubes, the lesions and the wasting, I could still see that special sparkle he always had in his eyes.

"You're the best sister anybody could have ever had." Tears spilled from his eyes.

I could barely breathe. "Thanks." We laughed about our shoe-shining career and the day we cursed like crazy together.

"I don't know what I would've done without you, Frankie. You always took care of me." I tried not to cry, but a couple of tears spilled out. He looked at me and smiled, "I had everything I wanted Frankie. I made it to Broadway. Better than that. I found true love. Someone who loved me no matter what I did. That's rare Frankie, but it's possible." He was having a hard time talking. "You'll find it, Frankie. There's someone out there right now waiting to love you. Once I get up there, I'm gonna help lead him to you." Patrick knew that I had never been able to fall in love.

"I love you, Patrick. I'm gonna miss you so much."

"I know, Frankie, but I'll always be with you." He was getting tired but pulled me in close and whispered in my ear "You gotta forgive Dad, Frankie. It's time. You know he loves you. You have such a big heart. Find it in there to let him in. Do it for you. You'll feel better, Frankie." I kissed him long and hard on his cheek. Our tears met in the middle. I knew it was time to say goodbye. "Could you get Michael?" He was at the end. I was certain Mom was getting a place ready up in heaven for her son. I knew for sure that's where Patrick was going. I must say there was a comfort in knowing Mom had already gone to the other side. It would help us all let go of Patrick a little easier. We would be passing a son back to his mother. Even he was happy to know Mom would be waiting to welcome him.

I kissed him and went to get his one and only true love. Michael's was the last face he wanted to see before he drifted into his endless slumber. He said if Michael were there, he would not be so scared to go. Michael whispered to him, "It's safe to let go now Patrick, you're gonna be okay. God and your Mom are waiting on a mountaintop. They're going to help you make the transition."

"I love you, Michael. I always have. You always had my heart." Patrick squeezed Michael's hand tightly, looked once more into his eyes, smiled, and let go.

He was gone. I ran my fingertips on the lining of his thin face, and I saw all of my frailty lying before me. Patrick's strength was to allow his vulnerability to shine through, which the rest of us fought tooth-and-nail to hide. I resolved to take that with me.

As I left his room, I thought about all the arrangements that had to be made, but I couldn't think about that right away. I needed to go for a walk.

I made my way down the hallway to the elevator. There was a man waiting for the elevator. He was crying too. He noticed me and smiled. I smiled back. I couldn't help but notice how incredibly handsome he was. He pulled out a handkerchief. "Please take this. I haven't used it. I brought extras."

"Thank you so much," I accepted.

As I blew my nose, I noticed the initials 'P.F.' sewn into the hanky. My heart stopped. I felt Patrick laughing above me somewhere. "Don't tell me, your name is Patrick."

He wiped his tears, "Oh my God, how did you guess that?"

"Well, your initials are here." I was floored.

"Oh right, but still, I could've been Peter or Paul or Philip."

"No, you definitely look like a Patrick to me." I started to cry again. I looked up thinking that Patrick might be watching.

"I'm sorry. Is someone you know sick?"

The elevator arrived. We both got on it.

"My brother, Patrick, just passed away. AIDS."

"I'm so sorry. I just lost my best friend. Cancer."

"I'm sorry."

We stood alone as the elevator carried us down. I had never felt so instantly connected to another soul. We'd both just lost someone, which made me think they were both in that elevator with us. They brought us together at this moment. I got such a tingle. My knees got weak as I held his blue P.F. handkerchief, moist with my snot in it. We reached the bottom floor.

He turned to me, very nervous. But I couldn't imagine he was as nervous as I was. "I don't know your name. I know that you know mine and it was the same as your brother's, I am so sorry..."

"Francesca."

He took a long deep breath and smiled into my heart. "Francesca, can I take you...would you like to have a cup of coffee with me?"

"Yes, I would love to."

We walked out of the hospital wiping tears of mourning and smiling about our meeting. We talked for hours, got ten refills of coffee and decided we'd better eat something to counteract all the caffeine. He offered to treat me to dinner at his favorite restaurant, One If By Land Two If By Sea. It was divine. As I looked at him across the table, I felt like I'd known this man for a hundred years. His eyes were familiar. Somehow, he put me at ease. Toward the end of dinner, I asked him what he did for a living. He told me he ran a shelter for abused children. Chills ran up my spine. I looked up to the sky again and smiled at my brother, Patrick. I told him that I was a chef at Dad's restaurant. He was impressed, but not as much as I was with his choice of work. All the men I had been dating were either construction workers or salesmen. I hadn't dated anyone who did anything but want to help himself. I had become completely disenchanted with the whole dating thing. It was also very hard for me to find a man who made me feel safe sexually. If I did have sex with them, it was for them not me. It was because I wanted them to love me. They didn't seem to care that I was crying or distant. Most of them didn't acknowledge my feelings. If I told them about being raped, they would act concerned for a moment and then say something like, "Well, you gotta move on. You can't hold onto the past." They just didn't get it, and I got tired of explaining. As I looked at Patrick Flannery through the candlelight, I thought, with him, it could be different.

We walked around Little Italy after dinner and made a plan to see each other after the two funerals. He grabbed my two hands in his as he looked into my eyes. "You're an angel, Francesca. You saved my life tonight." Those were my feelings exactly, but I couldn't speak. "Can I kiss you, Francesca?"

"Oh, please do."

He leaned in with his 6-foot frame and connected his glorious mouth to mine. Oh, my lord, I had never really been kissed before tonight! I wanted to sing in Italian, "I'm yours, Patrick Flannery, marry me now, tonight, right here in front of my Paisano Mario's Deli." But I didn't say a word. I could not believe what I was feeling. How could love happen so quickly? Maybe it is true what they say, "You just know when you meet the right person, it's love at first sight."

He smiled, "Goodnight, sweet Francesca Finnegan."

"Goodnight, Patrick Flannery."

On the morning of Patrick's wake, I woke up with the sun shining in my eyes. I took a moment to myself. I forgot for a moment that he was gone. All night I was dreaming of Patrick and Mom, happy. They blew me a kiss, turned and walked into the ocean. The phone rang. I jumped up and answered, "Hello."

"Hello, Francesca?"

"Yes."

"Good morning, it's Patrick."

"Hi."

"I just wanted to thank you again for last night."

"Thank you."

"I haven't been able to stop thinking about you."

"Really?"

"Really. Also, I wanted you to know that you and your family are in my thoughts today."

"Thank you, Patrick, and you're in mine."

"If you need to talk or if you need ten cups of coffee or anything, please call me."

"I will."

We laughed and said so long for now.

The house filled up quickly with my brothers and friends and family. We were all preparing for the wake. Ian, Seamus and Ryan were in the bathroom sharing the mirror as they usually did when dressing for occasions. I watched them. There was silence.

Ian put his tie around his neck. Then Seamus and Ryan did the same. As Ian went to make his tie his hands began to shake. He'd never made his own tie. He didn't know how. He struggled to keep his composure then he began to weep.

"I can't do my tie. He always did my tie."

Seamus did an okay one. "Look at mine."

Ryan laughed through tears, "It looks ridiculous."

The three of them were lost without their little brother. Michael walked in looking sad, but well put together.

"Let me help you guys. Patrick told me you're all hopeless with making a tie." Michael did each of their ties, one by one. They were impeccable.

Ian smiled in the mirror. "Boy, you fags really know how to make a tie."

They all laughed, knowing it was meant as a compliment to Michael.

Michael started to cry as he touched Ian's tie. Ian pulled him in and let him cry on his shoulder. Ryan hugged them from behind and Seamus squeezed into the side. There is such an inexplicable bonding between men that I have only been able to witness from the outside.

***

Patrick requested that we wake his body at Mr. Vannelli's, just like Mom. Mr. Vannelli was devastated. He had a bottle of Brunello di Montalcino waiting for me. All the people from Patrick's show came to pay their respects. Old friends from the neighborhood came, Nanny and Grumpy Finnegan came, but would not tell anyone they knew why he died. Still, their pride was more important than the truth. I had a hard time looking at them the same, but I kept it to myself. Nanny Juliano, Aunt Carmella, Uncle Louie, Virginia and all of Dad's brothers came with food, flowers, love and support. We put a picture of all of us together in the casket. He looked so peaceful in his bright blue suit. Michael came over and held his hand. He looked lost.

Patrick asked us to read his journal when he died. In it he made requests of each of us. He wanted Ian to paint a picture of him dancing on the Broadway stage. He wanted Seamus to fight for cures of all fatal diseases. He wanted Ryan to win the big boxing match he had coming up. He wanted Dad to forgive himself and he wanted all of us to forgive him too. He wrote, "Life is too short to waste your energy holding on to the anger of the past." He asked Michael to open his heart to falling in love again. He didn't want him to be alone. And me, well, he wanted me to get out our old shoe-shining box that we had hid, and to shine his shoes while he was in the coffin and he wanted me to curse like crazy the whole time I was doing it. Now most people might not understand the significance, but I did. I granted his request. It made me laugh and it made me cry. It made me remember who we were and where we came from.

We buried Patrick right next to Mom on a gorgeous day. Not a cloud in the sky. Peace swept over the cemetery. After we said our goodbyes, I walked over to visit Sean. I brought a flower for his tombstone and talked to him about my life. I told him I'd finally met someone who made me feel special. I felt Sean's approval as two bluebirds landed right next to me. It was Mom and Patrick for sure. I looked around at all the headstones that filled the cemetery. Each person who was buried under the earth had a story. I found comfort in that as I stood on top of them all. I felt like it was time to stop fighting so hard, to let people get close to me, to stop being ruled by fear and find my strength in love. I committed to walk through my life with my eyes wide open. Patrick's death brought me to Life. My fear was dripping off me like sad puddles.

I said hello to each headstone I passed and read some of the last words their families honored them with. There were loving prayers, poems and dedications all made in tribute of the special people beneath my feet. Everyone's life touches someone else's and changes it forever. I knew it was only a matter of time before I, too, would be part of the earth. I always thought cemeteries were creepy, but that day, I found them comforting, wondrous, and meaningful. I took all the energy of those fabulous souls and I let it rise through my shoes. The force that lived in the soil traveled up the veins of my legs, pumping a new warrior spirit into my being. I left the cemetery feeling alive and ready to live my life.

Chapter 18: ME AND FIVE GUYS

The following summer I went to Coney Island on Mom's birthday, June 12th and now 1986. As a present to her I decided to ride the Cyclone ten times in a row. I also thought it was a good way to get over my fear. I even rode in the front car. While the cars climbed to the top of the rickety old coaster, I let my memories of Mom fill each breath. I raised my arms. I saw Patrick's face. I saw Sean. I saw the Cuban man. I reached the top. Time to let it all go now. Wow, what a drop! It seemed endless, the ups and downs, the excitement, the fear, the thrill. Yes, I thought, this is life. After I finished my tenth and final time, I stepped off, a little shaky. Patrick Flannery stood waiting for me. We had been inseparable since the day we met. After the funerals, the courtship began. I told him about the Cuban man. He sat and listened. His posture was open. His eyes stayed with me. When I finished, he paused, took my hand, "I am so sorry that happened to you, Francesca. You didn't do anything to deserve that." The funny thing was I remember as a kid thinking I did, that it was somehow my fault. He then got a little teary eyed, "I know how you feel." I waited for him to continue. I knew he had something more to say. "I was raped as a young boy." My heart stopped. I never thought about that being possible. I mean, to look at him he didn't seem damaged. I felt like I wore my damage like a sign. I used to think it only happened to girls. It all seemed to make sense. It may sound crazy, but it brought me comfort to know that he and I shared the wound of being raped. Having that in common helped me surrender and with Patrick I never felt separate. Nothing I told him about myself or my family shocked him. He didn't run. He didn't belittle my experiences or make light of them. He said we had so much to give each other and so much time to heal together.

Patrick was the first guy I'd brought home who was completely accepted by my family. Maybe it was because I finally accepted myself.

My brothers tried to find fault at first - they were all so over-protective - but they had to admit he was a good match for me. We had so many things in common, I felt like we could talk forever and never get bored. I had never felt more like myself with anyone. I was actually learning more about myself through him. He was the home that I'd been searching for all my life. I trusted him so completely it terrified me. I didn't want him to be taken away.

One day I went to visit Mario. I still had my cart, wobbly and old, but it worked. I told him about Patrick. He asked if he liked Brunello di Montalcino. "It's his favorite."

He laughed, "A match made in heaven."

"He even likes my tattoo. He says it's sexy."

He laughed even harder, "Sounds like love," he said in Italian.

I brought Mario home grown vegetables from my garden. He was grateful that I kept my promise and our friendship.

"I told Patrick all about you. He can't wait to meet you."

"Does he speak Italian?"

"Not yet, but I'm teaching him."

"You bring him over. I make a nice lasagna."

They met over Mario's pesto lasagna. No one made it like him, not even me. They loved each other instantly, which I took as a good sign. If Mario approved, it was okay. When we left, our bellies were full of homemade Italian food, prepared with love, our hearts full of passion. We could still hear Puccini streaming out of the window when we got outside. The moon was full, and the air was warm. Patrick stopped and pulled me into him.

"Francesca Finnegan, I want to ask you, right here tonight in front of Mario's deli, will you marry me?" I was so taken aback I couldn't speak. "I don't want to be with anyone but you. I want to watch your hair turn gray, your eyes wrinkle. I want to have children with you and give them all the love we can. I've never been so sure about anything in my life and I can't stop talking because I'm so nervous." He got on his knee and pulled out a ring, "Will you marry me, Francesca Finnegan?"

I looked at his sweet blue eyes gazing up at me. I knelt down beside him. The couples walking by must've thought we were crazy, but we didn't care. I held his eyes in mine. Tears of joy poured out, "Yes, Patrick Flannery. I will marry you."

We kissed on our knees and practically fell over. He laughed and picked me up.

I yelled up to Mario's window, "Hey Mario, we're getting married." He popped his head out of the window.

"We're getting married! We're getting married." Patrick yelled too.

"Wait one minute." Mario ran back inside. I thought he was coming down to congratulate us, but then he came back to the window and threw down a handful of rice, showering us with his blessing. "Congratulations." He was laughing with joy.

We told our families and they were all very happy and supportive. We had lots of planning to do. We decided we'd get married next June. I wrote to Antoinette and asked her to please come and be in my bridal party. I had never given up on her. I knew from her letters that she was still in love with Ian. I had so much love in my heart, I wanted to spread it. I asked Ian if he would mind Antoinette being a part of the wedding. His face lit up. "Do you think she'll come?"

"I have a good feeling about it." I didn't want to build his hopes up, but I also wanted him to want her to come. I came to believe in the power of thought.

Patrick had been bringing me in to the shelter to talk with the kids. I found it rewarding and healing. "The kids really like you," he told me.

"I like them too."

"What would you say if I asked you to work with me?"

Secretly I prayed that he would ask me, but it did frighten me. Helping them brought up so many things for me. I knew if I said yes, I would have to commit fully. I was ready to make a shift with my work. The restaurant was running itself and it was no longer fulfilling. "Think about it." He didn't want to pressure me.

"I already have. I would love to work with you."

He smiled, "I have a reservation tonight at One If By Land. There's something I need to tell you."

I got scared. "What is it about?" I couldn't wait.

"It's about our wedding."

"Can you give me a hint?"

"No, you'll have to wait until tonight."

I went to Barney's of New York and spent a whole week's salary. I knew it was extravagant, but I wanted to look my best that night. When I arrived, he was waiting at the same table we sat at the first night we met. There was a bottle of Brunello di Montalcino opened. When he looked up and saw me, his eyes exploded with delight.

"Wow." He jumped up to pull my chair out, "You look delicious, I mean amazing."

"Delicious is good. I like delicious," I laughed as I sat down across from him. "You look pretty fabulous yourself." He blushed.

He poured us some wine, lifted his glass, "Here's to destiny."

I clinked my glass with his, "To destiny."

"Francesca, I have a confession to make."

Uh oh, here it comes. I got a pain in my heart and nausea spread in my stomach.

He continued, "I know you've been doing a lot of research, trying to find the right wedding hall for the reception, the right church, the right dress, the right price for everything and..."

I was dying. He was letting me down easy. The Brunello Di Montalcino was to soften the blow, "Go ahead." I said.

"And I want you to stop."

"What?"

"I want you to stop doing this all by yourself."

After he'd asked me to marry him, I said I would take care of everything. I didn't even give him a choice. I thought I was doing him a favor, saving him the trouble. Most men wanted the woman to take care of all the planning. He wanted to share the experience with me. He didn't want to be left out.

"Patrick, I'm sorry. I didn't realize."

He laughed, "I still haven't told you the reason I wanted to talk to you."

Shit, there's more, "Okay what is it?"

"I don't want you to try to save money. I want you to get the dress you want, the church you want, the honeymoon you want, the reception hall you want."

I didn't have much money and even though Dad was doing okay, I couldn't have some fairy-tale wedding. My dream was to be married at St. Patrick's Cathedral. Then I wanted a horse and buggy carriage to pick us up and take us to Tavern on the Green. I wanted to travel to Italy for the honeymoon, of course. I wanted to see my mom's house, ride in the canals of Venice in a Gondola, kissing under every bridge, then make a quick stop in Paris, glide up to the top of the Eiffel Tower, visit the museums and climb to the highest point of Notre Dame. This was my dream wedding. But Patrick worked with abused children and I would be doing the same. It was not a lucrative career. I really didn't care.

"Patrick, I don't care about all those fancy things, as long as we're together."

He smiled devilishly, "We can have all that and be together."

"What are you trying to tell me?"

"When my father died ten years ago, he left me two hundred thousand dollars."

"Wow, that's great, but we don't need to blow it all on a fancy wedding. I mean that could last a while."

He laughed out loud, "Francesca, I was young when my dad died. I didn't want or care about his money. So, I just put it into tech stocks. I didn't even know what I was doing."

I was trying to follow him, but I was lost.

"Well anyway ten years later..." He started to laugh even harder. "I turned it into a small fortune. So, you go ahead and get whatever you want. I'm gonna give you everything you ever dreamed of and more."

I didn't know whether to laugh or cry, "Why didn't you tell me sooner?"

"I was afraid. I was afraid you wouldn't love me just for me. So many women try to marry into money. I wanted this to be for love. I also thought if you knew you wouldn't like me. You wouldn't see beyond that. I never cared about the money. It just happened."

I started laughing, "So we're filthy rich?"

"Filthy."

"I can have St. Patrick's Cathedral, Tavern on the Green, Italy, Paris?

"You can have it all. We can have it all."

I started to cry. My first thought was, "What did I do to deserve this?" I figured my life was always going to be a struggle. That's what I was used to, that's what I was comfortable with. Then I thought, "No, I do deserve this. I deserve Patrick Flannery and all the love he wants to shower me with. This is my reward in life, and I wanted to breath it all in and just say FUCKING YES. Somebody sees me. Somebody loves me. Somebody wants to take care of me and I'm going to let him."

I told Patrick about Antoinette and Ian, hopeless romantic that he was, he bought her a round-trip, first-class ticket to our wedding. He said he made it round-trip so she wouldn't feel pressure. If she chose to stay, she could. He was smart.

We planned everything together. The wedding would be in June. I would be a June bride. The only thing I didn't let him do with me was pick out my dress. I wanted it to be a surprise. Virginia helped me choose the perfect one; a Vera Wang wedding gown. I wished Mom could've seen me. I felt like Audrey Hepburn. My maid of honor would be Virginia. I asked Patrick's two sisters, Colleen and Erin, to be my bridesmaids. If Antoinette came, she would be a bridesmaid too. Patrick had his brother John as best man and my three brothers as ushers. Little Isabella was the flower girl and Patrick's nephew, David, was the ring bearer.

* * *

One week before the wedding, Patrick, Ian and I were sitting at the table going over the seating arrangements. The doorbell rang. We looked at Ian. He got up to answer it. He swung the door open to reveal Antoinette, standing on the other side. "Ciao Bello!"

The sun streamed in behind her. The years had been very kind to her. She was such an elegant and beautiful woman. She threw her arms around Ian. His knees practically buckled. They both began to cry. Patrick and I felt like we were intruding, but they didn't seem to mind. She kissed every inch of his face. He didn't stop her. When she saw my face, she ran to hug me. Ian wiped his eyes and lifted her suitcase. She spoke to me in Italian. Patrick was impressed.

"Francesca, bella, you are as beautiful as ever." Bella jumped on her.

"So are you, Antoinette. I can't believe you're here."

"And I can't believe you're getting married." She smiled at Patrick.

Patrick stood up. "This is Patrick. The man I'm marrying." Saying those words sent chills through my whole body. I was certain he was the man for me.

She kissed me on both cheeks, "Bella, Bella." Bella kept jumping up when her name was called. We all laughed. Ian was delighted, and shocked.

As each day passed, Ian and Antoinette were rekindling the flame that was put out much too soon so many years ago. Clearly, the chemistry was still there.

Patrick surprised all of us by getting rooms at the Plaza two nights before the wedding. We would be staying until we left for our honeymoon. The whole bridal party and any out-of-town guest were all accommodated. He covered every little detail and made sure everyone was happy.

"I'm only going to get married once in my life Francesca, so I want to do it right." I loved him for saying that; He was as sure as I was.

On the night before the wedding, Ian called my room, "Frankie, come to my room. I have something for you." I walked down the hallway of the Plaza. This place was beyond my wildest dreams. Ian's door was open. Antoinette sat on the bed looking like a painting.

"Ciao," I smiled at her.

"Ciao, Bella," she said in her usual fashion.

Ian peeked out of the bathroom, "Sit on the bed and close your eyes." I felt silly, like a little girl, but it was fun. I could hear him moving toward me. "Okay, open your eyes, Frankie."

I opened them. “Mom at the Stove” stood before me.

"It's yours, Frankie. My wedding present to you." Antoinette cried too.

I had a huge lump in my throat. "I don't know what to say."

"You don't have to say anything." He knew what that painting meant to me. It was the best present in the whole world.

I tried to sleep that night, but it was impossible. I watched movies all night long. Casablanca, The Philadelphia Story, Roman Holiday and An American in Paris, West Side Story, all the movies that Mom loved. I was wide-awake and ready for my wedding day.

I sat in Central Park as the sun rose over Manhattan. Serenity washed over me. In a few hours my name would be different. I would be Francesca Flannery, not Finnegan. I liked the way it sounded.

All the girls in the bridal party arrived at my room and we had a professional hair stylist and make-up artist. We felt like movie stars. The photographer came shortly after and started snapping away. Someday I would show my children my wedding album and tell them my story, I thought as each flash exploded. The one picture that would be missing was the one of me and my beautiful mother.

There was a knock on the door. Antoinette opened it and in walked five guys in tuxedos. One of them looked at me and smiled.

"You must be the bride," he said knowingly.

"Yes, that's me," I said with pride.

They started singing, 'You Send Me.' All of the girls let out a romantic sigh. My heart burst and I couldn't wait to dance with Patrick at the reception. Then a bellhop delivered a bottle of Brunello di Montalcino with a note that said, there are cases more waiting at Tavern on the Green. I felt like a princess. The phone rang and it was Mario. I gave him my number in case he had any problems.

"Mario, is everything okay?" He was screaming in Italian, "Patrick said he was sending someone to pick me up." He finally slowed down, "There's a horse with a carriage on its back, waiting downstairs for me, Mama Mia." He had never ridden in one. I laughed.

They came upstairs to get us. As we exited the Plaza Hotel, there were several horse and buggy carriages waiting for us. We were all surprised. Not only did Patrick get a white one for us, but for the whole bridal party and for Mario.

St. Patrick's Cathedral looked glorious. Dad met me at the stairs as the church awaited my entrance. I looked up at the blue sky knowing Mom and Patrick were smiling down. Two bluebirds landed right on the front steps of the church, practically on my feet. I smiled. Dad took my arm. His eyes filled up with tears.

"My God, you're beautiful."

I smiled into his blue eyes. “Thank you, Daddy.”

“I love you Frankie, I always have.” He said it! The words I’ve waited to hear my whole life. It was worth the wait and couldn’t have meant more on this day in particular.

The music paused and then, “Here Comes the Bride” echoed through the church. I've heard stories about people walking down the aisle knowing that they’re making a mistake. I never understood how someone could do that to themselves or to their partner. I had no reservations. Patrick Flannery was my soul mate. My whole crazy life led me to this aisle on this day. Friendly faces smiled upon me with their blessing as I drifted by - Mario, Dr. Silver, Mr. Vannelli were among them. Aunt Carmella, Uncle Louie, Uncle Jim, Uncle Joe, Nanny and Grumpy Finnegan and Nanny Juliano beamed as I passed them walking down the aisle to marry the man I loved with all of my being. I pictured

Mom in her green dress, proud of her daughter and her new son-in-law. I saw Patrick up on the altar in his little altar boy outfit. I felt Sean smile down on us. The whole universe seemed to agree with this day.

Dad kissed me and handed me to my new husband and as he let go of me, I decided to let go, too. I forgave him. I looked over to my three brothers, Ryan, Ian and Seamus. I turned to kiss Dad. I looked at Patrick Flannery and realized something - it was still me and five guys.

About the Author

Trish Doolan started acting and modeling at the age of three, and graced many magazine covers as a child model. Trish moved to Los Angeles from New York by the age of 19 and began making the rounds as a working actress in Hollywood, in commercials, television and film.

A versatile, accomplished storyteller, Trish Doolan is an acclaimed screenwriter, playwright, director and actor. She wrote, directed, produced and starred in the film April's Shower, which was released by Regent Films and promptly won four best picture awards, two in the States and two in Europe. The New York Times called April's Shower highly "enjoyable" and "refreshingly volatile." The San Francisco Chronicle deemed it "expansive, talky and zany," and called Trish's storytelling "impressive."

Raised in Queens, New York and one of six children, Trish's strong Irish/Italian family provided much of the inspiration for her first novel, Me & Five Guys. The Running with Scissors-like Me and Five Guys is based on her real-life experiences coming of age. Her second novel, The Singing

Gardener, is a classic tale of forbidden love and the magic that occurs when we follow our hearts.

One of Trish's many screenplays, Me & My Cannoli's had been optioned by prolific Hollywood Exec Producer Lucas Foster (Mr. & Mrs. Smith, Crimson Tide, Man on Fire) Trish recently took this project back into her hands as a HER-I-CAN ENTERTAINMENT property. Two of her other screenplays, Dancing Fool and Next Stop are currently in pre-production stages. In late 2007 Trish wrote, directed, produced and starred in the short film, What's True; a controversial film posing the question... while innocent people are wrongly convicted and spending time in prison for crimes they did not commit "What is true?" The film was selected to participate in the Cannes Film Festival Shorts program.